THIS WOMAN

THE STORY FROM JESSE'S POV

JODI ELLEN MALPAS

Editing by - Marion Archer
Proofing by - Karen Lawson
Cover Design - Hang Le

PRAISE FOR JODI ELLEN MALPAS

"Malpas's sexy love scenes scorch the page, and her sensitive, multilayered hero and heroine will easily capture readers' hearts. A taut plot and a first-rate lineup of supporting characters make this a keeper."
—*Publishers Weekly on Gentleman Sinner*

"This book is JEM at her best, the secrets, lies, enemies... and tongue it cheek humour. It's all there on every single page! I had no idea where this book was going or how the book would end. The journey was as captivating as it was enigmatic." - *Kindle and Koffee Book Blog on Wicked Truths*

"It's just twist after dark and delicious twist; a completely, unquestionably unpredictable ride from start to finish. This is the kind of book where every page is important, because there is just SO MUCH going on, and it's an intricate dance from loathe to love for this couple." - *Jeeves Reads Romance on The Brit*

"So it's safe to say, Jodi has once again completely smashed it with another sensation making it the best read of 2021! Hold on tight you're about to be enthralled." - *Booksobsessive on The Enigma*

"The characters are realistic and relatable and the tension ratchets up to an explosive conclusion. For anyone who enjoys Sleeping with the Enemy-style stories, this is a perfect choice."—*Library Journal on Leave Me Breathless*

"The Controversial Princess is an all-consuming, scorching hot, modern royal romance with twists, turns and a jaw-dropping cliffhanger that will leave you begging for more." —*Mary Dube, USA Today HEA*

"A brave, cutting-edge romance…This is a worthwhile read." —*Library Journal on The Forbidden*

"Unpredictable and addictive."—*Booklist on The Forbidden*

"4.5 stars. Top Pick. Readers will love this book from the very beginning! The characters are so real and flawed that fans feel as if they're alongside them. Malpas' writing is also spot-on with emotions."
—*RT Book Reviews* on *The Protector*

"Super steamy and emotionally intense." –*The Library Journal* on *With ThisMan*

"Jodi Ellen Malpas delivers a new heart-wrenching, addicting read."—*RT Book Reviews* on *With ThisMan*

For my readers.
Thank you for the last ten years.

PROLOGUE

MAY 1991

Numbers. Fucking numbers. I stare down at the mock exam paper, the equations, fractions, and percentages all blending and blurring into one. I hate numbers. I can hear Mum behind us stirring a pot of soup and Dad in the garden mowing the lawn. I look up at the clock. Five fifteen. I have another forty-five minutes to get this shit done before I can escape.

Glancing across to Jake, I find his head down, his pen darting across the paper—as if his brain is working too fast for his hand to keep up. Probably is, the brainy bastard. I slip down my chair and kick my leg out, catching him on the shin. He stops writing. Looks up at me. His green eyes, a perfect match to mine, stare at me tiredly. I grin, harder when I spy his killer smile, and take my pen to my mouth. Slip it between my teeth. Start thrusting it back and forth. His lips purse as he tries in vain to hold back his laughter. He fails, snorting over his math paper. Of course, Mum's quick to whirl around, abandoning her soup, to find out what the disturbance is. And, of course, she's quick to reach her conclusion, despite it being Jake falling apart in his chair.

"Jesse." She clips me around the ear, and I flinch but smile wider. "Stop distracting your brother."

"I had a tickle in my throat," Jake says, fast to defend me as always. "It's fine, Mum."

"Sure you did." She gives him a fond smile and goes back to her soup. "You've forty minutes left."

I glance at Jake's paper. He's on the last page. Kicking him under the table again, I get his attention and then point to my own paper. The first page. Then I shrug. He shakes his head in despair, peeking across the kitchen cautiously. Mum's in the pantry, out of sight and earshot. Jake knows I could do this shit if I put my mind to it. I just can't be bothered; I have better things to do. And I want to get on and do them, for fuck's sake. Jake turns his paper over, back to the first page, and I lean across to see.

"What are you doing?" Amalie whispers, appearing beside me. "Cheating?"

"No. Using my initiative." I flip my little sister a wink and send her on her way after a quick peck on the cheek.

Thirty minutes later, I have all the answers I need. "Done," I say, slapping my pen down on the table. Mum looks over her shoulder, her face suspicious.

"Done," Jake mimics, refusing to look at her.

I jump up from my chair, keen to escape. "I'm going." I'm out of the kitchen before Mum can protest, grabbing my jacket and shrugging it on as I jog down the hallway to the front door.

"Jesse," she yells after me. "We have guests arriving."

"Which is exactly why I'm going out," I mumble to myself, not slowing my pace. I swing the door open.

And come face to face with our *guests*.

"Jesse." Dad's friend, Alan, thrusts his hand out to me,

smiling his usual jolly smile. He's a doctor. Thinks he's superior to the fucking world.

"Hi, Alan." I accept, because that's the polite thing to do, and try my hardest to avoid, Lauren's, his daughter's, eyes. She makes me . . . uncomfortable. We would never work, no matter how much my parents try to convince me—*and themselves*—otherwise.

"Are you going out?" he asks as I smile my hello to his wife, still avoiding Lauren's eyes.

"Meeting some friends." I skirt past them and make my way toward the lane. "Good seeing you," I call back, feeling untold guilt for leaving Jake at the mercy of our parents, their insufferable friends, and their daughter.

I pull out a pack of Marlboros, slowing to a stop when I hear Jake calling me. That's a crisis call. He wants saving.

I turn . . .

And crash into my father. *Fuck.* It was a warning call.

Jake gives me apologetic eyes. "Get back in the house, Jake." Dad's voice is cold, stoic, and nearly a whisper. It pisses me off, and Dad knows it. My irritation only multiplies when Jake backs up, his silent apologies multiplying. He has nothing to be sorry about.

I pull a drag of my cigarette and exhale over my words. "I did the math paper. I helped Mum chop veg for her soup. I swept the patio. What more do you want?"

"I want a respectful son."

"You have one," I say, pointing over his shoulder to Jake's retreating form. "Expecting two would be greedy."

"Don't give me your smart mouth, boy. You'll be out on your arse faster than you can blink."

I shake my head to myself and turn, getting on my way. He won't throw me out. He'd never be able to face the questions posed by his equally arrogant friends at the country club. "I'm just meeting some friends."

"We have visitors."

"I said hello as I left."

I hear Jake in the distance calling Dad, trying to appease our father, telling him to let it go. I hate that he's caught in the middle of our clashes. I hate that he's trying to protect me and at the same time keep our parents happy.

"It is not okay, Jake," Dad barks. "Go make yourself useful and help your mother get our guests drinks."

My hackles rise, and I pick up my stride before I blow my stack and do some true damage.

When I get to the end of the road, I stop and look back up the lane toward our house. Dad's nowhere in sight. Neither is my twin brother. My gut twists. I can't leave him there alone to put up with that shit. I flick my cigarette away and jog back, rounding the back of the house and peeking through the window. I growl under my breath when I see Dad throw Jake a warning look as he enters the kitchen. I circle to the next window, hoping I can get Jake's attention. Poor bastard is pouring tea for our *guests*. Fucking tea. Mum will have the biscuit tin on the table next. And as if she's heard me, it appears, covered in pictures of the Queen from each decade. The delight on Lauren's parents' faces makes me roll my eyes.

I become more alert when I see Jake leave the room. *Yes*. I dash around the side of the house.

And go arse over tit.

"Fuck!" My legs get caught up in the hose pipe hanging off the wall, and I land with a thud in Mum's flower bed, flattening her shrubs. I drag myself up and brush down my jeans, grimacing at the mud stains. "Bollocks," I mutter, trudging round to the window of the downstairs bathroom and finding the upended plant pot I always use as a step to reach the window. Except today when I stand on it, I overshoot the opening. Well, fuck. I've grown. I kick it aside and shove my head through the open window.

Jake jumps out of his skin, losing his aim and spraying the back of the loo seat with his piss. "Jesus, Jesse," he hisses, grabbing some toilet paper and wiping up his mess.

I laugh as I watch him, his dick hanging out. "Your dick has some catching up to do."

"Get stuffed," he grumbles, quickly tucking himself away. "What are you doing?"

"Rescuing you."

"Very funny." He flushes and washes his hands. "Dad will go through the roof."

"And?" I ask, seeing him falter as he grabs the towel. "Live on the edge."

"You live on the edge enough for the both of us."

"But I want to live on the edge with you," I whine, pouting pathetically. Jake laughs, his eyes sparkling. There's not much similar about our personalities, considering we're twins, but our laughs, eyes, and smiles are identical.

"It's not worth the hassle," he says lamely. It's a cop-out. He's desperate for me to take him to the wild side, and it pisses me off that he refuses to relent because of a misplaced honor. We're nearly seventeen, for fuck's sake. We're supposed to be out having fun, not revising for finals that are over a year away and eating custard cremes with the local snobs.

"Come on," I coo. "There's a house party. We won't be too late. Just a few drinks with my favorite brother."

"I'm your *only* brother, you twat."

I grin my megawatt smile and am rewarded with his in return. I've got him. Jake looks over his shoulder to the bathroom door. Thinks. And then he's up on the toilet seat, scrambling out of the window with my help. It's been a while since I escaped through this window, so I've neglected to consider that we've both grown considerably.

"Shit," Jake curses, his arms and legs all bent and twisted as I tug him. "I'm stuck."

"No, you're not." I start laughing as I dig my boots into the mud to get a better grip of him, imagining Dad barging in and being confronted with Jake's arse. "Turn a bit."

"There's no damn room."

There's nothing left for it. I increase my grip and heave with all my might.

"Whoa!" Jake dislodges and falls out of the window.

Right on top of me.

I grunt on impact, coughing. "You definitely weigh more than me."

"Piss off. We're the same size." He gets up and brushes himself down.

"You're not gonna pull the ladies looking like that."

"Like what?"

I stand and pull a few twigs from his blond mop. "Come on."

Both our heads snap toward the window when we hear the door in the bathroom open. *Oh shit.*

Lauren appears at the window, frowning, but her eyes light up when she finds the pair of us outside. "What are you doing?"

I grab Jake's arm and pull him toward the lane. "If anyone asks, we fell down the loo," I call, casting a smile over to Jake when he laughs, slinging my arm around his shoulder. Me and my brother. This is what makes me happy. That and girls. And a few beers. Tonight, I get all my favorite things.

"She fancies the pants off you," Jake says, and we both glance back to find Lauren still at the window, watching us.

I smile to myself. "Who doesn't?"

"You're a bighead."

"Weird, though, eh? Since you're the one with all the brains."

Jake nudges me, and I stagger a few paces on a chuckle. "I heard Curtis White screwed her in the pub toilets a few weeks ago."

I look back to the house again. Lauren is still at the window, still watching us. I shake off a weird shudder when she locks eyes with me. "Yeah," I say quietly. "And I also heard she threatened to spread nasty rumors about him if he didn't."

"You're kidding me?" Jake says, alarmed, swinging back to look at Lauren. He definitely shudders too.

"No kidding," I confirm, pulling him back. Call me paranoid, but that girl isn't right. There's some kind of crazy in her eyes. "Anyway, back to the matter at hand."

"What matter?"

"The party."

"I'm gonna get so drunk," Jake declares.

"Easy." I laugh, stopping us as we reach the main road. "Just a few," I reiterate, trying to sound serious, hiding my smile. The shackles are off; he's being himself. But he's not used to alcohol so I need to monitor him.

"Fine, just a few."

I reclaim him, slinging my arm around his shoulder again. "I love you, bro."

"Love you too, Jesse.' He moves stealthily and gets me in a headlock. "You're a cocky fucker, but I love you."

"Don't swear, Jake." He's too good to swear. Too pure. "It doesn't suit you."

"Yes, the good boy mustn't swear," he says tiredly. "For fuck's sake."

Wrestling my way out of the headlock, I throw him a sideways scowl. "Watch your fucking mouth," I grumble, and he breaks down in fits of hysterics.

I roll my eyes and give him a playful shove in the back.

I look down at the bottle of water in my hand. It's not what I had in mind for this evening, but as I see Jake chatting animatedly with a group of lads from school, I know that my sober state is worth it, just to see Jake relaxed and enjoying himself. He catches me observing him and breaks away from the group, joining me on the wall. "Why aren't you drinking?" he asks, claiming a shot off a nearby tray.

"Had enough," I lie. And so has he. He definitely wobbled a bit on his way over. I reach for the tiny glass, but he moves fast, necking it before I can confiscate it. "No more," I warn, and he grins.

"Quit complaining," he says. "You're the one who kidnapped me and dragged me here."

"Dragged? Give me a fucking break."

He laughs, and then he sighs. It's a deep sigh. "There's not one girl in that house who hasn't made a move on you tonight."

I glance around, seeing I'm under the scrutiny of many girls. They're probably wondering why I'm not flouncing around wreaking havoc but, and it's a revelation, I'm enjoying watching Jake let his hair down. "Jealous?" I ask with a cheeky smile.

"Kind of."

"Don't be. It's exhausting."

"Shut up. Your looks are one of your best assets."

"It's my *only* asset," I mumble quietly, taking a sip of my water. "And you can shut up too. You're beautiful inside *and* out."

There's silence for a few moments, Jake fiddling with his beer bottle. He's thinking. I can literally see the cogs of his mind whirling as he chews his bottom lip. I don't nudge him to speak his mind. He will eventually, and my twin senses know exactly what he's going to say.

"Why don't you resent me?" he asks, looking up at me.

And there we have it. I fucking hate the sorrow in his eyes. "Why would I resent you?" I love the clever fucker with everything I have. And more.

"Mum and Dad. They're so hard on you."

"I can handle them." I stopped trying to match Jake's academic ability long ago. It was exhausting, and the constant disappointment from my parents was hurtful. At least now they have a reason to be disappointed in me. But that's on them. It would *never* make me resent Jake.

"And what about when I'm at Oxford?"

"What are you talking about?" I ask seriously. "I'm going to Oxford too."

Jake's bark of laughter is warranted. "And what will you be studying?"

"Sexology."

"You don't need to go to Oxford for that. Just call Uncle Carmichael."

I laugh, grabbing Jake's hand when he reaches for another shot. *What the hell has gotten into him?* He scowls. I raise my eyebrows. "Enough."

"Since when did you become such a spoilsport?" Jake asks, but he relents, settling for his beer instead. "Have you met his new girlfriend?"

"Uncle Carmichael's?" I don't know why I'm asking. The whole family is talking about it. Mum and Dad looked like they were about to self-combust when Dad's little brother, Carmichael, rolled up in his swanky Aston to pick me up for a lunch date with his new, *younger* girlfriend in tow. Sarah. She's only a year or so older than I am. There are only ten years between Jake, me, and Uncle Carmichael, but still. Even *I* raised a brow, and not much shocks me when it comes to Carmichael.

Regardless, it's a moot point. She won't be around for long. They never are. "I've only met her a few times," I say. "She seemed nice." Almost too nice, to be honest. Very touchy-feely. It was slightly uncomfortable, but Carmichael seemed oblivious. Or perhaps his open-minded approach to all things didn't give a fuck. "You should've come with us," I say, giving Jake my attention. "Uncle Carmichael has a way of making everything so fucking right." Acceptance. No expectations.

"Mum and Dad ranted and raved for a solid hour after you left. If I'd gone too . . ."

He's right, of course. It's bad enough Uncle Carmichael could potentially lead the wild child astray. God forbid he got his hands on the saint. Shit, my parents' faces. They warned me. Told me if I left, I wouldn't be welcome back. The judgmental arseholes. Carmichael is the most accepting, kindhearted, patient man I've ever met. And even though my granddad and father hold him firmly in contempt, he does nothing but smile and be civil. He's a better man than I am. I want to be him when I grow up. So in control, respected, highly thought of, even if not by his family. Everyone else loves him. But I'm not allowed to see him. I mustn't be poisoned by his sinful ways. I'm not going to lie, what goes on at Carmichael's place always has my curious mind racing. I can't help it. He always looks so fucking happy. So free. So unbothered by criticism. I want some of that. I don't think he's an embarrassment; I think he's a fucking legend. Fuck society. Fuck expectation. Fuck my parents. I don't know what I'd do without Carmichael to vent my frustrations. "You know, if you want to do something, you should do it," I say wistfully. "We're nearly seventeen, Jake. You can't let Mum and Dad dictate every-thing." Guilt grabs me again. I hate leaving him at home, but I also can't stay in that house facing the constant disdain. Constantly trying to win their approval. So I'll be leaving the moment I can. "Come on." I get to my feet. Jake's starting to slur, and it's already going to take us hours to get home if I have to carry him. "Time for me to tuck you up in bed."

He rolls his eyes. "Let's get a few for the walk home, yeah?" He half stumbles half jogs to a nearby table and claims a few beers before returning with a big cheesy grin, handing one over. Instinct tells me to decline. To take the beers away—he's had enough. But since we're going home now, and I've only had two tonight . . .

We say our goodbyes and head toward the main road. "Tell me," I say, taking a sip of my beer. "Do you really want to go to Oxford, Jake?"

"Yeah."

"That's the lamest *yeah* I've ever heard." I put my arm around his shoulder to support him when I catch a slight stagger. "We're twins, remember? I can literally read your mind." I watch as those cogs start spinning again, and I wait for the answer I know I'll get.

"No," he breathes, as if the word is a hindrance he's glad to be rid of. "Shit, no, I really don't. I don't want to be a doctor. Jesus, I can't think of anything worse."

"But you *could* be one," I point out. "Quite easily. And you'd be really good at it." I can't deny I'd be super proud of him—to tell people my brother is a doctor. He's got that polite bedside manner people talk about when it comes to doctors. He's empathetic. Considerate. All those good things doctors need to be.

"But being capable or good at something doesn't necessarily mean you should do it." Jake's words are quiet, as if he's ashamed to admit it out loud. "Mum and Dad won't see it that way, though, will they?"

"They'd have to accept it."

"What, like they accept that you smoke, drink, and shag around?"

"They don't know I shag around."

"They really do, Jesse." He laughs, swigging the rest of his beer. "Do you know what I want to do?"

"Tell me." I smile, blinded by the excitement in his eyes, just from thinking about it.

"Superbikes."

"Build them?"

"Race them. God, Jesse, all that power between your legs. The wind in your hair, the freedom of the open road. The adrenalin, the speed, the race." He looks up at the black sky. "Could you imagine it?"

I smile, tossing my beer bottle in a hedge. I don't need alcohol. I need this. The truth. I've seen him watching Moto GP. I've watched his concentration. I've found the superbike magazines under his mattress that he's tried to hide from Dad like they're sordid porn shit. "Then fucking do it, Jake." He could do anything he puts his mind to. He's just that type of person. I pull him to a stop and take his arms, looking him in his drunk eyes, hoping beyond all things I've ever hoped for that he'll break free of the chains and do something he desperately wants to do. "You must do it."

His floppy blond hair falls across his eyes, and I knock it away, knowing he's probably incapable of coordinating his hands to do it himself. I'm going to have to start carrying him soon. "Yeah?" he asks, his grin crooked.

"Fuck, yeah."

"Will you tour with me? Help fix my bike? Ride with me? Me and you, together?"

Fuck, fuck, fuck, yeah. "I'm there, bro. All the fucking way."

He clumsily falls into me, giving me the fiercest hug. The mushy twat. But, of course, I embrace it. "We'll detail the finer points tomorrow," he slurs, breaking away and pulling a miniature bottle of whiskey from his front pocket, opening and raising it. "But for now, we celebrate." He downs the lot as he walks backward, taking him and the bottle out of my reach. "To freedom!"

he chants raising the bottle, stumbling into the road. "And doing what the fuck we want."

"Doing what the fuck we—" I blink, being blinded by the headlights of a car. And then I hear them.

Tires.

Screeching tires.

The sound of a horn.

"Jake!" I yell, my head snapping back and forth between him and the car. He's frozen. Looks startled. "Jake, get out of the fucking road!" I start running, but my legs are lead, not carrying me as fast as I need them to. "Jake!"

My heart. I can feel it cracking.

"Jake!" I roar. "God, Jake, no!"

The car hits him, hurling him fifty yards up the road, and I slow to a stop, suddenly paralyzed. "No," I whisper. "Please, no."

The sound of his helpless body hitting the ground is chilling.

A sound I'll never forget.

And the beats of my heart slow to nothing.

1

APRIL 2012

My nose wrinkles. My closed eyes clench. My waking brain pounds like a motherfucker. I open one eye and come face to face with an empty bottle, the damn thing practically touching my nose. I groan and roll onto my back, away from it. Good fucking God. My head feels like an army of soldiers is stomping its way through it.

I lift my hand on a sigh and rest it on my forehead, trying to compress the thuds. Painkillers. I need painkillers. And water. Get me some fucking water.

I drag myself up, resting back on my elbows, and peek around the room, searching for more evidence of my heavy night. I spy my clothes on the floor. But no others with it. No bra, no knickers. I hitch a brow in surprise. Don't tell me I went to bed alone.

"Water?"

I startle and look at the bathroom door, finding a naked woman—her name escapes me—leaning against the door with a glass in her hand.

"You look like you need it." Another woman appears behind her, also naked, except for the smile she's wearing. I definitely know *her* name. Fucking hell, what was I thinking entertaining Coral again? The woman is in love with me. I'm not assuming. She's told me. Repeatedly. I knew getting into bed with her and her husband to fulfill their wild fantasies was a mistake. Now she's left him. Now, I have a pissed off copper on my back. And now she'll take me however I come, always drunk and, last night, even with another woman.

"Want some help up?"

Make that another *two* women.

You're a fuck-up, Ward. A total, uncontrollable fuck-up.

I fall back to the mattress and pull the sheet over my head. "Any more of you hiding in there?" I ask. Jesus, I can't remember a thing.

I hear the bedroom door open. Then silence.

Then . . . .

"Okay, the orgy's over," Sarah says, sounding as unimpressed as usual. She's got a nerve. I bet she's been thrashing man after man all fucking night. "Out."

"I'm a paying member," one of them retorts, as indignant as fuck.

"Not if I cancel it," Sarah counters. I can hear the smugness in her tone. "No need to get dressed," she adds, and I peek out from under the sheet, seeing her gathering up clothes from the floor at the end of the bed and chucking them at the women. She's pissed off. Pissed off because there were three women in my bed last night, and she wasn't one of them.

She escorts them out, slams the door, and then starts collecting up various toys from the floor and shoving them in a basket ready to be cleaned. "Why didn't you stay at your rental last night?" she asks.

"It's lonely." I swing my legs off the bed and stand. And

wobble. And groan. Fuck me, why do I punish myself like this? On cue, a million flashbacks parade through my sore head, reminding me of my wrongs. As if I need reminding. But in case I do, my scar twinges too, and I rub at it as I wander to the bathroom. I can feel Sarah's eyes on my back as I go. "What time is it?" I call back.

"Too early for a drink."

"Fuck you," I mutter under my breath, flipping the shower on. It's never too early for a drink. *Never too early to escape.*

"You have an appointment with your lawyer at three, remember? To sign the papers for your new place. I've arranged for the transfer."

"When am I moving in?" I ask, stepping into the shower and standing there. Just standing there, letting the hot water wash away last night's shame, at the same time wishing this water could wash away my regret. My past. Wash away *me*.

"A week Saturday. The developers have the launch night on the Friday, then it's all yours."

I look at the bathroom door when Sarah appears, leaning on the frame. She seriously needs to stop with all that stuff she pumps into her face. It's having the reverse effect these days, making her look older instead of younger and fresher. "So my new apartment will be full of strangers wandering around messing it up?"

"It's in the contract. The developer has assured us it'll be left as good as new for you to move into."

I set about washing my hair. "What else?"

"We need to talk about the new rooms. Décor, design, layout, equipment, that kind of thing."

I work up a lather, closing my eyes and trying to enjoy the spray while Sarah bothers me. "John's sorting the equipment," I tell her. "As for the décor, call the company who did my new place."

"You want the Lusso designer?"

"Yeah, why not? All that Italian shit looks great." Really great. The penthouse I now own is fucking incredible, but the décor? Yeah, whoever did that knows what they're doing. It's good. Very good. Tasteful. And if The Manor is anything, it's tasteful. Past the orgies and illicitness, of course. I smile as I rinse my hair, thinking Carmichael would be proud of what it's become. Then it drops when I think about how disappointed he'd be by what *I* have become.

I flinch and shake my head free of those thoughts. "What's the time?" I ask as I step out of the shower. Sarah doesn't control her roving eye.

"Still too early for a drink." She pulls a towel off the rail and chucks it at me. "I'll call Rococo Union," she says as she leaves me in peace.

I frown. "Who's Rococo Union?"

"The designers of your new swanky penthouse," she calls. "What should I say when they ask what kind of establishment this is?"

I go to the mirror and immediately look away from the drained-looking man staring back at me. My green eyes look dull, my skin sallow. "It's The Manor, that's it. No need to give them a rundown of everything that happens within its walls, Sarah."

"Why? Are you ashamed?"

I don't entertain her. She knows I couldn't give a flying fuck what people think of me or my establishment. I just can't be bothered to feed their curiosity.

As I descend the sweeping staircase to the lobby, John wanders out of the bar. His wraparounds are perfectly in place as always, but I know his eyes will be narrowed behind them. I reach the bottom and stretch my hamstrings, nodding to staff as they pass. "All right?" I ask.

His face remains impassive. "Stayed the night again?"

I give him a tired look but hold back my retort, because if there's one man on this earth who deserves my respect, it's John. "I'm going for a run." I need to clear the cobwebs off. And the drink. And the sin.

I head for the doors.

"Just tell me," he says, pulling me to a stop. I don't turn around. "Why the fuck have you spent millions on a penthouse apartment when you crash here every night?"

It's a reasonable question. I turn to face him, pulling my heel to my arse to stretch my thigh. "It's an investment." What else should I spend my money on? My car's paid for, my bikes are paid for, this place is paid for, I don't need to pay for gym membership, food, and drink.

Or sex.

And I certainly haven't got anyone to leave my money to.

"We're here for a good time, John."

He shakes his head, and I know he's thinking Uncle Carmichael would turn in his grave. "Or," he starts, "perhaps you've bought it because a tiny part of your fucked-up brain, which makes a brief appearance most mornings when you wake up with a pounding head and a few women in bed, is telling you that you need to get the fuck out of this lifestyle." He turns and wanders toward the bar.

Yeah, and maybe that too.

"Go on holiday, Jesse," he calls back.

"I just got back from Cortina."

"That wasn't a holiday. That was a change of scenery." He disappears into the bar as I drop my heel from my arse. He's right, of course. But in my defense, I went with good intentions. A detox, if you will. Then I found the minibar and a few hot Swedish women. It spiraled from there.

My head is suddenly pounding again, and I glance around The Manor's lobby. Opulence and grandeur stretch to every corner. From floor to ceiling. Every inch of this place drips sophistication. I look up the stairs to the private suites. Why the fuck wouldn't I want to stay here every night?

Because it's slowly killing you.

Run.

I turn and break into a sprint. And I don't stop. Not for miles. My head empties and my body loosens, my mind focused on the feel of my feet hitting the ground constantly. Peace.

And that sense of freedom only intensifies the farther I get away from The Manor.

2

I WAKE up the following morning sprawled on a bed in the communal room, my staff cleaning around me. "Fuck," I mumble, propping myself up. "Morning."

"Morning, Mr. Ward," Rosa says cheerily as she strips the bed next to me. God love her, she doesn't bat an eyelid at my naked form.

I gather the sheets and stand, wrapping them around my waist. "What time is it?"

"Ten o'clock, Mr. Ward." She flaps a fresh sheet, and it whips the air, creating a deafening crack. I flinch, kicking a bottle out of the way as I leave.

I trudge down the stairs, around the landing, and into my private suite, shutting the door behind me and leaning against it. Why the fuck do I do this to myself?

Because you're a glutton, Ward. A glutton for alcohol and sex. And punishment.

And escape.

But there is no escape.

I hear the muffled sound of my mobile and scan the room. The bedsheets are everywhere, the floor littered with various pieces of leather lingerie. My mind fuzzes, a montage of naked bodies and entwined limbs, ransacking my brain. Moans of pleasure. Screams of ecstasy. Meaningless orgasm after meaningless orgasm.

Release.

But no release.

I fall to the bed and close my eyes. I shouldn't. I know what I'll see. What I'll hear. But I'm exhausted. Always exhausted.

Seven months. Seven months of hated but deserved solitude. Can't face a world where there is no Jake. I haven't left the house. Not once. Hardly left this room. We didn't share, not since we were fifteen, but he was always in here. Always reminding me I wasn't all bad, because we, Jake and I, were one, and everyone has two sides.

"We did everything we could." His words, his grave face.

The looks my parents gave me when the doctor uttered those dreaded words. They'll haunt me for the rest of my miserable life

I'm hollow. So fucking hollow.

No Jake.

Endless guilt.

Parents who hate me.

I hear a knock at the door, but I remain where I am, unmoving, unfeeling, unwilling. I hear it open. I know who it is; I heard them arrive a few hours ago. I'm surprised it took her this long to seek me out.

"Hi," Lauren says, closing the door and resting back against it.

Silence.

I don't have the energy to tell her to fuck off. To leave me alone. She wanders over to my bed and settles on the edge. Reaches for my shoulder. Strokes it a little. My dead eyes find her, my face as blank as my mind. Then she produces a bottle of vodka from her bag. Unscrews the cap. Takes a glug. My face remains impassive, but when she holds it out, I find some strength to take it and sit up. And I down half, forcing myself not to gag. The burn in my throat is welcome. It's something else to focus on. Something other than my unrelenting pain. I don't hand the bottle back. I work my way through it under Lauren's watchful eyes until it's empty, before slumping back to my mattress and closing my eyes.

I know what's coming next, so I remain unmoving when her hand slips under the sheets and finds my limp cock. "Condom," I mumble.

"I'm on the pill."

I open my eyes and find her top half naked. Reaching for her hand, I yank her into the bed and climb on top of her.

Numb.

Nothingness.

But it's a fuck load better than grief and guilt, and maybe all I'm good for anyway.

The easy lay.

Leave your feelings at the door.

I blink my vision clear, shooting up on the bed. My phone is ringing again, and I sift through the sheets and pillows until I locate it. Amalie's name glows on the screen. I drop my mobile back to the bed and head for the shower, the sound of her trying to reach me taunting me while I scrub last night's dirt away.

By the time I'm done, I have endless missed calls and a few voicemails. I delete them, but notice one from John. I dial him.

"I need you in the new wing," he says in answer.

"What for?"

"The beams. The carpenter wants to know if you're happy with them."

"They're beams. What could possibly be wrong with them?"

"Just get your motherfucking arse over here." He hangs up, and I laugh to myself. God, would I love to smash that fucker in the face from time to time. The feeling is probably mutual.

On a heavy sigh, I start to get into one of my finest suits, my armor, a mask to hide the cracks, rough up my blond hair with some wax, slip on my Rolex and brogues, and head to the new wing.

I find John in the farthest room, staring at the ceiling. "What's the problem?"

His head drops, and I get a rare glimpse of his eyes as he stares over his wraparounds at me. "Are you happy with them?" He motions to where four thick oak beams span the width at even intervals.

"They look great."

John raises his arms, and I frown, wondering what the fuck he's doing. Then he launches his big body upward and wraps his hands over the top of a beam, his huge, imposing frame dangling from the ceiling. I recoil. More so when I hear an almighty crack. "What the fuck?"

John drops to his feet. "Still happy?"

"There was no mention of reinforcements," the scrawny man next to him says, sounding panicked.

Well, fuck me. "How many of these have been installed?" I ask, mentally calculating the number of new rooms and how many beams are in each.

"All of them," John grunts, throwing an accusing glare the guy's way.

Oh. Well, that's fucking great. "We need to fix this," I say, looking across to the contractor who's frantically flicking through his phone, probably searching for the email that makes no mention of reinforcements. Whatever. We're here now and it needs sorting out. Jesus, I'll have personal injury claims thrown at me left and right. "We need to hang things from these, mate," I say, pointing to the ceiling.

"What kind of things?"

"People."

He recoils. "P . . . p . . . . people?"

"Yes, people." I head for the door, smiling to myself. Poor fucker probably thinks he's walked into a butchering house. "I'll be in my office."

As I pass through the lobby, a smile on my face, I see the local florist renewing the flower arrangement on the ornate, round showpiece of a table that holds court. I stop and admire the simple spray of calla lilies.

"Mr. Ward," she says, pausing with the tweaking of the tall stems. "It's a beautiful day."

I look at the imposing double doors that lead to the circular driveway. "I'll take your word for it," I say, returning my attention to her. She's smiling, all dreamy, and I dazzle her with my knockout beam. She gets herself in a bit of a fluster, returning to the arrangement that looks pretty fucking perfect to me. "They're beautiful," I say, reaching for one of the lilies and stroking the velvety white head.

She pauses again, her eyes falling to my fingers. She's wondering what these hands are capable of. I'll leave her with that thought. "Have a great day." I continue to my office.

Sarah is in the summer room when I pass through, talking to a woman I don't recognize. It's not unusual, what with new members joining every week. "Hi," I say as I pass.

"Oh, Jesse, this is Geraldine," Sarah says, and I stop. "She's a new member. I'm just showing her around. Geraldine, this is Jesse Ward. He owns The Manor."

My hand comes up as I take her in. Mid-forties, perhaps. Professional. A lawyer, most likely. She's got an air of supremacy about her. Uptight. Finds it hard to let herself go. She's come to the right place. "Welcome to The Manor." I dazzle her with my signature smile, and I see her throat bulge from her poorly hidden swallow.

She coughs, accepting my hand, and I give it just enough of a squeeze to have her mind race with curiosity. "Thank you." She smiles coyly as I flex my grip. "I look forward to spending time here."

I bet she does. "You'll never want to leave," I assure her, backing away. "See you around."

Her head cocks. "You will." She's wondering whether I dabble. She'll soon find out.

I don't have to look at Sarah to know her lips will be tight. "Let me show you the private suites," she says, virtually pulling Geraldine away.

I make it to my office and grab a water from the fridge, downing the lot in one fell swoop. My eyes fall to my drinks cabinet. Then to the clock. Back to my drinks cabinet. My jaw clenches. Back to the clock.

My phone ringing is my savior, and I answer as I wander to my desk and slump down in my chair. "Cathy."

"I'm at your rental. You're not here."

"I stayed at The Manor last night."

"You stay at The Manor most nights. There are only so many times I can clean the bathrooms and floors around here. I may as well be a housekeeper there."

I laugh. "You don't want to be a housekeeper here, Cathy, trust me."

"Why not?"

"It wouldn't suit you."

"Oh, I don't know. I used to ride horses in Ireland, you know. I'd whip that place into shape in no time using one of those floggers of yours."

I fall apart laughing at my desk, imagining Cathy, my dear,

wholesome housekeeper, cracking a whip in the communal room. "I know you would, Cathy. But I need you at my place."

"What for, boy? You're hardly ever here for me to cook for. You drop washing off sporadically. Honestly, finding your ski equipment here the other day was the highlight of my week."

I smile. I knew it would be, hence I dropped it off on my way through. She's indirectly telling me that I should be at home rather than lording it up here. I've tried being at home. Numerous times. It's torture of the worst degree. I'm not good at being on my own, especially when drink is added to the lonely mix which, inevitably, it always is. That rental has been sitting there for years, mostly unlived in. But it serves as a great crash pad on the odd occasion the boys and I venture into the city on a night out. My new penthouse at Lusso can't *just* be a crash pad. Not at ten million fucking quid. "Well, my new place is somewhat larger than the rental. It'll keep you busy."

"And will you be living there?"

"Yes," I reply. *You're a deluded prick, Ward.* "I plan on it, yes." I planned on staying at the rental too, but the rental is cold, sparse, and unhomely. My new place is anything but. I ignore the part of my brain that's currently telling me Lusso will just be another discarded part on my never-ending pile of attempts to fix myself. The car, the bikes, the apartments miles away from here. They're all supposed to help me escape. But they don't. Nothing helps me escape. I glance across to my drinks cabinet again. Well, not really *nothing*. Another glance at the clock.

"Ooh, I can't wait to see it," Cathy chimes. "When do you move in?"

"A week Saturday."

"Great. I'm off to polish your snowboard." She hangs up, and my eyes remain fixed on the clock, watching the second hand glide around the face. I roll my shoulders. Stretch my legs under my desk. Swipe a hand through my hair. *Run.* I should run. I rise from my chair to go change into my running gear just as Sarah strides in.

"Your noon meeting will be here soon."

My arse falls back down to the seat. "What noon meeting?"

"With the interior designer. I told you yesterday afternoon." She wanders across to my desk and slaps a file down. "But you had already started on the bottle."

"What's that supposed to mean?" I ask, glaring at her. "I have a drink most days. Is that a crime?" Listen to me, being all defensive. It's the first sign of guilt. But Sarah and I, we handle our guilt in different ways. She whips the fuck out of men, takes out her anger and frustration on them. Punishes them. Me? I seem quite content punishing myself.

"No crime," she muses, sashaying out of my office.

"Why can't you do the meeting?" I call.

"I've got memberships to deal with. When your meeting's done, we need to go over them." She stops at the door, looking back. "I'll be in the communal room tonight."

"And?" I'm not going anywhere near Sarah *or* her whip. Believe it or not, I do have a conscience, even if I lose it from time to time. I never lose it with Sarah, though. I won't make that mistake again. I flinch, and by the look on Sarah's face, she's read my mind.

"Have a good day, Jesse." She closes the door, and I clench my fists, trying to breathe through my anger, trying to keep my eyes off the bottles of drink across the room. Having them removed would be the answer. Clearing out my office and apartment of all temptation. But then, the bar is fifty paces from my office. And what would I offer mates to drink if we go back to my apartment?

Excuses.

I reach up and yank my tie loose, feeling suffocated. The last thing I need right now is a meeting. My head's fuzzy. My body strung. My mood low. Shit, I need a drink.

Glancing at my Rolex, like it might offer me a different time to the clock on the wall, I groan. Another hour, I can wait another hour. I stand, remove my jacket, and unfasten the top button of my shirt. Then I sit down and slump back in my chair and stare at the ceiling as I roll my sleeves up. *Another hour. Another hour. Another hour.*

There's a knock at my office door and my limp head drops as the big guy strides in. "Jesse. Miss O'Shea, Rococo Union."

Another hour. "Perfect. Thanks, John." My voice is hoarse. I'll get this meeting out the way and then, fuck it, I'm having a drink. Just one. I should've insisted Sarah deal with this. I'm in no mood—restless, cranky, and hot.

I watch as John slowly shifts. What's that look on his face? It's impassive, as always, unreadable with or without his wrap-arounds shielding his eyes. But . . . I cock my head.

And nearly choke when he reveals who's behind him. My limp body finds life and my back straightens.

What. The. Fuck?

I slowly stand from my chair, fully aware that her gaze rises with me. Is this her? Is this the woman who's filled my new place with all that Italian shit—Italian shit that inflated the price by another million quid?

I start walking around my desk, taking her in, every gorgeous little bit of her. Well, this is a pleasant surprise. The women around here, they're mostly mid-thirties plus. She's, what? Mid-twenties? Too young for me. *Way* too young for me.

I nibble my bottom lip, thinking, noting her eyes still firmly set on me. She looks a little . . . struck. I inwardly smile.

My legs are moving, but I can't feel the damn things. My mind is clean. My vision clear. My senses alert. Almost like when I finish a fifteen-mile run. I like those feelings, but I like them more when I've not had to nearly kill myself to achieve that sense of freedom. I reach up and feel my jaw. I should've shaved. Do I look older with stubble?

I close the distance between us, taking her in. Jesus, she's getting more beautiful the closer I get, her dark hair pinned up, her perfect little figure screaming for me to run my hands all over it. I want to remove those pins and plunge my fingers into those shiny locks. Her eyes, good God, those dark eyes.

Jesus, Ward, pull it together.

But . . . I'm not alone in my admiring. She's taking me in, assessing every part of me. I'm not what she expected either. What was she expecting?

John said *Miss* O'Shea, didn't he? *Miss.*

She's sublime. Completely and utterly sublime.

And so totally out of place around here. Lord, if any of the men of The Manor caught sight of her, they'd be fighting over who got her in the communal room first. It would be a frenzy, possibly even a bloodbath.

Smile at her. I should smile at her, but my trusty smile is nowhere to be found. I'm being failed by my magnetic asset, feeling like I've been sucker-punched in the gut. Her gaze. It's not pouring with longing for me, something that usually gets under my skin.

She's . . . unsure. Stunned into silence and stillness. I'm with her.

I finally convince my arm to lift, offering my hand. She remains motionless. Frozen. In a trance. I'm giving her three seconds before I'm moving in.

One.

Two.

Three.

I slowly lean forward and grasp her shoulders, my face going straight to the smooth, olive skin of her cheek. I could get drunk on her scent alone. I feel her tensing under my touch, and I laugh on the inside. These hands, lady, will give you hours of pleasure. My mouth, my tongue, my cock.

"It's a pleasure," I whisper. It really fucking is. A very *unexpected* pleasure.

She moans, and I smile, easing up on my grip, lowering myself so I'm at her eye level. "Are you okay?" I can feel my lips curving into a smile as she lifts those stunning chocolate eyes to mine. I'm so fucking happy in this moment. And it's . . . freeing, actually.

She suddenly seems to snap out of her trance and steps back, and my hands drop to my side. I inwardly pout. "Hi." She virtually coughs it out. "Ava, my name is Ava." She holds her hand out to me.

Her voice. Fuck me, I'm a goner. And I'm physically trembling. I really need to stop drinking. I take her hand and squeeze but pull away abruptly when I'm struck by an electric shock that flies up my arm and stabs at my heart, making it suddenly buck wildly.

What the fuck was that?

Dazed and massively confused, I repeat her name, it falling naturally from my lips, no other words coming to me. Oh Jesus, I need to be shouting that when I'm hammering into her. I want to make her scream, claw at me, bite me. She's just staring at me— this painfully beautiful young woman is staring at me, and for once in my fucking life, I'm stumped. No words. But plenty of thoughts.

I need to offer her a membership. She can have it for free. My heart is booming for the first time in years. Is it excitement? Anticipation? I don't know, but I tell you what I *do* know . . .

I've never seen a woman so clearly. Never wanted one *before* I've had a drink. This woman though? It's instant, uncontrollable attraction, and that is so very unfamiliar to me. So unfamiliar, in fact, I have absolutely no idea how to be.

"Yes. Ava."

I shake myself out of my useless state as I step away, aware I'm crowding her. I'm not dealing with the kind of woman I'm used to. I also slip my hands in my pockets, restraining them. Everything feels out of control—my mind, my mouth, my body. "Thanks, John." I glance across to him where he's standing by the door, giving him a look that tells him I'm in unchartered territory. But he knows that. He knew it the moment he met Ava O'Shea at the door.

He smiles. Leaves.

And my eyes fall back onto her, starving for more. *Jesus*. I shake my head to myself, searching for some direction. A seat. *Offer her a seat.* I motion toward the couches as I head for my drinks cabinet. "Can I get you a drink?" I stare at the endless bottles of spirits, my head totally bent. A drink? Did I just offer her an alcoholic drink in a midday meeting? I frown to myself and turn to find her.

She's looking at the cabinet too, her own frown in place. "No, thank you."

"Water?" I ask, unable to stop laughing on the inside at my own stupidity.

"Please." She smiles mildly, still standing where I left her. Is she experiencing the same level of uselessness as me? Shaky legs, brain malfunction?

I pull two bottles of water from the fridge as she finally makes her way to the couch, giving me the perfect view of the perfect silhouette of a perfect body in that perfect dress. *Good Lord, help me.*

I collect a glass. "Ava?"

She pauses. Looks back. And my cock, the one that usually only responds under the influence, twitches behind my boxers.

It's alarming. Unsettling. How old is she? I'm frowning to myself again. Actually, how old am I? I haven't celebrated a birthday since I lost Jake.

"Yes?" she asks, turning to face me.

"Glass?"

"Yes, please." She smiles and my dick very nearly fucking explodes. I work to talk it down as she settles and pulls something from her bag, setting it on the table before her with her phone, shaking her hands subtly as I wander over and sit opposite her. Right now, it's the best seat in the house, and there are some fucking amazing seats around here. I put the waters on the table and relax as she scribbles notes on a pad. I can't help but think she's distracting herself.

"So, where do we start?" I ask, trying to kill the awkward silence that's fallen. She looks up as I take a swig of water, her eyes falling to my lips. I smile, and she startles, distracting herself once again by pouring some water. I should have done that. Poured her water. *What kind of gentleman are you, Ward?*

"I guess you should tell me why I'm here." She braves facing me.

"Oh?" Yes, why is she here? My thoughts are all over the place, and she is dominating them. Just her. Nothing else. No shitty past. No guilt. No shame. No pain. Just her.

"You requested me by name?" she murmurs.

Ah. Interiors. This beautiful specimen is a dab hand at amazing interiors. "Yes." My smile is natural. Not forced. I just love how she's struggling to look me in the eye. She keeps taking a timeout, looking away, gathering herself, before facing me again. It's . . . fascinating. I know I affect women, but none of them try to hide their attraction. Perhaps, maybe—definitely— because all the women I encounter are members of my fine establishment. Inhibitions are lost. Beating around the bush is just a waste of time, when you could simply spell out your desires and get-fucking-on with it. Which everyone does at The Manor, including me. But this woman . . . that's not in her. Boldness isn't the way forward here.

But it's all I know.

I feel my forehead wrinkle again. *The way forward to what exactly, Ward?*

"So, may I ask why?"

"You may." I inch forward on the couch and rid my hands of my water, keeping my arse on the edge, my forearms on my knees.

"Okay. Why?" she asks, unsure.

"I've heard great things about you." Is she blushing? It's cute. And something else I'm not familiar with.

"Thank you. So why am I here?"

"Well, to design." I laugh to myself, my thoughts filthy. My answer could be *very* different.

"Design what, exactly? From what I've seen, everything is pretty perfect."

She's right, but as of now I'd have her redesign the entire place if it meant keeping her here for longer. Just to look at her. Admire her. Feel these odd tingles and be rid of the never-ending cycle of self-annihilation that is my life. "Thank you," I say. "Do you have your portfolio with you?" I'm dragging this out. I don't need to see her previous work. I've seen everything I need to see at Lusso to know she's the woman for the job. But, shit, I'm getting far more than I bargained for.

"Of course." She pulls it from her bag and sets it on the table, and I rise without thought and move to her couch, lowering beside her. She shifts subtly.

"You're very young to be such an accomplished designer." I start browsing the file.

"How old are you?" she blurts out, and my hand pauses turning the page. Jesus, and I thought *my* brain-to-mouth filter was dodgy. Hers is completely knackered. But, God love her, she's totally exposed her state of mind right now. Confirmed my thoughts. She's attracted to me.

Yet that question . . .

It tells me age matters. It tells me she's wondering. Fuck. How old do I look? My confidence in that department has been dented for the first time in forever. Maybe because I'm on unfamiliar ground with an obviously younger woman.

I start nibbling my lip, thinking. Avoid the question. Simple. I glance up at her. Her face, bless her, is bright red. "Twenty–one," I say, and she snorts, making my brows rise, part amused, but more insulted.

"Sorry." She swings her gaze back to the portfolio in my hand, and I start turning the pages again. And I'm smiling when the interior of my new apartment comes into view. "This, I like a lot."

"I'm not sure my work on Lusso would fit in here."

I find her eyes. *What about you, Ava? Would you fit in here?* "You're right; I'm just saying . . . I really like it."

"Thank you."

She clumsily grabs her water. She's modest. Reserved. It's refreshing after being surrounded by brash women my entire adult life. But she definitely needs to loosen up. Just a little, though. Not too much. Her disposition is endearing. Her awkwardness. Her terrible attempts to remain cool. That's refreshing too.

This is so strange, this feeling. My fascination. *Her* fascination. I smile at the photographs, feeling her eyes drilling into me. I move my knee a fraction and brush her leg, and she jerks, moving away quickly.

"Do you have a toilet?" She's up like a shot, faffing with her dress, and I slowly rise until I'm towering over her.

"Through the summer room and on your left."

"Thank you."

I remain exactly where I am, not giving her the space she

needs, forcing her to edge her way past. She's holding her breath. I'm definitely holding mine. My eyes follow her hasty steps all the way to the door until the wood separates us.

"Well, fucking hell," I breathe, falling to my arse on the couch and staring forward. Ava O'Shea. I don't know what I anticipated, but she most definitely wasn't it. I blow out my cheeks, scrubbing my hands down my rough face. Just ask her out. Simple shit. Except, I don't ask women out. I get plastered and fuck them in every filthy way imaginable, and something tells me she wouldn't be all too amenable to an offer to join me in my private suite. She's nothing like the women I'm used to, and I'm guessing Miss Ava O'Shea isn't familiar with this lifestyle. But is she curious? Could she turn after she's seen what I offer here? I pout.

Frown.

Recoil.

No. This place, it wouldn't suit her. She's too . . . lovely. She's more lace, not leather. More passionate lovemaking than animal- istic fucking. I sense she wouldn't settle for anything less than a fairy tale, and I know, better than anyone, that all I have to offer is a horror story. Darkness. Ugliness. Pain. Sin. Guilt.

She's out of your league, Ward.

The door swings open and I jump out of my fucking skin. "For fuck's sake, Sarah," I snap.

"Sorry. I finished earlier than expected. Want me to take ov—"

"No." I grab the portfolio and start flicking the pages. "I've got it, thanks." I risk a peek up at her, discovering exactly what I knew I would. A massive frown.

"Are you okay?"

"Yep." That's a lie. I don't think I am okay. I feel . . . weird. And gutted. Because Miss O'Shea doesn't fit into my box. "I'll find you when I'm done."

That frown doesn't leave her face as she closes the door. It's an achievement, considering the amount of shit she has pumped into it. I toss the folder on the table and start trying to master a plan because, and it's a fucking revelation, I am affected.

I've just *got* to know what's under that navy pencil dress. Got to taste those lips. Got to feel those hips. Get to know her. Woo her. *Then ask her out, Ward.* That's the correct etiquette, I believe.

All well and good, but I'm assuming she's interested. I might have read this completely wrong. Perhaps she's just off because she's found herself at an elite sex club in a meeting with a man who, I fucking hope, breaks the stereotypical sex-club-owner type.

My eyes fall to her phone on the table. Hmm.

Like I said, boldness is all I know.

I quickly claim it and bring up the home screen. Go to contacts. Add my name and number. And I dial myself so I can save hers. Stalkerish? Absolutely not. I'm just saving myself the time and hassle of calling the firm she works for to get her contact details. You know, just in case she forgets to give me her card.

I rest her phone back on the table, my eyes on her bag. I look back at the door. Think. I'm in her handbag before I know it, finding what I'm looking for quickly. I pull out her wallet, open it, my shaking hands not helping me. I spot her driver's license and pull it out, scanning the small card. And, horribly, my heart sinks a little. Twenty-six. She's twenty-six. It's confirmed. *Way* too young for me, and since she's asked the question, she's concluded I must be too old for her. "God damn it," I breathe, deflating.

I hear a knock at the door. *Fuck.* I shove her wallet back in her bag and quickly reclaim her portfolio.

She enters, and I look up on a smile. It's probably a guilty smile. *Yes, I just totally violated your privacy. Yes, I'm wondering what the fuck is wrong with me.*

My smile falls when I detect a change in her disposition. She seems more together. Resolute. I shouldn't have let her use the ladies'.

She walks to the couch opposite, completely disregarding me when I make space for her to pass and join me on this couch. So she's going to approach me professionally now, is she? Force herself to remain together?

Not if I have anything to do with it.

"Are you okay?" I ask, wanting her to know I've read the situation. That I'm aware.

"Yes, I'm fine."

I withdraw as a result of her snappy reply.

"Would you like to show me where your intended project is so we can start discussing your requirements?" she asks.

My eyebrows jump up of their own volition. I'd happily discuss my requirements all day long, and it doesn't involve any kind of designing. "Sure." I fetch my mobile from my desk and follow her to the door, quickening my stride to pass her. *Woo her in the traditional way, Ward.*

I bow as I hold the door open, unleashing one of my most dazzling smiles. She's not amused. *Oh, playing hard to get now, huh? Well, unlucky for you, Miss O'Shea, I'm quite taken by you. You only have yourself to blame.*

My eyes fall to the base of her back when she passes, and my hand is resting there before I can stop myself. Her shoulders jump up, her breathing becomes rushed, and she increases her pace, severing our contact, but she comes to an abrupt stop when she reaches the summer room. She doesn't know which way to go.

"Do you play?" I ask, pointing to the courts outside the window.

Her laugh is pure and joyful, and it feels good to know I did that. Made her laugh. She's loosening up. *A point to you, Ward.* "No, I don't."

I grin, happy with myself. More so when her smile widens.

Kill me now. Her beauty just increased tenfold. "You?" she asks as we walk on.

"I don't mind the odd game, but I'm more of an extreme sports kinda guy."

"What sort of extreme sports?"

The kind that'll make your eyes water. "Snowboarding, mainly, but I've tried my hand at whitewater rafting, bungee jumping, and skydiving. I'm a bit of an adrenalin junky. I like to feel the blood pumping." I need to do that shit more often. Get the adrenalin pumping in healthier ways.

I study her for a few pleasurable moments. This is nice. A normal conversation about normal stuff with a beautiful woman.

"Extreme."

I can't help myself. "*Very* extreme."

She loses her breath. She's struggling. Might even blurt out something inappropriate again. That façade she returned from the ladies' with? Bye-bye. "Shall we continue?" I ask. Her eyes close briefly—gathering herself—and when she opens them, I make sure the first thing she sees are mine. And she searches them. What is she hoping to find?

"Yes, please," she practically breathes.

I smile and lead her into the bar, not surprised to find Sam propped on a stool; he's a millionaire with nothing to do but fill his time with kink. But it's unusual to see Drew here at this time of day. I give them both a hello slap on the shoulder. "Guys, this is Ava. Ava, this is Sam Kelt and Drew Davies."

"Good afternoon." Drew, ever the cold one, takes Ava in from top to toe. *Yes, I agree, mate, she looks all wrong around here.*

"Hi," Ava says.

"Welcome to the pleasure dome." Sam raises his beer, and I roll my eyes. "Can I buy you a drink?"

"No, I'm fine, thanks."

"Jesse?"

"No, I'm good. I'm just giving Ava a tour of the extension. She'll be working on the interiors," I say, turning a smile to her. Perhaps I'm being presumptuous. Her taking the contract is not set in stone at all, but I plan on making it happen.

"About time," Drew pipes up. "There are never any rooms available."

"How was boarding in Cortina, my man?" Sam asks, steering us away from Drew's grievance.

I settle on a stool. "Amazing. The Italian way of skiing follows pretty closely to their laid-back lifestyle." I watch Ava as I speak. She's interested, wants to know more, and that in itself is appealing. So I reel off what I got up to in Italy. Minus the women and drink.

"You're good?" Ava asks quietly, her eyes now comfortably set on me.

At what? Fucking? Skiing? Wooing? "Very," I reply, and she nods, thoughtful, our eyes locked. She's wondering about the fucking part, despite the fact that, naturally, I didn't mention my extracurricular activities of that sort while I was in Italy. Or would she call it making love? Whatever. My dick inside her. All the same thing. "Shall we?" I get up and gesture the way.

She says her goodbyes to the lads, and I don't miss both their interested looks. Whatever they're thinking, I'm certain I won't like it.

"So, now for the main feature," I tease, taking the stairs, Ava following. We circle the landing. "These are the private rooms." I point to a few doors, my private suite included. Her. In there. I close my eyes briefly and try not to let the fantasy take hold as we reach the stained-glass window at the bottom of the stairs that lead to the communal room. I glance up, my mind off on another tangent. What would she look like up there? Hanging from a St. Andrews Cross? Shackled to a horse? Spread-eagled on a bed?

But then . . .

I look down at my feet, caught off guard by my next thought.

If she was in that room, every other man in this place would get to enjoy her. I chew my lip, my thoughts spiraling. All eyes on her. That doesn't sit well.

I force my feet forward, shaking my mind clear. "This is the extension." It doesn't sit well at all. "This is where I need your help." We enter the new wing, and I spy the carpenter in one of the rooms on a ladder, drilling into the ceiling.

"This is all new?" she asks.

"Yes, they're all shells at the moment, but I'm sure you'll remedy that. Let me show you." I seize her hand without thought and pull her to the last room, smiling at her when she doesn't protest. Because she feels it too. Whatever that odd sizzle is, she feels it.

"Are they all this big?" She tugs her hand free, and it's all I can do not to reprimand her for it. I don't get much pleasure in life. Sex isn't really pleasure. It's a necessity. A means to an end. A habit. A vice. But physical contact with her is pleasurable and, frankly, it's pretty fucking hard to let her withdraw from it.

"Yes," I answer, and she gazes around.

"En suite?"

"Yes." I lean against the wall as she disappears into the bathroom. These rooms are the last thing on my agenda at the moment. And at the top? How the fuck I'm going to convince this woman to have dinner with me. Somewhere else. Away from here. Away from the eyes of the male members. Away from the women who I absolutely *know* will take an instant dislike to her, because she's younger, fresher. And because I, the unfeeling, impenetrable lord of the fucking sex manor, am taken by her.

Ava emerges. Takes me in. Thinks. I'm suddenly wary, my eyes narrowing evidence of that, but I'm fucked if I can help it.

"I'm not sure that I'm the right person for this job."

Oh no she doesn't. Not a chance. No way. *Make normal*

conversation again, Ward. Talk about tennis. TV. Music. "I think you have what I want." And I say that. And I don't only say it, I say it quietly. Suggestively. *Boldness is all you know.* And, worryingly, I can see her withdrawing. So yes, fuck it, the gloves are off.

I know attraction when it smacks me in the face, and this woman is attracted to me. So why the heck is she trying to be all cool? Could it be this place? Is she wary of my elaborate high-end sex club? That's the stupidest question I've ever asked myself. Of course she is. Everyone unfamiliar with this lifestyle is wary of it. It doesn't usually bother me. Not with anyone—my parents, my sister, no one. But this woman? I care that she might think it's debauched. That *I'm* debauched. And worst, I care that she's right.

"I've always dealt in modern luxury," she says, gazing around. "I'm sure you would be happier working with Patrick or Tom. They deal with our period projects."

I don't know who Patrick and Tom are, but it's out of the question. I want her working here so I can work on her. "But I want you."

"Why?"

"You look like you'll be very good." *Jesus, Jesse, you couldn't be more diplomatic?*

Her eyes undeniably widen. "What's your brief?"

Oh, now we're talking. I'm quickly concluding that instinct is all I have here. I act on impulse. Always have. I smile a little. "Sensual, intimate, luxurious, stimulating, invigorating . . ."

Her frown throws me, I have to admit. "Okay," she says slowly. "Anything in particular I should allow for?"

"A big bed and lots of wall hangings."

"What sorts of wall hangings?"

"Big, wooden ones. Oh, and the lighting needs to suit."

"Suit what?"

"Well, the brief, of course." What's amiss here? She seems confused.

"Yes, of course." She looks at the ceiling. "Do all of the rooms have those?" she asks, looking back at me for an answer.

"Yes, they're essential." *When they're reinforced.*

"Are there any particular colors I should work to or against?"

"No, knock yourself out."

She glances up, startled. "Excuse me?"

"Go for it," I say around a smile. I couldn't give a fuck what colors she chooses.

"You mentioned a big bed. Any particular type?"

Big enough for me to tie you up. Big enough for us to roll around in. "No, just very big."

"What about soft furnishings?"

"Yes, lots." I've had enough of dancing around this obvious chemistry. I'm being suggestive at every turn and she's sidestepping it all. I need something she can't sidestep. Something unmissable. "I like your dress." *On my floor.*

"Thanks." She's off, virtually sprinting away. "I have everything I need. I'll get some designs together."

I stand like a plum for a few moments, my brain playing catch-up. Everything she needs? I go after her, because I definitely don't have everything *I* need.

By the time I make it to the top of the stairs, she's halfway down. Fuck, the woman moves fast. I shoot down after her, just reaching the bottom as she whirls around.

She's a hot mess. I'm there myself but concealing it far better than she is.

"I look forward to hearing from you, Ava." I offer my hand, and she takes it, if cautiously. The tingles are instant. And addictive. *Jesus, give me more of that.*

"You have a lovely hotel."

I withdraw. Hotel? What is she talk . . .

Realization slams into me like a hurricane. *What the fuck?* She doesn't know. Fuck me, she doesn't know what this place is. What we do. Is she that oblivious? That innocent? I don't know whether to be relieved or worried, because it's clearly not my establishment making her all awkward, but simply me. "I have a lovely hotel," I whisper, staring at her as the tingles ride through me at an epic rate. My heart kicks, like it's telling me it's still there. Always has been. Unfeeling, uncaring, but always there. Just dimly beating to keep me in this miserable life.

She yanks her hand free on a sharp inhale of shaky breath.

"It *really* was nice to meet you, Ava."

"You too."

I look around the lobby, thoughtful. Well, this certainly changes things. Should I tell her? My answer comes quickly. She can hardly cope with me, let alone my manor and all that happens here. She'll run farther and faster. I'll never see her again, and I really want to see her again. Feel all of these feelings. Smile and mean it. Talk because it's pleasurable. Observe her, even if she's simply working.

I spot the spray of callas the florist arranged earlier, stepping forward and pulling one free, inspecting it. If Ava O'Shea was a flower, she'd be this one. "Understated elegance," I say quietly as I hold it out to her, staring into eyes I'm pretty sure I could drown in.

I can't describe the euphoria I feel when she accepts it. "Thank you."

My hands go straight into my pockets where they're safe. "You're more than welcome." My eyes fall to her lips. How many men have kissed those lips? Admired them? Wanted to shove their cock past them?

I scorn myself for my depravity.

"There you are." Sarah's shrill voice has my hackles rising, but I refuse to take my eyes off Ava. She kisses my cheek, pissing me off further. "Are you ready?"

I say nothing, unable to get my eyes under control. They're greedy for every little bit of Ava O'Shea they can get.

Sarah drapes herself all over me. I know what she's doing. She's not the only woman around here with the balls to do it either. "And you are?" she asks.

"Just leaving. Goodbye." Ava retreats swiftly, turning and dashing away.

"Well," Sarah muses, her tone full of sarcasm, "it all makes sense now."

I ignore her and wander out of the doors, standing at the top of the steps, watching Miss O'Shea hurry to her car. I pull my phone out, knowing what I'm about to do is so far across the line but, again, I'm fucked if I can stop myself. I open the camera and take a picture of her. It's as if an instinct I never knew I had needs to capture this moment, needs it documented, because I'm pretty sure I'll wake up in the morning and feel like I've dreamt it all. Something just switched inside of me. Something significant. I'm scared of it. Intrigued by it.

But I'm damaged goods, and she is not only too young for me, but too good.

She deserves more than a hedonistic, alcohol dependent fuck-up.

And yet I'm not sure I'm strong enough to stay away from her.

3

I WALK BACK to my office in a bit of a daze, wishing I could relive every second of the past hour on repeat. The darkness feels like it's swiftly closing in again. I close the door and stare at the couch where she sat. Approaching, I collect the glass she drank from, seeing her nude lipstick on the rim. "Ava O'Shea," I say quietly, heading for my chair and lowering into it. I set the glass in the center and study it for a while, my mind mush. Then I get my phone from my pocket and pull up the photo. The photo of her literally running away from me. The thought is as depressing as fuck, and I cast my eyes across to the drinks cabinet. I feel nothing. No pull. No temptation. Drink is an escape. It makes me forget, and right now, I have something I really don't want to forget.

I pull up my contacts and dial Chris Clements, my estate agent. He answers on the first ring. "Mr. Ward," he says, thrilled to hear from the man who's earned him a heap of commission.

"Chris, how are you?"

"All good, my friend. All good."

Friend? Ten million bought me a penthouse, it didn't buy

Chris a friend. "I want to see Lusso again," I tell him, and I immediately sense his worry.

"Everything okay?"

"Yes, everything is fine." I smile as I reach for the glass and start turning it slowly on the spot. "Don't worry, I'm not pulling out. I want to show my housekeeper around."

"Name your time."

"I was thinking Sunday."

"Not a problem."

I nod, happy. "I'll confirm a time once I've spoken to her."

"Just let me know."

"Thanks, Chris." I hang up and rake a hand through my hair. It's the weekend. What will she be doing? Where will she be going? Who with? I fall into a daydream and walk my way through my meeting with Miss O'Shea, analyzing every look, every word, every move. Could I have played it differently? Absolutely, yes. Was I capable of playing it differently? Categorically, no.

I could change my approach now. But the question is, will I get the chance?

The deep ache inside gives me my answer. So does another quick look at the picture of her running away.

I swipe up my keys and head out, passing John as I stalk through the summer room. "Everything okay?" he asks my back.

No. "Fine," I call, passing the bar. "I won't be around tonight."

"What?" John blurts after me, uncharacteristically shocked.

"What?" Sarah asks, appearing before me, looking as if she's stumbled across alien activity.

"What?" Sam and Drew say in unison, pausing on their way up the stairs.

I reach the door and turn, finding a peanut gallery of surprise. I smile my signature smile, if only to reassure them I've not been possessed. Although, there's definitely something weird hijacking me. "I'm sure you'll survive without me." I wink at the boys, slip on my Ray-Bans, and break free of The Manor, taking the steps fast and jumping into my Aston. I rev the engine hard and pull off, kicking up the gravel behind me. My phone is ringing before I make it to the gates.

"What's going on?" Sarah asks. "Where are you going?"

"I'm staying at my own place for a few nights."

"Why?"

Good fucking question. "Sarah, let me breathe, will you?" I say as diplomatically as I can. If she's not trying to make me surrender to her fucking whip, she's suffocating me with her egocentric smothering. I'm not sure which is worse, to be honest. But, as I remind myself repeatedly, along with John, she needs to fuss over me. She needs that and her whip like I need alcohol and sex, and God help anyone who tries to take my escape away. "I'll be back," I assure her. "I have a few things to do." I pull onto the main road and put my foot down, heading toward the city.

"Like what?" she asks, quite rightly. She's not stupid. She takes care of most of my affairs. It's something else she needs, another form of containing me. But, again, I have to let her have it. The alternative isn't an option. She also saw my face, my persona, in the entrance hall of The Manor, probably even watched me give a woman a flower. And now I've gone AWOL. She'll be having me sectioned.

"I'm moving a week tomorrow. I have a few things I need to set up in the city, and Cathy wants to see the new place. I may as well stay at my rental."

"Right," she replies, very quietly. Suspiciously.

"I'm reachable on my phone if you need me."

"We were supposed to go over the memberships."

"I'm sure you've got it covered." I cut the call and turn the stereo on, cocking my elbow on the window and focusing on the road as Massive Attack's *Angel* fills the car and my mind wanders to unknown places. Ava—*my angel*—is definitely from above . . . although I know they'll be no love on the horizon.

On Sunday at one thirty, I pull up outside the Tesco local to Cathy's little terrace in Hampstead. I park on the double yellow lines to wait for her, tapping the wheel. I feel fresh. Awake. Alert. Fuck me, I haven't had a drink for two days, and that is fucking monumental. I can't even explain why. Or how I resisted. It was there, the same liquor that usually temps me back into debauchment daily, sitting bold as brass on the sideboard in my rental. I don't think I looked at it once. Weird. Very weird. I spent hours trawling the Internet for anything I could find on Ava O'Shea. That might have kept me distracted. And the morning and evening runs. And the dozens of times I went to call her but decided against it. Because, of course, it's the weekend and she'd have an excuse to either not take my call or answer and brush me off because she doesn't work on weekends. Because I'm a client. At least, I am for now.

I spot Cathy emerging from the supermarket weighed down with bags. "What the heck is she playing at?" I jump out of my car and jog across the road. Her beam could split her face when she clocks me.

"Jesse, my boy."

I claim the bags from her hands and let her smother my face. "Hey."

She squeezes my cheeks. "You look well," she says, taking a step back to assess me. "Really well. What's happened?"

I cock my arm out for her to link so I can walk her back across the road. Cathy knows my story. Knows everything about me. Every dirty detail. I managed to keep her in the dark for two years, not bad, all things considered, but eight years ago it all went to shit. It was my birthday. My thirtieth. *Our* thirtieth. I'm surprised I didn't kill myself with the amount of alcohol I drank that night. Poor Cathy found me in the morning. Called John, who called Sarah, who both turned up and said *way* too much in front of my sweet, wholesome housekeeper. I never expected to see Cathy again after that. "Nothing has happened," I say, spotting a traffic warden taking a picture of my car on the lines. "I'll put these in the boot." I leave her on the pavement as I pop the boot and drop her shopping in.

"You can't park here, sir," the warden says, starting to tap at his device.

I roll my eyes and guide Cathy to the passenger door. "I'm helping an old lady with her shopping."

I get a whack on my bicep for my trouble. "Less of the old, boy," she snaps, and the warden laughs. "Give him a ticket," she orders. "I'm perfectly capable of walking to the nearest car park, he's just being lazy."

I laugh under my breath and help her into the seat, hearing the warden laugh harder when she starts batting my helping hands away. "You in?"

"Yes, I'm in," she declares, and I close the door, turning to face the warden, holding out my hand for the ticket.

He shakes his head. "Go on, before I change my mind."

I smile and give him a friendly smack on his shoulder. "Good man."

I land in my seat and pull off a lot slower than usual. "Listen, this new place. It's rather large," I tell her, not wanting Cathy to be too overwhelmed by the size of my new penthouse.

"I don't understand it," she muses. "There's just you. Why do you need such a gigantic home?" She looks across to me. "Or do you have something to tell me?"

"Like what?"

"You know I live in hope that you'll settle down, Jesse. You can't carry on the way you do forever."

I face the road, feeling ashamed. She's right. I'll end up dead. But sometimes death seems like a much better option than navigating this unknown world. Especially without Jake. "Maybe one day," I muse, knowing deep down I'm deluded. There's not a woman on this planet who could take me and my demons on. Or, more to the point, would want to. This chilled Jesse, the one everyone sees, the laid-back guy? He's a shell. An act. Because acting like I'm fine is so much easier than admitting I'm fucked up. That I need help. Although I know waking up with a hangover each morning pretty much spells that out to everyone I know.

We make it to Lusso in good time, Cathy chatting the whole way. "Oh lord, oh my," she sings as the gates slowly open. "This is a bit fancy, isn't it?"

I laugh and pull into one of my allocated spaces. The car park is full of vans, tradesmen all working their nuts off to get completed on time. I round the car and open the door for Cathy, helping her, and she doesn't fight me. The Aston is low, and Cathy isn't a spring chicken anymore. She links arms with me, and I lead her in, past the concierge desk to the elevator where Chris is waiting.

"Mr. Ward," he says, extending his hand. I shake it and make the introductions.

"Cathy, this is Chris, the estate agent. Chris, Cathy, my housekeeper."

"Or penthouse keeper now," she says, and I laugh as Chris taps in a code to call the elevator. We board and yet another code is entered before we're carried to the penthouse.

"I'm sure Mr. Ward will give you the codes once he's changed them after he's moved in," Chris says, and I hear him and Cathy exchange a few words and laughter, but my mind is off again. She's been in this elevator. I'm beginning to regret not taking up

Chris's offer to oversee the interior taking shape. I may have encountered Miss Ava O'Shea much sooner than Friday.

Cathy's oohing and aahing continues when we get to the door, and once Chris has let us in, her awe notches up a few more levels. "Well, I'm very glad I didn't buy any perishables," she says. "My God, this tour will take a whole day!"

"Why don't you take a look around?" I suggest, smiling. I don't need to offer twice. She's off, poking in and out of rooms.

I wander into the kitchen, gazing around. I've neglected to appreciate just how amazing a job Ava O'Shea has done. There's not a detail she's missed, even down to dressing the place.

"Looking forward to moving in?" Chris asks, joining me.

"Yeah," I reply, for the first time actually picturing myself living here. Being here every night. Can I do that?

"So the launch on Friday evening," Chris says. "The developers wanted to showcase it before signing off. You know, get investors interested in their upcoming projects. It's also a good opportunity for all the contractors and companies who have worked on the project to network."

"Yes, Sarah mentioned it." I pull up, thinking. A launch. Showcasing. Networking. *She'll* be here.

"You should come."

Chris reads my mind, and I turn a smile onto him. "You know, I think I will." I back up into the open-plan lounge, looking up the back-lit staircase. The detail she's put into this. It's incredible.

"Actually," Chris says, pulling my attention back to him. He smiles, and I know what's coming. I laugh under my breath and head out the bifold doors onto the terrace. The jacuzzi, the limestone slabs, the sun loungers. All this would be wasted if I didn't stay here. The view over the docks. I didn't give that the time of day either. It's stunning. I feel like my eyes are open for the first time in as long as I can remember.

Chris follows me out, joining me to take in the view. "I

noticed you're . . . well . . ." He can't locate his words, and I find it highly amusing.

"You been looking into me?' I ask, slipping my hands into my pockets.

He chuckles. It's awkward as fuck. "We have to check the financial stability of anyone who offers on our properties, of course."

"Of course," I murmur. *Come on, Chris. Spit it out.*

"Well, anyway, it came to my attention that you own . . . run . . . have . . ."

This is getting embarrassing. I cast my eyes over to him. "The Manor," I say. "It's called The Manor."

"Yes. The Manor. And what would one do to become a member of The Manor?"

"One gets endorsed."

"How?"

"By other members who can vouch for them."

"Oh. I don't know any other members." He frowns at the view, and I smile.

"You know me, Chris," I say, putting him out of his misery. I'm done playing with him. "And lucky for you, I'm not just a member, by default, of course. I also own it." I reach into my pocket and pull out a card, handing it to him. "Call Sarah. She'll fix you up." The look on his face. Anyone would think I'd just given him a free pass to paradise. Yes, it's paradise for many. But it certainly won't be free. Perhaps his commission on this place will cover it. At least, for a while.

He takes the card and I head back inside. "I won't be too long."

I lied. I spent over an hour roaming the penthouse, taking in every little detail that I never noticed before. Like I said, open eyes. I drop Cathy home and take her bags into the kitchen, letting her kiss my cheek before I leave. Then I drive to my rental, stopping off at the supermarket on my way.

When I get back, I stand in the middle of the lounge, gazing at the cold, clinical space. It's unhomely. Because it's never been a home. Just a crash pad. A complete waste of money, to be honest, but my good intentions were always there when I rented it. Still are. I planned to stay here most nights but . . . well, it just never seems to happen.

I pull my T-shirt off and dump my bag on the worktop in the kitchen before pulling out a fresh jar of my vice and unscrewing the lid, tossing it on the side and dumping myself on the couch. I flick on the TV and surf the channels until I find something suitably mind-numbing to watch. Then I sigh and slump back as I have my first dip of the day.

I've worked my way through half the jar before I know it, and when I glance at my watch, I see it's only six o'clock. What the fuck am I going to do all night?

Alcohol.

I cast aside my peanut butter and stand, wandering over to the cabinet, assessing each and every bottle. My hands find the side of the wood, bracing there, my body bent over, my eyes laser beams. *Alcohol.* Alcohol kills time and guilt. But, right now, it'll also kill this revitalized feeling I've got going on.

Knock. Knock.

I straighten quickly.

"Jesse?"

My shoulders drop, my eyes turning slowly onto the door.

Fuck. Me.

I stalk across the room, feeling irritation flaring inside—it's unfamiliar, but not unwanted. How the fuck does she know where I am? I do not want the temptation of a woman and alcohol, so there will be no invite inside. I yank the door open. "Now's not a good time, Coral."

She pouts. "I'll make it a good time."

I can't even bring myself to smile at her suggestiveness. "How did you know I was here?"

"You've not been at The Manor." She goes to pass me, but I move, blocking her. She looks up at me in question, smiling, but it's unsure. "You're not going to let me in?"

I shake my head.

She cocks hers, thinking. "Let's have a drink," she says, pushing her way past me, and because I'm not an arsehole, I don't physically stop her. She scans the space, familiarizing herself with it, and heads straight for the vodka.

"How did you know where I live?" I ask, closing the door.

"You told me."

"I did?" I'm pretty fucking sure I didn't. "When?"

She pours two glasses, taking a sip of hers as she holds one out to me. "In the bar at The Manor."

When I was drunk. I feel my jaw tense, feel that irritation flare. *Why the fuck would she come here, and why the fuck would she wave vodka under my nose?*

Stupid fucking question.

"I don't want a drink," I say, plain and clear, pacing to the fridge in the kitchen and pulling out a bottle of water. "You should go." I turn to face her, my expression and words determined, and it's clear as day she has not one fucking clue what to do with it. "I mean it, Coral. Go." She needs to make amends with her husband. She needs to leave me alone.

She laughs and discards one of the glasses, slinking her way over to me, getting too close, her fingers tracing the planes of my stomach across my scar. I close my eyes, feeling the unbearable burn of her touch there. "Come on," she coos, leaning in and kissing my chest. I look to the ceiling, calling on all my willpower. Not willpower to resist her or the drink, but willpower to stop myself from manhandling her out of my apartment. "Let's have some fun."

I drop my head and come face to face with the glass as she lifts it. The edge of it skims my bottom lip, leaving behind the tiniest drop of vodka. My tongue darts out and licks it up without thought, and she smiles.

Poison.

Her *and* the drink.

"Get out, Coral," I say, my voice hoarse. "I'm not playing."

I see realization dawn on her. She's faced with a totally different man. A man in control. A man who is together. *Kind of.* I'm certainly still going mad, but in other ways.

She backs up, and I relax my strung muscles. "See you at The Manor." She places the vodka on the unit as she passes before letting herself out, and as soon as the door closes, I go straight to the kitchen and yank off a bin bag, then proceed to rid my apartment of all temptation, tossing all bottles, whether full or not, into the bag, not wanting to risk tipping the contents down the sink and catching a sniff. I should never have slept with Coral again.

Fucking hell, I'm a despicable arsehole.

4

IT HAS CATEGORICALLY, without doubt, been the longest weekend of my fucking life. But now it's Monday. A working week, and I am, as a client, perfectly within my right to call her and get an update on how her quotation for The Manor is progressing.

I hit fifteen miles and start to work down to a steady jog, the cobwebs well and truly blown off. Not that there were many this morning. I woke up fresh. Alert. Invigorated. That's a new sensation too. One that's both appealing and daunting.

I collect a coffee from Starbucks and pace down toward the docks, taking a seat on a bench to catch my breath. The water is still, the air fresh, a new day awaiting me. A good day? A bad day? I'm too used to the latter and, frankly, I'm fucked off with the continuous mundane cycle. And the energy it takes to pointlessly convince everyone around me that I'm good. Including myself. On Friday, I really did feel good. I want more of that. Way more.

I turn and gaze to the very top of Lusso. The morning haze is shrouding my penthouse, the terrace only just visible.

You'll amount to nothing, Jesse. You'll piss your life away on drink and women, you mark my words.

I stand and toss my cup in a nearby bin, Dad's words circling on repeat.

He's only part right.

Sarah is on me like a wolf when I arrive at The Manor, her long, leather-covered legs working fast to keep up with my strides as I head to my office. "You need to tell me what the fuck is going on," she snaps, chasing my heels.

"Nice to see you too," I mutter, pushing my way through the door. I come to an abrupt halt, and Sarah crashes into my back, jolting me. I stare at the drinks cabinet for a few moments. Just a few. "Get rid of the alcohol," I order. I land in my chair, read-justing my tie. It's tight.

"What?" she spits, impatient, her eyes drifting between me and the drink.

"I want it all out of my office." I open my laptop and bring up the new member requests that need approving before Sarah has a chance to ask. My eyes bug when I see Chris's name on the list. Fuck me, he didn't waste any time. I work my way through, scru-tinizing the endorsements as I go before checking them off. I can feel Sarah's incredulous glare burning through me, but I ignore it and move to the next spreadsheet. I frown at the list of bad debtors, dozens of them, but one name stands out. *Coral.* The direct debit for her membership has been rejected. Twice. "What's the deal with Coral?" I ask, looking up at Sarah, who has managed to talk her legs into making it to my desk.

Her smile is ironic. And annoying. "You're the one around here who's in the know about all things Coral," she replies, taking a seat.

I can't hold back my scowl. "That was a mistake." I return to the screen, and Sarah laughs.

"Which time?"

"Every time." I should never have agreed to that threesome. It was a disaster waiting to happen, but . . . alcohol. *Fucking alcohol.*

"Where are we with the works on the extension?" she asks.

I look up quickly and immediately kick myself for it. "I'm waiting for a quotation. I'll chase it up today."

She stands, sliding a file off my desk and tucking it under her arm, her shrewd stare studying me far too closely for my liking. "Or I could."

My eyes drop like stones to my laptop. *Fuck.* I always take any opportunity to pass off a job to Sarah. And she knows it. "It's fine," I say quietly. I have nothing else. "We had a good rapport." Stupid thing to say. "Work-wise, I mean," I add, hearing Sarah's interested hum. *For fuck's sake.* I drag my tired eyes up to her interested face. "I can deal with the new rooms." Jesus, if I passed this over to Sarah, which I absolutely will not, I wouldn't see Miss O'Shea for dust.

"Deal with the rooms," she asks, "or deal with the pretty little thing designing them?"

"Sarah, what point are you trying to make?" *Don't lose your rag, Jesse. Not with Sarah.* After being around her for the last twenty years, I know she ultimately has my back. Even if she is a total bitch when she wants to be. *Which is often.* Suffice to say, she's not exactly loved around here. Not by the women, anyway. The men, however, can't get enough of her and her talents.

"No point." She pivots and struts to the door. "Just keeping you grounded."

Grounded? Yeah, because I'm perfectly grounded when I'm legless. "Never felt more grounded in my life," I say to myself as she closes the door, my eyes naturally drifting across my office to where the alcohol lives. I swallow and look at the couch.

How old are you?

I look like I'm in my thirties but feel like I'm one hundred years old. Yet with her, for that brief time, I felt reborn. I spin my phone in my hand, my bottom lip getting a punishing chew. Call her. Check in. I pull up my contacts and scroll down. There she is. My thumb hovers over the dial icon, but before I pluck up the courage to hit it, my phone starts ringing. I don't recognize the number.

"Hello?"

"Mr. Ward, Patrick Peterson here, Rococo Union."

Oh? What's that funny feeling in my gut? "What can I do for you, Mr. Peterson?"

"I'm looking over the file for your upcoming projects."

He is? Why isn't Miss O'Shea looking over my file, and why the heck hasn't *she* called me? "And?" I ask, undeniably wary, maybe even standoffish.

"Ava has some great initial ideas."

"Yes, she will be a dream to work with." I wince the moment I finish speaking, all kinds of erotic images trampling my mind. Patrick Peterson chuckles, and my patience begins to fray.

"Yes, she is my best, I don't mind telling you that."

She'll be my best too; I have no doubt. "Her work on the Lusso project is phenomenal. It's why I want her." *Choose your words carefully, Ward.*

"I understand," he says.

Good.

"However, I will be taking over the project as of today."

No, you fucking won't. "Excuse me?" I find myself standing all of a sudden, my heart racing.

"We'll get the drawings together, incorporating Ava's ideas, of course, and then a proposal across for your consideration."

I stare across my office, motionless, my head in chaos. She's bailed? Abandoned the project? *You stupid fuck, Ward.* I came on stronger than a sex-deprived sex addict at a fucking orgy. But her face. Her composure. Her body language. I didn't misread any of that, and if I did, I'm more screwed up than I ever thought possible. She's running scared, because she felt it all too and, unlike me, it deters her rather than draws her in.

I need to remedy this little issue.

"Mr. Ward?" Peterson asks.

"Thanks." I hang up and head out, bumping into John as I take the steps to the driveway. "Morning," I say, trying to sound as normal as possible.

"Where are you going now?" He turns on the spot as I pass him, following my path to my DBS.

"Small crisis needs my attention." I hop in my car, hearing him calling me a stupid motherfucker. "Probably," I agree, racing away.

I pull onto Bruton Street and slip into a parking space across the road from the offices of Rococo Union, wondering what the fucking hell I'm doing. I won't need to worry about Sarah scaring Ava off at this rate. Seems I'm prepared to do a damn fine job of that all by myself. I tap the steering wheel, my eyes trained on the windows of the company's office. Is she even in there? God, would I love to be a fly on the wall of her brain right now. To know what she's thinking. What she's feeling. Is her mind circling constantly? Is she repeatedly swaying between the thrill of the chemistry, to the distress of being so utterly caught off guard by it?

I narrow my eyes. Something tells me yes, she is doing both, but clearly the latter is taking poll position, hence her withdrawal. I need to convince her she chose wrong. I'll do whatever it takes. I'm making it my mission objec—

Rap, rap, rap!

I jump out of my fucking skin, startled by the aggressive knocks on my window. "What the fuck?" I yell, making the traffic warden, whose face is currently glaring through my window, recoil. I grab the handle, yank it, and jump out of my Aston, my chest pumping with a mixture of fright and anger.

The poor fucker backs up, his eyes climbing my six-foot-three frame, regret plastered all over his face. "You need to pay to park, sir." He points to a ticket machine up the street as I work to contain my temper. What's wrong with me?

"I don't have any change." I pat down the pockets of my suit. Or my fucking wallet.

"Then you'll have to move on."

Move on? And park where, exactly? I could drive around London all fucking day and never find a space. It's pure luck I landed this one right outside her office.

I feel unfamiliar anger bubbling, and I am unable to contain it. "I'm not moving my fucking car," I growl, slipping back into the driver's seat.

"Then I'll have to issue a ticket, sir."

"Fuck off," I snap, slamming the door. *What the hell, Ward?* I rub my palm down my bristly face. My cheeks feel hot. Move my car? Not a fucking chance.

I realign my sights on her office, trying to regulate my breathing, and once I've cooled down, I dial her. My stomach flips a million times, my anticipation to hear her voice off the charts.

But she doesn't answer. I frown at my phone, thinking, imagining her staring at hers. She didn't miss my call. She wasn't otherwise engaged, I just know it. So she ignored me. My jaw clenches without thought, and I dial her again. Perseverance. I can do that. It rings and rings, and just when I reside myself to physically going into her office where she can't avoid me, she answers.

"Hello?"

And I'm bombarded by an inexplicable rush of pleasure. Pleasure without sex. So I can only *imagine* the heaven to be found with my body melded to hers, my cock in her pussy, my tongue in her mouth. I lose my breath just thinking about it.

But she sounded . . . uncertain. "Ava?" Why on earth did I pose that as a question?

"Who's speaking?"

I can't stop my laugh. Is she really going to play this game? "Now, I know you already know the answer to that question because my name came up on your phone. Trying to play it cool?"

"You added yourself to my contacts?"

Yes, yes, I did that. I still can't believe it but, as I've told myself one hundred times, and I will absolutely tell her when I have the chance, I'm acting on pure instinct, and my instinct is telling me to have her, one way or another. Easy or hard, and I have a horrible feeling she's going to make it hard. But I'm ready. I'm ready to remind her of all the bizarre feelings she had on our first meeting. "I need to be able to get hold of you," I inform her.

"Patrick should have contacted you." She sounds cool, calm, and collected. Waste of fucking time. "I'm afraid I'm unable to assist you, but Patrick will be more than happy to help."

I laugh on the inside. How many times has she talked herself round in circles over this? All weekend, I bet. "Yes, Patrick has been in contact. I'm sure he will be happy to help, but I'm less than happy to accept it." There. What have you got to say about that, Miss O'Shea?

"I'm sorry to hear that."

She is? She actually sounds a bit aggravated. "Are you?"

"Yes, I am."

She's not sorry at all, and I'm not sure I like it. A bit like she doesn't like my approach? Probably. But if Miss O'Shea insists on being stubborn and refuses to acknowledge or accept that we shared an equal attraction, I'll willingly convince her she's making a mistake. "I don't think you are, Ava. I think you're avoiding me."

"Why would I do that?"

Silly woman. She's asking for it, so I'll give it to her. Plain and simple. No more fucking around. "Well, because you're attracted to me." *Bam!*

"Excuse me?" She practically coughs over her words, and I smile. She has not one fucking clue what else to say. She doesn't need a repeat, but I'll happily oblige.

"I said—"

"Yes, I heard you. I just can't believe you said it."

Believe it, lady. And I'm not done. I have plenty more to say, and she is going to listen. I draw breath, ready to let loose on a few more home truths, ready to convince her she's wasting her time ignoring this attraction. It needs exploring. I *know* she's curious. She just needs—

"I apologize for not being available to assist with your work."

The line goes dead, and I stare at the screen, caught between annoyance and amusement. She hung up on me? She actually hung up on me. How rude. What is she so afraid of? She doesn't know about The Manor. My past. My issue with drink.

I wince, shying away from those thoughts, because they sure as shit won't help me here. I quickly tap out a message, spelling it out once more.

I notice you didn't deny it. You should know the feeling's mutual. Jx

I look up, settling back in my seat, waiting for a response. I'm kidding myself. She won't reply. And there I've learned something about the lovely Miss O'Shea.

She's stubborn as fuck.

I sit bolt upright when the door of her offices open, and lose my fucking breath when she appears. Jesus good fucking Lord. Just look at her. Sheer perfection. Her black trousers skim her dainty ankles, her cream blouse tucked in, showcasing her small waist. I look down at my hands. They'd circle it, easy. Her hair is down. It's longer than I thought.

I push my palm into my chest, my heart clattering. Tingles. Everywhere.

She swings her bag onto her shoulder and walks toward the end of the street, and I'm out of my car before I've registered I've even moved, my eyes stuck to her back.

"Your ticket, sir," the traffic warden says, and I blindly grab it, throwing it on the driver's seat.

"Thanks." I shut the door and follow her. It's impulsive, my brain working without thinking, my body more than willing to obey my brain. Just try to fucking stop me.

I jog across the road and round the corner, slowing when I see her up ahead. Her long, dark hair bounces across her back as she walks, the sway of her hips like magnets for my eyes. My big body feels restrained in my suit, in the groin area the most. I see her dip into a bar, and I come to a stop outside, wondering . . . what now?

I look at my reflection in the window. Straighten my tie. Brush down the lapels of my jacket. Run my hand through my hair. I look good, better than I did on Friday, and she struggled terribly to contain her awe then. So today? She's doomed.

I just need to pick up my feet, get my arse inside this bar, and knock her back with my smile. Kill her doubt with a swift reminder of our electric connection.

Yet ten minutes later, I'm still hovering outside, conflicted. She'll think I'm a nutcase, if she doesn't already. But . . . Just a chance encounter, that's all. I laugh to myself. I'm fucking deluded.

I push my way in, spotting her immediately at a table with a redhead. My eyes naturally fall to the glass of wine before her. Drinking on the job? I'm not sure how I feel about that. Or her drinking at all, actually. Alcohol makes you vulnerable. An easy target. It has you making stupid choices.

A waitress approaches and slides two plates on the table, and Ava rises. I dip into a recess, managing to keep her in my sights as she heads for the ladies'. Perfect. Get her on her own. Get close. Give her no option but to deal with the sparks that fly.

Remind her.

"Can I help you, sir?"

I turn around and find a frowning waitress hovering behind me. Can she help me? Can *anyone* help me? I'm stalking a woman, for fuck's sake. I lock and load my dazzling smile and blast her back ten paces with it. "Just waiting for a friend," I say smoothly, as she blinks rapidly and backs away, leaving me to continue with my stalking. I should punch my own face in. What the fuck am I even going to say? *Oh, fancy seeing you here? What a surprise?* She'll know. Of course she'll know.

I look toward the ladies'. She's been awhile, and I wonder if I've missed her coming out. Did she spot me and run for it? I pull my phone out and dial her, just as the door opens and she exits, rootling through her bag. I drop my mobile from my ear, smiling as she walks toward me.

It's all I can do not to laugh when she pulls her phone out and rolls her eyes at the screen. So cute. "Reject." She declines my call haughtily, tossing her mobile back into her bag as she marches on. *Reject?* Ouch. I put myself in the center of the corridor, filling the space, and her head starts to lift. My heart braces for impact.

And when it happens, my whole world goes up in smoke, and I inhale, feeling like I've been taken out by a boulder. My arm is out fast, holding on to her waist, not just to steady her, but to steady myself. I'm dizzy, my head spinning, her scent saturating my senses.

"Oh God, I'm sorry." She freezes, her face practically squished into my chest, and I drag in air, fighting for breath. This. This is why I feel like I'm going crazy. This feeling. This madness.

"Reject?" I whisper, looking down at the back of her head. She looks so right nestled into me. "I'm wounded." I really fucking am. In agony, in fact. *Reject.* She can't. I won't let her rob me of these new feelings. She's spiked them, so she can damn well deal with the consequences of them.

She pushes herself away quickly and laughs. Yes, I agree. *This whole situation is quite funny, Miss O'Shea, and if you knew me at all, you'd laugh even harder.*

"Is something funny?" I ask, wondering why she won't face me. *Look at me!*

"I'm sorry. I wasn't looking where I was going." She goes to move past me, and my hand shoots out in panic, grabbing her. *What?* There she goes again. Running. I'm not prepared to let her walk away without at least looking me in the eye, and when she does, I hope she sees what I need her to see. Want. Desire. Promises. *A desperate need to be fixed.*

I shake my head and silently implore her to face me. See me. But my silent prayers aren't answered. *Stubborn.* My natural magnetism fails with this woman. I can't smile at her if she won't look at me. Can't admire her if she avoids me. Can't talk to her if she refuses to listen. Fuck this. I've tried to be diplomatic. I've tried the softly, softly approach. I'm working my bollocks off here, stepping outside my box, and she's stonewalling me at every turn. Enough of the games. It's back to boldness.

"Just tell me one thing before you leave, Ava," I say quietly, and her gaze slowly climbs my body until we're eye to eye.

That's better. *Hear this, Miss O'Shea. Let's see you try to ignore this* . . . "How loud do you think you'll scream when I fuck you?"

"Excuse me?" Her jaw goes lax, and I smile, reaching forward and applying a little pressure, closing her mouth. It's doing me no favors hanging open like that. The things I could do . . .

"I'll leave that one with you." I release her, moving back, giving her space. The scowl she chucks me is fierce. It widens my smile. She's shocked? Good. I've felt constantly shocked since she stepped into my office on Friday.

I observe her as she walks away, far from stable, her hands twitching by her sides like she might reach out and take the wall for support at any moment. It's the nail in the coffin I didn't need. And my determination just skyrocketed.

She sits and virtually dives into her wine, and her friend, the redhead, gets her very own dose of lax-jaw syndrome, her blue eyes taking me in. I can't hear them from here, but when Ava's friend points her fork at me and Ava looks away, I can't stop myself from slipping over to introduce myself. *Charm her friend to death, Ward.* I need an ally. Someone to convince Ava, along with me, that she needs to give up the ghost and admit she fancies the pants off me.

I meander over, all casual, fixing my suit as I go. Ava's friend follows my every step, all the way to their table. But Ava? Her head is down, her fingers playing with her food, her body as stiff as a board.

"Ladies." I blast her mate back with my signature smile.

"Hi." Her eyes are widening by the second. Bless her. She's not trying to hide her awe at all. *I wish your fucking friend was as receptive.*

Speaking of which . . .

"Ava?"

I get nothing but a piece of her lunch waved at me. Good god, she's a gem. An increasingly infuriating gem. She doesn't just turn me on, she pushes buttons I never knew I had. She won't look at me? Fine. I'll soon fix that.

I pull the knees of my trousers up and lower beside her, casting my eyes across the table to her friend when she appears to start choking. It's all I can do not to laugh when I see her grab a napkin and wipe her mouth. I return my attention to Ava. Or her profile. "That's better." I don't think I've ever encountered a woman so fucking tenacious in my life. It's infuriating. I blow out air and offer my hand to her friend. "I'm Jesse Ward, pleased to meet you."

"Jesse?" Her friend nearly chokes on her food again, and I cock my head. "Oh! *Jesse.*"

Yes, *Jesse.* I watch, a little confused, as the redhead glares at a still mute Ava, who is now stabbing at her lunch. The penny drops, and I smile like a loon on the inside. She's mentioned me. She's talked about me. Well, doesn't that just inject me with even more fortitude.

"I'm Kate. Ava mentioned you have a posh hotel."

Hotel. Not quite. But I don't focus on that little issue. "Oh, she mentioned me?" I turn my smile onto Ava. And what did the lovely Miss O'Shea have to say about her meeting with me? I don't know. But I want to. "I wonder what else she's mentioned," I say thoughtfully.

"Oh, this and that."

"This and that," I mimic quietly.

"Yes, this and that."

I nearly fall to my arse when Ava suddenly decides to give me her eyes, even if she looks slightly pissed off.

I inhale.

"It was nice to see you. Goodbye." Her gaze falls to my lips. Her façade is laughable, and in an effort to prove it to everyone at the table, I lick my lips slowly, watching intently as her stare follows the trail of my tongue. She's imagining what I could do with this tongue, and I am desperate to demonstrate. I nearly drop to my arse again when she reciprocates. Whether it's intentional or not doesn't matter. It was natural.

"Nice?" I lift a little and lean in, getting as close as I can, my eyes closing. "I could think of lots of words, Ava." Pure bliss. Total gratification. Earth-shifting. Universe shaking. "*Nice* isn't one of them." Her cheek is millimeters from my mouth. Her leg inches from my hand. It's an opportunity I'm not prepared to pass up. "I'll leave you to consider my question."

I press my lips to her cheek and inhale the goodness, my hand falling onto her thigh. "Soon," I murmur, certain of that. She's exhausted. Exhausted from maintaining this pointless, annoying resistance. Good. So next time I call her, she'll answer. "It was nice to meet you, Kate." I surrender my touch and rise.

"Hmm, you too."

I smile at Ava's friend's pensiveness and stride away, heading for the men's room at the back. I need to splash my face with cold water. I'm hot.

And hopeful.

By the time I've gathered myself and once again recalled every look, every word every touch from another encounter with Ava O'Shea, I've lost half an hour. I blow out my cheeks, blink my dry eyes, straighten my suit, and head back to my car, so fucking curious about what was said after I left. I ignore a call from Sarah and dial Ava. I want her back at The Manor.

I don't know whether to be surprised or irritated when she doesn't pick up. After what just happened, she's not seriously still playing this game? Not after licking her lips and clenching her thighs. I try again. And again. And again.

And again, and again, and again.

Nothing.

I growl under my breath as I reach my car, slipping behind the wheel, but not starting the engine. I'm not averse to going into her

office and giving her a recap of our lunchtime meeting. The way
she looked at me. Her body was screaming so loudly, begging me.
It was impossible to ignore. Or not so impossible for her, it seems.
I growl again as I hammer out a text, my frustrated fingers
working fast, but I force myself to be reasonable.

. . . *ish*.

**Being rejected isn't very nice. Why won't you answer my
calls? Jx**

I give her thirty seconds to reply. Of course, she doesn't.
"Damn fucking woman," I mutter as my phone dings. Ah!

**If you need to discuss your requirements, you should be
calling Patrick, not me.**

I scoff, my thumbs a blur as they hammer their way across the
screen. "If I want to discuss my requirements?" I mutter. "Don't
try and turn on your professional switch now, Miss O'Shea."

**My requirement is to make you scream. I don't think Patrick
can help me there. I'm gagging just thinking about it. That's a
thought . . .
Will I need to gag you? Jx**

I smile as I click send. *Cheeky, Ward.* Very cheeky. But the
alternative was swearing my motherfucking head off and
demanding she stop it. Just stop it. She's sending me crazy. One
should question what the fuck I'm doing. I could go back to The
Manor, snap my fingers, and have a dozen women fall at my feet.
But all that will achieve is numbness. I might feel like I'm going
crazy right now, but at least I'm feeling *something*.

I quickly pull up my emails and send one to Patrick Peterson, insisting on having Ava working my project. *And working something else, hopefully.* I'm covering all my bases. Then I read my message to her again, biding my time, waiting for a reply. I bet she's laughing. Is she laughing? Or is she horrified? My face bunches. I hope not. A few suggestive, cheeky texts are nothing in the grand scheme of things.

After ten minutes of waiting and trying her mobile again, I resign myself to the fact that I've blown it. Again. Fucked it up. "Bollocks," I breathe, pulling up Google and finding the landline for the company.

"Good afternoon, Rococo Union."

"Don't hang up," I blurt, every inch of me tense, waiting for the line to go dead. It doesn't. She doesn't hang up. I exhale, reaching for my forehead and giving it a soothing rub. I've never had a headache without the assistance of alcohol before. It's something else new, yet this I *don't* like. Because there appears to be only one fucking cure, and she's refusing to share the antidote. "Ava, I'm really very sorry."

"You are?" The surprise in her tone is warranted.

"Yes, really, I am." A little. *More for me than you, though, lady.* "I've made you feel uncomfortable." *And worked my nuts off for nothing, it seems.* "I've overstepped the mark by a long shot." *Like, miles.* "I've distressed you." *And myself, because damn if your resistance doesn't only make me want you more. Make me wonder more. Make me ache more.* "Please accept my apology." *Please, please, please.* I reluctantly admit it's time to wipe the slate clean. Start again. Go back to Plan A. Woo her. Is there an online course for that kind of shit?

"Okay," she eventually murmurs. "So you don't want to make me scream or gag me?"

My eyebrows jump up. *More than anything I've wanted in a long fucking time.* "Ava, you sound disappointed."

"Not at all."

I smile. She's a terrible liar. "Can we start again? I'll keep it professional, of course."

"Mr. Ward, I'm really not the right person for this job. Can I transfer you to Patrick?"

For the love of God. Where does she find her control because I need some? Part of me admires her. She wants something desperately, I just know it, yet, rightly, she's denying it because she knows it's bad for her. She's fighting her want. I should take a leaf out of her book. I have the same toxic relationship with vodka. "It's Jesse," I mutter. "You make me feel old when you call me Mr. Ward." *How old does she think I am?* I can't believe I'm about to say this, but at this moment in time, I'm a desperate man. I need to get her in the same room as me. Where she can't escape. Where she's forced to face this madness and fucking well deal with it. "Ava, if it makes you feel better, you can deal with John." I should have perhaps run that past the big man first. "What would be the next stage?"

"I would need to measure the rooms and draw up some schemes."

I'm surprised how quickly she answers, but I certainly won't question it. "Perfect. I can get John to take you around the rooms. He can hold your tape measure." *Because we both know if I show you around, it won't be your tape measure I'll want to hold.* "Tomorrow?"

There's a slight pause. I don't like it. "I can't do tomorrow or Wednesday. I'm sorry."

"Oh." Fuck me, Thursday feels like years away. "Do you do evenings?"

"I can do tomorrow evening," she says quickly. That was another rather hasty reply. Has she adopted the same approach as me? Go on instinct? I smile. "Seven-ish?" she asks.

"Perfect." It's not perfect, The Manor will be busy, but if that's all she's giving me, then I'll have to work with it. "I would say that I'll look forward to it, but I can't look forward to it because I won't be seeing you." I start my car and pull out of the parking space, returning to The Manor a happy man. A very happy man. She backed down. I'm making progress. If she truly weren't interested, she would *not* be entertaining this. "I'll let John know to expect you at seven."

"Ish," she adds.

"Ish," I murmur. "Thank you, Ava."

"You're welcome, Mr. Ward. Goodbye."

I roll my eyes at her continued efforts to keep it business. We're way past that now, and deep down, she knows it.

I think.

I fucking hope.

ON TUESDAY MORNING before I head to The Manor, I make an impromptu stop off at Harrods to visit Zoe. She's delighted to see me, as always. "Have you been on holiday?" she asks as we walk through to the men's department.

"I was skiing a few weeks ago," I answer, browsing the rows of suits.

"I can tell. You look refreshed."

I turn a smile onto her and, of course, she swoons. I can't tell her my freshness has nothing to do with my holiday. "Ask me why I'm here, Zoe."

"Why are you here?"

"I need a new suit."

"Just a suit?"

I laugh as I wander to a display, eyeing the mannequin. "Yes, just a suit."

"And the occasion?" she asks, joining me.

"The reclamation of Jesse Ward," I murmur quietly, thoughtfully, looking across at her. She looks confused. I smile. "Something navy, I think."

"I have just the thing. This way." She's off and I follow,

taking my phone out of my jeans pocket as I go. "Oh, for fuck's sake," I mutter, and Zoe turns. I wave her off and answer. "Coral."

"Sarah's told me I can't come to The Manor, Jesse!" The panic in her voice is palpable. I step into the men's changing room when Zoe moves aside, and she holds her finger up for me to wait. I give her the nod, taking a seat on the chair, one leg crossed over the other. I can see it now. Sarah taking the greatest pleasure delivering the news to Coral. Just like the women of The Manor don't like Sarah, she's not all too keen on them either. Especially if they've been in my bed.

"You've missed your membership payment, Coral," I say as diplomatically as I can. "Twice. What do you want me to do?"

"Please, Jesse."

I wince, hating to hear a woman beg. *In this instance.* "What's the deal?" I ask. I might regret that.

"Mike. He's canceled all my direct debits and cleared our joint bank account. Since I told him about us, he's lost the plot. I'm getting it sorted. Please, just give me time."

Us? Now is not the time to tell a woman in despair that there is no *us*. God damn it, how do I end up in these situations? I have a fucking knack for it. I'm not a man to relish adding to a person's problems, so I'll probably regret this too, and Sarah will blow her stack, but . . . .

"I can give you until the end of the month." I look up when Zoe enters again, laden down with various suits. I stand and let her start helping me out of my polo shirt, dipping my head so she can pull it off, taking my phone away from my ear briefly. "But you don't murmur a word to anyone, okay?" I say when my phone's back at my ear. There will be anarchy. Members missing payments is commonplace. Me allowing them to reap the benefits of The Manor when they haven't paid for the privilege isn't. No exceptions.

"Of course," she breathes. "Thank you. I knew you'd understand."

I kick off my boots and flip the buttons on my fly, pushing my jeans down my thighs.

Coral's wrong. I don't *understand.* I'm the third in the three-some that's the cause for her marriage breakdown. *What the fuck had I been thinking?* And why the fuck am I doing this now?

"A month, Coral," I say sternly, lifting a foot in turn so Zoe can yank my jeans off. I look down where she's kneeling before me, my jeans in her hands. I hang up on Coral. "All right down there?"

She flips her eyes up, coming face to face with my groin. She's unmoving again.

"You know, Zoe, if you can't learn to control yourself around me, I might need to find myself another personal shopper. This is getting awkward." I give her a cheeky grin, and she shakes her head to herself, rising and claiming a shirt she's selected to go with one of the suits. It's pale blue. I nod agreeably and let her help me into it. She even fastens the buttons for me.

"So, tell me again what the occasion is." She passes me the trousers.

"It's the launch evening of the complex I just bought in." I get the trousers on and turn to face the mirror while Zoe holds the jacket behind me. I slip my arms through and pull it in, rolling my shoulders.

"A new suit for a party?" she questions on a raised brow, and I raise mine right back. "Last I heard, Jesse Ward didn't do mundane launch parties at apartment complexes." She's read between the lines. The fresh face. The new suit. Grabbing a tie, she lays it down my front. Her head cocks one way. Then the other. "No tie," she declares, her eyes falling to mine in the mirror.

I hold them, smiling, as I pull the cuffs of the shirt down. "If you say so, Zoe." I turn to face her.

"I'll just double-check the inseam." Her eyebrows lift as she lowers down my body. "Hmmm, could do with letting out a little."

"Sort it and have it delivered to The Manor?"

"Sure."

"Thanks, Zoe." I drop a friendly kiss on her cheek when she stands, so grateful she makes shopping as pain-free as possible, and I'm soon back in my own clothes, this time without Zoe's help. I flip the collar of my Ralph polo up and slip my shades on.

It's time to plan my seduction.

I pull up behind John's Range Rover, looking up at my rearview mirror when I hear the familiar sound of a Porsche. I pull my smile from nowhere and get out. "Sam," I say, making my way up the steps to The Manor. "It's a bit early, isn't it?"

He soon catches up, flanking me. "Thought I'd grab some lunch"—he casts a wicked grin across to me—"before I grab something else."

I laugh, looking over my shoulder when I hear another car rumbling down the gravel driveway. "What's he doing here at this time of day again?"

Drew swings into a space and gets out, pulling his suit into place as he heads toward us. His face is poker straight, his eyes focused past us rather than on our static forms by the door. "I'm stressed," he mutters as he passes, heading straight for the bar.

Sam and I give each other curious looks, following. Mario, my trusty Italian barman, has a beer on the bar before Drew can order one. "Put it on my tab," I say, settling beside him, as Sam takes a seat on the other side. Drew stares forward, knocking his bottle back.

"What's up?" Sam eventually asks the question burning my lips, but if there's one thing I know about Drew, it's that he doesn't do chitchat.

"The longest chain in the history of real estate just collapsed, taking my commission with it." He slams the bottle down, shrugs his jacket off, and casts his eyes over to me. "And that prick of an estate agent who you bought Lusso from swooped in and took the contract for the new development on Blackfriars." He scowls to himself, and I shrink on my stool, thinking it's probably best I don't mention that *that prick of an estate agent* is now a member of my fine establishment. Drew will find out soon enough.

"So my man needs to let off some steam," Sam chirps, giving Drew a smack on the back, just as he lifts his bottle to his mouth, making his teeth clash with the glass. Drew stills, his jaw tight, and Sam wisely moves back, away from the possible swing of Drew's fist. Me? I do a terrible job of suppressing my laughter. "Sorry," Sam mutters, throwing me a wary look. "But you know what the answer to all this is, don't you?" he goes on, and I shake my head. He needs to shut the fuck up, or that possible swing of Drew's fist will become a certain swing. "Quit."

"What?" Drew spits.

"Don't work," Sam clarifies, nodding to Mario in thanks when he's passed a beer. "Live the stress-free life like me."

"We don't all have dead parents who left us millions," Drew retorts, and I flinch on Sam's behalf, although Sam simply smiles that cheeky smile. I know he has his demons. Drew, however, is plain filthy, no demons so to speak. But while Drew is self-made, Sam was left his millions when he lost his parents in a tragic car accident at nineteen. He and Drew go way back, and Drew has been a member here for over twelve years. He introduced Sam to the lifestyle, brought him here, to escape I suppose—I can relate —and we've been mates ever since. We just connected, despite them both being a few years younger than I am. I love Drew's straight-talking. He doesn't say much, doesn't talk for the sake of it, so anything he does say carries a certain weight. As for Sam, I suppose we clicked because of our histories, since I also lost . . .

I shake that thought away before it can take hold and have me diving across the bar for a drink.

"Sorry," Drew mutters, finding solace in his beer again.

"No sweat." Sam reaches to give Drew another slap on the back, but he soon retracts, thinking better of it. "I don't mind sharing my millions with you. I don't like seeing you stressed, man."

Drew finishes his drink and stands, fixing his suit. I don't know why. It'll be ripped off in a few minutes, given a willing woman or two will be waiting for him in the communal room. "The answer to my problems isn't to quit. I own the fucking company. But do you know what *is* the answer?" he asks, and we both tilt our heads. "Fucking." He stalks out of the bar. "The answer is to fuck."

I laugh as Mario slides a glass toward me, and my amusement dries up in a nanosecond. I stare at the clear liquid. It isn't water. I swallow as I push it back to him, feeling Sam's eyes on my profile. "Thanks, Mario, but I'm not drinking."

There's no mistaking his shock, and I can feel Sam's beside me. And then an awkward silence. I look out the corner of my eye to my mate. He looks like a deer caught in the headlights. "Not drinking?" he eventually manages.

I shrug, accepting the water Mario has replaced the vodka with. "It's no big deal," I say, but we both know it's a huge deal.

"That's great, man." Sam offers a small smile, but reading past his cute, boyish expression, I know he's desperate to ask more. "Good for you."

"Thanks." I'd better get used to this reaction.

"And you've been staying at your own place more," he points out casually. "Is that no big deal too?"

"No big deal," I reiterate, and he grins.

"Nothing to do with the pretty little thing who was here on Friday?"

I get up, not prepared to be interrogated. I'll get that enough from John and Sarah. "No big deal," I say again, striding away.

"Hey, Jesse," he calls, pulling me to a stop by the door. He toasts the air, his face now straight. "When you're done with her, I wouldn't mind a little play with her in the communal room."

I could have just been electrocuted, my entire being vibrating, my jaw feeling like it could snap. My fists ball. "Forget it," I virtually growl, my chest expanding.

Sam's expressionlessness face transforms into a shit-eating grin. "No big deal," he says, that smile wrapping around the neck of his bottle as he takes a swig. *Fucker*.

I flip him a snarl and leave. Ava in the communal room? I shudder. Fuck, no. Ava in *any* room here? Not a fucking chance. Unless I'm with her. And we're alone.

My pace increases, my aggravation uncontainable, and I enter my office and slam the door, forcing my breathing to straighten out. "You look like you're about to launch something," John says from the couch, where he's fiddling with a small box.

"What are you doing?" I ask irritably.

He holds up a little device. "Fixing the CCTV hard drive. Who's rattled your cage?"

"No one." I find my way to my desk and slump down into my chair as John shakes his head, going back to his task. "What's happening?" I ask, trying to steer things away from my simmering rage. Fuck me, that caught me off guard. But it was unstoppable. Completely unstoppable. "And where's Sarah?"

As if she heard me, she appears at the door.

"There," John says without looking up.

"Oh, the hobo returns." She saunters across to my desk and takes a seat.

I'd tell her to fuck off if my conscience would allow it. I pull my laptop forward and start working my way through emails. She can't be here when Ava is here. She'll sniff her out. Potentially ruin my strategy, and I need all possible obstacles out of my way. "What are you doing around seven this evening?" I ask, keeping my eyes on the screen, all casual.

"Why?"

"I need a favor."

"What?"

Fuck. What do I need? *Think, Ward, think.* "Packing," I blurt, peeking up at her. I smile, mild and awkward, hearing John chuckle under his breath. He can fuck off.

"You want me to pack up your rental?" she asks, as insulted as she should be.

"Yeah."

"You hardly ever stay there. Until recently," she adds, her face accusing. John chuckles again, and I throw him a contemptuous glare. "What do you need packed?"

I've got her. Of course I've got her. Sarah will pretty much do anything I ask of her, and I'm taking advantage of that right now. "Ski stuff, clothes."

"Fine." She stands. "I have an appointment at five in the city. I'll head over after."

Perfect. "An appointment for what?"

"None of your business."

Which means she's having something tweaked. Probably her lips. "Thanks. You still have the spare set of keys?"

"Yes." She wanders past John, and he nods before going back to his hard drive. "By the way," she says over her shoulder, not looking back. "If I revoke a member's membership, don't reinstate it without talking to me."

I wilt slightly. "I gave her a couple of weeks. Give the woman a break."

"Will *you* give her a break?"

"What?"

"She's only here for you, you fool. You've made your life more difficult and given her the wrong impression."

She wouldn't say that if she'd seen what happened Sunday night. "I can handle Coral," I mutter, going back to my emails.

"Good. Handle her now. She's in the bar." The door closes. *Fuck, fuck, fuck.* And John's laughing again.

"Fuck off," I snap, earning a deadly glare. I can literally see the burn holes through his wraparounds.

"You're a stupid motherfucker," he rumbles, tossing the hard drive on the coffee table and rising to his full, intimidating height. I should be buttering him up, not pissing him off. Because I need a favor from him too. I give him my dazzling smile. "No," he says, walking away. "Whatever it is, no."

I'm out of my chair fast, going after him. "John, please."

My beseeching tone halts him in his tracks, and he turns, looking over his glasses, giving me a rare peek of his eyes. "What the fuck have you done?" he asks, wary.

Good question. "I have someone coming at seven. I need you to handle it."

"Who?"

"Ava O'Shea."

He laughs. Then he stops abruptly. "No." He takes the handle of the door, as I rummage through my mind for more pleas, anything to convince him to help me. I find nothing. *Fuck it.*

John comes to another sharp stop, his big body facing me. "Whatever you're planning, unplan it."

"I can't."

"Why?"

"Because I can't stop thinking about her," I admit, the frustration apparent in my words. "Fucking hell, John, she's embedded in my brain, and I'm fucked if I can dig her out."

He frowns, dropping his hold of the door handle. "Why have I got to handle it?"

I look away a little sheepishly. "Because she only agreed to come back if she can deal with you."

"Why?"

"I may have come on a little strong."

"How?"

Yeah, I'm not telling him that. I'm ashamed. "It doesn't matter." I shove my hands in my pockets, feeling the stress rising. "I just need you to escort her to the extension so she can measure whatever it is she needs to measure. And don't let anyone talk to her."

"Why?"

I give up the ghost. *For fuck's sake.* "She thinks this is a hotel."

An eruption of laughter bursts out of him. It's so sharp, so powerful, he's forced to bend and brace his hands on his knees. *Fucker.* I'm glad he's finding this funny. Although, I admit begrudgingly, it's oddly satisfying to hear and see John laugh. No one else sees this rare side of him, only me. The man's my rock. And I need him now. Begging isn't beneath me, not on this occasion, yet whenever have I had to beg for anything in my life?

Except for forgiveness.

Except for mercy.

Except for peace.

"You done?' I ask, irritated, going back to my chair. I settle and look across to the drinks cabinet. It's still loaded with alcohol. Why hasn't Sarah done what I asked her to do? I want it gone.

John's quiet now, and I look up to find he's also looking at the drinks cabinet. "And once I've assisted in helping Miss O'Shea measure whatever it is she needs to measure, I do *what* with her?" he asks. "Escort her back to her car?"

"Not exactly," I murmur quietly, sinking my teeth into my

bottom lip. He tilts his head, making the light hit his bald head and bounce off. "You then escort her to my private suite."

"What?"

"Tell her to have a look around. Get a feel for the place."

"And where will you be?"

"Waiting for her."

"Hell, no." The door is yanked open and he's gone, slamming it behind him with brute force. The whole fucking office shakes, and I drop my head back, looking at the ceiling in despair.

See? Stupid idea, Ward. Fucking stupid. But it's all I can think of to remind her. To show her. I'm about to go after John, not prepared to give up—he is quite literally my only hope—but he bursts back in again, slamming the door *again*. The office shakes. *Again*.

"Of all the stupid motherfucking shit you do, Jesse, this takes the cake." He throws his arms out. "Trapping the girl? What kind of fucked-up shit is that?"

If only he knew what I'd been up to so far. I remain mute, completely defenseless, as he rants on.

"If you're that obsessed about fucking your interior designer, take her to fucking dinner."

"John," I say on a sigh. "The closest I've come to taking a woman to dinner is when I wanted to screw the captain of the school hockey team and gave her a piece of my fucking chewing gum. You know I don't do dinner. Besides, she'd only refuse."

"Maybe because she's not attracted to you, you dumb motherfucker."

I balk at him, and he rubs at the wrinkles on his forehead. The cheeky bastard. Every woman is attracted to me. "She most certainly is, and not even *you* can argue that. You were here. In this office when she showed up." He stood there, observing, watching. He probably even had to duck out of the way of the sparks that were flying. I'm taking drastic measures, but it'll be worth it. I know it'll be worth it.

"What is it about her?" he asks out of the blue.

I pull up, startled by his question. "Apart from not being able to get her out of my head?" I hit my temple with the ball of my hand a few times, demonstrating, like I'm trying to physically knock her out.

"Yes, apart from that," he says, reconciling himself to taking a chair opposite my desk and settling in.

I try to locate the words I need, but I'm struggling to find a way to explain. Plus, I'm a little shell-shocked by the whole situation myself, still trying to navigate exactly what the fuck is going on with me at the moment, so I really don't have much hope of enlightening John. But I must try. I sigh. "On Friday, for the first time in as long as I can remember, I felt my heart beating, John." He recoils, and I laugh lightly. Yes. It was weird as fuck. "There was the initial attraction, of course, but after that, I found my mind focused on one thing, and it wasn't alcohol. It was her. She set something off inside, and I'm fucked if I know what to do with it."

"Maybe don't corner her in your private suite in your exclusive sex club. And perhaps, maybe, tell her it's a motherfucking sex club."

Tell her? Is he mad? If Ava O'Shea is deflecting me now, she'd run for the hills if she knew what this place is. Not an option. "I'm not trapping her. I'm making her see."

"See what?"

"I don't know," I grate, my hands going into my hair. "All I know is she makes me feel good and, like the drink, it's becoming a bit addictive."

"Becoming?"

"Is," I admit. "It *is* addictive. *She's* addictive." Fuck me, I've not even been inside her. If I feel this pull toward her now, what will I be like after I've made love to her? *Made love?* Fuck. After I've *fucked* her. "Do you know how frustrating it is to want something but be refused for no good reason?"

"I think Miss O'Shea has plenty of good reasons." He stands. "She just doesn't know what the fuck they are." He walks away from me. "Yet," he adds, exiting my office. "You're acting like a crazy motherfucker."

I drop my forehead to my desk and roll it from side to side. "I fucking feel it," I admit. But this sense of crazy is so powerful, it clouds everything else. And that is addictive too.

I've avoided leaving my office all day, especially since I know Coral is knocking around The Manor. My arse is well and truly numb.

I stand and stretch, glancing at my Rolex, and my stomach flips when I see it's six thirty. She'll be on her way, oblivious of what's waiting for her. I hum to myself as I round my desk. That's not strictly true. She knows what's here at The Manor, namely *me*. And she still agreed to come.

In the evening.

Out of hours.

If that isn't a sign, I don't know what is. She's curious about me. My fortitude gets another quick boost with that thought, and I exit my office, making my way through the summer room. I need to shower. Brush my teeth. Change. I cock my head in thought. Clothes? No clothes? Presenting myself naked might be pushing it. But, on the other hand, it could seal the deal. I glance down at my shirt-covered chest with a smile, diverting up the stairs and pulling my phone out to call John. "Where are you?" I ask when he answers.

"Extension. Checking the beams." He hangs up, and I round the gallery landing, listening for any activity behind the closed doors. There are a few moans, nothing major. I just hope it stays that way.

I make it to John, finding him with a thick piece of rope in his grasp, the end tied to one of the beams, a stepladder set to the side. He's removed his black suit jacket and tie.

"Want some help?" I ask, and he stops tugging, handing me the rope. I accept, happy to assist, giving it a few firm yanks before I reach farther up and wrap it around my fist. I let my feet leave the ground, hanging there. "Solid as a rock," I confirm on a smile.

He grunts and sets about pulling off some more rope to try another beam. "Are you in?" I ask, finding my feet, chewing my lip. He never actually confirmed he'd help me earlier, although I know deep down his parting words were an agreement without actually agreeing.

He doesn't look at me, continuing to measure the rope through his hands. "I will, but only because I prefer this obsessive, uptight motherfucker to the old, laid-back drunk motherfucker."

"Uptight?"

"Yes, uptight." He looks at me. "You're uptight. Moody."

"I'm stressed." But all this frustration will be gone just as soon as Miss O'Shea stops fighting me.

"Whatever. It's better than plastered." He goes back to his task. "But if your plan to seduce her fails and she really doesn't feel whatever the fuck you think she's feeling, you leave it. You hear me? No more crazy shit. You leave the girl alone."

"Promise," I agree without hesitation. But my plan won't fail. "Sarah gone?"

"Left a while ago."

"Good. Ava will be here at seven." I back out of the room. "Ish," I add, frowning to myself as I take in the rope and beams. "Probably wise to take her to the room at the far end." Where there are no ropes hanging from the beams to test they're strong enough to take the weight of a human body. "And could you let me know when she's here? Text me?"

He hears me, but he doesn't answer.

"Thanks, John."

"Fuck off."

I smile and leave him to it, making my way to my private suite. I go to the cabinet and pull out a pair of jeans and a T-shirt, then take a shower. I kill time, running through my plan as I wash. Which is, basically, get her steaming drunk on lust. Make it impossible for her to walk away. Be gentle. Patient.

I step out and dry off, pulling on my jeans. I hear the door open. John appears in the bathroom doorway, and I frown. "What are you doing here?" Shit, hasn't she turned up? I mentally locate my phone on the unit and push past John to retrieve it, my insides churning.

"She's here."

I swing around before I make it to my phone, my insides now on fire.

"I left her in the bar."

"Why?" I ask, horrified. The place is heaving.

"I told Mario. Don't worry."

"You could have text me."

"I can't convince you to rethink if I text you."

Oh. So that's why he's here. To talk me out of it. I scoff and pass him, going back into the bathroom to grab my toothbrush. "My mind is made up." It's the only way. "If you'd ever felt like this, you might understand."

"The butterflies? The tingles? Yeah, been there."

My toothbrush stops halfway to my mouth, my shocked eyes finding him in the mirror. *What the fuck?* John's been single for as long as I've known him, which is basically forever. It's never cost me a thought, to be fair. He's hardly a cuddly bear pouring with affection that a woman couldn't resist. "You have?" It's all I can think to say, and judging by his scowl, he regrets opening his mouth.

"Who?"

"It doesn't matter who it was."

"And what did you do?"

"Ignored it." His eyebrows pop up above his glasses. "Because it wasn't reciprocated."

I sag. How many times have I got to tell him? "She feels it. She just needs a little . . . nudge."

"Make sure it's just a nudge," he warns, backing out. "And for the love of God, whatever happens, keep your cool."

"What makes you think I won't?"

"Stupid motherfucker," John mumbles, bringing the wood between us.

And I'm alone again. Alone with my pulse racing and my heart booming. I rest my hands on the edge of the sink, staring at myself. I should listen to John. If this fails, if she rejects me again, I need to let it go. And then what? Back to seeking solace in drink? No. I haven't had a drink for five days and I feel great. With the exception of this awful anxiety, obviously.

I swallow and nod, mentally promising myself I'll walk away from her. Because at this rate, I'll have a fucking heart attack.

I finish brushing my teeth, rake a hand through my wet hair, and go into the suite to wait. How long will she be? I pace in circles for what feels like forever, the soles of my feet becoming warm from the friction on the carpet. I dump my arse on the chaise in front of the window. Get up. Pace some more. Fucking hell, have I ever felt so nervous? I don't do nervous. It's not in my DNA. It's yet another sign that there's more to this.

And then I hear something.

John.

On impulse, I go into the bathroom, closing the door behind

me. If she walks in and sees me standing in the middle of the room, she'll walk right back out.

I stand still.

Listen.

The door closes.

I breathe in, my heart going like the clappers, just with the thought of seeing her. She's mere feet away from me. There's a door between us. And I'm buzzing.

I brace my hands on the sink to get my breathing under control. I have to be together when I open that door. Calm but determined. I reach up to rake a hand through my hair, knocking my tin of hair wax to the tile floor as I do. *Shit.* My eyes fly to the door. It's now or never. On a deep breath, I edge forward, take the handle, and pull it open.

She swings around and gasps.

And there she is.

My lungs fail me.

Her bag hits the floor, and the sound is deafening in the silence. I keep my mouth firmly shut and let her drink me in. She's fidgeting, but she's not running. Will she submit to me?

"Is this some kind of joke?" she asks over a nervous laugh, no doubt at my boldness. I can't quite believe I'm doing this myself, but I need to have this woman. Fuck, I've got to have her. The fight stops now. I've never needed to go to these lengths. A woman has never done this to me, so here I am, half-naked, cornering my interior designer, desperate for her to admit the crazy chemistry we shared.

Her eyes wander all over my chest, and I just stand before her, letting her take me in, my eyes lowered slightly and burning with the need to blink. But I won't blink. I don't want to miss a moment of this look of awe on her face. I don't want to miss the second she stops fighting me. She's imagined this. She's imagined my naked chest. What it would be like to kiss me. Be with me.

She's going to find out.

Her chest pushes against her fitted black dress as she takes a deep breath. I'm not going to be able to stand here much longer. I'm desperate to move in.

Shifting again, her neck flexes, the taut expanse of smooth flesh at her throat begging me to place my mouth there. She's psyching herself up. But she's still edgy.

"Relax, Ava," I say softly. "You know you want this." I take tentative steps toward her, my hands twitching, ready to take hold of that small waist. Our eyes are locked. I'm not breaking this connection. My body is singing, my headspace flooded with her and her alone. I feel wobbly with the rush of returned sensations. Unstable. High as a kite on lust and anticipation.

When I'm a few feet away from her, I see her tense more, but she doesn't look away. Instead, her gaze drifts upward as I get closer until I'm towering over her. I don't touch her. Instead, I get our bodies as close as I can, but it's taking every fucking bit of effort I possess not to grab her.

"Turn around," I order softly.

I let out a quiet, relieved breath when she slowly pivots, giving me her back and the zip of her dress. My eyes skate the length of her spine, my blood burning. I feel wary and euphoric.

I'm enthralled. Spellbound.

I've not touched her, am almost scared to, because something deep and unsettling inside is telling me that if I do, I might not ever let go. I need to maintain this rapture. I need to feel my heart beat this hard every day.

I watch as her shoulders solidify and hear as her breaths turn harsh. I'm matching her reactions with my own.

She makes to turn back toward me, and my hands fly up fast, my palms resting on her shoulders. We both jolt with the contact, and I clench my eyes closed, blood starting to whoosh in my ears.

I slowly release a hand, silently pleading for her to stay exactly where she is. She does. No fight.

Reaching forward, I scoop her hair up, the shiny, dark locks that match her eyes, feeling like silk on my palm. I let it tumble down her front, my eyes fixed on the bare skin of her nape, and as much as I want to kiss it, I need to take this slowly. I'm not doing anything that will freak her out. I should laugh at my own audacity. I've cornered the poor woman and presented myself to her half-naked. You don't get more audacious than that. And yet . . . she's still here.

But still so tense. I need to soften her up, so I start slowly rubbing away the tightness in her shoulder, smiling to myself when I see her head roll and then hear a slight purr coming from those lips—the lips I want to devour. She likes it, so I increase the pressure and move my mouth to her ear.

When her face turns into mine and her pants of hot air spread across my face, I lose the battle not to voice my lingering fears. "Don't stop this."

She starts trembling under my hold. "I don't want to." Her answer is soft but sure, and I deflate, my perplexing anxiety leaving me. I knew deep down she was with me in this, but those words have filled a huge void of doubt. And every amazing thing I feel when in this woman's orbit intensifies.

"It's a good job. I don't think I'd let you." I push myself into her back, my mouth falling straight to her ear again. "I'm going to take your dress off now." I catch her nod and clamp down lightly on her lobe. "You're too fucking beautiful, Ava." I skim my lips across her ear.

"Oh God," she breathes, leaning on me and pushing her lower back into my groin.

Good lord, I'm suddenly throbbing, my jaw ready to shatter like glass from the harshness of my bite. "Do you feel that?" I push into her, and she moans. "I'm going to have you, lady." I'm sober and the most turned on I've ever been. She's magic. A cure.

My savior?

I blink and place a fingertip at the top of her spine, drawing a perfect line down her back, nodding mildly as the signs of her craving moves up a level. Her skin is on fire beneath this dress. I can feel her need, smell her anticipation. I take the zipper, placing my free hand on her hip. She jerks, and my grip firms up, making sure I hold her in place. She can't run, not now. I gently tug the zip down and slide my hands onto her bare flesh beneath it, flexing my fingers before pushing the material away from her body and letting it drop to the floor.

Oh fucking hell.

I knew it.

Lace.

I can't control the sharp breath that's just escaped. "Lace," I whisper. God, she is fucking glorious in lace. Grabbing her waist, I lift her slight frame, freeing her ankles of her dress. She feels so right in my hold, like she's been molded to fit perfectly in my grasp. I need to see her face again. Need to see the lust in her eyes, her craving, her desperation. And, God, she really needs to see mine.

I turn her around slowly, taking in every inch of her skin as I do. She's focused on my lips. She wants to kiss me. I've got her, and I'm going to take my sweet time savoring every fucking moment of this.

My hand rises and finds her breast, my finger painting perfect circles around the rim of her nipple. Her body concaves with her tiny gasp, her eyes studying my fascinated face. I want to touch her as much as I want to slam into her. I want to run my hands over every square inch of her body, kiss her from head to toe, lose myself in her, and hold her while we both recover from what I know is going to be a universe-shaking experience.

I take her other breast, and I'm slightly shocked when her hands lift and rest on my chest.

Shit. Fucking shit.

I'm the one flinching now, and the look of satisfaction that flashed across her face is like a shot of adrenalin. She knows she's affecting me too, but does she know that this is absolutely unheard of?

I turn her around. "I want to see you," she breathes.

I smile to myself. "Shh." I unclasp her lace bra before sliding my hands under the straps. Her skin is like velvet. I want permanent access to this. My heart is not easing up on the persistent, thundering pounds. It feels too good.

I push her bra away from her body, breathing heavily in her ear. "You. And. Me." It's the perfect combination, I was certain of it, and now I've had it confirmed that this woman will be my undoing. I can't hold back anymore. I spin her around and kiss her, my body folding under the pleasure of our lips connecting. I coax her mouth open and take her like I really mean it, and I really fucking do. She flings her arms over my shoulders and yanks me closer, and I can't help grinding my hips into her, trying desperately to cool the incessant throb in my cock. I moan, my hands drifting all over her bare skin until they reach her hair, my fingers spreading across the back of her head and my palms cupping her cheeks. I force myself to pull away, needing her eyes again, needing to check she's real and this isn't some cruel dream. She swallows, blinks, and scans my face. I can't control my heaving chest, and I've given up trying to regulate my breathing. I'm a fucked-up mess of a man. She's just blown everything I know and live by right out of the water. My forehead falls to hers, my eyes closing as I try to figure out some of this shit. I can't. I haven't the first idea what the fuck this is, but I'm sure of one thing. We'll be doing this again.

"I'm going to get lost in you." Already am. My hand falls

down her back until I'm grasping the back of her thigh, and with one gentle tug, she obliges my demand and lifts her leg, cradling my hip. I want her wrapped entirely around me . . . forever.

We stare at each other, and I try to bat away the ridiculous notion that she's been sent to save me. "There's something here." I have to say it, and even though it wasn't a question, I need confirmation because I feel like I'm going fucking insane. "I'm not imagining it," I say, and again I'm begging for an answer.

She's quiet for a few moments, but then she draws breath, and I hold mine, waiting, praying she says what I need to hear. "There's something," she whispers as she watches me.

The relief is inconceivable, the need to kiss her overwhelming. Except this time, it won't be hard. It won't be greedy. It'll be a different kiss. A slow, soft, meaningful kiss. I claim her mouth, gently swirling my tongue. It's heaven. Pure, unmistakable heaven, and heaven is not a place where I ever thought I'd find myself. It's a million miles away from the hell that is my life, and for that reason alone, I want to tape my mouth to hers. The need coursing through me isn't letting up, it's multiplying by the second, each look, every word, all the touches, only deepening everything. As I predicted, I'm lost.

But found.

I will never doubt my instinct again.

But then I hear something, and I find my relaxed form tightening.

Oh fuck, no.

Please, no.

The sound has me kissing Ava more aggressively, my groin involuntarily pushing into her, and I really don't mean to. "Oh, Jesus." I don't let her lips free. "Don't ruin this."

I hear her again. Sarah. Damn that fucking woman. What the fuck is she doing here? *Forget about her. Ignore her.* I'm not letting anything stop this—nothing.

I feel Ava's nails digging into my shoulders, and I moan. Fuck, that feels good, but I know I'm freaking her out with my sudden urgency to devour her. I let her leg go, grab her hips so she can't move, and tear my lips from hers, gasping for air. Her head drops. "The door's locked." It's not locked—fuck, I should have locked it—but I'm trying my hardest to reassure her. My damn hardest.

This doesn't end yet. This *never* ends.

I take her jaw and pull her face up. "Please," I beg.

Beg. I'm fucking begging. And if necessary, I *will* get on my fucking knees.

She shakes her head, and I fail in my attempts to stop hardening my hold, shaking her slightly, desperate to keep her with me.

"Don't run," I order harshly, my heart now pounding with panic. *Do. Not. Run.*

"I can't do this," she whispers, and my hands fall away from her, a severe, unstoppable growl of frustration erupting.

"Jesse?" Sarah's shriek makes my blood begin to boil, and I watch in a daze of horror and complete fucked-up devastation as Ava dips and gathers her clothes before running into the bathroom, slamming the door behind her.

My eyes drop and dart across the floor, my head in my hands. I can hear Sarah calling me in the distance, but I'm in a total stupor. Gutted. Hurt. Furious. My eyes land on Ava's lace bra. I scoop it up and stuff it in the top drawer of the cabinet, just as Sarah bowls in. I swing around, fighting to regain my composure *and* hold back my anger. "What are you doing here?" I ask quietly.

"I got a call from a member who needed some attention. I'll sort your apartment tomorrow."

"Fine," I reply, willing her to fuck the hell off, trying not to be hostile and failing miserably.

"Are you okay?"

"I'm fine." I glare at her, and I can see she's desperate to know what the fuck's gotten into me. I motion to my bathroom. "I'm busy, Sarah."

Her eyes drift across to the door, where I suspect Ava is beyond having a full-blown meltdown, full of regret. But why? And why the fuck did Sarah have to interrupt and give Ava that time to backpedal?

"Oh, I see." Sarah smiles. She thinks I've got one of the ladies of The Manor in there. Good. "See you later." She closes the door, and my head goes straight back into my hands.

Fuck.

Fuck, fuck, fuck.

My body heavy, I drag my feet to the bathroom. I can turn this around. Talk to her. Ask her what's going through her mind. Reassure her. Get her back to where we both want to be. I feel my body reheating with that unfathomable rage.

Because of Sarah.

Fucking hell, Ward, keep your cool. Approach carefully.

I swallow and knock on the door. "Ava?" My voice is gruff, sounding a bit impatient. So, not surprisingly, she doesn't answer. I close my eyes and try to reset, try to find some calm.

And then I hear the door lock click, and my hands are out before I've even registered they've moved, shoving the door open, my body naturally filling the doorway. Instinct.

She glances past me, probably checking the coast is clear, as I wonder where the fuck she got the willpower to abandon that moment because I couldn't have, not for anything. Her pretty face looks at me in contempt, and I'm absolutely stunned by it. She pushes past me aggressively, and my body turns, following her path.

"Where the hell are you going?" I blurt without thought.

She ignores me, snatching up her bag and hurrying out of my

suite. *What the fuck?* Nothing? No explanation? No words at all? After all that, she's really going to leave without talking about this? My face must be expressing the incredulity I'm feeling, my forehead heavy as fuck from my confused frown. "Fuck," I yell, snatching up my T-shirt, shoving my feet in my shoes, and grabbing the file she's left, going after her. *Not a fucking chance, lady.* She doesn't get to take me to heaven and then send me to hell. "Ava!" I bellow, flying out of the suite, wrestling with my T-shirt as I do.

I see her reach the bottom of the stairs, going into the bar. I'm down the steps in a few reckless leaps, wide-eyed members everywhere stopping and staring as I go.

I land in the bar, out of breath and disheveled, my fear escalating when I find Sarah crowding Ava near the bar. For fuck's sake, didn't she have someone to whip?

I feel her interested stare pass between Ava and me. I'm going to be grilled as soon as she has me alone. I'll make sure it isn't anytime soon, if only because I can't promise I won't rip her head off for fucking it all up. I feel like I'm back at square one, and by the look on Ava's face, her beautifully flushed face, I am. Her eyes glance at me briefly before looking away, her attention turning to Mario who's approaching.

"Miss O'Shea, here, you must try." He thrusts a shot glass containing one of his potent concoctions toward Ava, and I find myself scowling at him. She's driving, for fuck's sake.

"Do you have my phone, Mario?" Ava asks.

"You try." He thrusts it forward, all smiley, and she grabs it and knocks it back, her flinch an indication of the strength. I bristle.

"Wow," she says over a cough.

"It is good?" Mario asks, hopeful, freeing Ava's hand of the glass and replacing it with her phone.

"Yes. It's very good."

Yeah, well, don't be getting used to it. I make a mental note to have a quiet word with Mario about testing his concoctions on Ava.

Sarah casts her eagle-eyed glare my way—she can fuck off, this is all her fault—as Ava fusses with her dress, breathes in, and lifts her chin, facing me.

"You left this upstairs," I say, holding up her file, my eyes rooted to hers, my mind a riot of pleading words. *Come on, Ava. Don't walk away, not now. I need to finish what we started. And then do it all over again. And again. And again, and again, and again.*

"Thank you."

I feel her pull against the file, but I refuse to let go, my teeth going overtime on my lip, thinking, thinking, thinking. Just take her into your office. Talk it through. But before I can suggest that, she's gone.

"Goodbye," she says, leaving me standing like a twat, open-mouthed, Mario looking interested as he pours a drink, Sarah still studying me. If she breathes a word . . .

"Want to explain?" she asks, accepting the gin being handed over the bar. In my head, I tell her to fuck off a million times. "No." I look at Mario. "When she was in the bar earlier, what did she have?"

"A wine."

I'm off after Ava, and not only because she's had a drink and she shouldn't be driving, but because I deserve an explanation. She can give me that explanation while I drive her home.

I jog to the front doors and down the steps, hearing the engine of her car. Is she fucking stupid? "Ava!" I roar, incensed.

She screeches off, demonstrating she's not in control, and the alcohol is only half the reason. "Fuck," I bellow, flinging my arms into the air. Is it possible to desire a woman and want to fucking strangle her too? Because I do. I really fucking do.

I race back into The Manor, flying through like a bullet to my office. I grab my keys and sprint back to my car, people jumping from my path. I land in the seat heavily, start the engine, and pull off, sending the back end drifting across the gravel. "Fucking woman." While it's my mission to prove she's as desperate for me as I am for her, it seems her mission is to send me to crazy town in *every* fucking way.

Her Mini comes into view, the gates stopping her escape. "Good try," I say, coming to a stop behind her, getting out and walking over. I know my face is displaying every ounce of anger I feel as I swing the door open. She has her head resting on the steering wheel. Don't tell me she's exasperated? She has no fucking idea. I take her arm firmly and pull her out of the car, taking the keys out of the ignition too. "Ava." My jaw buzzes, my aggravation blazing when her nostrils flare in annoyance. "You're half pissed. I swear to God, if you'd have hurt yourself . . ."

She flinches, looking away, ashamed. God damn me. I soften, taking her jaw and turning her to face me. Look at her. Still flushed with desire. Her eyes still begging for me, even if her lips refuse to say it. *Say it, woman. Find that resolve you had back there when I had you in my arms. Accept me.*

She tugs her face away, and I sigh. "Are you okay?" I ask gently, now calm. It's because she's here, within touching distance. I reach for her again, but she withdraws. I take it on the chin. She looks . . . emotional.

"Funnily enough, no, I'm not," she snaps. "Why did you do that?"

"Isn't it obvious?"

"You want me."

"More than anything," I admit, unapologetic.

"I've never met anyone so full of themselves." Is she laughing? "Did you plan this? When you rang me yesterday, was this your intention all along?"

Did she honestly think I'd be able to stay away? And did she honestly want me to? Good lord, if I'm full of myself, she's full of fucking shit. What I've done is as obvious as how I feel. But in case she's truly missed all of that, I spell it out, loud and clear, no holding back. "Yes. I want you."

She shakes her head. *No, I can't believe I'm here either, but I am, and so are you. So, deal with it before I go certifiably mad.* "Can you open the gates, please?" She marches off, and I watch her, ignoring her request. There's no way I'm letting her out of here, and I wouldn't even if she hadn't had a drink. Not until we've talked. Sorted this shit out. Found a middle ground. *Which is what, Ward?* She flies around, fuming mad. "Open the damn gates!"

"You honestly think I'm going to let you go wandering aimlessly out there when you're miles from home?"

"I'll call a cab."

"Absolutely not. I'll take you."

"Just open the fucking gates!"

What the actual fuck? Why is she speaking like a whore when she's a fucking lady? "Watch your fucking mouth!" I roar, and she recoils in shock.

"I'm not prepared to be a notch on your busy bedpost."

I'm beginning to think she's the crazy one here. A notch? Oh, she will be no notch. "You actually believe that?" I ask, astounded. Hasn't she heard anything I've said? Does she think I say this shit to every woman I bed? I'm about to ask, but my phone rings. I dig it out of my pocket and answer. "John?" I try to walk off some of my stress, pacing in circles.

"All right?" he asks, probably having gotten word of me flying around The Manor like a madman.

"Yeah." I'm not going into it now. I cut the call and face her with a stare that she better not mistake as anything less than determined. "I'll take you home."

"No, please, just open the gates."

I shake my head. She can beg all she likes. I'm not backing down. "No, I'm not letting you out there on your own, Ava. End of. You're coming with me."

She looks away quickly, and I follow her eyes, seeing a car pulling in off the main road. "Fuck," I shout, scrambling for my phone and dialing John. I see Ava's body engage, her legs getting ready to run, and I make a grab for her, but she dodges me, dashing to her car and grabbing her bag.

"John, don't open the fucking gates," I bellow down the line, seeing her getting farther away.

"I'm nowhere near a gate control panel."

Sarah. "Well tell Sarah not to."

I go after Ava, the gap now big enough for her to squeeze through. And she does. Damn her for being so tiny. I'll have to wait too many seconds for it to be large enough to get my big frame through. Not that I'll have the chance to wait. They start closing. "Bollocks." I run back to my car and scratch around for my fob, smacking the button to open them again. I'm fucking exhausted.

I stalk after her, my strides long, eating up the distance between us. She's on her phone by the time I reach her, and I swoop in, throwing her onto my shoulder, not prepared to try and reason anymore. I've never met such a difficult woman in my life.

Her scream of surprise is endearing.

"You're not wandering around on your fucking own, lady." I take us back into The Manor grounds.

"What's it got to do with you?"

"Apparently, nothing." *You stubborn mare.* "But I do have a conscience. You're not leaving here unless it's in my car. Do you understand me?" I drop her to her feet and give her an expectant glare before escorting her to my car and physically putting her in the seat. My final look tells her she'll regret it if she even *thinks* about getting out.

I go to her Mini, squeezing myself in behind the wheel. "Jesus Christ," I mutter, feeling around under the seat for a lever to push the seat back. And even then, I feel like I'm squished into a can of sardines. "This can't be safe," I say, starting it up and moving it to the side of the drive to allow cars to pass.

I stomp my way back to her and throw myself in the seat. Is she smiling? What the fuck is there to smile about? I'm fucking livid, and not only because she stole a rare piece of heaven from me.

I start my Aston and fly out of the gates. No matter how much I try to talk myself down, I can't, but if I don't take this unwarranted, unusual, unwanted anger out on the road, then Ava will cop it, and that would be a sure-fire way of severing any possibility of fixing this fucking mess.

I glance across the car to her. She's looking out of the window, quiet. Tense. Do I *want* to fix this? Yes, the feelings I felt *were* amazing, but this? This anger? It's not me, and it doesn't feel good at all. How can someone drive you to the highest heights of desire and to the deepest depths of despair?

I return my attention to the road, mulling that over for the rest of the journey as Ava gives me short, snappy directions. I've still not found an answer by the time we're in her neighborhood.

"It's left at the end of the road," she says, clipped. I do a left. "Just there on the right."

I pull in, and she's out of the car like a bullet. "Ava," I call, reaching for her keys to hand back. The door is slammed, and she's up the garden path to the front door fast. I peer up at the house. It's small. Modest. Cute.

I look down at her keys in my hand, thinking.

Just for a second.

Then I throw them on the seat and roar off.

6

I FALL BACK against the door of my rental, looking at the ceiling. My fucking jaw is aching like a bitch, my body still wired, every inch of me tense. My eyes land on the cabinet, the surface bare. I close my eyes and breathe deeply, in and out, in and out. She ran. It's time for me to walk away.

But there's something. I know I'm a total fuck-up, but I'm not completely delusional.

I hope.

My hands come up to my head, and I attempt to force the images and words away. My heartbeat feels sluggish. My head aches. My stomach is constantly twisting, whether with anxiety or anticipation. I can't let this rule me. I feel more destructive now than I ever have.

Self-sabotage. I'm a master at it, and it seems Miss O'Shea could be both a cause and the cure.

My hands are shaking. Drink. I need a drink. "Fuck." I stalk to the fridge, grabbing a jar of my vice and taking it to the couch. Tossing the lid aside, I scoop out a huge dollop and shove my finger in my mouth, pulling off the peanut butter and closing my eyes. Rest. I just need to rest my eyes and my mind for a moment.

Jake frowns at me across the lounge as I work my way happily through the jar. "You're gross," he mutters, disappearing out of the room and returning a few moments later. He drops down on the couch next to me and unscrews the lid of his own jar. "Crunchy all the way." He shoves his finger in his pot of crunchy peanut butter and shovels out a big helping, wrapping his grinning mouth around his finger.

"Fucking weirdo," I mutter, unable to hold back my smile. "Smooth. It's got to be smooth."

No!

I snap my eyes open.

Inhale.

And throw the jar across the room on a thunderous roar, my head going into my hands, trying to suppress the torture. Trying to shy away from a time just before my life fell apart. Just before the downward spiral started. I can't escape. And I don't deserve to.

I jump up from the couch and take myself to the bathroom, stripping out of my clothes on my way. And I stand in front of the mirror, gazing at my reflection, my eyes drifting to my scar. I rest my finger on the edge and trace the jagged line. I'm beyond hope. Broken.

And I'd be stupid to think she could fix me.

I spent Wednesday hiding. Hiding from the world, from my friends, from my thoughts. I ignored endless calls from endless people, buried under my duvet.

Hiding from the alcohol.

They can't see me like this.

The moment I open my eyes on Thursday, I throw the sheets back and force myself out of bed, pulling my shorts on quickly and heading out the door. I run. I run so fast, so hard. I lose all feeling in my legs, and if I run even harder, even faster, I'm hoping I will lose all feelings *everywhere*. Be rid of this madness. Be numb.

Yet with the wind whooshing past, my eyes trained on the path before me, endless, tormenting flashbacks hound me, goad me, remind me of that extreme sense of unrestrained abandon. One by one, my bastard memories of Tuesday evening play out, a few agonizing splinters of my history joining the chaos in my head. "No." My pace increases. Run away from them.

There's something.

"Fuck!" I yell, my legs failing me, slowing, taking me down to a slower jog. Sweat pours from every pore, running into my eyes, and I come to a stop, rubbing into the sockets, the sting killing me. I'm forced to sit myself down on the grass, unable to see clearly. I also need to catch my fucking breath. I'm a mess. A broken, fucked-up mess, and I feel no better for having nearly killed myself running fuck knows how many miles.

I fall to my back and stare at the sky. I can't run away. I'm trapped.

Lonely.

I'm at the mercy of my demons and, fuck, I could cry my fucking eyes out.

Helpless.

My phone rings, and I blindly reach into my pocket, pulling it out, hoping it's Ava. The only voice I want to hear. Of course, it's not her.

"Sarah," I breathe, my lungs tight.

"I'm at your apartment," she snaps impatiently. "Where the hell are you?"

In Hell. I don't bite. I know she'll be worried. I drag myself to my feet and start the long walk back to my rental. "Running."

"Why is her car at The Manor?"

I bristle. I'd forgotten about her car. She's not collected it? Will she *ever* collect it? "Drop it, Sarah." Her huff of indignation rattles me more. I'm still blaming her for fucking it all up for me. "I'll be at The Manor later. Go back. I'm sure you'll survive without me until then." I hang up, and the small pang of guilt only serves to piss me off more. Because if there's one thing I'm certain of amid all of this uncertainty, it's that Sarah really can't survive without me.

I pull up at The Manor just past noon. John is in the driveway talking to a man in a white van, pointing at the cameras that line the front of The Manor. "Hard drive's fucked," he mutters as I approach, turning away from the guy and looking me up and down, assessing me. I look smart. I made a point of looking smart in an attempt to halt the barrage of questions that I know are awaiting me. I'm fine. Totally fine.

I pass him without a word, bypassing the bar and striding to my office. I walk in and close the door, finding a suit bag hanging on the back. I frown, my lagging brain failing to enlighten me. I reach forward and pull the zip down, and it finally comes to me before the navy suit is revealed. The Lusso launch tomorrow. I let out a light, sardonic puff of laughter. I think we can safely say I won't be welcome.

"Jesse?"

The door flies open.

And smacks me in the face.

"Fuck," I yell, the wood ricocheting off my forehead.

"Shit. Sorry." She's on me like a wolf, checking me over. "Why the hell are you standing behind the door?"

I bat her fussing hands away and rub my nose, checking for blood. Shit, my eyes are watering. "I was checking my new suit," I grumble, going to the couch and sitting down, holding my throbbing nose. "If you've broken my fucking nose, I'll—"

"You'll what?" she asks tiredly, halting my empty threat in its tracks. She closes the door and checks out my suit. "Nice. Special occasion?"

"No, I just fancied a new suit." Or a new mask. I glare at her back. "Did you want something?"

She turns slowly. I don't like the thoughtful look on her face. "Something's been playing on my mind."

Don't ask, Ward. I narrow my eyes and go to my desk. Sarah joins me, crossing one leather-clad leg over the other, sitting back, getting comfortable, her accusing eyes nailed to me. "You didn't need me to pack your apartment up at all, did you?"

"No, and it's a good job since you didn't fucking do it." I start smashing at the keys on my laptop. What is it with her, sticking her fucking nose into my business all the time? Although, Sarah has always stuck her nose into my business. Not that I have much business outside the walls of The Manor. I've never been so defensive before. But now . . .

"What is it about her?" she asks.

It's exactly what John asked. Except I can't share with Sarah. Won't. And it's a moot point now, anyway. Ava walked away. I'm done. It's finished. "I don't know what you're talking about." I can't sit here under her interrogating stare. "I have things to do." I get up and round my desk, mentally scratching around for what it is I need to do exactly. Nothing. Everything here is fine, always is, whether I'm absent in mind or body or not.

"Tomorrow night," she calls, and I frown, keeping up my stride. "We have a meeting with a few members about another member."

"Can't make it," I call without thought, my frown deepening.

What the fuck else am I going to do? My eyes land on my new suit as I take the handle. "You'll have to manage it on your own."

"Why, where will you be?"

Probably punishing myself. "Otherwise engaged," I say, turning and flashing her a smile that won't fool her. I close the door, my smile drops, and I rest my forehead on the wood. I cannot go to the launch. I cannot call her, see her, pursue her.

There's something.

Oh God.

I want to see you.

My fist comes up and pushes into the wood firmly, my eyes clenching. "Just fuck off out of my head, woman."

Don't stop this.

I don't want to.

"Then why the fuck did you?" I ask quietly, squeezing my fists as I push myself off the door. I pull my phone out. Dial her. "Answer, baby," I whisper, mentally praying. I know I'm praying for a miracle. I'm not even blessed with fairness, so a miracle is way out of my reach. "Come on, come on." I turn my face to the ceiling. Is there a god? Would he hear me? Listen to me?

No.

It goes to voicemail, and my face screws up in agony at yet another rejection. I punch the door, angered. She's scared. Scared to talk to me, scared to face me.

And I know why. It was insane. Our kiss. Our skin touching. The look in her eyes and undoubtedly mine. This isn't just attraction. There's more. So much more. It's something inexplicable. Something fucking huge.

A connection that I can't dismiss.

The door of my office swings open, and Sarah's mouth is locked and loaded, ready to ask why the fuck I'm beating the door. Then she catches my expression. I can only imagine how I must look. Despaired. Desperate. Hopeless.

She withdraws, her mouth snapping shut, and I breathe in, turning and walking away. She doesn't ask me where I'm going this time. Doesn't throw any sarcasm or snide remarks at me.

She lets me go.

Good. Because I've thought of something I really have to do.

That explanation I'd accepted I would never get from Ava?

I want it.

Now.

7

IT TAKES everything in me not to storm her office and start throwing around my demands. I haven't got much willpower at the moment, as most of it is being used to resist my craving for a drink. Seven days without a drop. *Fucking incredible.*

I settle on paying her a visit at home.

"How the fuck does she drive this thing?" I mutter to myself, yanking her Mini into reverse and backing into a space outside a convenience store not far from Ava's place. I virtually crawl out of her car. I must look ridiculous.

The lady behind the counter beams at me as I approach, her eyes sparkling with delight. I have no energy to dazzle her further with a smile. "I need a disposable phone, please." I pull out my wallet, my eyes lifting to the shelf behind the counter, automatically landing on the vodka.

"No problem," she sings. "Do you need a SIM as well?"

My eyes don't move from the vodka. "Yes."

"That'll be thirty pounds, please, sir."

Give me a liter of vodka too.

"Thanks." I slap a few notes on the counter, snatch the phone and SIM, and get out of the store, feeling my brow dampen. I throw them on the passenger seat, wedging my body behind the wheel again, and pull off quickly, getting far, *far* away from the temptation. Heading for another lure. A more powerful lure.

I pull onto her road and glance up at the house as I pass, seeing the lights on the first floor are on. Swinging into a space, I cut the engine and flip open the glove compartment. I look through the CD's she's got stashed in there, smiling when I see Blur in her collection. I pull it out, eject the Ibiza dance tracks—definitely more her genre than mine, another reminder of the age gap—replace it with Blur, and skip to the track on my mind, my smile growing. But it falls when I stare across the road, wondering what reaction I'll get this time. Has she been thinking about me?

I want to see you.

The breathy *Oh God* was acceptance. She royally fucked up when she said that.

I reach across to the other seat and take the phone and SIM, putting it together, not quite believing I'm stooping to this kind of low. I key in her number, lifting the phone to my ear as I look back up at the window. As it starts to ring, I break free from the confines of her little car and stretch my muscles, glancing at my trousers. They're stupidly crumpled. They match my fucking brain.

"Ava O'Shea."

My head snaps up, her voice sliding over my skin like silk, momentarily rendering me incapable of replying or moving.

"Hello?"

"Are you alone?" I spit the words out fast, not thinking about how I sound. Angry. I sound angry. I'm not thinking straight.

I can hear movement and sudden heavy breathing. "No." She rushes the word after way too long.

For the love of God, does she take pleasure from this? "Why

are you lying to me?" I ask, my vocal cords hurting from the strain to hold back from growling my words.

There's more movement, and my mind conjures up images of her darting to the window to look out, so I gaze up, seeing her shadow behind the blinds. Every modicum of sense remaining is telling me to walk away before this kills me, but that tiny side of my fucked-up mind, the side that's dead set on making my life fucking miserable, is stamping all over it.

The line goes dead, and I pull the stupid, cheap, disposable crap away from my ear, looking at it in disgust. My ego wants to believe that the piece of shit is broken, but I know damn well she just hung up on me. Again. *Breathe, Ward. Breathe.*

Slightly concerned by the building anger, I dial her again, my mind invaded by those images of her standing before me in that lace. The words she uttered. The desperation, the want, the acceptance.

She doesn't answer, and I resist throwing the phone to the floor, texting her instead. I know she'll read it. She might not reply, but she'll read it. I don't think about what my thumbs are bashing out. They just bash away, a mind of their own.

Answer your phone!

Just as I click send, I yell in frustration at my own abruptness. I'm trying to fucking win this woman, not scare her half to death. I dial her again, but she doesn't answer. *Again.* "For fuck's sake," I curse, re-dialing. I'll call her all night if I have to. I'm not leaving until she faces me and explains what the fuck happened. "Fucking answer!" I demand.

She doesn't. "Fine," I say to myself, resolute. She doesn't get to do this. Every second she refuses to acknowledge me is enhancing the truth of it.

She's scared.

Admittedly, I'm scared too. Fucking terrified. She can soothe me, just like I know I can soothe her. I cross the road toward the house, as the piece-of-shit phone screams the arrival of a text. My stomach turns, my stomach actually turns, and my brow breaks out in a light sweat. I open her message.

No.

No.

Just . . . no.

Bollocks to this shit. I pick up my stride, hammering out another text, my march determined.

Fine, I'm coming in.

It's mere seconds before my phone is screeching in my hand, and I look down at it, smiling to myself as I answer. "Too late, Ava," I say quietly, approaching the front door and cutting the call, my heart feeling like it could punch its way out of my chest. Her fault. And with that thought, I start hammering at the door like a fucking madman, but I feel like it, totally consumed with desperation to make her admit our chemistry.

"Open the door, Ava." I continue banging, not bothered about disturbing the peace or drawing any attention to myself. She will answer. "Ava, I'm not going anywhere until you talk to me, please."

Bang, bang, bang.

"I've got your keys, Ava. I'll let myself in." What the hell am I saying? Will I?

I halt with my incessant beating of the door and think for a moment. Will she make me resort to that too? *Jesus, please don't.* I bang some more, but stop quickly, my back straightening, my ears listening carefully. And then I hear the thumping of footsteps. She's coming down, and she's mad.

Good. I need someone in this with me.

I rest my hands on the doorframe and wait. Breathe in. Swallow hard.

The door swings open, and I'm instantly gulping back air, taking in every fragment of her. Her hair is piled high, her smooth, olive skin glowing. I don't care that it's in anger. Even the lounge pants have me trembling.

She's not unaffected herself, although clearly trying to be. My eyes drift back up her legs lazily. I feel weak all of a sudden. The strength required to absorb her is almost too much. I could fall to my knees, and I wouldn't give a shit about what she thought of that.

I release an uneven breath, struggling to maintain any kind of sanity. I feel like I'm losing my fucking mind. "Why did you stop it?"

She balks. She has a fucking nerve. "What?" she spits back impatiently, like she doesn't know what I'm talking about. It makes me madder, my teeth clenching to a point I could crack one of the fuckers.

"Why did you run out on me?"

"Because it was a mistake." She doesn't hesitate with firing that gut-punching declaration at me. A mistake? It was fucking amazing. Amazing things can't be mistakes.

"It wasn't a mistake, and you know it," I breathe. "The only mistake was me letting you go."

Her eyes widen, but no words fall past those full lips, and I know it's because she has no clue what to say. But then the door starts shutting, her face quickly disappearing from my sight. Oh no. We're getting somewhere. Her lack of a reply speaks volumes.

My hand flies up and pushes against her, but I'm conscious of my strength and her petite frame. I could break her in half. "Oh, no, you don't." I'm in the hallway fast, shutting the door behind me. "You're not running this time. You've done it to me twice already, not again. You're going to face the music." I look down at her. I'm failing on every level to talk without sounding like I'm out of breath. And patience. And sanity. She starts backing away. She can't cope with our closeness. Is she scared she'll give in to the attraction? *Go on, Ava. Give in.* I move with her, not letting the distance grow between us.

"You need to leave," she blurts urgently. "Kate will be home in a minute.'

I stop, my face screwing up in annoyance. "Stop lying," I warn, pushing her hand away from her hair where her fingers are twiddling wildly. It's a habit. I've worked that much out. A tell. She plays with her hair when she's lying, and she's lying through her teeth now. "Quit the bullshit, Ava."

Throwing me a filthy glare, she turns to walk away from me. "Why are you here?"

I'm quickly in action, grabbing her wrist and spinning her around to face me. She can't ignore me when I'm forcing her to look at me, to touch me. "You know why."

"Do I?" Her perfectly arched eyebrow arches higher.

She can't be serious. "Yes, you do." She's not going to make me spell it out, surely? Not again.

My grip is missing her wrist within seconds as she yanks it away and backs up, meeting the wall in just a few steps. "Because you want to hear how loud I'll scream?"

"No," I yell incredulously, but I have no right to sound so shocked or annoyed by her question. That was not the sort of line I should've delivered to this woman. She's worthy of so much more. But this is what she does to me. She makes me irrational. Drives me wild.

"You are undeniably the most arrogant arsehole I've ever

met," she yells, and I flinch at her harshness. "I'm not interested in becoming a sexual conquest."

"Conquest?" I snort, swinging away from her and marching up the hallway, digging deep for some control. "What fucking planet are you on, woman?" There's no control to be found.

"Get out!" she shouts from behind me, and I freeze before turning to find her. She's fuming. Join the fucking club.

"No," I bark, continuing with my moody march. Oh my God, I could strangle her.

"I'm not fucking interested." And then she swears like that, pushing more buttons, and it feels like pins being poked into my skin. "Now, get out."

"Watch your fucking mouth!"

She recoils, looking at me like I've lost my mind. I might have. "Get out!"

Never. I look at the space between us. There's too much.

I have a moment of realization.

I'm not close enough to her. Let's see how fiery she is when I'm up close and personal. Our encounter in my suite was torment —a perfect moment cruelly snatched from me. Let's remind her of that ecstasy.

"Okay," I say surely. "Look me in my eyes and tell me you don't want to see me again, and I'll go. You'll never have to lay eyes on me again." The very words tighten my gut and have every inch of my hard-muscled frame praying that she gives the right answer. But would it be right, or would it be wrong? I don't even know.

It seems like an eternity passes, and she still doesn't speak. She doesn't say it. She can't say it, so I move in. Three paces puts me before her, the closeness making my head spin, my heart smashing violently, my breathing accelerating to a stupid rate.

"Say it," I whisper, sparks of desire firing all over the place. "You can't, can you?" I place my finger lightly on her shoulder, making her twitch and me smile, and I trace a perfect trail up her taut, smooth flesh until I'm gently pressing the pad of my index finger on the soft void below her ear. Her breath noticeably hitches. Her pulse quickens. Her heartbeats match mine.

Heavy. Frantic. So alive.

"Boom . . . boom . . . . boom," I whisper. "I can feel it, Ava."

She's as stiff as a board, pushing herself into the wall. "Please, leave."

"Put your hand over my heart." *My black, dead heart.* I take her hand and rest it on my shirt, just so she can appreciate exactly how I'm responding to her. This isn't a one-way street. I need her to know that.

"What's your point?"

"You are one stubborn woman." It's infuriating. "Let me ask you the same question."

"What do you mean?"

"I mean, why are you trying to stop the inevitable? What's *your* point, Ava?" I force her to meet my gaze by gently encasing her neck with my palm, bringing her face to mine with the lightest of pressure. I dip and ghost my lips over her ear, enticing a breathy gasp. Oh God, help me, her smell. "There it is," I whisper, the relief of hearing that tiny sound of submission emboldening me, sending my mouth on a leisurely tour of her sweet skin. "You feel it."

She does nothing to stop me. She lets me at her, finally, and I continue to work her with my mouth, making my way across her jaw, my target those soft, beautiful lips. I'm nearly where I need to be.

Nearly there.

Just a few more pecks and my tongue will be meeting hers.

My pace quickens at the thought, until the squawking of a phone suddenly breaks the delightful sound of her ragged, sex-fueled breaths.

My lips aren't on hers anymore, and her palms are set firmly on my chest. "Stop, please."

I sag, pulling my phone from my pocket and looking down at the screen. Sarah? Does she have a radar on me? "Fuck." I stab at the reject button, send it to voicemail, and return my attention to Ava. "You still haven't said it."

She hesitates but then draws breath, and I dread the words I'm about to hear. "I'm not interested," she whispers, sounding desperate, but I can't work out if she's desperate to get rid of me or desperate for me to prove her wrong. "You have to stop this. Whatever you think you felt, what you think I felt, you're mistaken."

A burst of laughter flies from my mouth. "Think? Ava, don't you dare try and pass this off as a figment of my imagination. Did I imagine that? Just then, was that my imagination? Give me some credit."

"You give *me* some fucking credit."

My shoulders tense. What's the matter with this woman and her foul language? "Mouth!" I yell, wondering what the hell *my* problem is. Hearing such harsh words fall from those lovely lips is really rubbing me up the wrong way. Something so beautiful —*so pure*—shouldn't be swearing, and especially not at me.

"I told you to leave," she repeats, dragging me back to the present.

"And I told you, look me in the eye and tell me you don't want me." I stare at her, watching for any sign of a falter.

"I don't want you," she says quietly, but she's not avoiding my eyes. No, she's glaring at me, completely resolute.

"I don't believe you." I catch her fiddling fingers shifting quickly from her hair. She's lying, she has to be.

"You should," she affirms, a cold sheen glazing her dark eyes only strengthening her order.

Pain sears me.

We're staring at each other, her jaw clenched, her expression resolute, me doubting myself—doubting all my thoughts and assumptions. Because no woman in the last two decades has said no to me. And I don't know how to handle it.

I run my sweaty hand through my mess of hair, but frustration overrides my disbelief and anger sets in. Red-hot anger. And if I don't leave now, she'll see a side of me I'm not familiar or comfortable with.

But this isn't done. I just need to restock on some calm and energy because this woman is draining me, and I'm about to lose my shit completely with her.

I stalk out of her house, slamming the door behind me and throwing the disposable phone to the ground with all the force I can muster in an attempt to dispel some of my fury. I stand, my body heavy, fighting to get my ragged breathing under control, and slowly turn, looking up at the house, feeling in my trouser pocket. Her keys. I pull them out and play with them for a few moments, before shaking my head and walking back to post them through the letterbox.

I pull out my other phone and start pacing down the street, dialing the big guy to come get me. "We have a problem," he says in answer.

"What?"

"You could call it a domestic, I suppose."

He doesn't need to say anymore. "Coral and Mike." I need this like I need a hole in my fucking head.

"Yeah. Sarah's tried calling you. Probably best you don't turn up at The Manor and add to the prickly mix."

For fuck's sake. "We need to get rid of one of them." Because as long as they're both members, there will be constant clashes.

"You had your chance," John reminds me, and I roll my eyes.

"I was thinking specifically Mike, actually." The guy, under-standably, hates me. He blames me, and I know my short fuse at the moment won't allow me to handle the situation with anything other than a fist in his face.

"I'll see what I can do. Where are you, anyway?"

"My apartment." At least, I will be. I turn onto the main road and start looking out for a cab.

"Alone?"

"Yes."

"Car returned?"

"Yes."

"All okay?"

No. "Yes."

"Fine. See you in the morning." He hangs up, and a cab pulls over the lanes and up to the curb. I jump in and flop back, feeling exhaustion take hold. I reach for my throat. It's rough and scratchy. My heart actually hurts from the relentless pounding. My skin is sore from the constant bombardment of heat.

And yet it's still feels like a far more appealing kind of hell than being blind drunk.

Or have I simply forgotten how blissful that nothingness is, even if only temporarily?

8
_____

I HAVE ABSOLUTELY no desire to go to The Manor today. It
seems I'm constantly dealing with shit, dodging shit, and
getting myself into shit. John's fat fingers are drumming the
steering wheel when I slide into the passenger seat, and he's
humming.

His fingers stop. His humming stops. He looks across the car
to me. "You look like shit."

"Thanks."

"Why?"

"Didn't sleep." I don't know what contributed to my insomnia
more. Ava or alcohol on my mind. One would have eliminated the
other. And yet, having a drink feels almost like letting myself
down, and I've never had that direction of thought before.
"What's the situation with Coral and Mike?"

John pulls off. "Put your belt on," he grumbles, and I sigh,
doing as I'm told. "Mike's pissed. Coral's pissed. Everyone is
pissed." He turns his deadly glare onto me. "Don't get involved
with a married couple ever again, you stupid motherfucker."

I blow out my cheeks, rubbing at my forehead. I doubt John
has ever called me a stupid motherfucker as many times in the

space of one week. Can't say I'm loving it. Deserve it? Yes. "Don't worry, I won't."

"There's something in the bag on the floor for you." He motions to my feet, and I reach down, dragging up a Tesco bag. "Looks like you need it."

I pull out a jar of peanut butter and smile for the first time in what feels like days. "Cheers, bud." I dive right in.

"So you and the girl? It's done?"

"Not by a long shot," I say without thought and immediately regret it. I shove my finger in my gob to shut me up. I don't need him to nag me. Not today. Not ever. "She's stubborn."

"She's sending you off the deep end, that's what she's doing." He turns his shades onto me as I plunge my finger into the jar again. "You were there last night."

I don't look at him. "Briefly."

"And she welcomed you with open arms, right?"

I breathe out, already exhausted by the day. He knows the answer to that. "Why are you so averse to this? Are you and Sarah working in cahoots?"

He frowns at the road. "What's Sarah got to do with this?"

"She has an uncanny habit of appearing, calling, or texting whenever I'm a heartbeat away from . . ." I wonder how to put it without sounding like a total creep.

"What?"

I shake my head and screw the lid of my vice back on. "It doesn't matter."

"I'm not averse."

"Then what are you?"

"Worried."

"Why?"

He hums, not so quick to reply this time. I'm not drinking. I'm not shagging. He should be happy for me. "Give me one good reason why she's a good idea," he says.

"Because she makes me feel," I answer without delay, and John looks across to me. I don't give him a chance to question me. "Because the moment she walked into my office, my skin buzzed. My brain spun. My mind was elsewhere, and by elsewhere, I mean not at The Manor or at the bottom of a bottle of vodka. If there's not something in that, I don't stand a chance of ever being able to repent my sins or live a normal life."

"You want to live a normal life?" He laughs. "You own The Manor, Jesse. You can't lure a woman into falling for you without telling her who you really are."

"Maybe The Manor isn't who I really am," I say quietly, looking out of the window. "And *lure*? You make me sound like a fucking predator."

John huffs a sardonic burst of laughter, and I scowl at the streets of London as they whizz past. "Have you tried talking to her? Conversation?"

"Yes."

"You sure?"

I think hard, revisiting every encounter with Ava O'Shea. I find plenty of stalking and not much talking. In fact, with the exception of our first meeting when we chatted briefly about interiors and extreme sports, which was beyond pleasurable, the rest of our encounters have been lacking in the conversation department. "No," I admit.

"Women like to talk."

"Not always true." I smile, and he sighs.

"You're not dealing with any of the ladies of The Manor now. You're thinking about a normal life with a normal woman? Then start acting normal, motherfucker."

I sink into my seat. Normal. What the fuck is normal, anyway? "Did the CCTV get fixed?" I ask, diverting the conversation to other places. He nods, thoughtful, starting with the drumming of his fingers again, obviously done with talking. So I shut up and try my fucking hardest not to think. Impossible. It's Friday. Lusso launch day. I should stay away. Give her space. Let me play on her mind. Perhaps she'll reach out to me.

I wedge my elbow on the door and rest my thumping head in my hand. *Stubborn.* There's no way I can stay away from my new apartment knowing she's in there. I'm going. End of.

And normal? Ava isn't normal. Normal for me is what I'm used to, and Ava isn't what I'm used to. Or what I deserve.

"You will marry Lauren," Dad says, pacing the kitchen as Mum, ever still and quiet these days since Jake died, hollow and lost, says nothing. "Of all the stupid things you've done, Jesse. All the stupid things!" His fury is palpable, his face red with it. "Are you trying to ruin us?" His hands slam on the table with force, making Mum jump, and he leans across, his lip on the verge of a snarl. I take no pleasure from the stress and hurt I have caused. Just like I stopped fighting to win their approval when Jake was alive, I've stopped fighting to win forgiveness. I have nothing left in me, so rather than fight, I will surrender. I'll do what I should do and hope it redeems me in some way. Hope it alleviates this unbearable pressure on my shoulders. Hope it brings peace. For all of us.

"I will be a good husband, Dad. A good father." I won't throw my weight around. Apply unnecessary pressure upon my kids. Make them feel useless.

He snorts. "I won't hold my breath."

"Hey." John's distant voice brings me back into the car, and I turn my eyes onto him. "You okay?"

"Yeah," I say, blinking away my memories. "I'm fine."

. . .

As we rumble down the driveway toward The Manor, I feel myself tensing, and my tight muscles only get tighter when I see Coral's car. I hope and pray she had too much to drink last night to drive and called a cab, but the turn of my gut tells me otherwise.

"She stayed the night," John says before I can ask, coming to a stop and turning off the engine. "Drew and Sam calmed Mike down. She had nowhere to go." He gets out and walks away, his ominous frame telling me in every way not to question him.

"What are we, a fucking hotel now?" It comes out before my brain engages, and John stops, slowly turning back to me, his persona deadly.

"Maybe if the *Lord of The Manor* stopped allowing sleepovers in his fucking bed, we wouldn't have this fucking problem."

I can't hold back my curled lip. "Fuck you," I spit, stalking past him, waiting for a dig to my ribs.

"I'll let that slide, since you're obviously not yourself these days."

Myself? Who the fuck am I, anyway? I keep my attention forward and immediately wish I hadn't. Coral falls out of the bar, literally, and makes a beeline for me, throwing herself into my arms. I have no choice but to catch her or leave her falling face-first to the floor. "You're here," she slurs, and I look down at the back of her head incredulously where it's buried in my chest, her body limp and heavy. "I missed you."

I inch round with Coral hanging off my front to find John, my face undoubtedly expressing my disbelief. It's morning and she's plastered. John just shrugs and walks off. He's not seriously leaving me to handle this? "Wanker," I mutter, virtually dragging her back into the bar. "You need to go home, Coral." I negotiate her useless form onto one of the chairs, resting my hand on her shoulder to stop her from tumbling off as I pull out my phone.

"Mike wouldn't let me." She drops her head back, looking up at me. "And I wanted to see you."

"You're drunk." Have I ever stated something so obvious?

"I'm not drunk." She reaches up and clumsily tucks her hair behind her ears, straightening her slumped body. It's a feeble attempt to convince me she's sober. I don't think I've ever seen a woman so rat-arsed. It's ugly. "Where have you been?" She tries to focus on me, blinking. "You're never here anymore. Why?"

I laugh under my breath and dial Sarah, mentally praying she doesn't let me down. It goes to voicemail, and I curse as I dial again. Nothing. "For fuck's sake." I lean as far as I can, trying to see outside the bar when I hear footsteps. I spot Drew coming down the stairs fastening his tie, and I frown. Fuck me, in my absence this place really has turned into a hotel. "Oi," I call, and he looks up. His face twists. "Some help?"

His eyes fall to Coral, his face twists more, and he carries on his way. "Fuck you," he calls back, and my mouth falls open.

"I'll revoke your membership!" I yell, shifting quickly to catch Coral when she slips farther down the chair, dozing off.

"Fine by me," Drew yells. "I don't share my fucking space with dickhead estate agents who steal my business."

I roll my eyes and try Sarah again, thinking I need to get myself some new friends. It's all I can do not to yell my elation when she answers. "Where are you?"

"I'm . . . why?"

"I need some help."

"Dealing with that drunk tart? No. I've been dealing with it all fucking night. Your problem." She hangs up.

"For fuck's sake," I yell, disturbing Coral from her slumber. She looks up at me and drunkenly grins.

"I've been looking for you." Her hand lands on my stomach and strokes. "Take me to your room."

"I'd rather eat razor blades," I say to myself, resigning myself to the fact that I'm alone in this. I should have stayed at my rental and tore myself apart with my uncontrollable thoughts. Dipping, I lift Coral from the chair and get her on my shoulder, heading out of the bar. I don't have time for this.

I take the stairs, bypassing my suite and entering the next room. It's a mess, the cleaners yet to venture in here. I dump her on the bed, batting away her grabby hands when she tries to pull me down with her.

"I left him for you, you know." She looks me straight in the eye. "Because what we shared, that was special."

I turn and walk away. Special? No, it was *fucking*. I felt nothing. She's seeing what she wants to see.

I pull the door closed behind me, stopping in my tracks, thinking, Ava's words hitting me for the millionth time since last night.

Whatever you think you felt, what you think I felt, you're mistaken.

I recoil. Shit, am I to Ava what Coral is to me?

No.

Laughing, I head to my office, pulling up Google on my way. *Think?* I don't *think* anything. I know. Maybe John is right, though. Women love to talk. But not all women. The women of The Manor don't want to talk. They don't want to be treated reverently. Be romanced and sent flowers.

I find a florist and order some flowers, having them sent to Lusso with a note.

Sarah is at my desk when I get to my office, and I ignore the look of interest she gives me. I'm not speaking to her. Landing on the couch, I start sifting through a pile of paperwork on the coffee table, just for something to do.

"*Forgive me,*" she says, and I look up, confused. She turns my laptop around, showing me the screen, where an email with my order confirmation from the florist is open. A confirmation that states what I want to be written on the card. *Forgive me.* "Why?" she asks. "What did you do?"

I close my eyes and breathe in. It's never been an issue that she has access to my email account. She has access to everything. Everything but my black heart. "Mind your business, Sarah," I mutter, done with this place already. I get up and grab my suit off the back of the door.

"Is that where you've been recently?" she asks. "Fucking the interior designer?" There's laughter in her tone, and it gets right under my skin. "Jesus, Jesse, she must be ten years younger than you."

My jaw ticks, my eyes burning holes through the door before me. *Don't bite.* "I'm not *fucking* her," I grate, incensed by her assumption. Although, painfully, I have no right to be annoyed.

She starts laughing, and it's like blades cutting my flesh. "Then what are you trying to do? Woo her?" She laughs some more, and I slowly pivot, my suit hanging from one hand, my face straight. Her eyes sparkle delightedly. The twisted bitch is getting a sick thrill out of baiting me.

"Shut the fuck up, Sarah."

She smirks, standing, the bodice she's wearing pushing her fake tits up to her chin. "You know only this life, Jesse." Her hands rest on my desk when she bends, leaning in, getting closer. "You'd be a fool to think you can manage without it."

"Or without you?" I ask, swinging my suit bag over my shoulder. "That's what you mean, isn't it? You think I can't survive without you." She's right to an extent. Keeping Sarah close, looking out for her, defending her when she upsets someone—which is a lot—has always offered me a twisted sense of redemption. Because despite what I did to Carmichael, despite what *she* did too, he would want to know she's okay. That's just how he was. Always happy. Always forgiving. Always compassionate. *Never* held a grudge, and my father's contempt for him was proof of that. So was Sarah's attraction to me. He knew how she felt. I knew he knew. She knew he knew. Everyone knew he knew. But he'd smile it off. Tell me he trusted no one in the world more than me, that Sarah was a natural-born flirt, and her confidence was one of the things he loved about her. Their relationship wasn't exclusive. But it didn't stretch to me.

I let him down.

I know he'd forgive me for being weak. For betraying him. For falling into Sarah's clutches. But I wasn't blessed with his clemency. He didn't have the opportunity to absolve me of my wrongs, because he died, and that is entirely my fault.

Like Jake. Like Rosie.

All my fucking fault.

"No woman will accept you as long as we're together," she retorts, though there are threads of doubt in her words, and they are warranted.

"But we're not together, Sarah. Never will be. You need to get your twisted, fucked-up mind around that," I yell, and she flinches. Guilt eats me up inside, and I bite my tongue, holding back on hitting her with more scathing truths. She's spent the past sixteen years trying to bend me to her will. Trying to convince me in one way or another that we need each other. Trying to make me see the devastation and pain we caused wasn't entirely for nothing. It's never been hard to resist her advances, or her fucking whip. But I've never lost my rag. I've always maintained my cool, laughed it off, shook my head in despair sometimes. Not today. Today, I'm done.

"Stop believing in something that has never been there. Wake up. See the truth. I am *not* yours." I yank the door open and leave, closing my eyes when I hear the unmistakable sound of her sobbing.

Fuck!

John is on his way down the corridor toward me, and he pulls his wraparounds off, revealing his deadly glare. "What did you do?"

"Told her some home truths," I snap, barging his shoulder as I pass. It wasn't a conscious move, but his body is wide, and this corridor isn't.

"Watch it, boy," he warns menacingly, his threat palpable. "Don't think I won't kick your motherfucking arse all over this place."

"I'm out of here." I pick up my pace, itching to escape.

"Be wise," he calls. He's not talking about my lack of respect for him. Of course he's not.

"I'll call you tomorrow."

"I might not answer."

He'll answer. John always answers. I make it to my car and sling my suit on the back seat, before getting behind the wheel and revving the engine hard a few times, taking out my frustration, my fury, my hopelessness, on my car.

All I can hear is Sarah's laugh. All I can see is her amusement.

Am I that laughable? That . . . beyond hope?

I rub at my forehead, lifting my arse from the seat to dig out my phone. "I'm sorry," I say to myself as I message Sarah. I am literally all that woman has. And she's scared. I get that. But she needs to face the truth and let me go.

It's not the first time I've needed a woman to do that.

I've always looked at Lauren and wondered what goes through her mind. Now more than ever as she prances around her parents' home, her belly swollen, my baby growing inside of her, looking like the most content girl alive. Ignoring my despondency. Ignoring my lack of affection or effort. Ignoring the fact that she lied to me about being protected. Trapping me. Every day, I wake up and take a few moments to register that Jake isn't here anymore. Then a few more moments to register that in a moment of weakness, of pure stupidity, I accepted a bottle of vodka from Lauren, downed the lot, marveled at the numbness it offered, and then fucked her. At that moment, with drink dulling my pain and my dick inside a welcoming pussy, I was out of my body. Away from my grief. Four months later, I'm married to a girl I do not love. Hardly even know. Definitely don't understand. Or trust. Or feel comfortable around. But it's all I'm good for now, and doing what is expected of me feels . . . right. Especially after all of my wrongs. And yet, all I feel is empty.

I hear a horn honking outside, and I'm up out of my chair in a heartbeat, my spirits lifting. I see Uncle Carmichael pull up and get out, slipping his shades on. John is with him, the big burly bloke looking as foreboding as always. Oh, thank God. They're here to get me away from this hell for the day. I head for the kitchen door, ignoring Lauren's calls, but when I open it, I'm faced with her father.

"You can't see him," he says. "You're a husband and soon to be a father. You should be here, looking after my daughter."

"It's our . . . it's my eighteenth birthday." Over a year without Jake. "He always comes to see me on my birthday," I say, passing him, half expecting to be pulled back. I'm not. At least, not by him. But Lauren grabs me.

"Oh my God, Jesse!" she practically screams, and I turn to find her clenching her belly, her eyes watering.

My stomach drops. "What? What is it?" I ask, scanning her up and down, trying to figure it out as she cries and yelps. "Are you hurt? Is it the baby?"

"Look what you've done now," Alan snaps, leading Lauren to a chair and sitting her down. "Now, now, darling, what is it?"

"Pain," she cries. "It hurts."

I stand like a useless fool while Alan tends to her. Stand and listen to her cry and wail. Puff and clench her belly.

Torn.

Guilty.

Lauren's father takes his time with her, calming her. The tears subside. An ambulance arrives. The baby's heartbeat is perfect. No bleeding. Nothing wrong with the baby, or with Lauren.

"What a fright," she says, smiling, reaching for my hand.

Was she fucking faking?

"Get out of my house," Alan barks, making me turn toward the doorway where he's looking.

Carmichael's there, and John is looming behind him, looking ominous. Of course they didn't leave. Perhaps they wondered about Lauren too.

"I'm here to speak to my nephew," Carmichael says, looking at me with . . . sympathy. It's fucking sympathy.

"He's busy tending to his wife and unborn child." Alan remains unmoving.

"There's nothing wrong with his wife and unborn child."

Now, Alan moves forward, and as a result, John passes Carmichael and steps into the room. "We're here to speak to Jesse," he says, removing his shades, something that never happens unless he wants someone to see the threat in his eyes. And it's there. Boy is it there. And so is something inside of me.

Hope.

The only two people in this world whom I can depend on are here.

Rescuing me from this madness.

9

THE CONCIERGE OPENS the gates for me, and I pull into the car park of Lusso, my stomach doing cartwheels. Did she get the flowers? Did she like them? What did she think?

I park, get out, and straighten my new suit, taking in a deep breath, repeating the same mantra I have all day. *Gently, gently.* Talk to her, dazzle her. Show her she would be making a massive mistake if she doesn't indulge me and explore the butterflies.

Butterflies.

Can't say I've ever had them but, God, it's a pretty fucking incredible feeling.

I stroll into the foyer and spot the concierge desk decorated with an elaborate spray of white calla lilies, and I can't help but laugh under my breath, shaking my head to myself. Impossible woman.

"Sir." A man appears from behind the desk. He's short, gray, and his eyes travel up my front until his head is dropped back, looking at me. "Can I help you?"

"I'm here for the launch party."

"Your name?"

"Ward."

He goes to his clipboard, running a pen down the list. "I'm afraid you're not down."

"There must be a mistake."

"No mistake," he chirps. "And as the saying goes, if your name's not down, you ain't coming in." He chuckles then stands tall, and it's all I can do not to sigh. "It's guests only." Something tells me the concierge and I aren't going to get along, especially if he tries to stop me going up to my own fucking penthouse. Especially now, when Ava's there. I can virtually smell her in this building, in every crevice, her creative mark everywhere.

"I'm not a guest," I tell him, walking to the lift. "I'm the owner."

"Oh?" He peeks down at his clipboard again as I look back, smiling on the inside. "The name again, sir?" he asks, giving me his attention.

"Peter Pan," I reply, and he scowls. "Ward. It's Ward. Jesse Ward, owner of the penthouse." I'm going to lose my patience in a minute. "Now, would you mind?"

"I'm going to need to see some identification." His chest puffs out, his chin high.

"For fuck's sake," I mutter, dragging my wallet out and flashing him my driver's license. "Happy, Kojak?"

He approaches, taking it, inspecting it. I express my boredom with a drawn-out sigh, my jaw ticking. "Welcome, Mr. Ward." He beams up at me, and I laugh my disbelief. "Let me show you up."

"Thanks," I grate, reminding myself that the concierge is old and here to serve me for the foreseeable. *Don't burn your bridges, Ward.* "Very kind of you." I smile, completely over the top, and he narrows an eye, reaching past me to call the lift.

I board and watch him enter the code for the penthouse. "Enjoy your evening, sir." He exits, leaving the doors to close.

"I will," I say, inspecting myself in the mirror, ruffing up my hair.

"Hold the lift!"

I freeze, my hand in my hair. *What the fucking hell?* Did she not fucking hear me? The doors open, and Sarah appears, dressed in her usual skin-tight trousers and boob-enhancing top. I give her a tired look, and she smiles knowingly, stepping in. Not surprisingly, the bulldog concierge is hot on her heels. "She's with me," I tell him. I should have kept my mouth shut. Let him bite at her ankles and drag her out, because I do *not* want her here. He backs off and the doors start to close again. "You just couldn't fucking help yourself, could you?"

"I want to see your new place." She goes into her purse and reapplies her red lipstick.

"You've seen it."

"I've forgotten." She smacks her lips and gives me a coy smile. "You trying to impress someone?" Her eyes travel the length of my new suit.

"You will be nice," I warn.

"Of course." The lift opens and she's out in a shot, smiling and sashaying through my new home, which is currently bursting at the seams with people. Fuck me, it's heaving. I stare, stunned, wishing them all the fuck out of here. All except Ava.

I ignore the waitress who offers a tray of champagne as I enter, but accept the brochure handed to me by another guy. I don't waste my breath telling him I don't need one.

Chris, Drew's estate agent nemesis, spots me, hurrying over, probably to fill me in on his adventures at The Manor. "Mr. Ward," he says, offering me his hand. "Good to see you."

"How are you doing, Chris?" I ask, my eyes darting, searching for her.

"All right now, if you know what I mean." He chuckles goofily, smacking my shoulder. My body jolts, my jaw tensing of its own volition, irritation flaring. What the fuck is wrong with me? Laugh with him. Humor the twat.

"I know," I say. I just don't give a flying fuck.

I turn, scanning every nook and cranny. Where is she? I can feel my disappointment building, and then . . .

I inhale, my skin tingling. She's standing in the kitchen, her back to me, but I would know that shape anywhere. My heart starts to pick up. My pulse thuds.

"Isn't that right, Jesse?"

I frown and turn my eyes to Chris. What the fuck is this idiot rambling on about? Drew's right. Total prick. I shake my head and find her again, studying her red-covered body closely. I admit, it's a lovely dress, but it's on the short side. I look around at all the men here, watching for straying eyes. I soon force myself to stop when I spot more than one perv eyeing up my girl.

I frown. *My?*

"It was honestly surreal," Chris harps on, and I nod, hardly hearing him. All I'm hearing is an unconvincing, lust-filled voice telling me she's not interested. I should never have left her place last night, not until she relented and admitted she's consumed by thoughts of me too. I'm standing in my new home, surrounded by strangers, resisting the urge to set off the fire alarm to clear the place so I can have her alone.

I smile to myself when I see Ava's redhead friend look my way, her eyes widening when she clocks me. She's smiling thoughtfully. She remembers me, and Ava turns and clocks me too. Her eyes do more than widen—they nearly fall out of her head. I don't have a chance to flash her my smile. She swings back around, clearly shocked by my presence. But her friend's grin? It speaks volumes.

Ignoring the arsehole next to me, I make my way over to Ava, lip-reading her friend's words. She's telling her I'm coming. *Oh yes, lady. I'm coming.*

Ava refuses to acknowledge me, and her friend is clearly

amused. Not horrified or shocked but amused. I'm not out of this fight just yet.

"Nice to see you again, Kate," I say smoothly. "Ava?"

She doesn't acknowledge me, and Kate's eyes are shooting between us in delight. "Jesse." She nods, pursing her lips. "Excuse me. I need to powder my nose." Placing her glass on the counter, Kate leaves us alone, and I smile smugly on the inside. Because if Ava's friend believed she wasn't interested, she sure as hell wouldn't leave her alone with me. I am fucking delirious, and that boost to my confidence I was feeling? It just rocketed into outer space.

After a few seconds of waiting patiently for her to acknowledge me, I accept she isn't going to budge. Because she's a stubborn sod. So I slowly circle her until I'm looking at her exquisite face. I have to force myself not to reach out and touch her. "You look stunning," I say quietly, running my eyes over every perfect inch of her features. I've tasted those lips. I don't know what I'll do if I don't get to again.

"You said I wouldn't have to see you again."

"I didn't know you would be here," I lie, nibbling my lip. I wouldn't blame her if she took out a restraining order on me. I'm tempted to have one slapped on myself.

Ava looks at me like I'm stupid. She might be right. "You sent me flowers."

I fight to keep the cheeky—guilty—smile from my face. "Oh, so I did."

"Please, excuse me." She goes to pass me, and I panic, quickly moving to stop her.

"I was hoping for a tour," I blurt, laughing privately at my own audacity. I know this place inside out.

"I'll get Victoria. She'll be happy to show you around."

"I would prefer you."

"You don't get a fuck with a tour," she retorts harshly, making me recoil. She's standing in front of me, looking like she's literally fallen from the heavens, and she's using vulgar language like that?

"Will you watch your mouth?"

I expect her to tell me where to go, but she doesn't. "Sorry," she mutters instead. "And put my seat back when you drive my car."

Now, I really can't help my smile, and I'm filled with immense satisfaction when she starts shifting uncomfortably.

"And leave my music alone."

"I'm sorry," I whisper. I bet she loved my joke. I watch her awkwardly shifting from heel to heel, her eyes working hard not to look at me. A hunch is telling me it's because if she looks at me, she'll fold. *Look at me.* "Are you okay? You look a little shaky." I lift my arm, desperate to feel that smooth skin again. "Is something affecting you?"

She pulls back, and my fortitude takes a kick in the nuts. "Not at all," she murmurs, looking away. She's lying. I can see her hand twitching by her side. Her tell. "Did you want a tour?"

My smile broadens. "I would *love* a tour." And a kiss. *And a night worshipping every inch of you.* And maybe breakfast. And more kissing. And lunch. I'll feed her until she could burst, then rub her tummy until she's ready to eat again. Or kiss again. I smile to myself. Sounds like heaven. I just need to convince her that it absolutely will be. She's as blindsided as I am, albeit less willing to crack. Imagine how she'll be when she *does* crack. When she accepts and embraces this.

I watch her virtually stomp out of the kitchen, frustration leaking from every pore of her gorgeous body. That dress is definitely too short, and I glare at a guy across the room when he catches me observing him staring at her. He blinks and looks away, his smile falling. Wise man.

I follow Ava, and she starts waving her hand around

aimlessly. "Lounge," she declares, not giving me time to look around, not that I need to. So I keep my eyes on the gentle sway of her hips as she leads on. "You've seen the kitchen," she calls over her shoulder, giving me a small peek of her luscious lips. "View." She points across the terrace before trekking back into the penthouse and stalking across the open space towards the gym. I smile, placing the catalogue I'm still holding on a table as I pass. People try to stop me, say hello, shake my hand, and I ignore every single one of them, my pace quickening to keep up with her.

"Gym," she mumbles as she enters, before leaving as soon as my Grensons cross the threshold. I laugh as I follow her up the stairs, my eyes nailed to her arse. How I want to get my hands on her and haul her into a bedroom.

After opening and closing every door and shortly declaring what rooms lay beyond, she marches into the master suite. My bedroom.

Oh fuck, if she only knew she'd just entered the lion's den.

"You're an expert tour guide, Ava." *And sexy when you're stroppy.* I arrive in front of quite a boring piece of art, but there's something about the shabby old rowing boats—something charming. "Care to enlighten me on the artist?"

"*Giuseppe Cavalli,*" she practically sighs, but it's not a tired sigh. It's one of admiration. She likes this painting. A lot.

"It's good," I say, studying the piece as she remains behind me. "Is there any particular reason why you chose this artist?" Talk. Conversation. I can't believe I'm taking advice from John. The man who has been eternally single.

She's silent for a while, and my skin's hot under her scrutiny. She likes what she sees, and she likes what she felt when I had her in my arms. I imagine that's what she's thinking about right now. Not the painting.

"He was known as the master of light," she replies quietly,

joining me in front of the art. I look at her, willing her to talk and indulge me more. This is nice. It's calm and peaceful. "He didn't think that the subject was of any importance," she goes on. "It didn't matter what he photographed. To him, the subject was always the light. He concentrated on controlling it. See?" She points out the reflections across the rippling water. "That's what's so fascinating. It's the light."

I nod thoughtfully to myself, impressed and quite charmed, but what's standing beside me is more intriguing. More beautiful. And, ironically, the source of light she radiates is really fucking fascinating. I turn my stare back to her as she continues. "These rowing boats, as lovely as they are, are just boats, but see how he manipulates the light? He didn't care for the boats. He cared for the light surrounding the boats. He makes inanimate objects interesting, makes you look at the photograph in a different . . . well, a different light, I suppose." She cocks her head thoughtfully, lengthening the column on her neck, revealing perfect, smooth, taut skin. Jesus, the woman is like nothing else I've seen. And what she just said about that painting rings so fucking true for how I'm feeling recently. Seeing things. Imagining myself in a different light. Her light. Because it's fucking bright and blinding, and within her light, I'm just as inconsequential as Cavalli's boats.

I let her finish her observations, quite happy to watch her, admire her, but then she looks up at me, and my bubble is popped. She's back in the room with me, and I can see her mental battle has returned.

"Please don't," she whispers.

"Don't what?" I know damn well what, and she needs to understand that there is absolutely nothing in this world that could stop me. Except her. She could stop me again, and I would be crushed.

"You know what. You said I wouldn't have to see you again."

"I lied." I'm honest. I've got to be honest. "I can't stay away from you, so you do have to see me again . . . and again . . . and again." I say it slowly, and she inhales as she starts retreating. She's trying to escape the sparks flying. They're everywhere, uncontrollable and violent.

"You persistently fighting this is only making me more determined to prove that you want me." I keep my eyes on hers. "I'm making it my mission objective. I'll do *anything*."

The bed halts her escape, and she throws her hands up. "Stop," she blurts, panicked, and I do. Of course I do. Because she's clearly upset. Emotional. Frustrated. "You don't even know me." She's desperately trying to convince herself that this is crazy. It is, and it scares me too, but at least we'll be scared together. At last I won't be alone in this madness.

"I know you're impossibly beautiful." I walk forward, thinking I can make her feel so much better if I can just hold her. "I know what I feel, and I know you're feeling it too." I stop as our chests brush, and my body responds, the fire inside blazing. I can feel her heartbeat through her dress. Her need. "So, tell me, Ava," I ask quietly, "what have I missed?"

She drops her face, and I waste no time pulling it back up to mine, feeling like a total bastard when I see tears in her eyes. "I'm sorry." I slide my hand onto her cheek and gently wipe her tears away.

"You said you would leave me alone."

"I lied," I say, apologizing again. I couldn't leave her alone if my life depended on it. And, strangely, it feels like it does. "I can't stay away, Ava."

"You've already said that you're sorry, yet here you are again. Am I to expect flowers tomorrow?"

My strokes of her cheeks pause, and it's *my* face that hides now. I really am a bastard, but I wouldn't be doing this if I didn't know that she wants me. I'd buy her flowers every day forever, and hopefully they won't all be apology flowers. There's nothing left for it. I've got to remind her—remind her of how it felt when we kissed. Touched.

I lift my eyes.

And slowly lower my lips to hers.

I need to be gentle.

Gentle and slow.

She doesn't stop me, and when our lips skim, she's the one who takes the lead, grabbing my jacket. *Oh my God.* My body is immediately wracked with shakes, her surrender like the air I need to breathe. It's as if she's stretched the elastic band of restraint too far and it's finally broken.

"Have you ever felt like this?" I ask, pulling her closer, working my mouth across to her ear.

"Never."

Fuck, me neither. "Are you ready to stop fighting it now?" I ask softly, licking my way up her ear and back down until I'm at the smooth flesh that meets her neck.

"Oh God," she gasps, and I swallow her words of submission, tenderly plunging my tongue into her mouth, silently grateful when she accepts it, relieved I really haven't been imagining this. I'm out of my body already. She's air and water.

"Hmm," I hum, breaking our kiss reluctantly to get a solid confirmation from her. "Is that a yes?"

"Yes."

A million sparks light up inside of me, hope that I don't understand bombarding my entire form. I nod and proceed to show my appreciation by scattering light kisses all over her face. She's with me. I have never felt such a powerful surge of faith. Everything this woman does to me is addictive. "I need to have all of you, Ava." Every little piece and more, and not just her body. I want her words, her smiles, her passion. "Say I can have all of you."

She hesitates, but only briefly. "Take me."

Fuck. Yes.

I curl my arm around her tiny waist and lift her slight frame from her feet, carrying her to the wall and gently pushing her against it as our lips become more frantic, more desperate. We're both on the same page, and something tells me it could be a beautiful story. My hands are everywhere, frenzied and hungry, my mouth the same. I refuse to release her lips, so when she starts pushing my jacket away from my shoulders, I step back only a fraction to give her room.

I shake it off and reclaim her, thrusting her back into the wall, a bit harder than I intended, but she doesn't seem bothered by my eagerness. She's meeting my urgency perfectly.

"Fucking hell, Ava," I breathe. "You make me crazy." I circle my hips to alleviate the throb in my cock, pulling a quiet cry from her. Her hands are clenching at my hair, the feeling out of this world. I yank her dress up to her waist and roll into her once more, nipping at her bottom lip before I pull away, breathing uncontrolled bursts of air as I deliver another grind, delighting in her moans of pleasure, smiling at her drowsy eyes. Her head falls back against the wall, and she pants. The temptation of her exposed throat is way too much to resist. I'm lost. Fucking lost, and I don't want anyone to ever find me.

"Jesse."

I'm only mildly aware of her panting my name as I bite my way across her skin, my mouth on a tangent, my mind seized by anticipation of what's to come.

"Jesse, people are coming, you have to stop." She starts squirming in my embrace, rubbing up against my solidness.

Fuck!

"I'm not letting you go, not now." I groan the words out, silently begging her not to stop this.

"We need to stop."

"No." Not a fucking chance in hell. I sound demanding, but I can't help it. I know there are people wandering around, and I fucking hate them for it. Of all the times and all the places she could have submitted to this madness, she chooses today in a packed open house with no privacy.

"We'll do this later."

I laugh to myself. "That leaves you too much time to change your mind." I carry on biting at her neck, unwilling to release her from my grasp for fear of never getting my hands on her again. But then my jaw is grabbed and she pulls me from my happy nuzzling, winning my eyes. I've never seen her looking so determined, not even when she fought to resist me.

"I won't change my mind." Our noses are touching. "I will *not* change my mind."

She means it, her words full of grit . . .

But I'm not chancing it. She's swayed from acceptance to denial too many times already. I need to make it impossible for her to ever try and wipe me from her memory. I push my lips hard on hers. "Sorry, I can't risk it." I scoop her up and carry her to the bathroom. And, God, she feels amazing in my arms.

"What?" she cries. "They'll want to see in there too."

"I'll lock the door." Problem solved. I grin at her. "No screaming."

Her eyes widen momentarily before she smiles. I'm glad she's smiling about it. The delivery of such a tactless line to such an exquisite woman should've put me out of the race immediately. "You have no shame." She laughs, and damn if my aching dick doesn't dance as a result. It has never gone so long between fucks. Never.

"No. My cock has been painful since last Friday, I finally have you in my arms, and you've seen sense. I'm going nowhere, and neither are you." End of. I kick the wooden door of my lovely new bathroom shut and place her gently on the double sink unit before hastily returning to lock the door. *Nothing* is interrupting this.

When I turn to face her, she's looking at me, her eyes shimmering with hunger. I've never in my life seen anything so beautiful. So exquisite. And the way she's looking at me? Kill me now, for I will certainly die a happy man.

I slowly start unbuttoning my shirt as I walk casually toward her, as if I'm not falling apart with unbridled desperation. As if my heart isn't screaming. As if this isn't the biggest moment in my life in forever. But I'm not rushing. I don't need to. Because she has submitted. This is happening. Not once. Not twice. This will happen over and over again.

I leave my shirt hanging open and watch her, holding my breath when she places her finger in the center of my chest, dragging it lightly down the middle, my hands instinctively finding her waist and my body moving to between her thighs. I'm on fire, burning.

I glance up and find her observing closely, and my lips twitch in . . . happiness. For the first time in too long, I feel happy. "You can't escape now," I tease.

"I don't want to."

"Good," I mouth, dropping my gaze to her lips as she continues with her drifting finger, back up my chest, my throat, until it rests lightly on my bottom lip. I bite down, my happiness intensifying tenfold when she smiles at me and works her hand into my hair, feeling me everywhere she can.

"I like your dress," I say, skating my eyes down the gathered material at her waist until I'm focused on her lovely thighs.

"Thank you." Her voice is husky, sexy as hell.

I don't know how much longer I can continue with this slow seduction. "It's a bit restrictive." And short, but now's not the time to express my concern over the lack of material. I pull at a piece of the red dress playfully, smiling to myself when I sense her breathing quicken.

"It is."

"Shall we remove it?" I tilt my head thoughtfully.

"If you like."

If *I* like? Oh, she's a treasure. She's ready to rip clothes off to move this along, but I'm having fun, enjoying seeing her need escalate the more I keep up this game. "Or maybe we leave it on?" I pull away and hold up my hands—a stupid thing to do. I already miss the feel of her, so I immediately run my palms around her back to find the zip. "But then again," I whisper in her ear, "I have firsthand knowledge of what's under this lovely dress." *And it's fucking incredible.* I breathe heavily as I slowly draw down the zip. "And it's far superior to the dress. I think we'll get rid of it." Is this what being seriously pussy-whipped feels like? Because I like it.

I pick her up off the counter and set her on her feet, pushing the dress away, revealing a sight that has been carved on my mind since Tuesday. I kick the redundant material to the side and absorb her for a few moments. More lace, and it sends my knees weak. I lift her back onto the counter, the feel of her in my arms as satisfying as looking at her. I want to carry her everywhere, have her glued to me.

"I like that dress," she says, full of false indignation.

"I'll buy you a new one." *A longer one.* I take up my position between her legs and take hold of her petite bum, tugging her closer and rolling my hips while we study each other. My cock isn't going to hold out much longer. I unclasp and remove her bra, sighing when my eyes are blessed again by her pert, perfectly formed breasts. And then the little temptress leans back on her hands, accentuating the subtle push of her chest toward me. She knows what she's doing.

I raise my eyes to hers and cover her entire throat with my

palm. "I can feel your heart hammering." I'm enthralled. She completely captivates me.

Slowly, I glide my hand down her front until it's resting softly on her flat tummy. I find her eyes again. "You're too fucking beautiful, lady." *Please, if there is a god, let me keep her. Let this feeling last forever.* "I think I'll keep you."

When she arches her back, I smile, and then let my mouth drop to her nipple, taking her other breast in my spare palm, massaging gently as I suck her into my mouth. She's moaning immediately, her body going lax as my aching cock rubs delicious circles into her. I'm fighting to keep control, but I need this time. I need to use every second to blow her mind repeatedly, to make it impossible for her to ever deny us again. She's unpredictable. It worries me.

She starts getting frenzied, her breathing erratic and rushed, so I slip my finger into the side of her knickers, resisting the temptation to rip them off. My finger brushes her saturated core. Good lord, she feels perfect everywhere.

"Shit," she yelps, her body flying up, her hands clenching my shoulders.

"Language, lady," I warn, taking her mouth and thrusting my fingers deeply into her, gasping at the rightness of her internal, hot muscles grabbing me. She's moaning, pushing her body into mine and greedily contracting around me. I sense her desperation. I know her already—a stupid thought, given my limited time with her—but the perfection of this moment, my awareness of her body and the language it's speaking, is only enhancing my feelings and hopes. This every day? This and not the nightmares or pounding head? Am I worthy of that?

And will she oblige me?

My questions are pushed aside when I feel her body tighten. She's there. Fuck, she's there. "Come," I demand, pushing deeper and higher, pressing my thumb on her pulsing clitoris, my heart hammering wildly as I watch her disintegrate into a mass of twitching nerves. Watching her orgasm? It's something else.

When she yells, I quickly tackle her mouth, soaking up her moans as she shakes in my arms. Her eyes are closed while I devote my time to easing her down, kissing her face everywhere until she finally opens them and gazes at me on a sigh.

Fuck . . . me.

My heart isn't only racing. It's breaking. But for her or for me? Because she knows nothing about me. She doesn't know what she's just let herself in for. Who I am. What I could do to her. Yet my guilt for holding back is superseded by my serenity. I lean in and kiss her again, her whole form like a magnet to me. I can't get enough of her. "Better?" I slip my fingers out and smile when she hums, running them across her full bottom lip as we watch each other.

And when her palms lift and smooth down my cheeks, I'm powerless to stop myself from turning into it, kissing it tenderly before letting my eyes find her again. Understanding. Acceptance. Possibly even adoration. It's all staring back at me, and I ask myself again . . . do I deserve her? This bright, beautiful young woman. A woman who could have any man she could dream of. Could that man be me?

I hate the tug of my heart. Hate it.

She gasps, and it throws me for a moment until I realize someone is trying to get into my bathroom. *Oh no.* I'm far from done. I slap my palm over her mouth and smile at her shock.

"I can't hear anything," someone says, and Ava's eyes widen farther. They're not interrupting this. Ava is not stopping this. Make her forget there's someone outside. So I release her mouth and replace my palm with my lips, hushing her quietly.

"Oh God, I feel cheap," she cries, her forehead falling to my shoulder.

Cheap? She's the furthest you could get from cheap. "You're not cheap. Talk crap like that, I'll be forced to kick your delicious backside all over my bathroom." I immediately realize my error. Fuck, did I just say that?

"*Your* bathroom?"

Her puzzled face makes me smile. It's time to confess. At least, confess one small detail. "Yes, my bathroom. I wish they would stop letting strangers roam around my home."

"You live here?"

"Well, I will as of tomorrow. Tell me, is all this Italian shit worth the outrageously expensive price tag they attached to this place?" I love the Italian shit she's loaded it with. I hope she loads The Manor with it too.

"Italian shit?" she coughs, and I can't help laughing at her shock. "You shouldn't have bought the place if you don't like the *shit* that's in it."

"I can get rid of the shit."

Her eyebrows lift, but soon lower into a scowl.

"Unravel your knickers, lady," I say. "I wouldn't get rid of anything in this apartment." I land her with a forceful kiss. "And you're in this apartment."

She's mine again, meeting my hard tongue lashes stroke for stroke, her hands shooting to my shoulders and clinging harshly. And she didn't contest my claim, instead eating me alive, her mouth working fast and hard. I can't wait any longer. I've never needed anything so much in my life. And now I know beyond all doubt that she wants me too.

Game over.

Lifting her from the counter, I yank her knickers down her legs, my gentle approach fast disappearing. I cast them aside and ease her back down, making quick work of removing her shoes and mentally thanking her for taking the initiative to start on my clothes. Her awestruck face doesn't escape my notice, and neither does her flinch when she spots my scar. *Fuck.* I don't need her prying into the whys and wherefores of that. She's just staring at it, but, thankfully before I'm forced to distract her from it, she rips her eyes away, curious eyes, and screws my shirt up, tossing it to the side.

"I'll buy you a new one," she says casually, making me smirk.

Relief washes over me, but I know there are things she's going to have to know. Eventually. But now?

Leaning forward, I home in on her lips again and moan when I feel her hands working my trousers, but soon pull away on a surprised furrow of my brow when she yanks my belt free and the bathroom is filled with a sharp thrash of leather.

I'm trying to hide the shock. "Are you going to whip me?"

"No," she replies slowly, before discarding the belt, her uncertainty reassuring. But then I'm seized by the waistband of my trousers and hauled forward. "Of course, if you want me to . . ."

I fight a smile. She's playing with me. God, she has no fucking idea. "I'll bear that in mind." *Never*.

Her eyes burn as she unfastens me and mine clench shut when I feel her small palm skim across my throbbing cock. Oh sweet Jesus, I'm twitching uncontrollably, sending a silent prayer to the ceiling to maintain my control, struggling further when I feel the unmistakable heat of her tongue licking up the center of my chest.

"Ava, you should know that once I've had you," I murmur drowsily, "you're mine."

"Hmm," she hums, licking my nipple and pushing my boxers down my thighs, finally freeing my painfully stiff cock.

She gasps, but I waste no time removing my remaining clothes, as equally rapt by the nakedness before me as she is. I didn't think my pulse could race any faster . . . until she reaches forward and rolls her thumb over the head of my dick.

"Shit, Ava." I take her hips to steady myself, and she gasps. "Ticklish?"

"Just there," she blurts, tensing in my hold.

"I'll remember that." I smash my lips back to hers, my body tingling, my hips thrusting when she starts stroking me. It's becoming urgent, and when she inhales sharply, I clamp down on her lip. "You ready?" I gasp, my cock set to explode. I should wonder if my lack of action for eight days straight is contributing to my urgency, but I know it's simply the anticipation of her.

Her nod fires me into action, and I bat her hand away, grab her under her arse, and pull her up and forward, straight onto my waiting dick.

She cries out.

And I nearly *pass* out with the instant pleasure. *Oh, my fucking God.*

"Okay?" I wheeze, my eyes crossing. "Are you okay?" Fucking hell, I can feel every tiny bit of her around me, every pulse, every twinge, every spasm.

Pleasure with no alcohol.

Pleasure with no darkness.

Pleasure with complete alertness.

Pleasure with someone I'm utterly enchanted by.

It's new. It's amazing.

"Two seconds," she breathes. "I need a few seconds." Her legs circle my waist, and I swing her around, pushing her against the wall, my forehead dropping to hers as I give her the time she needs to adjust. I'm sweating, panting, as I ease out of her gently. Then I plunge forward, controlled and carefully, giving her time and space to accept me.

"Can you take more?" I fight the words through my breathing, and her breasts push into my chest, a silent message, but I need the words. This isn't going to be slow. "Ava, tell me you're ready."

"I'm ready," she whispers, and with that, I rear back and drive forward purposefully. And I don't stop. Can't stop. I'm growling in appreciation as I pump into her time and time again, my body not my own.

"You're mine now, Ava." The words roll out with no prompt from my brain, my thoughts, my body, my soul, all being hijacked by this moment. This feeling.

She doesn't object, filling me with contentment—something that I've never felt. "All mine," I reiterate, meeting her forehead with my own and retreating before I really let rip, pounding forward repeatedly like a crazy man, desperate and sweating.

I relish in her repeated cries of pleasure, feeling her muscles tightening around me as I take her mouth again, our sweaty bodies slipping and sliding. "You're going to come." I can feel it. She's pulsing and squirming.

"Yes!" She bites me.

Fucking hell. "Wait for me," I order, increasing my pace.

She screams. Shit, she's going.

And so am I.

It creeps up on me, and I fight to remain standing.

"Now, Ava!"

I push into her, holding myself deep and high, heaving into her neck. I'm a wreck. A fucking mess. "Oh, fucccckkkkk," I groan, my dick exploding as I lazily circle my hips, wheedling every scrap of pleasure, her moans into my shoulder tired and drowsy. *Jesus, Lord above, what the fucking hell just happened?* We're doing this again *very* soon.

"Look at me," I demand gently, needing to check once again that she is real. When her heavy head lifts and her face finds mine, I look straight into those eyes and know for certain that something really special is happening here. And for the first time, I wonder whether to be delighted by it, or afraid.

Softly circling my hips, I kiss her. "Beautiful." I push her back into the warmth of my chest and take her to the counter, resting her down gently and reluctantly slipping out of her.

I cup her face with my palms and kiss her. "I didn't hurt you, did I?" I scan her face, searching for any signs that I may have. She seems so delicate. She's not fragile, not at all, but I feel like I need to be careful with her in every way. And I'm fully aware of the reason.

She answers by pulling me into her arms and squeezing me tightly, my face naturally finding its place in the crook of her neck and my palms feeling her back. I feel an overwhelming sense of . . . belonging. For years, I've stumbled randomly and blindly, doing things without thought or consideration. But this? Leaning into her neck, being held not constrained? It feels so fucking right. It's as if I've finally fallen upon something I really want. Something I can see so very clearly.

But then I realize what I've done.

Idiot.

Pulling back, I stroke her heated face with my knuckles. "I didn't use a condom." I feel so ashamed and, actually, surprised with myself. No matter how drunk I've ever been, I've always protected myself. Always. After being trapped, it's inbuilt. "I'm sorry, I got so carried away. You're on birth control, right?"

"Yes, but the pill doesn't protect me from STDs."

I smile, not in the least bit insulted. I have no right to be . . . not that she knows. "Ava, I've *always* used a condom." I peck her forehead. "Except with you."

"Why?" she asks, puzzled, and I can't blame her. I'm quite befuddled by all this myself. I'm acting out of character in so many ways.

"I don't see straight when I'm near you." She knocks all rationality right out of me, has me thinking stupid thoughts and behaving like a total nutjob. And I adore her for it.

Taking one of the fancy face cloths from the shelf by the sink, I run it under the tap, hating the idea of wiping myself away from her. When I turn, I find her legs are closed tightly. She's feeling awkward, and with a small frown, I separate them again. I never want her to feel uncomfortable with me, which is a ridiculous claim, given my recent behavior. She's still here, though. And now she can never deny how incredible we are together.

"Better," I mutter, placing her palms on my shoulders while I reluctantly sweep the cloth across her skin, cleaning her up and flicking a glance up every now and again, each time catching her regarding me carefully. I would bet my bottom dollar on what she's thinking.

Age. She's wondering how old I am.

"I want to toss you in that shower and worship every inch of you, but this will have to do. For now, anyway." As soon as I get her back to my rental, there will be plenty more worshipping. Her issue with age will be lost amid my capabilities and her craving. I give her a quick kiss, resenting having to cover her. "Come on, lady. Let's get you dressed." I love that she lets me do it all, and I love how she tenses and spasms when I can't resist another taste of her neck. She'd better get used to my lips all over her, because I don't plan on putting them anywhere else ever again.

My shirt is handed to me, and I shake out the creases as best I can. "There really wasn't any need to screw it up, was there?" I grin as I dress myself, and she watches closely.

"Your jacket will cov—" Her eyes widen. "Oh."

"Yes. Oh." I snap my belt, and grin when she flinches, only because she seems alarmed by it. Absolutely no idea. Thank God. "Okay, you ready to face the music, lady?" I signal for her hand, and she wastes no time giving it to me. Smart girl. "I'd say quite loud, wouldn't you?" I break out in a full-on, blast-her-back smile when she darts her wide eyes to me.

But she's distracted from her shock when she catches sight of her face in the mirror. I don't know why; she looks just flawless. "You're perfect." I unlock the bathroom door and pull her out, scooping up my jacket as we pass.

As we take the stairs, I know I have a certain spring in my step, my body feeling the lightest it has in as long as I can remember. I look across to Ava. All because of her. But my contentment falters when I feel her trying to pull away. Instinct tells me to keep hold of her.

So I do.

"Jesse, let go of my hand."

"No," I fire unreasonably and shortly.

I stop when she does and turn to look at her on the step above. She's nervous, her earlier blissed-out state gone. I'm tempted to take her straight back in that bathroom to remind her of what we just shared together. She can't have forgotten already. She can't possibly think we'd walk out of there and that would be the end of it.

"Jesse, you can't expect me to parade through here holding your hand. That's not fair. Please, let me go."

I gaze at our hands, seeing the evidence of the firmness of my grip by the bulging veins. I'm not hurting her, I'd never hurt her, but I have a solid hold and I have no intention of letting go. "I'm not letting you go," I whisper sullenly. "If I let you go, you might forget how it feels. You might change your mind." It sounds irrational, but that's how it is. And it scares me. It scares me to think that she could rob me of this. That it's out of my control.

"Change my mind about what?"

"Me." I can feel her eyes scanning my nervous form, confirming my fears. She could never appreciate this unshakable fear I'm developing, and she doesn't give me time to explain. Or, at least, try to. My arm jolts, she's suddenly free, and I watch, feeling a mixture of anger and agony, as she escapes me, running into the arms of some girly twat at the bottom of the stairs. *Who the fuck is that?*

I'm only mildly uncomfortable with the rage flying through me as I charge down the stairs, watching another man all over her.

For the most part, I'm consumed with an unreasonable need to reclaim her and ensure she never has the opportunity to escape me *ever* again.

Reclaim?

Ensure she never has the opportunity to escape me again?

"Fuck me, Ward. You have issues," I mutter, taking mild comfort from the fact that I'm recognizing that. My eyes are nailed to the man's hands resting on Ava's shoulders as I approach them, my jaw virtually in spasm from the effort it's taking me not to growl at the fucker. He spots me, and his eyes definitely widen. Good. Yes, you should be very worried. *Get your fucking hands off her.* He leans into Ava and whispers something, and she's quick to shrug off his hold. Good girl. She's also quick to turn and find me. Good girl. Then she rolls her eyes at me. Not such a good girl.

"Tom, this is Mr. Ward. Mr. Ward, Tom." She motions to the man, who looks less wary now, more delighted. "He's a colleague," she tells me. "He's also gay."

I don't have a moment to offer my hand. He's on me like a lion, his lips on my cheek. *Whoa, mate.* I remain still, as stiff as a board. He's a bit . . . friendly.

"It really is a pleasure," he chants, pulling away and copping a good feel of my biceps. "Tell me, do you work out?"

It's me rolling my eyes now, and I scowl at Ava when she laughs before pivoting and leaving me with her very enthusiastic work colleague. "From time to time," I say, reminding myself that this guy is obviously friends with Ava, and I need all the support I can get.

"You're very well formed." He steps back, smiling at me. "If it wasn't obvious you've got your sights set on someone else, I'd ask if you'd like to join me for a drink."

I can't help my small smile. Oh, I have my sights set on some-one, make no mistake. I cock my head when I see Ava disappear into the kitchen. "Nice talking, Tom," I say, moving past him and heading toward the kitchen.

"Where the hell have you been?" Sarah intercepts me, her eyes accusing. "I'm bored out of my mind. Can we leave now?"

"Feel free to leave when you want." I see Ava approaching an older man, who passes her a glass of champagne. How many has she had this evening? I could taste it on her tongue, and I saw her car outside. She better not even *think* about driving anywhere.

Sarah moves in my peripheral vision, turning to see what has my undivided attention. "Ah. The designer," she purrs. "The *young* designer."

I wish she would shut the fuck up. I toss her a tired look, am about to tell her to clear off back to The Manor and go whip the living daylights out of some poor, sick bastard, but someone catches my eye. And I'm all stiff again, holding back my growl. "What the fuck?" I murmur.

"What?" Sarah asks, her attention back on me.

"Nothing." Fucking hell, I need to leave before I go on a rampage and drag Ava out of here.

Mikael Van Der Haus moves in, his smarmy, suggestive smile being lavished all over Ava. I wouldn't be worried, but Van Der Haus's marriage is over. And I know that for a fact because his wife told me. And she told me because she was a guest at The Manor.

Ava glances over her shoulder and spots me, and I fight to soften my features. She looks away before I can. They chat for a bit, and the tension inside me builds and builds. My feet are shifting, my fists clenching. "I'm going to the bathroom." I leave Sarah and take the stairs back to the main suite quickly, closing the door behind me. Removing myself from the situation was my only option. Jesus, he knows what The Manor is, what goes on there. His wife has been in my bed, something I hadn't cared about given his *out-of-marriage* activities. Cluing Van Der Haus in on my relationship with Ava would be bad news. Shit, it's one thing after another, a pile of problems adding to all the fucking issues I have already. I've never questioned my lifestyle. It was the only way for me to deal with my torrid past. The only way to temporarily eliminate the torment.

I look around the space I had Ava in not twenty minutes ago. But it feels like centuries. The rush has disappeared completely. I need it back.

I go to the mirror and splash my face with cold water, hoping it'll cool me down in many ways. Then I head back downstairs, praying Van Der Haus has fucked off so I can get Ava and leave. The place is still bustling, people chatting, drinking, eating canapes, laughing. But no Ava.

"Looking for someone?" Sarah asks, joining me as I continue to scan the space.

"Don't be a dick, Sarah. Have you seen her?" I pull my phone out, ready to dial Ava and track her down.

"She left."

I swing my worried eyes onto Sarah. "What?" She left without even saying goodbye? And more to the point, she left without *me*?

"Five minutes ago." She points her champagne flute toward the doors, and I'm off like a rocket, pushing my way through the crowds, wishing, once again, that they'd all fuck off out of my penthouse.

I nearly take an old chap off his feet. "Sorry," I say, making sure he's steady.

"You in a rush?" he asks, holding out his hand. "Patrick Peterson."

Ah, Ava's boss? "Nice to meet you." I leave his hand hanging and hurry away, smacking the button for the elevator repeatedly when I get there, like it might arrive faster under pressure. "Come on, come on," I chant. I rush in as soon as the doors are open wide enough and hit the button for the ground floor. Why did she leave? I start pacing the small space feeling a sweat coming on and reach up to my chest and apply a bit of pressure, trying to force my heart into slowing down. Don't tell me what I just shared with Ava will be it. Don't tell me I won't ever experience lightness like that again.

The doors open, and I dart out, nearly taking the concierge off his feet too. "Sorry," I call back, landing outside the foyer, my eyes scanning. I see her car, but I don't relax. She was drinking. She wouldn't have driven anywhere. Good girl. But is she walk-ing? Alone?

I scrub my hands down my face, slumping back against her car. This isn't how I expected the rest of my evening to pan out. I pull up her name in my phone, but as my thumb hovers over the dial icon, I hear something.

Ava?

I frown, glancing around.

And I spot her, sitting on a bench on the docks. She's on her phone. I look at mine. I don't know why; she won't be calling me, and that fucking hurts. I wander over quietly, coming to a stop a few paces behind her.

"Oh, Kate," she says on a sigh, her head dropped back. I can sense her despondency from here. Can feel her regret. "I've made a monumental fuck-up," she whispers, and I flinch. How can she say that was a mistake? It was nothing short of perfection. "I'll be home soon."

My heart in tatters, I hit dial on my phone, as if I need her to ignore my call and give me the agonizing confirmation that she's talking about me. Of course she's talking about me.

But she *does* answer. And it throws me. "Hey," she says quietly.

My mouth is working before my brain. "Where are you?"

Please don't lie to me. But her hand goes straight to her hair and the frantic, unconscious twiddling begins.

"I'm at home."

I'm crushed. Fucking crushed. "Okay," I murmur, hanging up before I say something stupid. Why is she doing this? It's even fucking harder to understand now. She can't give herself to me like that, make me feel like that, and deny me the chance to ever have her again. It doesn't work like that.

My head spins as I watch her on the bench, sitting quietly, wondering what on earth is going on in her head. She needs to tell me. Maybe then I can reassure her. *Or continue lying to her.*

I cringe that thought the fuck away, focusing on the here and now, and she stands. Turns. Our eyes collide, and the second they do, I know beyond anything I've known before that this is it. She is it. Whatever I've been waiting for to redeem me, to rebuild me, to cure me, is standing before me, her eyes welling, her entire being yelling that she wants me. I am smitten, and whatever she's set alight inside me can only burn if she preserves it. And that means I need her. And to need her is to keep her forever, and to keep her forever means I have to start being honest about who I am and what I have done. It's a terrifying prospect. More terrifying because the chances of her running for the hills when she finds out everything there is to know is more likely than her accepting me. All thirty-seven years of me.

I need to make her need me. Make it impossible for her to ever walk away from me.

If only it were that simple.

After an age of us staring at each other, she breaks down, and my dead heart cracks. She feels hopeless. Overwhelmed by this crazy connection. I should take comfort in her inability to shield herself in this moment, to keep her vulnerability and conflict hidden, and instead wield her determination. But I don't. I just feel like a first-class wanker for reducing her to despairing tears.

I move in and take her in my arms, holding her tightly and relaxing, feeling untold comfort in her embracing me, burying her face in my neck, her arms clinging to me firmly.

I let her be, give her time to let it all out. It's all I can do in this moment. That and hope. Hope with everything I have that this isn't a goodbye embrace. Because it's amazing. Having her in my arms is amazing. Comforting her when she's sad. Holding her when she needs to be held. *Purpose.* I reach up and massage the back of her head, sighing deeply.

The jerks of her body lessen slowly. "How long have you been here?" she eventually asks.

"Long enough," I reply, holding her tighter, preparing myself to ask the question I'd like to avoid. "What's all this about a monumental fuck-up? I hope to God you weren't referring to me."

"I was."

"You were?" Unexpected annoyance drifts into my tone. I'm putting it down to surprise. I'm surprised she's being so brutally honest with me. I should follow her lead. Open up. Yet everything is telling me it's too soon. She's swaying back and forth without knowing all the details, without really knowing me, leaving me concluding that the age difference must be one of her issues, along with this fierce intensity. Because it really is quite frightening. "Will you come home with me?" We'll talk. I'll remind her. Take her back to the places we went to only an hour ago.

"No."

I sag, fucking knackered by the walls she keeps adding more fucking bricks to. "Please, Ava."

"Why?"

Why? Isn't it fucking obvious? I release her a bit, but not too much. "It feels right. You belong with me." The words just come, with no hope of being held back. I'm being honest. It's a step in the right direction. Although her monster frown is a little worrying.

"So who does Sarah belong with?"

"Sarah? What's she got to do with anything?"

"Girlfriend," she says, and I gape at her, completely stunned. Girlfriend? *What the* . . . Oh no. She thinks . . . Sarah? Good God, how did she come to that conclusion?

"Oh, please don't tell me you've been ignoring my calls and running away because you thought . . ." I force myself to release her, aware that my hold is tightening by the second. "You thought me and Sarah were . . . Oh, fucking hell, no."

"Yes," she yells, and I move away, stunned. Sarah? "She's not?" she asks, her beautiful face a picture of confusion and . . . relief. There's relief. Jesus, how did I allow her to believe that? How did I not see?

No woman will accept you as long as we're together.

Fuck.

Frustration grabs me, and my hands go to my head, gripping it, stopping the mammoth headache from taking hold. "Ava, whatever made you think that?"

She's on the verge of laughter. I have no idea why. This is the least funny thing ever. I've been going out of my mind trying to figure out how she could brush me off so easily. My age. The sparks. I considered it all. But Sarah? "Oh, let me see." The smile she hits me with is pretty fucking insulting, to be honest. Like I'm stupid. "Maybe it was the kiss in the hallway of The Manor. Or when she came looking for you in the bedroom." She looks up briefly, as if mentally recalling every valid reason. "Or it could be her frosty reception to me. Or perhaps it's the fact that she's with you every time I see you."

I unwittingly flinch, remembering each and every one of those times. There was nothing in any of them. Maybe that's male ignorance on my part. I have no clue how women's minds work. But I'm learning. Fuck me, what a nightmare.

"Who is she?" she asks, furious.

She doesn't want to or need to know. But, bloody hell, let's set the record straight on something. I take her hands and hunker down a bit so I'm close. And clear. Very, very clear. "Ava, she's a little friendly." Mostly with me. She's also a mega-bitch from hell when she wants to be. But that's Sarah. Always has been. I'm used to it, but I've had a very swift reality check. Ava doesn't know Sarah like I know Sarah. I need to remember that.

"Friendly? That woman is not friendly."

"She's a friend." I feel at her cheek, ignoring her look of ire. Enough about Sarah. She's not an issue anymore. Now the issue is Ava and me and how we move forward. "Now we've clarified Sarah's position in my life, can we talk about yours?"

She frowns. "What do you mean?"

I'm glad she's asked. "I mean in my bed, beneath me." I can't help my smirk. I'm so fucking happy. All that unnecessary stress was for nothing?

I pull her into me and sigh when she snuggles deep. "At The Manor?" she asks, and I balk at thin air before me. At this time of night? Jesus, no. It'll be heaving.

"No, I've an apartment behind me, but I can't move in until tomorrow." I smile a little. I cannot wait to get her back in there and christen every surface, room, and floor. "I'm renting a place on Hyde Park. You'll come."

"Yes."

I close my eyes and bury my face in her hair. She still smells of me. I smell good on her. "Come on," I say, maneuvering and tucking her into my side, walking us over to my car.

"My stuff," she says, pointing to her Mini.

"Open it." I leave her by my Aston and hurry over, collecting her bags off the front seat before she locks it again. "You left your flowers?" I ask, my head cocked as I load her bags into the boot of my car. Her persona screams awkward, her shoulders jumping up on a shrug. "So do you?" I ask, helping her into the passenger seat.

"Do I what?"

I crouch beside her, resting my hand on her knee. "Forgive me."

Her smile is small. "I'm here, aren't I?" she says, looking away. *What was that?* An answer without answering? I cock my head, thoughtful, rising and closing the door. My relief, apparently, was short-lived. She's still uncertain, and as I make my way around to the driver's side, I wonder what else could be the cause. My age? I don't know, but I will find out just as soon as I get her home.

10

"I'M on the first floor. We'll take the stairs," I say as I direct her through the doors into the main building from the car park. We climb the stairs, and the silence is constant. Has been from the second I pulled away from Lusso. I'm slowly figuring out if I give this woman too much space to think, she'll talk herself in circles. Talk herself out of this. So I need to stop giving her space. The notion is lovely, if impossible. I realize that.

I let us in and turn to look at Ava, cringing when I see her expression. Not surprisingly, given her profession, she doesn't like it. "It's a pit stop," I explain, placing her bags on the floor. "I bet you're really offended." I force a smile, trying to dent the awkward atmosphere. The car was bordering unbearable, Ava silent, me not knowing what to say. Talk, John said. I've never appreciated how hard it is to do that. I never usually have to.

She smiles meekly. "I prefer your new place."

"Me too."

She braves coming farther in, glancing around, taking it all in. "I don't keep alcohol." *Anymore.* "Do you want some water?"

"Please."

I take two bottles from the fridge and turn to find she's settled at the island. She looks small and uncomfortable. Like she's questioning being here. It grates on me. She's finding a problem for every solution, and I'm trying so hard not to let it rile me. I pour her water into a glass and remove my jacket, looking down at the mess that is my creased shirt. I want to smile. I can't. I want to relish in the memories. I can't.

I pull a stool close to her and pass her the glass, and I watch her as I sip. She's fidgeting, refusing to look at me, playing with the glass. What the fuck has happened? She clung to me like I was life outside of Lusso.

I breathe out heavily and she freezes, looking out the corner of her eye as I rid my hand of my water and take her glass, setting it gently down on the counter. I don't only want to see her face when she gives me the answers to my questions, I want to feel her body react. So I reach for her stool and tug it closer, turning it slightly so she's facing me. My hands fall to her bare knees. I need to talk. I *have* to talk. "Why did you cry?"

She shakes her head mildly. "I don't know."

"Yes, you do. Tell me." *Don't make me force it out of you, Ava.*

I keep her in place with my expectant stare, willing her to dig deep and be honest with me. I'm a fucking hypocrite.

"I don't know," she says again, and I sigh, my eyes narrowing, discontent flooding me. And I want her to know it.

"Would I be right in saying that your misinterpretation of mine and Sarah's relationship wasn't the only reason you were avoiding me?" There. Let's move this conversation along, because if I wait for Ava to find the courage to speak up, I'll be waiting forever. Enough. I flip the catch on my Rolex and slip it off my wrist, waiting.

She looks away. "Probably."

I nod to myself. "That's disappointing." So what obstacle is she going to put in our way now?

Fuck it. I'm done with talking. Because I hate what she's saying. Let me communicate with her in another way. A way that will leave no room for misunderstandings.

I seize her and get her onto the counter, moving in between her legs and slamming my mouth on hers, not giving her the chance to prepare for me. Nothing will prepare her for this. I don't think anything can prepare me either. I hear the sound of smashing glass through the instant rush of blood to my head, my body singing, my skin blazing, my cock dripping. Just from a kiss. I reach for her arse and yank her tighter into me, my groin inadvertently pushing into her, an attempt to ease the throb.

The sounds she's making are quiet, but the loudest I've ever heard. I rip myself free of our overwhelming kiss to find her eyes, my breathing shot. She's alive with want. For me. "Let's establish some things here," I practically wheeze, desperate to get my mouth back on hers and my dick back in her glorious, sweet pussy. But as desperate as I am for that, I'm just as desperate for her to understand I'm figuring her out.

I slide her off the counter, feeling her legs tighten around me. "You're a shit liar." I drop a gentle kiss on her lips, pushing my tongue gently into her mouth. She accepts. Of course she accepts. And she moans. She moans so loudly. "You're mine now, Ava." No more fucking about. No more games. I grind into her, feeling her stiffen in my arms. "I'm keeping you forever." I thrust once more, and when she responds by kissing me, I take that as a resounding yes. Yes, she's good with that. Yes, I can keep her forever. Yes, she's on the same page as me. Good.

Time to consummate that. "I'm going to possess every single part of you." *Mind and body.* "There will be nowhere on this beautiful body that won't have had me in it, on it, or over it." I've never desired something so much. Craved it so much. Never felt this fucking dependent. It's possessing me, and there is nothing I can do to control it. Only sate it.

I drop her to her feet and turn her, trying not to be too rough. But . . . her breathing is heavy, her whimpers endless. Desperate. I grab the zipper on her dress and tug it down, pushing it from her body to the floor. The bra is next. Gone. And her skin? It glows, pulling my lips to the back of her neck. I kiss her gently, smiling when I feel her shudder, her neck flexing. She can't cope. *Me neither.*

I turn my mouth into her ear. "Face me," I whisper.

She's looking at me quickly, her dark eyes blazing, and I lift her, setting her on the counter again. Her hands land on my shoulders. I quickly seize them and guide them down to the edge of the counter. "The hands stay here." She's going to need something to hold on to, and I can't guarantee I'll be stable enough. "Lift," I order as I take the sides of her knickers, dragging them down her long legs.

And she's naked. Gloriously naked. And I am held rapt by the vision of her sitting here on my countertop, waiting for me to blow her mind.

She reaches for my shirt, and I move back. *What the fuck am I doing?* Torturing myself? "Hands," I order, and her bottom lip juts out. It's cute. But I'm happy taking this part slowly. Happy to watch her gradually disintegrate with an impatience I'm all too familiar with. "You want me to remove my shirt?" I ask, casual but cocky.

"Yes."

She's out of breath. It's too satisfying. "Yes, what?" I ask around my grin. She will beg for me. Make up for all the lost time and stress she's caused.

"Please," she virtually snarls, her eyes boring holes into my smug form. I give her what she wants and start unbuttoning. Slowly. Watching her. Relishing her building impatience.

I'm surprised she manages to restrain herself. I'd be damned if I could sit and watch her slowly strip. Has she suddenly become compliant?

I flex my shoulders and remove my shirt, kicking off my shoes and dipping to pull off my socks. And as I rise, I watch as her gaze falls to my stomach. I want to think she's admiring my form. But I know different. I'm not up for questions on how I came to have a mammoth scar there, not now, so I move into her quickly, placing my hands on her thighs. I have her again, her attention diverted.

"Where to start?" I ask thoughtfully, dragging my thumb across her bottom lip. "Here?" I slide the tip into her mouth, smiling when I feel her tongue circle the end. She's doing anything she can to break me. I move my touch to her cheek and then lazily down her throat onto her chest. "Or here?" I ask, cupping her breast, looking to her for a reaction, tracing the edges of her nipple. Her gasp nearly has my dick breaking free from my trousers. "These are mine," I tell her, moving to her flat stomach, circling a few times, before continuing down to her thigh. I tease her for a few moments, softly stroking her, feeling the warmth of her pussy. *Soon, Ward.* You'll be back there again soon. I find her arse. "Or here?" I ask, and she stiffens. What will she say? Will she let me? "Every single inch, Ava." *Every. Single. Inch.* I return my hand to her front, smiling when she relaxes. "I think I'll start here."

Her rush of relieved breath is short-lived. I take her face, getting close. "But I did mean *every* inch," I assure her, preparing her, getting her used to the idea. She's never had it before. And I want to claim that part of her. *Every* part of her. I'm going to leave my mark everywhere, making it impossible for her to forget. Consume her. *Make it impossible to leave me.*

I wedge a hand on the counter to hold me up, the very thought making me unsteady. My dick in her arse. That's a sure-fire way of ensuring she never forgets me.

I rest a finger in the snug warmth of her pussy and drag it up, and she folds, her forehead meeting my shoulder. "You're drenched," I rasp, pushing my finger inside her and clenching my eyes closed. Fuck, her condition makes every attempt to push me away laughable. "You want me." I withdraw, circling, spreading her pleasure, before diving deep again. She cries into me. "Tell me you want me, Ava."

She's spent already. It's fulfilling and worrying. She's got a long night ahead of her.

"I want you," she cries, and I moan my happiness.

"Tell me you need me," I demand.

"I need you."

I look to the ceiling in gratitude. *And I need you, baby.* Fuck the whys and wherefores. It is what it is, and I'm happy with that. "You'll always need me, Ava. I'm going to make sure of it." *Any way I can.* "Now let's see if we can fuck some sense into you."

I remove my fingers from inside her and drag her off the counter, turning her around and positioning her hands on the edge.

"I want to see you."

I ignore her and start getting her to where I want her, crowding her from behind. "Shut up and soak up the pleasure," I whisper, grinding into her, reaching forward and taking her wrists. "No talking unless I tell you. You got that?"

She nods, and I smile on the inside. So stubborn. But so amenable. She's becoming more perfect by the second. I brush my touch gently up her arms, working my way onto her shoulders, massaging away the last scraps of tension I can feel.

I drop my mouth to her neck, dotting soft, delicate kisses there. I've never found it so easy to be tender. "Your skin is addictive." She hums quietly, the sound nothing short of orgasm provoking, and I laugh softly. "This good?" I continue tracing my mouth all over her neck, her jaw, her cheek. She turns to look at me, and I read her want, kissing her lips, my hands drifting down to her sensitive hips. "Keep your hands where they are." Releasing her, I step back, my eyes never leaving her as I remove my trousers and boxers. I reclaim her. Slowly walk her back, my breathing more strained by the second. I take hold of her nape with one hand, my cock in the other, guiding it to her pussy. The second there's contact, my knees begin to shake. I lower my mouth to her spine and lick a long trail up to her neck, finishing with a kiss. "Are you ready for me, Ava?" I ask. Am *I* ready? "You can answer."

"Yes," she murmurs, and I exhale, advancing forward, clenching my eyes closed. Good God, I can hardly breathe. I'm struggling to move, being held captive by the pleasure she gives me.

I release my dick, taking the counter again for support, bracing myself for my next move. I don't get a chance to make it. She jolts back, and I sink deep and hard, nearly choking as a result. "Fuck, Ava," I bark, gasping for breath. "You turn me inside out." My grip on her nape tightens, my other hand reaching for her breast. Staring down at her back, I fight off the urgency building, my compulsion to take her hard overwhelming me. It's no good. Seeing her like this. Hearing her, feeling her, smelling her. "I can't do this slow." I squeeze her breast, withdrawing and pounding forward on a grunt.

"Jesse!"

I slip out lazily. "Quiet, Ava." And enter her hard again, jolting her forward. I see her white knuckles flex, and when I'm sure she's got a solid hold of the counter, I give in to my need and piston in and out of her like I might never get the chance to take her again. That thought. This moment. I shake it away and focus of blowing both our minds, moving my hold back to her hips and powering on, sweating, breathless, every muscle working harder than they ever have before. The walls of her pussy relentlessly grip me, increasing the friction. I'm out of my fucking mind. She lets out a little yelp, her body solidifying. No. She's not going yet. "Not yet, Ava." I need her to last the distance, to come with me. I pull out without thought, my face screwing up, both in pain and loss. There's a better way, and it'll be a check off my list.

I look down as she whimpers, my finger drawing a line down the center of her arse. She's immediately a statue. "You can do this, Ava." Just talk her through it. Reassure her. She has to let me take this from her. I move my hand to between her thighs and gather some of her pleasure, smiling at how saturated she is. No prep required. I spread it far and wide, making sure she's ready for me. But she's still a little stiff. "Relax, we'll take it slow." I continue working her, mentally willing her to loosen up. *Come on, baby. It'll hurt if you don't ease up.* I circle my thumb around her opening, watching her closely. Her shoulders rise. "Ava, relax."

"I'm fucking trying," she retorts, her fists clenching. "Give me time, damn it."

"Watch your mouth," I say around a smile, knowing I'm asking the impossible. Her sass makes me chuckle as I return to her pussy, working her a little more. She's not denying me.

"Don't you need some lubricant or something?"

"You're soaking, Ava. That's enough." I will slip right in there, and I can't fucking wait. If her pussy is tight, her arse will be . . . I shudder at the thought of my impending pleasure. "You're not very good under instruction, are you?" I go in for the kill, pushing my thumb past her tight ring of muscles. We've gone backward. Moments ago, she was compliant. Docile. Not anymore. But I'm prepared to accept a little feistiness if it means I get to give her this experience. She trusts me. "Relax, woman."

"Oh God," she wails. "This is going to hurt, isn't it?"

"Yes, at first." But not for long, she has to believe me on that. "You have to relax. Once I'm in, you'll love it. Trust me."

Her head becomes floppy, her breathing even more labored. I

reach for her neck and massage some more as I continue to get her ready to take me. She softens, and I mentally praise her, moving my hands down to her arse cheeks and pulling them apart. My teeth sink into my lip, my body tingling with anticipation as I guide myself to her tight hole. The second my dick meets her, she's tense again, resisting my invasion. "Easy, lady. Let it happen," I say, softly circling the tip of my cock across her skin.

I try again, my attention split between the back of her head and her arse, and I grit my teeth, advancing, moving my hands to her shoulders. "That's it, Ava," I whisper encouragingly. "We're nearly there." I can barely get my words out, my body sweating profusely, my dick sliding deeper and deeper.

"Shit!" she yelps, and I convulse, blinking rapidly to try and clear my distorted vision.

"Oh God, you're so tight." I start to vibrate, feeling her resist me again, every muscle in her arse clenching around my dick. "Stop fighting, Ava. Relax."

And she does. Every part of her softens, and she moans.

"Jesus, that feels good." So fucking good. "I'm going to move now, okay?"

She nods, and I breathe in, reclaiming her hips. "Real slow, Ava," I assure her, slipping free, my teeth clenching.

"Jesus, Jesse."

"I know," I pant. Fuck, do I know. I quickly find my pace, slipping in and out easily, watching her body roll with the unexpected pleasure she's finding from this. She's felt nothing yet. "You feel amazing, Ava. I could stay here all fucking night, but I'm losing it." I'm losing it fast.

She pushes herself back onto me, and I gulp. "Keep going," she orders.

"Yes, baby. Are you close?"

"Yes!" She smashes back onto me, and I bark out my surprise, finding her pussy and stroking her to help her along. "Harder!"

"Oh fuck, Ava." I circle her clit, powering on, my pace increasing naturally.

She tosses her head back. "I'm there!"

Fuck! "Wait." I piston on, urgency taking over, my world spinning wildly, and I finally bark my order for her to let go. My cock lunges inside her, my lungs shrink, my head spins, my world explodes.

Fuck . . . ing . . . hell.

She falls forward, and I have no choice but to fall with her, landing on her back, squishing her to the marble. I can't get my breathing under control. Can't get my thoughts to align. Can't fathom what the bizarre throb is in my chest. Yet I've felt it before. And I never thought I'd be blessed enough to feel it again. The question is, though, am I blessed enough to have someone return these feelings?

Or is this heaven just a brief break from the hell I'm used to?

11

NEVER HAS a silence so loud been so comfortable. I'm dazed, confused, but high on hope.

I sigh, nuzzling into her hair. "Are you okay?"

"Am I allowed to speak?"

I smile as I squeeze her hip. Yes, she can speak, so long as she speaks from her heart and not her head, which I know is telling her I'm a bad idea. The obvious age gap won't be helping either. Is it still an issue? I snort to myself. I'd wipe the floor with any twenty-something self-proclaimed stud. "Don't be smart."

"I'm well and truly fucked."

I scowl at her back as I rest my arms over hers, wondering how the fuck I can stop her from swearing all the time? It's like razors over my fucking skin. I cock my head in thought. Gag her? "Ava, please watch your mouth."

"I am, though."

I'm glad. Really glad. She won't be forgetting that little encounter in a hurry. "I know, but you don't have to swear. I hate you swearing." It doesn't suit her.

"I have to endure *your* blue language."

If I could see her face, I know it would be full of indignation.

"My language is only blue, lady," I whisper, "when you make me see red." Which is a lot.

Her body deflates on a tired sigh. She can sigh all she likes. I *will* get my way. "Okay."

She's appeasing me. It's a step in the right direction toward my stability. What else will she appease me on? Everything? Will she agree to be nailed to me for all time? I smile into her skin as I stroke over her arms. She might say no, but what I've learned about this woman is that no doesn't always mean no. Sometimes it means: *I really want to, and I need you to show me why.* I'll show her. Every day. Which basically means I get to make love to her daily. I smile again. She can't possibly dispute perfection.

Letting me take her in the arse showed me something solid. She trusts me. She was willing to give herself to me in *any* way. I need to explore every possible avenue, hunt down every sign that she's completely and utterly in this unchartered territory *with* me. I'm terrified. For myself, but more for Ava. She's given me a gift unknowingly, and I need to treasure it. For the past week, I've only found peace when I'm touching her.

How on earth am I going to balance that? How am I going to make sure I give her what she needs while ensuring I get what I need to maintain this bliss? I'm reasonable enough to accept it's going to be tricky.

"Jesse?" she whispers, my name loaded with a million questions. And I know what one she will ask.

"Hmmm?"

"How old are you?"

I inhale and flex my hold on her arms. It doesn't matter. *So why won't you tell her, Ward?* "Twenty–two." Soon. I'll tell her soon. I slowly inch my way out of her as I kiss her back, my face strained in discomfort. "Come here." I avoid her hips for risk of her jerking out of my hold, taking her waist instead. I frown, looking down, my sated dick deciding it's not so sated anymore, twitching and standing to attention again. *Fuck me, haven't you had enough?*

I turn her and lift her onto the counter, catching her slight alarm when she sees my condition. She'd better get used to that. I can't stop myself from responding to her, and I don't want to. I take her arms and rest them over my shoulders as I move between her thighs, absorbing her face. It's been too long since I've seen it. And her eyes. She's real. I could never refute that when they're sparkling so madly. "Are you okay?"

Her smile is gorgeous. Satisfied. "Yes."

"Good." I move in, hugging the shit out of her. "I'm not finished with you yet."

She wraps everything around me, legs, arms, and all. "I noticed."

"You have this effect on me."

Her face goes straight into my neck. That's amazing too. Everything with this woman is amazing.

I exhale my contentment and free up my hold, leaning back slightly to get her in my sights. Her cheeks are flushed. Beautifully flushed, and I can't help giving them a light caress. "Are you hungry?"

"Ish."

"Ish," I mimic, and she grins. Amazing. "You have a cheeky grin. I love it." I drop a light kiss on her mouth.

"Shit!"

"Mouth," I grate, giving her displeased eyes. "What's the matter?"

She looks worried, and in turn, *I'm* worried. "I told Kate I'd be home," she says, her body tensing, ready to free herself. "I better call her. She needs my car to visit her gran in Yorkshire."

She's out of my arms before I can stop her, and I have to reason with myself before I yank her right back. She's just making a call. Let her make the call. I pout, my naked body feeling lost without her attached to it. I'm in more trouble than I thought.

My hand goes to my chest. The contented heartbeat is now more of a panicked thrum. Jesus, I need to get a fucking grip. *She's right there, Ward.*

I stand stock-still, watching her as she retrieves her phone and bashes out a text message before she pulls some jeans out. She's dressing? Why?

"I've got to go," she says as she starts to put them on.

What?

"Go?" I yell without thought, and she jumps, but she still carries on dressing.

"I've got one set of car keys and Kate needs them."

Tough fucking shit. I need her here more than her friend needs her keys. She's staying. End of. *Are you hearing yourself, Ward?* I stalk over and seize her, throwing her over my shoulder.

"What are you doing?" she yells. I ignore her, focusing on getting her into my bedroom. "Shit!" she curses, only serving to piss me off more. I'll be asking Cathy to pick up some soap when she's next at the supermarket so I can wash Ava's mouth out. "Jesse, put me down!"

Not a fucking chance. I grab the leg of the jeans she managed to get halfway on, pulling them off and tossing them aside. And for good measure, I give her arse a stinger of a slap.

"Ouch!"

"Mouth," I yell, pushing the door open with a bit too much force. I see the bed, maneuver her on my shoulder, and toss her onto the sheets, diving on after her and pinning her down. My cock falls straight to where it should be, and I inhale, waiting for her to get her bearings and find me. She better see the annoyance in my eyes. "You're not fucking going anywhere." My voice is hoarse, and when I swivel and plunge, I bark out my pleasure, hearing the muffled sounds of her scream.

My heart settles.

I have to take a moment, my head limp, every inch of my skin sizzling with need. How does she do this to me? I lift my gaze to hers, pulling out, relishing the want in her eyes. And I pound back in on a grunt, making her head lash back. Her scream is epic. "Look at me," I order, and she does, her breathing chaotic. "That's better. Now, do you need a reminder?"

Her eyebrows jump up in surprise, her expression questioning. But the defiant little temptress still swivels her hips, egging me on. I will not cave under her tactics. This isn't about what I want or need right now. This is about showing her what *she* wants and needs, and she doesn't need to fucking leave. She needs this. Me. "Answer the question, Ava."

"Please," she says in a breathy whisper, and I smile my satisfaction, withdrawing and powering forward. And I don't stop. She caused this urgency. She can soak it up.

"You're mine, Ava," I say, unable to stop my thoughts from rolling out of my mouth, my control gone. She closes her eyes, robbing me of the glorious sight of her brown orbs glistening in pleasure. "Open your fucking eyes," I demand, thundering on, sweat pouring, my heart back to hammering, but for all the right reasons.

I can see the effort it takes her to comply, but just the fact she does speaks volumes. The bedroom is my domain. I hold the power.

She crumbles under my touch, my mouth, my attention. I maintain our locked stares. I wouldn't be able to look away if I tried. So much is being communicated in this moment. Does she realize that? How much I'm saying as I fuck her into oblivion? This never ends. Not for me.

Her legs come up to my waist, constricting hard, sending me deeper and higher. I hiss, feeling her internal walls tightening. Fuck me, I'm a goner. In every way.

"Jesus, Ava, you okay?"

I'm forced to release her wrists, worried my strength and grip is hurting her. I smash them into the mattress, getting my balance without hampering my pace.

"Don't stop," she yells, grabbing at my upper arms.

"Fuck."

Her nails sink into my flesh, my hips buck wildly, and her head is tossed back. No. None of that.

"Damn it, Ava," I roar. "Look at me." She needs to see me.

Her eyes drop, and I feel beads of sweat trailing down my cheeks. I'm absolutely insane with adoration for this woman. What she can do to me. How she makes me feel. I want to kiss the living daylights out of her, and as if she's read my mind, she grabs my hair and yanks me onto her mouth, our tongues battling uncontrollably.

"Jesse, I'm going," she says against my lips.

"Fuck. Together, okay?" I find the strength I need to get us both there, pounding on, my dick almost sore with the friction. *Come on. Come on.* "Now!"

I sink in one last time, air gushing from my mouth, and I come so fucking hard, my sight fogs and my hearing distorts. "Jesus Christ," I blurt, stilling, clenching my eyes closed as I sustain the sensitivity, my body in spasm. I lose all strength, everywhere, my arms failing me, and I collapse, dripping wet, my hips gyrating without instruction, rolling, grinding, relieving me of the pressure. My forehead falls to hers, every piece of me useless. I'm done. Knackered. Good for nothing.

Fuck.

Me.

I feel her shift beneath me, and it takes everything in me to drag my eyes open. But, God, it's worth it when I find her. I use a bit more strength and pull back, wanting to get her entire sweaty face in my sights. Fucking beautiful. Every inch of her is beautiful. I sigh and kiss her swollen lips, before settling back into her neck again, the feel of her light fingers tracing the planes of my back making me sleepier. I give in to my exhaustion and space out, relaxed in her hold. Calm in her hold. At peace in her hold.

I don't know how long I snooze for, but it's the most tranquil snooze in the history of snoozes. This. Every day. And then in my subconscious state, I notice the soft feel of her strokes is suddenly gone. But I can still feel her hot walls hugging my dick. I lift my hips, hissing as I pull out of her.

"You sent me to sleep," I rasp, my throat scratchy.

"I did."

I smile and take a lock of her sexed-up hair. "You're too beautiful."

She reaches for my forehead and smooths out the frown line I hadn't realized was there. "So are you."

Me? No. I'm ugly. Marred. I don't ever want her to see that, don't ever want to disappoint her. My smile is half-hearted, and I pray she doesn't notice it.

I look at her boobs. Perfect distraction, for me and for her. I dive in, wedging my face in and taking a deep inhale. "Consider yourself reminded, lady." And I'm available to remind twenty-four/seven if necessary. Part of me hopes it *is* necessary.

I get to my knees and hold out my hands for her to take. She comes with ease, and I settle her on my thighs facing me, before moving myself up the bed to rest back against the headboard. Just look at her, magnificently naked and all over me. She looks good all over me. Attached to me. Touching me. I take her hips and circle my thumbs across the sensitive spot, smiling when she grabs my hands, stopping my movements. "Spend the day with me tomorrow." That was supposed to be a question, not an order.

"I have things planned."

Things planned? It's Saturday, so unless it's work, it can be canceled. And if it is work, I'll find a way to cancel it myself. I pout, hoping she caves into my cuteness so I don't have to convince her in another way that spending the day with me is quite compulsory. "What things?" I ask, starting to circle my thumbs under her hold. Another way might be tickling her to death until she agrees. Or I could just fuck her again until she agrees. A persuasion fuck, if you like. It'll work quite nicely alongside the reminder fuck, and she took to that quite well.

Her grip on my hands increases, her face warning. It's laughable. Is she trying to regain some control here, now I'm not buried balls deep inside her, blowing her mind? How quickly she forgets. Silly woman. "I need to sort my stuff out," she tells me, and I frown.

"What stuff?"

"Kate's place is temporary accommodation," she says on a little shrug, and my frown deepens. "I've been there for four weeks—everything is everywhere. I need to sort it out for when I get my own place."

Her own place? Maybe that's not necessary. But . . . . "Where were you four weeks ago?"

"With Matt."

"Who the fuck is Matt?"

"He's my ex-boyfriend."

And what the fuck is that inside now? Relief? "Ex?"

"Yes. Ex."

I'm unable to stop my body from softening. So she has an ex. Matt. *Of course she has a fucking ex, you dickhead. Look at her.* But how and why did it end? And does it matter now that it means I get her? How old was he? I snarl to myself.

"Jesse, I need to get my car. I can't leave Kate to drive Margo all the way to Yorkshire. She rattles and shakes all over the place; it won't be safe."

Margo? "Don't worry," I assure her. Who the fuck is Margo? "I'll take you to get it in the morning."

"She's leaving at eight-ish."

"Ish," I mouth, grinning, getting one in return. She likes that word. Translation: Not committed. So long as she doesn't use it when discussing us.

She shifts my hands a few inches, away from her tickle spot, and starts feeling around in her hair. I don't know what the fuck she's doing, but it's making her boobs thrust forward, and that's uncalled for. I scowl, and she smiles, probably wary.

"What?"

She knows what. "You refuse to spend the day with me, and then thrust those fabulous boobs in my face? That's not playing fair, Ava." I flick a nipple, my scowl transforming into a smile when it hardens. One fleeting touch. Her body responds in the most pleasing way.

"Hey," she yelps, covering her boob. "I need to take my grips out. They're digging into my head." She slips one between her teeth and starts feeling at her head again. I have an overwhelming urge to help her, so I sit up, taking the grip from between her teeth with mine and spitting it out. Now, back to the boobs. I hold her around her back and haul her onto my face, closing my eyes in bliss. I could stay here with her soft, warm skin all over my face forever. But . . . hairgrips. I begrudgingly pull out and give each nipple a peck before turning her around on my lap, letting her settle between my bent legs.

"Let me." I start feeling through her hair, pulling out the little metal things one by one, locks of her hair tumbling down with each grip I remove. "How many have you got in here?" I ask, dropping another into her palm.

"A few. I have a lot of hair to keep up."

"A few hundred?" I ask on a light laugh, finding more and more. I massage her scalp, ensuring I've caught every one. "There, I think I got them all." I relieve her of the grips, leaning over to place them on the nightstand, and then pull her back to my front, encasing her completely in my arms, ensuring she can't go anywhere. Her hands land on my shins and start stroking, her head limp against my shoulder. *God, I love how she touches me.* Her breathing pattern has changed. She's tired, but she still strokes me, and it makes me realize that it's been years since I've been touched with such gentleness and care. It's not a touch to incite sex, just gentle movements.

"How old are you?" she asks sleepily, and I laugh softly, wondering if she will ever let this go. Probably not. The fact she's asked twice in an hour is evidence that it's playing on her mind. And that hurts. It really does matter.

"Twenty-three," I reply quietly, running my hand through her hair, the silky, soft strands slipping through my fingers easily. I look down at the back of her head, swallowing, breathing in, trying not to think it.

But it's inevitable.

I'm terrified she's going to slip through my fingers. Walk away and take everything I've always craved with her.

Peace. Calm. Serenity.

Please don't walk away.

I reach down and pull the covers up over her waist before wrapping myself around her again, my nose finding its place in the crook of her neck.

And I decide here and now, with her warm in my arms, I need to do everything in my power to guarantee she doesn't slip through my fingers.

12

I'VE WOKEN up with plenty of women in my bed. I've woken up and cringed my way from under the covers. I've woken up and mentally shot my brain out. I've woken up and been desperate to get out into the fresh air to clear my head.

But I have never woken up with a woman in my arms. I've never woken up and immediately smiled. I've never woken up and thought *fuck it* to my morning run. Actually, I've never woken up and not felt like I *needed* to run.

This. Is. Unprecedented.

She's still, peaceful. I'm peaceful with her.

Bliss.

But then I feel her shift, and my arms lock down of their own volition. "Don't even think about it, lady," I mumble. I'm not moving, not for a long while, and neither is she.

"I need to use the bathroom."

"Tough," I grunt, probably unreasonably. But this is so nice. "Hold on to it. I'm comfy."

"I can't," she says, somewhere between laughter and exasperation, trying to pry my arms from around her.

I shrug her hands away with ease. I'll always win. She needs to get used to that. Especially when she is the prize. "I'm not letting go of you." *Not ever.*

Sensibly, she relents, and I smile on the inside, placing a kiss on her cheek before relaxing back again, my eyes closing. I could stay here all day. This is unbelievably amazing, just . . . being, but I feel her body solidify. She's going to try and escape me again? When will this woman learn? I move fast, spinning her onto her back, kneeing her thighs apart, and nailing her wrists to the bed.

Job.

Done.

Well, almost.

I push my groin into her, feeling the corners of my lips twitching. She's breathless. Staring up at me in wonder. One touch and she's mine. I mentally file that knowledge away and get down to the business of maintaining our bliss, as well as keeping Ava in her blindsided frame of mind. I'm lacking many things as a man —we won't go into details—but one thing I have on my side is my talent in bed, and I will wield that power to my advantage when I need to, no apologies. Like now when she needs to pee. She'll soon forget that.

I pout, dipping and circling the tip of my nose with hers. "Sleep well?"

"Very." She rolls her hips, and I pull back, my eyebrows hitting my hairline when she thrusts up. I try to contain my smug smile. Try. And fail. She wants me. She wants me so fucking bad.

"Me too." I glide my mouth across hers leisurely and softly, working her up, making her body beg for more. I'm lazy as I kiss her. Gentle, slow, and infuriatingly unrushed. But I don't need to rush. I have to keep reminding myself. She's seen the light.

And with that thought, I release her wrists and work my touch down her torso, feeling her writhe, buck, squirm. My tongue rolls languidly through her mouth, corner to corner, her moans constant, her palms on my arse trying to instigate my movements.

She gets her way. I lift, letting my dick fall into place. "I completely lose myself in you, lady," I whisper, surrendering her lips so I can watch her as I dive slowly and deeply into her. The vision. The pleasure on her strained face. The whimpers of indulgence. Her hands leave my arse and land on my back, her eyes closing. *Oh, no, no, no.*

I hold back from setting the pace, the willpower draining my lungs of air, every muscle locking down. Not until she's looking at me. I'm not moving until she looks at me.

"Look at me, Ava," I grate, my teeth about ready to pop from my harsh bite.

Thank God, she listens, giving me her eyes, and I gaze into them, feeling nothing but wonder. *Real.* This is all real.

She wants me to move, her hips flexing in invitation, and I sigh and talk my muscles into loosening, retreating from the heat of her pussy and driving forward slowly. The friction is a blissful torture.

"I love sleepy sex with you," I whisper, hoarsely.

She answers by thrusting upward, and I gulp, fighting to regain control when my dick jerks its delight.

"Is that good, Ava?" I keep our eyes locked, and she has no problem maintaining this level of intimacy.

"Yes."

"Faster?" I ask.

"No, just like this, please, just stay like this."

Good answer, and highly satisfying, because she's consumed by this moment too. Now, *this* is making love. And that is exactly what I'm doing. Literally. Creating love. Fuck me, what I felt last night wasn't a whimsical throw-away thought. As I feared, it was a very real, very serious thought. I always believed it would be impossible to love again. Now I feel it's impossible *not* to love this woman. Cupid has rammed his fucking arrow through my heart, the sadistic bastard, and reminded me that I do, in fact, have one.

I feel frustration grip me, and I try in vain to shake it away. Ava's legs come up and circle me, her touch feeling like it's getting lighter.

Love.

Should I cut my losses now? Minimize damage control? Because how the fuck could this woman love me back?

Fuck.

I stop moving and gaze at her confused face. So beautiful. "Enough of the sleepy sex," I declare, pulling out and ramming back into her brutally, letting my frustration take over. She cries out.

Damn my fucking history.

I retreat, smashing forward again.

Damn my stupid fucking choices.

I draw back and hammer home.

Damn my fucking life.

Bang.

Damn my weaknesses.

Bang.

Damn my darkness.

Bang.

Damn my black fucking soul.

Bang.

I take pleasure in Ava grabbing my hair and pulling it, take comfort in the pain. And when I kiss her and she bites my lip, I will her to bite harder. Hurt me. Make me suffer here and now, but please, *please* accept me. My hips work overtime, pounding into her, my head ready to explode with the pressure of my thoughts *and* my pleasure.

"I'm never letting you go," I say as I kiss her wildly.

"I don't want you to."

I still, the words knocking me out of my hysteria. She doesn't want me to. *Listen to her, Ward. Don't doubt it. Cut the self-sabotage bullshit.* I look at her, and she withdraws, looking away, telling me I've failed to wipe the irritation from my face. Damn me.

"Look at me now, Ava," I order harshly, wishing I could control this frustration. It's not her, it's me. All of this is me. I force my face to relax, to soften and hopefully ease her. "We're going to have this conversation when you're sound-minded and not crazy with lust." I find my pace again and get us back on track to our morning highs before I let my crazy thoughts ruin it. But there's the problem. They're not crazy thoughts.

Shit, kiss her.

I let my mouth plummet to hers, struggling for air. Unable to breathe steadily.

Is it panic?

Pleasure?

Both?

My eyes close, and I concentrate, whimpering like a fucking baby when she strokes through my hair. "I'm going to come." So damn hard. "Come with me, Ava. Give it to me."

I up the ante, hitting her cleanly and precisely, hammering away the negativity. And then she screams. And I jerk. "That's it, baby." And my dick detonates, filling her to the fucking brim, my release coming and coming, not letting up, not relenting, not giving me a second to catch my breath. *Oh, my fucking God.*

My muscles call it quits and leave me collapsing onto the bed in a heap on top of her. "I don't know what to say," I murmur quietly, shell-shocked.

And it would appear she doesn't either, because she's silent, and it starts to get slightly uncomfortable. Again, my fault. All my thoughts, my mood, my harsh words when she said something I really wanted to hear.

"Can I use the bathroom now?" she asks, wriggling beneath me. I sigh, sliding out and falling to my back on the bed. *What have I done?*

She slips out of bed and walks quietly but hastily across the bedroom, and my eyes don't leave her fleeing form until she shuts the door behind her. The only reason I'm letting her go is because she's headed to the bathroom. Had she tried to leave, I can't promise I wouldn't have dragged her back to my bed like the caveman I appear to have become.

"Fuck," I hiss, grabbing a pillow and smashing it on my head repeatedly until I'm at risk of splitting the damn thing and sending goose feathers everywhere. I toss it aside and look at the bathroom door. What is she doing in there? What is she thinking? *Stupid, Ward. So fucking stupid.* I growl at myself and slump into the mattress, arms splayed.

I hear the chain flush and drop my eyes to the door. She appears, awkward as hell. "I should go. Kate will be wondering where I am."

Make it right! "Maybe I'd like to keep you here." So I say that? Jesus, I need to get myself a fucking psychiatrist fast before I fuck this chance up good and proper.

Her questioning face is warranted. Poor thing looks completely lost. Goes for me too, because since she escaped my bed, I feel like my arms have been ripped off.

"She needs my car," she goes on, ignoring my statement, as she should. Because it's unreasonable. "Will you take me?"

I drag a smile from nowhere and mentally vow to pull myself into line. "What do you say?" I ask teasingly.

Her grin is like a pressure release in my head. "Please."

I jump up. "Good girl. Give me five." I land a smacker of a kiss on her lips as I pass her to the bathroom, keeping our lips touching as I walk back. She moves with me, prolonging it until we're in the doorway.

Back. In. The. Game.

Now I just need to ensure I stay in front.

I wretch myself away, and she staggers forward a little, dazed, breathless, and flushed. I leave her exactly like that, grinning as I turn and flip on the shower. I'm fully aware I'm rushing, eager to get back to her and make the most of the time I have left with her today. Which isn't fucking long. But I need to be patient. Don't crowd her too much. I laugh at myself as I grab a towel and dry off, not bothering to trim my stubble. It'll take up valuable time. I throw on some shorts, a Ralph polo, and flip the collar up as I assess myself in the mirror. I look younger. Fresher. Alive. It's no wonder. Last night and this morning, minus that little blip, was the most incredible experience.

I fetch my phone and my mood dips in an instant when I see endless missed calls from Coral. I need to block her number. Maybe even get a restraining order. *Fuck my life.*

I go in search of Ava, finding her crouched on the floor in the kitchen. She looks up. Practically drools. My chest expands. I'm smug. *Yeah, I thought I looked good today too.* Younger. Hotter. It's Ava. The effects of Ava.

I quickly pull my swelling head out of my arse when I realize what she's doing.

"I need to go," she says, her hands full of glass.

For fuck's sake, has she no regard for her well-being? I inhale my annoyance, swallowing it back. The last thing I want to do is leave her on a bad note. No. I'll be leaving her to wish all day that she hadn't been a stubborn minx last night and refused to spend the day with me. "Here." I dip and cup my hands for her to transfer the shards to me before I tip them in the sink. "You should have left it, Ava. You could've cut yourself." I brush my hands off and grab my shades. "I'll sort it later." I take her hand, get my keys and her bags, and lead her out.

"Are you working today?" she asks, and I grimace.

"No, not much goes on at The Manor during the day," I say, wiping away yet more annoyance and flipping her a cheeky wink. I don't know where the fuck that came from. Why the fuck am I winking? Probably to stop myself from growling. I don't want to go to The Manor. I want to spend the day with her.

I open the door and find the removal men outside. "Mr. Ward?"

I walk Ava past them. "The boxes in the spare room go first. My housekeeper will be here shortly to assist with the rest. Be careful with the ski and bike equipment."

"You have a housekeeper?" Ava asks.

"She's the only woman I couldn't live without." Literally. "She's off to Ireland next week to visit her family. It'll all fall apart then."

"Fall apart how?" she asks, and I throw a smile back at her.

"I'm not the most domesticated man in the world." Will that be another reason to add to her list of reasons to repel me? Does she want a house-trained bloke who will cook, clean, and iron? I laugh to myself. Every modern woman wants that. But surely bedroom skills trump domestic skills? And if it doesn't, it should. Because I'm a master of former, and I'm pretty fucking certain Ava will agree. "I'm better at sex," I mutter to myself, returning my attention forward.

I help her into the passenger seat and put her bags in the boot before jumping in beside her. "Sure I can't convince you to spend the day with me?" I dazzle her with an irresistible smile, reaching for her knee and gently caressing it.

"I'm sure," she says slowly, narrowing her eyes, taking my hand and removing it.

I scowl playfully, but deep down it's a thorough, pissed-off scowl.

Stubborn.

. . . .

When we pull up outside Lusso, I get out and breathe in the clear air, looking up the front of the building. I've got a good feeling about this place. I get Ava's bags out, passing her purse before I load the others in her Mini, all the while my mind spinning with potential ideas to change her mind. I don't know when I'm going to see her again, and I have a horrible feeling she'll keep me hanging. I turn and find her attention on her phone, and I sink my teeth into my lip, thinking. *What to do, what to do?*

She looks up. Stills. Takes me in. Then visibly shakes herself out of her awestruck state. God, she's infuriating. She opens the door of her Mini and slips in, but before she can pull the door closed, I'm crouched beside her.

"I'll take you for lunch," I declare surely, mentally daring her to refuse. Just lunch. A few hours to break up my day.

"I told you, I've got stacks to get done."

Fuck's sake. "Dinner then," I try.

"I'll ring you later."

Everything in me sags, most of all my heart. What point is she trying to prove here, other than she's a defiant pain in the fucking arse? I know she wants to see me. "Are you refusing me?" *Yes, Ward, didn't you hear her?*

"No, I'll call you later."

I reach for her thigh, a tactical move, and then lean in and kiss her into oblivion. Another tactical move. "Make sure you do," I order, rising, leaving her dazed, and walking away, smiling to myself. I can feel her desire smacking me in the back as I go. "Have a good day, dear," I say to myself.

"How old are you, Jesse?"

My smile drops. Are we really going to do this again? After last night, she's still thinking about that? I pout, turning, but I keep moving, walking backward. "Twenty-four," I call.

She noticeably sags. "How many times have I got to ask before we get to your real age?"

I'm not cocky enough to be insulted. Clearly, I'm not twenty-four. "Quite a few, lady," I say, flashing a cheeky grin as I turn and stride away. *Quite a few.* She'll keep asking, but how long can I evade?

I jump in my car and roar off, mentally planning my day. It needs to pass quickly so I can call her tomorrow. That's if she doesn't call me first. Will she call me first?

My phone rings and I sigh. Back to real life. "Sarah."

"Where did you disappear to last night?"

Like she needs to ask. "I spent the night with Ava." I don't beat around the bush. She'll see the spring in my step when I get to The Manor anyway.

"Oh," she breathes, and I frown as I cruise down The Embankment. She *is* surprised? "Jesse . . ."

"Don't do it, Sarah," I warn, my tone automatically deadly. Talk about a drastic change in mood. Not only am I being deprived of Ava for a guaranteed twenty-four hours, but I also have to deal with endless shit that makes me feel like shit—while being deprived of the one thing that doesn't make me feel like fucking shit. My fists clench around the steering wheel. "I'll be there soon." I hang up and put my foot down, blowing out my annoyance.

The moment I land in my office, I get straight on my laptop and look up a member of interest in the system. I dial the number we have on record and relax back in my chair, drumming my fingers on my desk.

"Hello?" Her accent sounds thicker over the phone.

"It's Jesse Ward," I say, and I hear her surprise in the form of a subtle inhale. "Hope you don't mind me calling." *And picking your brain to bits.*

"Of course not. How are you?"

I didn't call for a pleasant catch-up. The last time I saw this woman, she was naked in my bed when I woke up. I need to get to the point before she assumes—or hopes—I'm calling for round two. "I'm good," I reply, trying to keep it pleasant. "You?" I stop drumming my fingers, listening carefully. "I've not seen you around here for a while." I cringe the second I say the stupid words, but I need to know what the deal is with her husband. I'm mentally praying to every god in existence that the reason she's not been around here lately is because they've made amends and Van Der Haus has promised to keep his dick in his pants. And in return, she'll steer clear of my establishment.

"I've been in Denmark," she says. "Visiting my mother."

"And your husband?"

"Is a disgusting womanizer."

I sag in my chair. I don't need to ask anymore.

"We're getting a divorce," she goes on. I want to cry on the inside. I saw the way Mikael Van Der Haus looked at Ava.

A low, rumbling growl works its way up from my toes. I have to know what I'm dealing with here. "Does he know?"

"About us?"

Why do women say that? Us? Like there's more to it than a good fuck? "That we've fucked, yes."

"Why do you ask?"

I close my eyes, my head heavy, my fingertips ironing out the creases on my forehead. How do I answer that? Do I tell her I've recently acquired a woman whom I've become a little obsessed with, and I'm concerned that her slimeball husband will find out and exact revenge? Would Ava be attracted to him? Lord, she's getting her knickers in a twist over *my* age, and I know Van Der Haus is at least mid-forties. But he's got that smooth, suave thing going on. And an accent. All refined and gentlemanly. I inwardly pout. I can be a gentleman.

When I want to be.

One thing's for sure, though. He won't be a snitch on me in the bedroom. So why am I starting to sweat? "I ask because I don't want The Manor being dragged into your mudslinging match in court." Because make no mistake, she'll be trying to rinse him dry. Do I need to remind her of the contract?

"Don't worry. I would like to retain my membership, thank you."

My lip curls. Great. "So?" I prompt.

"He doesn't know you tied me up, gagged me, and fucked me from behind, no."

I flinch in my chair. "Good to know," I murmur, beginning to feel drained already, and I've only been here five minutes. "Good talking." I hang up and pull up Ava's number. Call her. Just to hear her voice. Just to level out my mood. I look down at my Rolex. It's only been an hour since I left her. Too much?

I drop my forehead to my desk, giving it a good whack, my phone clenched in my fist. I give that a good whack on the desk too. All she had to do was spend the day with me. It's not too much to ask.

There's a knock on the door, and someone strolls in. I remain slumped over my desk, but I manage to lift my head a bit to see who. John looks over his glasses at me. Shakes his head. And leaves without a word.

I pull my laptop closer. Flowers. Send her flowers. Loads of flowers. I need to constantly send her flowers or books or . . . anything, just to remind her I'm here. Or one flower. The flower that reminds her of me. *Understated elegance.* I smile, relaxing back in my chair, seeing her in my mind, gazing at me as she accepted the single calla. How much more will she accept? The flowers, yes. My body, yes. This unrelenting need to see her every day? I hope so. My Manor? I gaze around my office, my eyes falling on the cabinet that's still loaded with alcohol. My history? I swallow, my hand naturally resting on my lower stomach. *History, Ward.* It's all history. And it'll stay that way.

I dive back on my laptop to order the flowers, looking up when Sarah strolls in, her eyes on her phone. I snap my laptop shut. "You're here," she says without looking up.

"I'm here," I confirm, wishing I fucking wasn't. "What's happening?"

She glances my way. Definitely recoils. "You look . . . stressed."

I stand and round my desk. It's this place. Obviously I can't deal with it when I'm sober. "I'm moving today," I say lamely, passing her. "A lot on my mind." I haven't once thought about the fact that I'm moving today. Not once. I need to call Cathy. "How are the rooms coming along?"

Sarah follows me, her heels clicking the floor. That irritates me too. "All of the beams are now reinforced. What about the designs? How are they coming along?"

Good question. I need Ava back here, and not just to design. Close. Keep her close. She's young, beautiful, ambitious. It's only a matter of time before a more suitable match comes along and sweeps her off her feet. A younger, unbroken man. I frown. Not happening. "Great," I lie, as we pass through the summer room. "And the anniversary party?"

"Invites have gone out."

Our annual glamorous shindig/gigantic orgy is four weeks away. I'll confess to Ava before then. Tell her what this place really is, and then she can come. Be my date. Obviously, she won't leave my side. Or step foot in the communal room. I nod agreeably to myself. Four weeks. I can do that.

"How was last night?" Sarah asks as I take the stairs.

I look over my shoulder, finding what I knew I would. Curiosity. "The launch? You should know, you were there." I round the gallery landing, heading for the new wing. I am not talking to

Sarah about Ava. I might say something I regret like yesterday and be forced to apologize by guilt.

"She doesn't know what goes on here, does she?"

My teeth scrape together. "Not yet." If she laughs, I can't promise I won't lose my shit. "But she will," I add, wondering how the fuck I'm going to tell Ava. She thinks I'm a hotelier, for fuck's sake.

"Planning on keeping her around, then?"

I stop just shy of the entrance to the new wing, turning to face Sarah. "I need you to back off."

Her face softens. That pisses me off too. "I'm just looking out for you."

"I don't need you to look out for me, Sarah." I motion up my tall, well-built frame. "I'm a big boy, in case you haven't noticed."

She looks at me tiredly. "You're vulnerable."

I laugh. "What?"

"In case you've forgotten, you're a bloody millionaire, Jesse. And she's a lot younger than you."

I wince, disgusted. "Are you insinuating she only wants me for my money? Kick me in the gut, why don't you?" I motion down my body. "This body is the most desired around these parts, so take your conclusion on Ava's intentions and shove it up your tight arsehole." I turn and stalk off, hearing Sarah laugh as she follows.

"This arsehole isn't very tight after last night, actually."

I grimace, pushing my way through the final door. "Too much information," I say, but at the same time, I smile, remembering last night, the kitchen, the bedroom, the ecstasy. Ava's flushed cheeks. Her wonder. How easily she accepted me into her body. All positive signs. But what about her heart? Will she accept me into that?

"I'm just pointing out the obvious," Sarah goes on. "As I'm sure many will."

I sigh, deflating. Many can go fuck themselves. Besides, it's a moot point, because Miss O'Shea has done everything she could to resist me. Too bad for her, I'm irresistible. And persistent. If she was interested in my money, she would have jumped into bed with me at the first opportunity. She's not like that. She's different from what I know, and that's just making her more wonderful. "Do me a favor, Sarah," I say, inspecting the finished beams. "Stay out of my relationship with Ava."

"So it's a relationship?" she asks, shocked. "You? In a relationship?"

My shoulders drop. I can't be affronted. It is quite amusing. "I'm done here." I leave, finished for the day. "I've got to collect Cathy from my rental."

"What about the membership renewals I put on your desk?"

"Get John to deal with it." I can't think straight, my mind bouncing between deep-rooted fulfilment and contentment, to dread and self-doubt.

I need a distraction, and I'm not getting it here.

13

CHRIS THE PRICK meets us at Lusso to give me the codes I need for the gates and elevator. He definitely has a spring in his step. Apparently, the concierge isn't in until tomorrow so security will be covering and I should request a code change ASAP.

After seeing him off, I take Cathy up to the penthouse, smiling at her constant sounds of awe. "I've bought the essentials," she says, wandering into the kitchen and opening the fridge. She starts pulling out jars of peanut butter and setting them on the shelf. "But you'll have to do a supermarket run for other supplies." She shuts the door and smooths a palm over the countertop, then tuts, rubbing her fingers together. "This won't do," she mutters, magicking a bottle of kitchen cleaner from her bag and attacking every surface in sight. I'm glad. There were dozens of people here last night, and I'll be glad to have all their fingerprints cleaned off my . . . home. Not a rental, not a crash pad. A home.

I leave Cathy to it, placing her bags on the side and heading for the lounge. Boxes are stacked everywhere, and I blow out air, wondering where the fuck I start.

"When do you go back to Ireland, Cathy?" I call, grabbing a random box and pulling off the tape.

"In the morning, boy," she says, and I sigh. The boxes just keep appearing—in corners, under tables, behind the couch. "We'll get as much done today as we can. Then you'll have to survive without me until I'm back."

I crouch and pull the box open and immediately wish I hadn't. Of the hundreds scattered everywhere, I picked this one? My heart squeezes as I pull out a framed photograph of Jake and me. My eyes sting. My throat clogs. He stares at me, his eyes twinkling madly, his smile bright. Alive. And like I'm not sad enough, I pull out another picture. A little girl gazes back at me. My hands start to shake, my vision blurred.

"Jesse?" Cathy asks softly, and I quickly clear my throat, scrubbing at my cheeks roughly. I look up at her, and she smiles sadly. I can't take it. I stand and take the pictures to the nearest sideboard, pulling a drawer open and slipping them away. Jake and Rosie don't deserve to be hidden, but I just can't right now. Cathy doesn't murmur a word. Never does. She knows better than to raise a conversation I never want to have.

"I'll start on my wardrobe," I say, making my way up the stairs. I don't go to the wardrobe. I head straight into the bathroom and close the door, roughly wiping at my cheeks as I sniff back the suffocating hurt. God, I miss them. Every fucking day.

I fall back heavily against the door, my head in my hands, my palms squeezing my temples in an attempt to push the visions away. *Alcohol.* Drink it all away. Fuck your way through the pain. "Fuck," I breathe, my eyes landing on the vanity unit.

Ava.

She's everywhere in here. She's everywhere in the whole penthouse. My heart kicks. Jesus, I've got it bad. Whatever *it* is.

I meant what I said. I knew that once I'd been intimate with her, she would be mine. She better believe it.

I suddenly jolt forward, courtesy of the door being pushed from the other side. "Yo, Jesse, my man, you in there?"

I clear my throat. "Yeah." I move back as Sam swings the door open. He looks as crumpled as always. "Christening your new loo?" he asks, grinning.

No, I was having a minor breakdown. I pass him and pull one of the suitcases onto the bed. The obscenely colossal bed. She'll be in it soon.

"Fuck me, man, this place is something else," Sam says, poking around in my bedroom. "I can see why you'd sack off The Manor." He lands on my bed, arms and legs spread.

I pull out a pile of jeans and take them into the wardrobe. "Where's Drew?" I'm mentally planning an impromptu house-warming as I find a home for my jeans, just the three of us. Here. Tonight. It'll keep me busy for a while longer until it's acceptable to call her.

"He's at work this morning. Said he'd be here later." Sam appears in the doorway, his hands stuffed deep in his pockets. "You okay, mate?" he asks, his concerned eyes running up and down my form. "You look . . ."

If he says I look stre—

"Stressed," he finishes, cocking his head. "Come on, tell Uncle Sam."

I laugh under my breath, welcoming Sam's attempts to lighten my mood. "You're thirty. Stop talking to me like you're double that." I edge past him into the bedroom.

"What's going on with the pretty little interior designer?"

I stop at the bed, searching for what to tell him. "Nothing." I take out a stack of black T-shirts, hearing him chuckle to himself. "So you came here last night to network, did you? Offer free memberships to The Manor?"

I frown and face him. "How did you know I was here?"

"John," he says, and I scowl. "I'm worried about you, man. You've not been around The Manor much this past week. Every-one's talking."

"Let them talk." I go back to the wardrobe. "Nothing is going on with the interior designer."

"Sure," I hear him say on a sigh. He hands me a stack of gray T-shirts, and I avoid his eyes as I accept them, setting them in a drawer below the black ones. I'm not sure why I'm being so cagey. Or maybe I do. Sarah's reaction stung. "So what's the plan?" he asks.

"Unpack, eat, and chill the fuck out."

"High five," he sings, raising a hand. I leave him hanging but nudge his shoulder playfully as I pass, spiking a chuckle.

"Jesse," Cathy calls. "Jesse, where the flaming heck are you?"

"Master suite," I yell, zipping up the first empty case and setting it aside as Sam retrieves another.

"Ah, there you are. It's like finding a needle in a haystack," she says, taking out her duster and having a quick polish of the door handle. "A man called. I answered the little phone thing by the door. There's someone here to see you."

I look up sharply. "Who?"

"A lady. I told him not to let her up because I don't know who it is. She's waiting in the foyer." She tucks her duster back in her apron, and I silently thank her for being so cautious.

"Name?" I ask, feeling Sam's interested look on my profile.

"She wouldn't say."

"Fuck me, they've sniffed you out already." Sam laughs as he starts unzipping the second case. "Or could it be the interior designer?"

"Shut up, Sam," I mumble, giving Cathy an appreciative rub of her shoulder as I pass, heading downstairs.

"Interior designer?" Cathy asks, with way too much interest in her tone. "Who's the interior designer?"

"She's the interior designer," I call as I take the stairs, hearing Sam laughing again. Ava's one of the only people who know where I live now. Could it be her?

My pace increases and the journey down in the elevator is the longest of my life, but it gives me some time to reason with myself. Of course it's not Ava. Why would she withhold her name? Or . . . does she want to surprise me?

The doors open. My hope builds.

And dies.

Mikael's wife gets up from one of the chairs. "Jesse," she says.

"Freja," I breathe, my legs unwilling to carry me out of the lift. "What are you doing here?" Stupidest fucking question ever asked.

She approaches, cautious, as she should be. "Can we talk?"

"What about?"

"Us," she says, coming to a stop outside the lift.

"There is no us, Freja." I back up, reaching for the button, but her hand comes out and stops the doors from closing.

"Why the call this morning?"

"I told you why."

Her head cocks, her blonde hair falling over her shoulder. Her eyes look glassy. Sad. And damn my heart for feeling these days. I breathe in and step out, motioning her to one of the chairs in the foyer while checking we're alone. The flowers I sent Ava catch my eye, still sitting pretty on the concierge's desk. My nose wrinkles. They should be in Ava's bedroom. She should be looking at them and thinking of me.

Freja sits, looking suddenly hopeful past her sadness, and I resign myself to spelling it out. I take the chair opposite her, having a quick rub at my forehead. "How do you know where . . ."

"You live?" She's looking at me like it's a stupid question, because, of course, it is. Her soon-to-be ex-husband is one of the developers of this building, and I bought the fucking penthouse.

I lean forward, resting my elbows on my knees. "You need to

pretend what happened never happened," I say as softly as I can. Lord knows, there are plenty of men around The Manor ready to tie her up if that's what she wants. I just can't be one of them.

"Easy for you to say."

She's right. It is, and I'm in no position to question why that is these days. "I won't be around The Manor as often as I used to be." *Or drunk like I used to be.*

"Why?"

"I have other interests filling my time at the moment." Listen to me. Other interests? Who do I think I am? I sigh, flopping back in the chair. I'm no good at reasoning with women. They can't be reasoned with.

"May I ask what?" she presses.

"No," I reply flatly. "Freja, The Manor isn't a place you go to find love. It's a place you go to fuck."

"I'm in love with you now?" she asks, her shoulders straightening. "Who said anything about love?"

"So you just want me to tie you up again, do you? Because there are hundreds of members of The Manor prepared to do that. Are you going to show up at their homes asking to talk?"

She wilts a little, looking away, and I find myself rubbing my forehead again. "Freja, concentrate on you for a while." *What am I, a fucking life coach?* I laugh to myself, standing from my chair. "I have visitors."

Freja rises, slinging her bag onto her shoulder, refusing to look at me. I feel like shit. Being sober brings on too many emotions I don't know how to deal with. She turns and walks away, head held high, trying to claw back some self-respect. The door is pulled open from the other side, and Drew stands back, letting her through, ever the impassive gentleman. His eyes follow Freja's path, a heavy frown falling into place.

He recognizes her. Great. "Hey," I say, pulling his attention to me. I've never known a man to look constantly and consistently pristine. He's been at work all morning and looks like his suit has just come back from the dry cleaners. And his hair? Not a strand out of place. His blue eyes look tired though. "Late night?" I ask, strolling to the elevator. Every night is a late night for Drew.

"What was she doing here?" he asks, catching up with me and getting in the elevator.

"It's not what you think."

"It's never what anyone thinks," Drew says flatly. "So what was she doing here?"

"She's in love with me."

Drew scoffs. "It must be so tough being a stud."

I dazzle him with a smile that could light up the building. "Want some tips?"

"Fuck off." He rolls his shoulders, pulling at his suit jacket, and I laugh. I've made myself clear to Freja. It's one less thing to worry about amid the dozens of things for me to worry about. I only have to hope Mikael doesn't find out I slept with his wife, find out I'm seeing the pretty interior designer who I just know he has his eye on, and tell said pretty interior designer that I slept with his wife. Actually, it's not so much that I slept with his wife, as I didn't know Ava then. Mikael knows what The Manor is and that's bound to come up in conversation with Ava. Jesus, he might even think she's a member. Sexually adventurous. Open to a come-on from him. *Jesus.*

So, yes. Mikael cannot know about Ava and me.

"If anyone around here is giving tips," Drew says, "it's me."

I'm about to ask if he has any tips for a clueless man who thinks he might have found *the one*, but then I remember who I'm talking to. Drew wouldn't know love if it slapped him around the face with a dildo. The man's impenetrable. Probably more clueless than I am. And definitely kinkier. In fact, he's pure filth.

Says the man who fucked a woman up the arse with no prep to test her boundaries and feelings for him.

The lift opens and Drew's out, leaving my frowning form tucked away in the corner. I wasn't testing her boundaries. Was I? I shake my head, following behind my friend. No, I was testing how responsive she is to me. How much she trusts me. How much she's into me. Her acquiescence. Because one thing I know is that if a woman wasn't majorly into a man, she definitely wouldn't let him take her arse. Unless, of course, she was a member of The Manor. Which Ava isn't.

"What a total pit," Drew says, completely deadpan, as he walks through the lounge to the kitchen. "And do yourself a favor and get rid of Coral." My eyes widen as I follow him into the kitchen, finding him with his face in the fridge. "Peanut butter? Is that all you've got to offer?"

"Step away from the peanut butter," I warn as the door is slammed in disgust. I barge him out of the way and open it again, helping myself to a jar. Fucking hell, I'm beginning to feel stressed again. I whip off the lid and dive in. "What happened with Coral?"

Drew rests his arse against the counter. "Steaming drunk. Again."

"Last night?" I ask, and he nods, his face in his phone. "Sarah didn't mention it."

"Sarah didn't have to deal with it. She was busy in the communal room. John dealt with her. Took her home."

"He didn't mention it," I muse, slowly sucking my finger clean, thoughtful, as Drew taps away at the screen of his phone. Why didn't he mention it? I need to know this kind of shit.

"He said he didn't want to trouble you." He looks up, tucking his phone away. "Said you've got enough on your plate." His head tilts. "Anything to do with a pretty little interior designer?"

I shove my finger in the jar and into my gob, buying some time. What can I say? Luckily, I don't have to say anything. Sam rounds the corner into the kitchen with Cathy in tow, their hands full of cleaning stuff. Their timing is impeccable.

Drew looks on, horrified. "I'm not cleaning," he declares, and Cathy laughs. "I came round to chill the fuck out before I go let off some steam at The Man—" He snaps his mouth shut, eyeing Cathy.

"At The Manor, dear?" she asks on a laugh, dumping her bucket on the counter. She pulls one rubber glove off, and it snaps, piercing the air. "Think I'll fit in?"

I fall apart laughing, as does Sam, and Drew's eyes widen dramatically. "Like a dream," he murmurs, giving me a pleading look, like, *get me the fuck out of here.*

"Now," Cathy says, giving us all a moment of her eyes. "How about I cook you boys dinner before I go pack for my trip?"

"Where are you going, Cathy?" Sam asks, settling on a stool.

"Ireland, dear. Visiting family for a few weeks."

"A few weeks?" He looks at me. "You'll be missed, I'm sure, since Jesse's suddenly decided to move out of The Manor."

I scowl, and Drew looks at me with interest. "Fuck you," I snap, having one last dip of my vice before replacing it in the fridge. "I'll survive just fine." I go to Cathy and give her a kiss on the cheek. "Thank you for the offer, but you should get home to pack. I'll drive you."

"You're a good boy, Jesse." She gives my cheek an affectionate rub before taking a bottle of bleach and leaving the kitchen. "I'll just finish the bathrooms."

"So, what's the plan?" Sam asks, clapping his hands together and rubbing. "Oh, and who was the visitor?"

"No one," I answer.

"Freja Van Der Haus," Drew pipes in, holding back a rare smile, motioning to my brooding form. "She's in love with bighead over there."

"Same day, different story," Sam mutters, going to the fridge and opening the door. "Peanut butter? Is that all you've got to offer?"

For the first time, I notice both the boys have turned up empty-handed. I turn questioning eyes onto them. "You didn't bring any beers?" I ask. They always bring beers.

Sam looks at Drew. Drew looks at Sam. What's going on? "I'm driving," Drew announces. "I said I'd be at The Manor later."

"Yeah, and me."

"Get a cab," I suggest. They usually do.

Both my friends start shifting awkwardly, and the penny drops in my lagging brain. "You're fucking kidding me," I say, stalking past them and grabbing my keys. "I'm going to the shop to get you two dicks some fucking beers." I can't be pissed off with them. They're friends. Good friends. "And I'll drop you at The Manor later myself."

"Why's that?" Sam calls. I look over my shoulder, finding him smiling mildly.

"Because I'm not drinking," I answer, disappearing around the corner to the door.

"And why's that?" Drew yells.

I don't bother answering them this time. I don't need to. I'm a mug if I believe they're not onto me. Maybe later I'll open up to them. Talk. Get their thoughts.

I laugh. Only pussies discuss woman prob—

Wait . . .

Have I got woman problems?

14

IT WAS good to spend time with the boys somewhere other than The Manor for once. Really good. We tucked into a takeout dinner, talked like women, and laughed. Their help in distracting me was more appreciated than they'll ever know. Or perhaps they do know. Of course they know. But alcohol isn't the only thing I'm trying to avoid. I'm also trying my fucking hardest *not* to call Ava. I wouldn't want her to think I can't let her breathe.

I could tell both Drew and Sam were itching to get their deprived arses to my place of pleasure after a few hours of humoring me in my new home, so I drove them over. I didn't go inside. I dropped them off in the driveway and got my backside away from there before any more women came crawling out of the woodwork. I may have driven past Ava's place on my way home. I may have stopped and looked up at the window where the light was on. I may have imagined her in bed. Was she in bed? What was she doing? Surely being cuddled up with me would have been better.

You cuddle now, Ward?

I drove back to Lusso with a moody face and fell into bed. And I stared at the photograph of the boats for an eternity, constantly wrestling with my mind's demand to call her. Just call her. Or text her. Text her and tell her you're thinking of her.

I fell asleep with the soft sound of her laugh haunting my dreams.

On Monday, I wake up in a foul mood. Yesterday was pure hell, spent kicking my heels around my new place, constantly fighting with my swaying mind. Call her. Don't call her. Text her. Don't text her. Honestly, it could have driven me to drink. If this is her playing hard to get, I fucking hate it. It's stupid. And pointless. So today things change. She's had enough breathing space. And since, apparently, I need her to keep myself breathing comfortably, I'll be seeing her today, whether she likes it or not. I'd rather she likes it, of course.

After my morning run, I shower, change into my finest gray suit, and take myself to the bookstore I googled earlier. I pay, then take myself to the nice florist lady. I write a note, smiling the whole time, and give her specific instructions and an address. I leave feeling rather pleased with myself. See? A gentleman. Romantic. I can do that.

When I arrive at The Manor, I find John in the bar. He looks like he's about to go on a slaughtering mission, his face cut with irritation. I'm almost afraid to ask. "All right?" I say lamely as I perch on a stool next to him.

"Fuck you, motherfucker." He necks a water, turning to face me, and looks up and down my suit as I balk at him. Then he jerks his head in the general direction behind us. I crane my neck and find Coral on one of the bench seats, her face squished into the plush material. "Sort it out," he hisses. "Because I ain't fucking here to deal with drunken love sick women." He slams his glass down, and I flinch. "If you don't revoke her member-ship, I will."

Well, welcome back to The Manor.

I exhale tiredly, slumping over the bar. I need to stay away from Coral or she'll get the wrong idea. I look back again when I hear stirring from behind me. Shit, she's waking up. I can't be here. I get up and hurry out of the bar, hearing John cursing his arse off behind me. "Sorry, mate," I mumble. I'm very fucking tempted to let Sarah loose on Coral if this carries on. *For fuck's sake.* I reach up to my forehead and rub away my frown lines. I must have aged ten years in the past week, and aging isn't something I need to be doing anytime soon when I'm trying to woo a twenty-something woman.

I see Sarah at a table in the summer room with another lady, looking over some brochures. "Ah, here he is," she says, jumping up from her chair.

"Indeed he is," the woman muses as she gets to her feet, her tits definitely pushing out, her smile coy. "Mr. Ward, what a plea-sure to see you again."

Again? I've never seen her in my life. Sarah must catch my frown because she saves me from insulting the woman, who looks pretty fucking delighted to see me. "Chrissie helps me plan the anniversary party each year."

I still don't recall her. Jesus, I really am looking at the world through new eyes. Sober eyes. "Nice to see you again." I blast her with my smile. Literally. She staggers back, taking hold of the edge of the table. "I'll be in my office."

"I have piles of contracts I need you to sign."

"I'm only here until five," I call back, having decided to collect Ava from work. Like I said, enough is enough. I'm going stir-fucking-crazy. Friday night feels like it was another life ago. "Make the most of me until then."

"Why? Where are you going?"

To heaven. "Home."

If Botox weren't a thing, Sarah would be scowling right now.

By five, I'm both relieved and agitated. Relieved it's time to go pick up Ava, even if she doesn't know I'm picking her up, and pissed off because the florist confirmed delivery of my gift and I've not heard one peep from Ava. No call to thank me. No text. Nothing.

I drive back into the city like a madman, my foot naturally heavy on the accelerator, my Aston beautifully responsive. *Bundle her in my car. Take her home. Get her into bed. Ravish her.*

I pull up down the road from her office, having to double park with the lack of spaces. I'm not driving around the block; I might miss her leaving. I'm about to cross over to go meet her when a bright pink van virtually shakes its way past me. I'd recognize the redhead behind the wheel anywhere. Fuck me, the fumes coming out the exhaust pipe choke me. I cough, flapping a hand in front of my face to waft away the smoke.

It stops outside Ava's office, and the next thing I know, she appears. "Ava," I call, but a dickhead in a Merc zooms past, honking his horn, and I jump out of his way. *What a cock.*

By the time I can cross the road, Ava is clambering into the passenger side and the pink thing is banging its way up the street. "For fuck's sake," I mutter, watching as it takes a turn onto Berkeley Square. I run back to my car and jump in, pulling off fast, earning a collection of hand gestures and horns from various motorists that I cut up in my urgency. "Fuck you," I hiss, skidding away. "Fuck you all."

I spot the pink monstrosity on the other side of the square, its indicator blinking to take a turn.

I have absolutely no shame or regard for my fellow drivers. Now *I'm* the cock, as I undertake them, weave in and out of them, all the while wondering where Ava and her friend are going. That damn van looks like a death trap. She better have her seatbelt on.

I twitch, a stressed sweat coming on, no matter how hard I try to reason with myself. I've been looking forward to seeing her all fucking day, and now I'm on a wild goose chase across London, trying to catch her. I take a sharp left, seeing the van up ahead in the traffic. There's no chance of me losing it; I'll just have to follow the cloud of smoke it's leaving in its wake.

I tail them all the way to Belgravia, nowhere near Ava's home, only increasing my curiosity. It turns into a street, and I start impatiently smacking my wheel, willing the Sunday driver in front to put his fucking foot down, at the same time checking ahead in the road for a chance to overtake him. I spot a gap and zip out, slamming my foot on the accelerator. The sounds of horns ring out everywhere as I zip back into the right lane, just missing an oncoming car. I reach up and wipe my brow. Fucking hell, that was close.

The turn the van took comes up on the left, so I indicate. *Good boy.* Check my mirrors. *Good Boy.* See the lights up ahead turning to amber.

Fuck.

I can make it. I can make it.

I put my foot down and spot a little old lady step into the road, oblivious to the Aston speeding toward her. "Fuck!" I slam on the brakes and brace my arms against the wheel, my face screwing up in dread, my eyes partially closing. The sound of my wheels screeching stabs my eardrums, and I eventually close my eyes completely. I wait for it, the sound of her hitting my bonnet. But it doesn't come.

My car stops.

I gingerly open one eye.

And exhale, seeing the old lady still crossing the road, in a world of her own. She's got to be deaf. And perhaps a bit blind

too. I blow out my cheeks, relaxing my arms and glancing around.
The looks of disapproval come at me from all directions. *Yeah,
yeah. I know. Total twat.* I take a moment to breathe, working my
heart rate down. I can't see her again if I'm dead.

Dead.

I flinch.

Slow the fuck down.

The lights turn green, and I pull into the tree-lined side street
and come to another stop. "For fuck's sake." I crane my neck to
see what's holding up the traffic. The pink van is stationary in the
middle of the road. Broken down? I wouldn't be surprised. I scan
the street for somewhere to park. Nowhere. The gods seriously
aren't playing ball today. "Fuck this," I mutter, pulling over and
parking as considerately as I can. My phone rings as I get out. I
consider, only for a second, ignoring John. But he's already
fucked off with me. "John," I say as I start pacing down the street
toward the van.

"Where the fuck are you?" he asks.

*Trying to get myself killed just so I can find out where the fuck
the object of my affection is goi*ng. "Shop," I mutter. "Then
home." *To remind the object of my affection how amazing we are
together.* "Why?"

"Get your arse here and deal with this shit, Jesse. I've had it
up to my motherfucking eyeballs."

"She's back already?" I ask, my eyes unmoving from the van,
the scream of car horns hurting my eardrums.

"She never fucking left, so get your shirking motherfucking
arse here and sort it out or I'm out of here."

My sigh is heavy. I'm tired of this bollocks, but I know when
John is serious and he's serious now. Enough is enough. *Fucking
Coral.* My mood takes a nosedive as I slowly accept that I *need* to
deal with the remnants of my past. Freja is sorted. Now it's
Coral's turn. I just hope no more women pop up and declare their

undying love for me. Unless it's Ava. That would be fine. "On my way," I confirm quietly before I hang up, feeling my mood lift when I spot Ava by the side of the van. I stop. Take her in. Grin from ear to ear. *There's my girl.*

But my smile falls like a rock when I see a man up in her face, yelling, making her back into the side of the van. Then he grabs her arm.

He grabs her fucking arm.

My blood goes from cool to red-hot in a nanosecond, my head ready to explode. "Get your fucking hands off her!" I bellow, breaking into a sprint. Mother of *God*, what is this rage inside me? I have the urge to kill, and that bald fucker holding Ava is going to sate my urge. I see Ava look up, followed by the guy, who quickly releases her and backs off.

Wise man.

But I'm still gonna kill him.

His eyes get wider the closer I get, and I crash into him, taking him out, tackling him to the ground like a rugby player and giving him a few jabs on his nose, ignoring the sound of it cracking. *You call this being a gentleman, do you, Ward? Calm the fuck down, for fuck's sake. You'll be locked up. Then you'll never get to see her again.* "Get off your fat arse and apologize," I yell, wrestling his fat body up from the road and thrusting his alarmed form in front of Ava. I can't appreciate the shock on her face. I'm too shocked myself. "Apologize," I bellow. *Or so help me God.*

He stammers his apology as I shake him, hoping to shake my rage away too. It's not subsiding. I feel lethal.

"Lay a finger on her again," I breathe, getting my face close to his ear, "I'll rip your fucking head off. Now, fuck off." I release him before I do more damage and grab Ava, if only to occupy my hands.

The turmoil and anger within settles in an instant. Gone. Like it was never there. And then I feel her body jerk and hear the muffled sounds of her sobs, and that anger returns. "I should have finished the bastard off." I look over my shoulder to check he's gone, praying he has for his own sake. "Hey, stop the tears." I can't bear to hear her cry. "I'll get crazy mad." *Because you're not already, Ward?*

"Where did you come from?" she asks, looking up at me.

Ah.

Umm . . . "I . . ."

"You followed me, didn't you?" she asks over a gasp, her body tensing.

I have no other choice but to step into defense mode. "And it's a good job." God knows what that creep would have done if I'd not intervened. "Where's Kate?" Just as I ask the question, she appears, asking what's going on.

Can't she hear the fucking horns? *Keep your cool.* We'll be dealing with the van matter later. "I think you need to move your van, Kate."

She looks up the street, her shoulders jumping up, as if she really couldn't give a shit that she's holding up London with her heap-of-crap van. "Oh, okay."

I shake my head, pulling away from Ava and checking her over. Her feet are bare. "Where are your shoes?"

She brushes at her nose. "They're in the back of Margo," she says, motioning to the pink van. I frown. *Margo?* "The van," she explains.

Margo's a van? I've heard it all. Well, she'd better say goodbye to Margo because she isn't going to be around for much longer. I dip and scoop Ava up, taking her to a wall and placing her on it. "I'm not even going to ask how they got there," I say, convincing myself, wisely, not to add to my grievances.

"I'll get them," Kate declares, and a few seconds later she's handing Ava her heels. I focus on those and those alone. They're very nice heels. Would look lovely around my neck.

I leave Ava slipping them on and go to the van, yanking the door open. "What the fucking hell?" I say, taking in the mess inside. It's filthy, magazines and coffee cups everywhere. This thing is ready for the scrapyard, which is exactly where it's heading. I drag Ava's bag off the seat and make my way back over, seeing the girls talking quietly. What are they saying? My man brain wants to know, but they both shut up as I near, Kate looking cautious. I can only imagine my face is still burning red.

"Kate, you need to shift that van before war breaks out," I say as Ava gets to her feet, wincing. I frown. "I'm taking Ava with me."

"You are?" Ava asks, sounding shocked.

"Yes, I am." She shouldn't defy me on this. It seems I've got a temper where she's concerned, and I'm not afraid to use it.

Kate smiles, moving in and kissing Ava before sauntering off. I can't find it in myself to say goodbye or even look at her. I'm too busy wondering why the fuck Ava winced when her arse met the wall.

"Why are you flinching?" I ask brusquely as she stands again. And winces again.

"My backside hurts." She claims her bag. "I was holding Kate's cake up in the back of Margo."

The back of the van? Wait. "You didn't have a seatbelt on?"

"No." Her eyeballs roll into the back of her head in an epic display of mockery. "You don't get seatbelts in the backs of vans, Jesse."

For fuck's sake. Reckless *and* sarcastic. Neither suit her. I growl and pick her up, mentally lining up a very stern conversation about safety and cynicism as I head back to my car. She doesn't argue or insist on walking. Good. I've had enough of being pissed off today. Now? Now I just want to lose myself in her. And I can't. I fucking can't, which means any chances I had of not being pissed off for the rest of today have gone up in smoke.

Ava's head meets my shoulder, and she clings on, her entire being relaxing in my arms. God, I would carry her anywhere she wanted to go. I needed this. Her acceptance of my presence. *Her.*

My heart is back to beating steady and strong. "You didn't call me. I told you to call."

"I'm sorry."

"So am I."

"What are you sorry for?" I feel her curious eyes lift to my face.

"For not being here sooner," I say quietly. "Don't do stupid shit, Ava. And call when I tell you to." I sound petulant. It's unstoppable. But if this relationship is going to work, someone needs to be reasonable.

And it isn't me.

Instinct told me to insist she spent Saturday with me. Instinct told me to call her yesterday. Instinct told me to call her today. Instinct told me to intercept her outside her office before she got in that fucking van. *Fuck the cock in the Merc. He better hope he doesn't meet me in a dark alley.* If I had done any of those things, she wouldn't have been roughed up by that bald prick. The course of events leading to that moment would have changed. She wouldn't have been so distressed. She wouldn't have felt pain when he grabbed her. She wouldn't have sustained a barrage of abuse. And I wouldn't have had a million heart attacks.

So I vow from this moment, I won't hold back from doing what instinct tells me. If I'm going to remain sane, it's necessary.

Like I should have trusted my instinct over twenty years ago when Jake sucked down that last drink.

I flinch and inhale. I should have trusted my instinct.

My legs become heavy, and it isn't because I'm carrying Ava. I make it to my semi-abandoned car and deposit her carefully in the front seat, pulling the seatbelt across and securing it, giving it a tug as I raise my brows at her, as if emphasizing the need to wear it. She doesn't roll her eyes externally, but I can tell she's exasperated on the inside. Tough. Like I said, she'd better get used to it.

When I hop in beside her, my hand goes straight to her knee and remains there the entire way to Kate's place. She's quiet, and my mind is racing with what she could be thinking. But regardless of her silence, she seems . . . settled. Happy I'm here.

I pull up to the curb by her friend's house and look up at the window. How long does she plan on staying here? Because I have a huge place with just me rattling around in it. Wouldn't it make sense?

I'm snapped out of my thoughts when I hear her open the door, so I get out and round the car, swooping her into my arms again. Her weight is perfect. Her head at the perfect level for me to smell her hair. Her arms go straight around my neck, and I walk up the path, damning everything to hell and back. We shouldn't be here. We should be at Lusso. In my bed. Naked. High on each other.

"I can walk," she says over a laugh, but I ignore her, negotiating her body to take the keys from her hand. She doesn't need to walk with me around. *Look after her. Keep her safe.* I open the door, kick it shut, and succumb to the inevitable, placing her on her feet and pulling her into me. My mouth finds hers. It's like everything that's ever troubled me drifts away into a haze of nothingness, and there is only me. Me, her, and this incredible kiss. I exhale happily, my eyes closing, feeling her welcoming tongue circling with mine. The way she holds me. Her peaceful sigh. Don't tell me this is a dream. Don't tell me I might wake up.

"Thank you for the book," she murmurs around my mouth, and I smile, breaking our kiss and looking into her eyes. Does she know she's my peace? Her touch is magic, the effect she has on me so settling.

"You're more than welcome." I kiss her again, her mouth a magnet.

"Thank you for saving me."

My smile is unstoppable. "Anytime, baby." But there will be no need to save her again. *But what about from you? Can you save her from you?*

I wince back those thoughts as Kate bursts through the door. She eyes us. Mouths an apology. Then shoots up the stairs, leaving us alone. There was a happy twinkle in her eye. I laugh under my breath, my groin pushing forward against Ava, my forehead meeting hers. Her breathy pants warm my face, her eyes glistening. "If we were alone," I whisper, feeling every part of her body responding. It's incredible. *One touch.* "You would be against that wall, and I would be fucking you stupid." My appetite for this woman is ferocious.

"I can be quiet," she breathes, applying pressure where it counts, begging for me. "Gag me if you must," she adds, and I inwardly balk. Gag her? No. Listening to her scream and moan is one of my new favorite things.

Her desperation for me is reassuring. I grin, thoroughly pleased with myself. "Trust me," I murmur, "you'll be screaming. No gag will stifle it."

She inhales, her body beginning to vibrate. Jesus, tomorrow I'm going to eat her alive. No question. "Now, tomorrow." Let's make some arrangements to ensure my sanity. "I'd like to make an appointment."

Her eyebrows raise. "An appointment to fuck me?"

I laugh loudly, the sound pure and rare. I like this Ava. Accepting Ava. Willing Ava. "I want you back at The Manor so you can take the details you *really* need to start working on some designs." And then I will fuck her. Make love to her. Kiss her. Cuddle her. Eat my fucking dinner off her.

My body responds to the very thought, and I'm taking her mouth again, getting everything I can before I have to leave and sort out Coral. My kiss hardens, frustration aiding it. I rip myself away and breathe down on her dazed form. "I don't make appointments to fuck you, Ava," I murmur, making sure I'm clear. "I'll be doing that when I please." Whenever, wherever. That's something else she must accept.

I look toward the stairs, wishing Kate away. Luck isn't on my side today. "The Manor at noon." I have to touch her just one more time, stroking her flushed cheek as she nods her agreement. "Good girl." I give her one last affectionate kiss on her forehead, marveling at the heat of her skin for a moment, then I have a brief argument with my legs before they relent and carry me away. I close the door behind me and drink in air, placing my hand on my chest to feel the consistent, steady beat.

Alive.

I'm so alive. And despite having to leave her, I'm blissful.

How does Ava O'Shea do that to me?

15

DREW IS COMING down the steps of The Manor when I arrive, and my pace falters slightly when I catch the expression on his face— a look of pure filth that could turn me to stone.

"I come here to relax," he snaps as he passes, annoyed as he opens his car door with a vicious yank. "It's like a fucking soap opera in there."

I look to the doors of The Manor, just as a female member, Natasha, breezes out. Her smile is instant as she struts down the steps, stopping before me. "Oh," she coos, resting the tip of her finger in the center of my chest and circling it slowly. "I'm just leaving, and you've just arrived. Shame." She blinks slowly, running her tongue across her bottom lip. I move back, out of her reach, shying away from her touch. It feels all wrong.

"What's going on?" I ask, looking away from her, finding my mate. His face is still screwed up in repulsion.

"I'm taking Natasha back to mine to relax." His head cocks. "If you get my drift."

Natasha brushes past me, pulling on her jacket. "Care to join us?"

I scoff. Never have I fucked with a close friend. And never

will I. "Have fun," I mutter, not needing to ask them why they're taking their pleasure outside the walls of The Manor. "For fuck's sake." I gingerly take the steps and brace myself for what I'll be faced with.

It's quiet. I glance around, listening carefully, not hearing any commotion.

Sam appears at the top of the stairs, fastening his fly, a smile on his face. I cock him a questioning look and take the few steps needed to get me to the bar entrance. I look through the doorway, seeing someone slumped over the bar, a tumbler of amber liquid in their grasp.

Mike.

I quickly backtrack before Coral's husband sees me. I need to know what I'm dealing with. "Drama," Sam says from behind me, and I sigh.

"Where's John?"

"Your office." Sam heads into the bar. "Put your armor on. He's not a happy bunny."

"Bunny?" I laugh, and Sam grins over his shoulder, settling on a stool next to Mike, whose head starts to lift with some effort. I make tracks to my office, wary, still looking around, still listening. It's quiet. Which means John has calmed the situation down or Sarah has sewn Coral's mouth shut.

I walk into my office and the first thing I see is the big man with a face like thunder. Then I see Coral on one of the couches, her face a tear-stained mess. And guarding her, Sarah, leaning against a cabinet, her arms crossed over her leather bodice, her lips twisted in displeasure. She shakes her head at me. "Glad you found it in yourself to return to sort out your shit," she spits, dipping and picking up her whip off the floor and stamping toward me. She stops by my side, looking up at me. "You need to get your priorities in order." She carries on her way, slamming the door with brute force. *Oh boy.*

"Jesse," Coral sobs, jumping up from the couch and throwing herself into my arms. I hold my breath, catching her, not at all comfortable.

"What's going on?" I ask John, who's rising slowly from the chair, removing his wraparounds to ensure I see the fierceness in his glare.

He raises his hands, holding up all ten fat fingers. "Number of members who canceled their memberships this evening."

My eyes widen. "Ten?" That's unheard of.

John steams past me. "Outside," he orders, swinging the door open, obviously not prepared to let Coral free from my office. I negotiate her dead weight over to the couch and ease her down, the smell of alcohol, both new and stale, wafting up, making my nose wrinkle and my eyes water.

She flops back against the cushion on a whimper, and I hear John growl, prompting me to follow him out of my office. He closes the door. Slips his shades back on. Stuffs his hands in his trouser pockets. I remain mute, waiting for him to give me a thorough dressing-down for all the things. Only John can.

"Coral was engaging in some activity with another male member this evening. Mike didn't like it."

My eyebrows rise, and I can't help but think this is a good thing. Coral's shifted her affections to another man? Great. This means she'll leave me alone. Right? "Okay," I say slowly, waiting for more information I'm hoping won't burst my bubble.

"Mike's asked me why Coral is still here, given he knows she's not meeting her contractual payments."

I cringe, resting back against the door. "Oh."

"He wants to know who's giving her the free pass."

"Oh."

"And she didn't mind telling him when they were screaming at each other in the communal room."

"Oh."

John's shoulders drop. "You are your own worst enemy, you stupid motherfucker."

"I know," I reply lamely, rolling my body until I'm facing the wall, giving my forehead a few deserved whacks.

"Coral thinks you have feelings for her, and now Mike does too."

Bollocks.

"So you need to make yourself clear. To both of them."

I hear the sounds of his heavy steps leaving. Leaving me to deal with the mess I've created. *Fuck my life.* An hour ago, I was on cloud nine. "John," I call, and he stops but doesn't turn around. "Miss O'Shea will be here tomorrow at noon."

"Miss O'Shea?" He spins around faster than his big body should allow, his lips straight. "Have you taken the poor, oblivious young woman to bed yet?"

I start shifting on my feet, dropping my eyes to my shoes. "What's that got to do with anything?"

His groan is epic, and he stalks back toward me, forcing me to back up until he's got me pinned to the wall by his deadly glare. I remain where I am out of respect. And because, despite his strange way of showing it, he cares. And he's always right. "It has everything to do with it." He throws his arm out to my office door. "In there is a woman who is head over heels in love with you after you merely fucked her. No emotions or feelings. Yet she loves you. *And* your infamous Manor." His other arm shoots out, pointing away from my office. "Out there, somewhere in London, is a young woman, *Miss O'Shea*, who knows fuck all about you. You're giving her a side of you no woman has ever seen before. A softer side. A committed side. A side that cares, even if it's driving you fucking crazy. And me, by the way. It's driving me fucking crazy too, because you're not thinking straight, you stupid motherfucker." He takes in air as my eyes increasingly widen. "That woman out there? She's falling in love with you, Jesse. Like every other fucking woman you've had. Except probably harder. Probably faster. And that"—he jabs me in the chest hard—"is plain fucking cruel when she doesn't know who the fuck you are."

"You think she's falling for me?"

His big shoulders drop. "I can't deal with your stupidity." He turns and walks away, and I nibble my lip, contemplating John's words. Is she? Falling for me? I let my head meet the wall behind me. I don't know. But I do know he's right. And I hate that. But everything he said is the fucking point of my silence. I have way more chance of keeping Ava if she's in love with me, especially when she discovers what this place is. Who I am. Where I've been, what I've seen. It's easy to fall in love—that I know for sure. It's hard to fall out of it, and that is my saving grace. Because having had this clean euphoria, there can be no going back. So I have to do what I have to do, and telling Ava what happens at my *hotel* isn't a priority right now. Making her unable to survive without me, however, is.

The door to my office swings open and Coral's eyes dart around, eventually finding me propped up against the wall. She goes to speak.

Then throws up at her feet.

I jump away. "For fuck's sake, Coral." The smell is instant, and so are my retches. And yet, I'm alone in dealing with this. It's my penance. But I'll clear up puke every day if that's my punishment. I can cope with that. It's far better than the alternative.

No Ava.

I lose my breath at the very thought, which is probably a good thing as I approach Coral, sidestepping the splattered carpet and taking her arm. I hold her up as I escort her to the couch, placing her back down. Her eyes roll. She grins, reaching and grabbing at thin air for me. There is absolutely no point trying to reason with her now. She won't remember a thing, and I'll only have to go over the same rigmarole again in the morning when she's coherent. So I lift her feet onto the couch before removing my jacket and rolling up my sleeves. It's time to stoop to an unbelievable low.

I leave Coral and go in search of a bucket and disinfectant. The surprise on my staff's faces is warranted as they watch me scrounging through the cleaning closet. "Can I help you, Mr. Ward?" the sous chef asks, venturing from the kitchen to find out what I'm doing around these parts.

"I need a bucket, Paulo," I say, moving endless things around on the shelves. "Any idea?"

"Let me get Rosa for you."

"Rosa?" I ask, stopping with my search and turning my attention onto him. "What's she still doing here?" It's knocking on eight o'clock. Way over the end of her shift.

"There was a mess that needed cleaning up in the communal room, sir." He looks wary as he tells me, and guilt flares inside. Someone else suffering the consequences of my poor decisions. I should clear up that mess too.

Paulo disappears to find Rosa, and I continue with my search. I'm not familiar with the cleaning closet and isn't that fucking obvious now. I can't find shit. "Fuck's sake," I mutter.

"Since when have you become Mr. Domestic?"

I look over my shoulder and find Sarah. "Still talking to me, then?" I ask, returning to my search. "Where the fuck is the antibacterial stuff around here?"

Sarah nudges me out of the way and pulls down a bottle from the top shelf. "Need to cleanse yourself?" she asks, handing me the bottle.

She's about as funny as the vomit all over the carpet outside my office. "Bite me," I snap, squirting a bit in her hair before stalking off.

"Mr. Ward," Rosa says, hurrying through the kitchens toward me. "Let me, let me."

"It's fine, Rosa. I can deal with it. You should get off home."

She snatches the bottle from my hand, giving me a fierce look. "I do," she snaps, her Spanish accent thick, "my job." She magics a bucket from nowhere and starts filling it with hot, soapy water.

I turn to Sarah. "Give Rosa a raise."

"Fine. Where's the loony bitch?"

"In my office."

"Do you want me to put her in your suite?"

I frown. "No. I don't want anyone in my suite ever again."

"Why?"

"I just don't, Sarah." I walk away. "She can stay on the couch in my office until she's sober." Then we'll be having some serious words. This ends now.

John is outside my office admiring the pile of puke when I get back. "I'm getting it sorted," I growl, taking the door handle, keen to escape before I have more brutal—truthful—words thrown at me.

"Jesse."

"What?" I don't face him.

"Have you thought this through?"

"I've thought of nothing else, John," I assure him. "Trust me, she's on my mind constantly."

I feel his hand meet my shoulder, and I look out the corner of my eye, seeing his big fingers gripping me lightly. "I hope she can accept you."

"She has to," I say, turning to face him. "Because what's the alternative?" He knows what the alternative is. It's alcohol and wasting my life away with meaningless woman after meaningless woman. Looking as pathetic as Coral. Hopeless. Irreparable.

"A woman more on your wavelength, perhaps?" His words are too soft for such a big, mean-looking bastard.

"On my wavelength?" I ask on a laugh. "You mean like Sarah was to Uncle Carmichael? Because that turned out well, didn't it?"

We both flinch. "You've got to stop blaming yourself," John grates, his anger rising, the subject guaranteed to spike it.

"How can I, John? It was my fault."

"No." He takes both of my shoulders in his big palms and shakes me. "You deserve more than this self-sabotage."

I can't agree. I don't deserve more. I just need some good in my life. Some peace. Some fucking forgiveness. I rest my hands over his and smile mildly. "Maybe Ava is the *more* you speak of," I say, throwing his words back at him, and given what he's just said, he can't possibly challenge me. And his body shrinking slightly tells me he knows that. "She makes me feel good," I say, lifting his hands. "I don't deserve her, but I want her." I let myself into my office and rest my back against the door, leaving John on the other side, probably with his head in his hands. I've always expected too much of him. And it would be too much to expect him to understand. I realize I'm merely replacing alcohol and an unhealthy, hedonistic lifestyle with something else. That itself is unhealthy. Ava and me, though? Together? That's glorious, and it feels so incredibly right. My dependence, however? I know that's not right. Or healthy.

I sigh wearily and take myself to the free couch, kicking off my shoes and watching as Coral flips her body over and snuggles deeper. She's going to feel like hell in the morning. Worse still after I hit her with reality. I get comfortable on my back and fold my arms behind my head, propping it up, tiredness taking hold.

This is the last night I will spend without Ava.

End of.

16

HER HEAD IS BURIED in my naked chest. Her palms are resting on my shoulders. My arms are wrapped around her waist. She's nervous, and I don't know why. But I do know it's making me edgy. "What's wrong?" I ask into her hair, brushing my nose through the strands, taking comfort from her natural scent. She clings to me tighter, as if she can't bear to let me go. "Ava, baby, tell me." I gently push her away and find her eyes. They're overflowing with tears. Tears of despair? Of joy?

What?

My heartbeat slows. I can't quite catch my breath.

"I can't be with you," she murmurs, her voice cracked and rough. She looks away, and my heart feels like it stops beating completely.

"What are you talking about?" I ask, taking her chin and forcing her to face me. I hate the desperation I see in her beautiful eyes. "We're perfect together, Ava. Me and you. We're perfect."

"I can't love you." She breaks away from me, getting up off the bed, leaving me a useless, stunned mess of a man. We just made love. It was beautiful, full of sentiment and tenderness. "I can't save you," she whispers, and I reach out for her, desperate

to pull her back, desperate to get her in my arms again. But I'm
grabbing at thin air. She's fading.

Fading.

Fading.

Gone.

My eyes snap open.

My chest constricts.

My body feels heavy, like something unshakeable is holding
me down. I can't breathe. *Fuck, I can't breathe.*

Air.

I need air.

I try to sit up, grappling at the back of the couch for something to hold on to. I can't move. "Fuck." My forehead's damp,
my whole body is clammy. *Why the fuck can't I move?*

"Morning," a groggy voice says, a face appearing above me,
hovering. Smiling. I blink away the fog and Coral's face comes
into view. I look down my front. She's straddling my waist, her
body naked, her hands working the belt of my trousers.

"What the fuck, Coral?" I croak, the feeling of suffocating
worsening. "Get the fuck off me." I push her away, firmly but
gently, scrambling to my feet. "What the hell are you playing at?"

She slumps back on the couch, half smirking, half indignant.
"You were dreaming."

I rake a hand through my hair, my body now drenched under
my shirt and trousers. I wasn't dreaming. It was a fucking nightmare, and reality is no better in this moment. "Get out," I seethe,
throwing my arm toward the door. "Now."

She shrinks back, shocked, but slowly stands, grabbing her
dress and holding it against her front. I turn away, my eyes bleeding, my hands ready to rip all the hair from my head. I feel dirty.
Tarnished. I hear the door to my office open. "No, wait," I shout,

facing her. She's halfway out the door, still naked, thoroughly wounded. I drop my eyes to the floor. "Get dressed," I say more softly, my palm sliding onto my nape and massaging away some of the tension as I turn away from her. "We need to talk."

The door closes, and I hear the sounds of her shuffling into her dress. I look to the ceiling, exhaling. This is not how I planned on spending my morning. "Coral, this needs to st—"

"I've told Mike I want a divorce."

I swing around, stunned. "Not on my account, I hope."

Her head cocks, her jaw tight. I can't believe she has the nerve to look indignant. After everything she's thrown at me? "You don't realize yet, Jesse, but you will. You and I are meant to be together."

"Oh, for the love of fucking God." I laugh, my head falling back. "Coral, how many times have I got to go over this with you?" I drop my serious eyes to hers. "I fucked you. In case you didn't notice, that happens a lot around here." I wave a hand in the air, deranged. "People fuck." I take a step forward, my jaw ready to snap. "And if you've read too much into it, that's your problem, not mine." I'm done with this fucking circus. I shouldn't even be here, and just the fact I am, dealing with her bullshit fantasy world, is only escalating my bad mood. I've tried. I've tried so fucking hard to be reasonable and compassionate. No more. "I'm not interested in you." It's not a slap in the face, but it's close. "Now get the fuck out of my Manor and do not come back. Understand?"

"Understand," she says through gritted teeth, dipping to slip her shoes on. Then she exits without another word, leaving me heaving in the middle of my office, feeling no less harassed now she's gone. "Fuck!" I yell, bracing my hands on the edge of the drinks cabinet and working hard to cool myself down. Obstacles. At every fucking turn, there's an obstacle waiting for me to fail. *And why the fuck is the drinks cabinet still here? Stocked?* My gaze lifts to a bottle of vodka. "Fuck you," I spit, pushing myself off the wood and stalking to the door. I need a shower. A fresh suit.

I need her.

I also need to run.

I go up to my private suite and change into some shorts.

And I run. I run until I can no longer feel my legs and my head is full of nothing but racing-hot blood.

But, of course, as soon as I stopped running, the unwanted tension came right back. Someone needs to call the fucking shrink, because I feel like a need a sedative. I shower, change, and land at my desk. I order flowers for Ava, relaying exactly what I want written on the card, and pay extra to have them delivered before eleven, which is when she'll be leaving her office to come see me. That brings a little smile to my face. Then I tackle something that's been bothering me since I saw Ava get into that shit heap, bone-shaking van. I spend a few hours trawling the Internet, but after coming up with nothing, I call a local dealership, tell them what I'm looking for, and express my thanks when the salesman ensures me he'll find something suitable. "Make sure it's pink," I say before hanging up.

I glance at my Rolex. Did time ever tick by so fucking slowly? I get up, walk circles around my office, sit down, stand up, pace some more. *Not long*, I tell myself. Then I can relax. She can get her work done, I might even sit and watch her, and as soon as she's finished, I'll take her home. I drop my head back. "Make time go faster, please," I beg, fishing around in my pocket when my phone dings. And then I nearly throw up all over it when I read the message.

Cancel?

She's canceling on me? "I don't think so," I say, smacking the dial button, pacing some more. "Pick up, Ava. Don't do this to me." It goes to voicemail. "Fuck!" I hammer out a text.

Cancel for what?

I take a seat on the couch, having to put my fucking head between my legs to remedy my dizzy spell. What kind of pussy am I? I feel sick. Injured. Panicked.

My phone dings, and I scramble to get it. I literally cannot believe what I read. "Give you time?" I've given her loads of fucking time. Time that's felt like centuries. "This is too intense?" I go on. "Too quickly?" I stand, my eyes rereading it over and over, my heart sinking more each read. "It's also fucking amazing, Ava," I whisper, taking my phone and pushing it into my forehead, clenching my eyes shut. I am not going back to square one. No fucking way. I dial her again, and it goes to voicemail again.

And again.

And again, and again, and again.

"Fuck this." I stride out of my office, the floor shaking under my feet from the impact of my determined pace. People clock me. Move from my path. Wise people. All except John, who blocks the doorway out of The Manor.

"You're going to do something stupid," he says, widening his stance, standing firm.

"Move," I growl, and it's a fucking surprise, but he does. Albeit slowly and with a despairing sigh.

I get in my car and skid my way down the driveway, dialing Ava on repeat, and each time it goes to voicemail, I curse and smack my steering wheel.

The traffic is diabolical. It matches my mood. I spend over an hour stopping and starting, not seeming to get anywhere fast. "Come on," I growl, poking the nose of my car out of the traffic every now and then to try and see what the holdup is. I'd get there faster walking at this rate, and I'm not opposed to doing that. She needs to cancel. Needs? She doesn't *need* to do anything. She wants to. Why? After everything, why? I yell my frustration, looking at my dashboard when my phone rings.

"What?" I bark down the line to Sam, pulling out of the lane again but quickly zipping back in when I see a bus coasting toward me. The driver sounds his horn, flipping me the finger as he sails past.

"Good to hear your voice," Sam quips, and my lip curls at the bumper-to-bumper traffic ahead. I'm not in the mood for his happy-go-lucky disposition today. It's been a shitstorm from the second I opened my eyes—even before, actually—and the one thing that was guaranteed to improve it has canceled on me. "Where are you?"

"Stuck in traffic," I grunt. "On my way into the city." To talk some sense into someone. Or maybe I'll fuck some sense into her.

"Yeah, traffic's shocking today, mate."

"Did you just call for a chit-chat?"

"Fuck me, who's shat in your coffee this morning?" he asks, and I roll my eyes, giving my horn a few irritated smacks.

"Sam, what do you want?" I ask.

"I'm meeting Drew for a lunchtime pint."

"That's nice," I say, full of sarcasm. "You two lovebirds have fun."

"We would, but he's just called me to cancel. Something about sealed bids and a deadline."

"I haven't got time for a quick pint." I'm too busy going crazy. And has he forgotten I'm not drinking? Although, admittedly, I could really fucking do with one right now.

"That's not why I'm calling. You wouldn't believe who's in here."

I frown. "Who?"

"Your pretty little interior designer and a particularly fiery-looking redhead."

I sit up straight in my seat. She's having lunch with Kate? She canceled *me* to have lunch with her friend? "What bar?" I ask, edging out again, seeing the line of cars up ahead beginning to move.

"Baroque on Piccadilly. So, who's the redhead?"

"Kate. She's not your type."

"She looks very much my type from where I'm standing," Sam muses. I'd laugh if I was in the mood. Sam's type drops their knickers at the drop of a hat. Usually at The Manor. I don't know Kate all that well, but I get the feeling she'd play hard to get. A bit like her annoying friend.

"I've got to go," I say when the traffic finally breaks, giving me space to put my foot down. I hang up on Sam and overtake the car in front, my Aston screaming. It's not the only thing.

I make it into the city *finally*, park illegally, and stalk my way to the bar, hammering out a text as I go.

There better be a GOOD fucking reason for you standing me up & needing time isn't one. Someone had better be dying. I'm going out of my fucking mind, lady. NO KISS

I push my way into the bar and find her immediately. And as if it's backing me up, my heart starts galloping. It pushes all reason out of my mind. It makes me resent her more for depriving me. Sam's at the table too, flashing his cheeky smile left and right.

I'm glad he's providing the comedy. I'm about to provide the angst.

Ava stands, collecting her bag and phone, as I heave like a

gorilla behind her. I can see her profile. She's smiling. And doesn't that just wind me up more? What the fuck is there to smile about?

She turns, still smiling.

Sees me.

Stops.

"Who's dead?" I bellow, stunning her. "You don't get to fuck me off, Ava."

She blinks, looking back at her friend and Sam, seeming lost. Like she doesn't know what to do. As if she thought I'd happily accept her piss-poor excuse for standing me up and not come after her.

"I have to get back to work," she eventually says, dropping her eyes and passing me, hurrying out of the bar. *What the fuck?* Didn't she note how rattled I am? Didn't she consider for a moment how to change that?

"Jesse," Sam says, pulling my confused form around to face him. He cocks his head in question. "Breathe, man."

Breathe? Yes, breathe. But when I try to drag air into my lungs, my chest goes tight. And there's the problem.

I leave Sam and Kate in the bar with alarmed looks on their faces, going after Ava. I spot her on the pavement, her stride fast, her hair bouncing across her back. She rounds the corner onto Bruton Street and arrives at her office door too quickly for my liking. I'm about to call out to her when she zips inside, and I laugh out loud, part disbelief, part infuriation. She thinks she's safe from having to face me? She thinks I won't go right on in there and bring her back out? This woman needs to remember that when it comes to her, I have no shame or boundaries.

Apparently.

I burst through the door, stalk to her desk, and catch her before she can take a seat, throwing her over my shoulder. Her squeal makes my damn fucking cock twitch. Even blood-boiling mad, I'm still hard for her.

"What the bloody hell are you doing?" she shouts as I pass her colleague's desk, his eyes wide as he follows my path. I get her outside and find a suitable wall. "Jesse, fucking hell! Put me down now!"

I cringe. Good lord, won't she stop cursing like a fucking sailor? I reach back and start to slowly ease her down my front, making sure every inch of her front slides across every inch of mine. With my arm wrapped around her waist, I hold her off the ground, our noses nearly touching, my raging erection pressed in her lower stomach. *You feel that, baby? That's for you, even if you don't fucking deserve it right now.*

She groans as my eyes dart across her face, drinking in every exquisite piece of her desire. I didn't need this confirmation. But I wanted it. What game is she playing?

She swallows and looks across to her office window, wincing. Fuck them.

"Mouth," I whisper, pulling her face back to mine. "You stood me up." I kiss her chastely, and everything inside of me softens. My world stabilizes. My heart announces its presence. And as I stare at her, my life seems to tunnel into an oblivion of her. All her.

She looks away, as if she can't stand the intensity of our eyes being locked. "I'm sorry," she murmurs. I'm sorry too. I'm sorry she keeps ping-ponging between acceptance and denial. I'm sorry she can't hack the whirlwind of our connection. I'm so fucking sorry. And frustrated. And lost. And, fuck me, dependent on what only she appears to be able to give me.

It's a shitty situation to be in. For me, *and* for her. But it is what it is. I've accepted it. It's time, once and for all, for her to stop fucking fighting it. Just feel it. *All* of it.

I slam my mouth to hers, swallowing her whole with my kiss,

my passion, my need. She doesn't deny me. She can't possibly when we're touching. A crowbar couldn't pry us apart, so Ava fighting would be fruitless.

I push my groin into her stomach hard, showing her something else she does to me. The irrational reactions are out of my control. My craving. My obsession. My frustration. "What do you need time for?" I ask, and she sighs on a mild shake of her head.

"To think."

Think? She needs to stop thinking. It'll drive her nuts like it does me. "Don't think, Ava," I say sternly. "This is how it is. Accept it." I force myself to break away, my dick aching, willing me to bury it inside her. Right fucking time, wrong fucking place. I reach out to steady her when she sways, my smile unstoppable. *Go on, baby. Deny it now. Tell me I don't turn your world upside down.*

She hisses in pain, and I recoil.

I drop her, stepping back, my eyes like lasers on the collection of bruises on her arm. My jaw goes into overdrive, my teeth gritting, my breathing going to shit once again. It's something else I can't control where Ava O'Shea is concerned. This newfound anger.

There are two instructions running on repeat through my head. Just two.

Find that bald prick.

And kill him.

She quickly covers the source of my rage, her hand settling over the marks. It's a pointless effort. They're imprinted on my mind. "I'm fine," she says quietly, shifting awkwardly before me. "I need to get back to work."

I stare at her, this beautiful, oblivious woman, and something uncomfortable shifts inside of me. Guilt. Except this guilt is unfamiliar, yet it hurts just as bad. It turns my stomach. It makes me want to punish myself. Knowing she's hurt kills me, whether physically or emotionally, and as I stand here, looking at the woman who has knocked me for six, I have the most unbearable realization.

I can hurt her the most. I've only ever hurt the people I've loved. I could kill her spirit. Her faith. Her trust.

That woman out there, she's falling in love with you, Jesse. Like every other fucking woman you've had. Except probably harder. Probably faster. And that is plain fucking cruel when she doesn't know who you are.

I try to ignore John's words. I can't. Because while I'm sure this woman can fix me, it could break her in the process. And, Jesus, I can't do that to her.

I move back, dazed, confused, and feeling even more broken than I have before.

She's a cure. I'm a disease.

Walk away. I should let her have the man and life she deserves. I'm not that man. And I can't give her that life.

My anger returns tenfold, and my feet carry me back, away from her, my body working in line with my brain. I can feel Ava's confused expression resting on me.

I. Am. Beyond. Help.

I was a fool to think even for a moment that Ava could save me. Because if saving me means breaking her, I'm out.

I blink, my eyes stinging, and turn, walking away from her.

I fight with my urge to look back, and lose.

She looks dazed. Confused.

It's better than fucking destroyed.

I don't bellow my despair to the heavens until I make it back to my car.

17

I DON'T REMEMBER my drive back to The Manor. Massive Attack played, and when *Angel* came on, I turned up the volume to its maximum, trying to drown out my thoughts and the image of her looking at me, lost and stunned.

I park my Aston haphazardly and walk up the steps of my manor on numb legs, my mind focused on the only thing that can get me out of this hell. I pace through the rooms, ignoring everyone I pass, and John comes out of my office with Sarah as I approach, his face grave when he sees me. I start shrugging my way out of my jacket and pulling my tie loose.

"Don't do it," he says as I pass him and enter my office. "Don't do it, Jesse."

"Why?" Sarah asks. "He looks like he needs to relax."

"Shut the fuck up," John barks, but I'm too focused to appreciate how angry he must be to talk to Sarah like that. He never talks to Sarah like that, no matter how much of a bitch she can be.

I head to the drinks cabinet and brace my hands on the edge, my breathing labored, my eyes scanning the bottles. "Leave me," I order, feeling John's presence still behind me. "Just leave me the fuck alone."

The door closes, and I continue to stare at the bottles, every shitty thing that's happened in my life running circles in my head, cruelly reminding me of my innumerable shortcomings. Of my stupidity. Of what I've lost and what I can never have. *Ava.* She's at the top of the list, but then there is also purpose, hope, peace . . . freedom.

Forgiveness.

None of those things will ever be mine.

My nostrils flare, and I swipe up a bottle, taking it to my desk and dropping to my chair, placing it in front of me. I can smell it. I can smell the relief, the numbness, the emptiness. I slam my palm into my temple, clenching my eyes closed. I see Jake. I see Lauren. I see Rosie. I see Carmichael. I see the knife, the alcohol, hear the hateful words.

The horror movie that is my life plays before my eyes, every unbearable detail, every awful moment.

And at the end, before the curtain falls, Ava's face.

The end.

I grab the bottle, unscrew the cap, and take it to my lips, swigging back the respite within my reach. I gasp, wincing, the burn fierce. *More.* I take it back to my mouth, glugging the vodka, determined to get lost in the bottle.

How old are you?

More vodka.

I'm never letting you go.

I don't want you to.

More vodka.

I'm going to get lost in you.

More vodka.

Once I've had you, you're mine.

More. Fucking. Vodka.

The seconds blur into minutes, and the minutes into hours.

Every moment painful. I work my way through the entire bottle, getting angrier with every recollection taunting me.

Every moment when I was offered wasted hope.

Fuck knows how long later, I glance out of the window, seeing the sun going down. I reach up with a wobbly hand to unfasten the top button of my shirt as I get up and go to the cabinet. There's a knock at the door. "Go away," I mumble.

More vodka.

I'm ignored, and the door opens. Sarah walks in, her eyes falling to the bottle in my hand. "Want some help unwinding?"

"No, I want to be alone," I snap, not that my drunken slur penetrates her thick skin.

She says no more and closes the door behind her, and I stagger to the couch, flopping down, the soft cushion feeling like iron against my pounding head. It's not pounding with the effects of alcohol. It's still fucking pounding with visions, memories, and fucking feelings. How much do I need to drink to make this all go away? Will it ever go away? Will I ever return to the welcome place of nothingness?

More vodka.

Restless, I get up and start pacing my office, my legs unstable, my big body swaying. Why the fuck am I still hurting?

More vodka.

Knock, knock.

"I said—" I look at my office door when it opens.

And stare at Freja Van Der Haus on the threshold.

She pulls the tie of her overcoat. Shrugs it off. My eyes drop down her bare body.

"Shut the door," I order harshly, placing my bottle on the cabinet as she obeys. I scrub my hands down my rough cheeks, wrestling away the fact that she looks nothing like Ava. At least twenty years older. More meat on her bones. Blonde hair. Too much makeup. She couldn't be any more different. "Come here."

She wanders slowly over, and even through my drunken eyes, I see her body lighting up. She stops in front of me.

Forget.

Eliminate her.

Do whatever it takes to free myself of this nightmare. And, more importantly, free Ava of me. And the daze of the alcohol kicks in—*yes, this is familiar.* A willing woman. No fight. *This. Is. How. I. Fuck.* It doesn't matter which pussy. Just a willing fuck. "Turn around," I say, my voice groggy. She slowly turns, looking over her shoulder coyly. She wants foreplay. A build-up. An extended session to blow her mind.

I haven't the inclination to please her, just the desperate need to escape. I grab a condom and clasp her neck with one hand, walking her across my office to the sofa, applying pressure, encouraging her to bend over as I unfasten my belt and yank my trousers open. My limp dick falls into my hand. I stroke it, willing it to life, begging it to harden, the strain and effort almost too much. I slip the condom on with some effort, and with my hand on her back, I guide myself to her wet, begging pussy and push my way inside her with no warning or consideration. She's ready. Always ready.

They always are.

I grunt, taking her hips, ignoring how wrong she feels. How wrong all of this is. She cries out, I bite down on my back teeth, and I start thrusting, my head dropped back, unwilling to look at her, unwilling to reason with myself. Fuck her hard. *Do what you do best, Ward.* I'm not capable of loving. I'm only capable of fucking. It's all I know, all I'm good for.

You deserve nothing more than this meaningless pleasure.

Leave your feelings at the door.

I bellow at the ceiling, starting to pound her hard, my fingers clawing into her hips. This isn't pleasurable. It's not serving its purpose. Sarah was right to laugh at me. To think I could have Ava. That's why she sent this woman here.

I feel a hand on my back and drop my head, looking over my shoulder. A seductive smile greets me. I growl, pulling free of one pussy, and drag the woman in front of me, bending her over the couch beside Freja and burying my dick in another on a yell. She screams her delight, her head thrashing around immediately.

Sweat starts to seep through my shirt, my face strained, my dick sore. I force my eyes to the woman's back. Then to Freja, who's watching, waiting for her turn again. I blink when her face starts to distort, my vision fuzzy, my brain feeling like it's smacking against the side of my skull as I try to bang myself free of my cage.

They're. Not. Who. I. Want.

Trapped.

"Fuck!" I bark, pulling out fast and swinging around, my hands delving into my hair. "Get out," I bellow, stalking to the door and swinging it open. "Get the fuck out!"

Both women scurry away, their faces expressions of pure shock, and I immediately hate myself more. They didn't deserve that. But I'm in no fit state to right my wrongs.

I slam the door behind them.

Punch it.

Bellow obscenity after obscenity.

Then I stalk to the cabinet, swiping my arms across the surface on a yell, sending the glasses and bottles crashing to the floor. I yank the mini-fridge open and grab a bottle of water, glugging it back manically. I toss it aside when I'm done, immediately grabbing another and downing it. Then another. Then another. I keep going, drinking water like it can cleanse me of the alcohol and my sins, bottle after bottle. My stomach eventually revolts, and I grab a bin, throwing up into it, coughing, spluttering, and retching.

I'm done.

But I'm not done.

I take hold of the cabinet at one end and drag the solid piece across my office, blocking the door, barricading myself in. Stopping me from leaving. And anyone from coming in.

Then I fall to my knees, my eyes welling with hopeless tears.

I can't escape. I can't be free of this self-sabotage. I'm my own worst enemy. A failure. The deadliest kind of poison. Out of my mind in all ways.

And hopelessly in love with a woman I can never have.

Or deserve.

"Why did I fucking live and they all died?" I roar, consumed by self-hatred.

Why? I should be dead. Not them. *Not. Them.*

Because I'm a fuck-up, just as my dad has always said. A total, unsavable fuck-up.

That thought has me sifting through the bottles on the floor to find some more vodka.

I just need this all to end.

18

WHAT HAVE I DONE? How could I? What will my punishment be for that mistake? Can I redeem myself?

Questions run amok in my mind, one after the other, all questions with answers I can't face.

John has come and gone. Sam and Drew have come and gone. Sarah followed me back after I released myself to use the toilet. All have stood on the other side of that door trying to force it open, calling out to me. I text them all. Told them I'm fine.

I'm far from fine. I'm a wreck. Plagued by guilt. Haunted by shame.

But while I'm suffering, at least Ava isn't. *Especially clear given she hasn't text once.*

I drag myself onto the couch, pulling my phone off charge. Saturday. I've been festering in here for days. I finished every drop of vodka I had for the first two days. Safe. Barricaded in my office to be numb, with no risk of more meaningless fucking, dropping off to sleep now and then, but only for an hour or two before my nightmares woke me. Then the vodka ran dry. And all that was left for the past two days was a hangover, regret, and memories of the brief time in my life when grief and guilt didn't rule it. The hangover has passed, but I still feel like death. It's the first time ever alcohol isn't responsible.

I toss my phone aside and scrub my hands down my face, feeling my overgrown stubble scratching my palms. Every one of my muscles feels tight. I gingerly stand, cringing through the discomfort, stretching. I smell like death too, my shirt crumpled and stale. I need a shower. Maybe ten.

I look at the door, at the cabinet blocking it. Each time I've been forced to move it so I can use the toilet, it's become heavier and heavier. I'm desperate for a piss now. But, again, scared to leave. Not because I'm afraid of what I might do or who might be out there, but because leaving means facing my reality. A reality without Ava.

A reality where I put my dick in two other women. A reality where I might go straight to the bar to drown my misery.

I sigh and go to the cabinet, taking the edge and engaging my body to pull it away. It doesn't budge, not an inch, and I'm quickly out of breath trying to make it. "Fucking hell," I murmur, flopping back against the wall, feeling weak.

The sound of something hitting the window pulls my attention to it, and I find Sam's face squished up against the pane, his eyes searching inside my office. My usually cheerful mate looks worried, and when he eventually finds me slumped by the door, he shakes his head. I drag my tired body across the room and open the window, exhausted, my hands falling to the ledge to hold me up. "Hey." My voice sounds strained, my throat sore.

"Mate," he says on a sigh, his worried eyes running up and down my bedraggled form. "What on earth?"

I close my eyes, inhaling, trying to soothe my straining lungs. Even breathing hurts. "I don't want to go back to this shit, Sam," I say to my darkness, unable to face him. "I *can't* go back to this shit." I'll be dead before I'm forty, and now I've had a taste of heaven, I feel like I'm eternally screwed. I can't survive this hell.

"Then don't go back," he says, as if it's that simple, and I look up at him. He smiles mildly. "Don't go back, Jesse."

"I need help." It's the first time in my life I've admitted it. "And I have no idea where to turn."

He reaches through the window and takes the top of my arm. "We're all here for you, mate."

All. That's not true. Ava's not here. But I appreciate his sentiment.

I inhale and push myself upright, noticing Sam's in his running kit. "Been or going?" I ask.

"Been. Come on, we need to get some food inside you." He backs away, and I look back to my office door.

"I can't move the cabinet," I admit, pulling Sam back to the window. He looks across to the door and rolls his eyes, clambering up into my office. "Thanks," I say quietly as he paces across the room, me following slowly. He takes one side, me the other. He knows I'm not just thanking him for his help moving this lump of wood.

We shift the cabinet back into place, and I take an encouraging breath as I leave my office. The Manor is quiet as we walk through side by side. "Full English?" Sam asks when we make it to the bar.

I blow out my cheeks. I should be hungry after days of only a liquid diet, but I'm not sure I can stomach it. "Just some toast." I take a seat in the corner while Sam orders, looking at the screen of my phone and clearing the endless texts and missed calls. None from Ava. *Still.*

Sam returns with coffees, loading mine with sugar and setting it in front of me. My hands shake as they carry it to my mouth, and it doesn't escape Sam's notice. "Talk to me," he orders softly. "What the fuck happened?"

"I realized everything is impossible," I admit, looking past him when I see John in the foyer. He clocks me, sees Sam too, and nods, impassive, before carrying on his way.

"Is drink the answer?"

I shake my head. "There is no answer."

"There's always an answer." He stirs his coffee, his full attention on me. "You're in love with her."

I glance away. "I don't know what love is."

"Don't bullshit me," he says, sounding a little irate. "You know what love is. Love is scary. It hurts and, correct me if I'm wrong, you are in agony right now."

"What are you saying?"

He moves in, resting his elbows on the table. "I'm asking you if it hurts more with her in your life, or without her in your life."

"Stupid fucking question."

"Then why the fuck are we having this conversation?"

My fist balls, my knuckles turning white. "We're having the conversation because even though I'm in agony, I know Ava is not. She's—"

"How do you know?"

I sit back, frowning. "What?"

"How do you know she's not hurting?"

"Sam, she spent over a week doing everything she could to avoid me. Every time I thought we'd made progress, she'd back away again."

"Yes, because she's probably falling in love with you and, like I said, love is fucking scary."

His words, a near mirror image of John's, have my mouth snapping shut. "Then why hasn't she called?"

"You walked away from her."

"How do you know that?" I ask.

"I may or may not be having a little text banter with that fiery red-headed friend of hers. And she said Ava is a walking corpse at the moment. Lost. Miserable." He nods down my seated form. "Not unlike yourself."

She's suffering? She's not . . . relieved that I'm gone from her life? "She doesn't know what happens here, Sam. She knows nothing of my history. She's completely in the dark."

"Then tell her."

I laugh, and then cough, my throat sore. I feel like I've swallowed a bag of nails. "Everything?"

He shrugs. "She needs to know."

"She doesn't need to know. Not everything. Fucking hell, Sam." He knows I can't talk about that stuff. I'm sweating just thinking about it.

"I know your past is fucking tragic, mate, but I hope to fucking God you can find it in yourself to share that shit with her. But that's on you." His blue eyes soften. "The happenings of The Manor, though? That shit's here now, Jesse. And it's right under her nose, just waiting for someone to spill. That someone needs to be you."

He's right, of course. If she's going to know, it has to come from me. I shake my head. We're talking like she'd even entertain a conversation, and I seriously doubt that. Plus, the happenings of The Manor isn't the only confession I have. "I've fucked up." Regret is a vise around my lungs, squeezing them, preventing air from getting in.

"Yeah, you're a dick. But I get it."

"Will she?" I ask, looking at him hopefully. His silence speaks volumes, and I wedge my elbows on the table, my head dropping into my hands. Of course she won't get it. "How do I fix this?"

"You can only show her how you feel. Everything else will come naturally."

"What seems to come naturally for me with that woman is a one-way ticket to fucking crazy town." And a two-way ticket to rapture.

Sam laughs. "You're passionate about her. It's quite refreshing."

"I don't think she sees it like that," I grumble, bringing my coffee to my lips, the caffeine so needed.

"Then make her."

My eyes lift from my cup. "She won't want to see me."

"For fuck's sake," he mutters, standing. His chair scrapes the floor, the sound ringing in my ears. "I'm meeting Drew for a coffee when he's finished work."

"Coffee?" I laugh a little. "What are you, two old women?"

Sam ignores me, accepting the toast from one of my staff, Pete, when he brings it over. He slides it on the table. "We were actually meeting to discuss an intervention."

"For what?"

"You, you tart." He sighs, nodding to the plate. "Eat. Shower. Sort your shit out." He leaves me to munch my way slowly through half a slice of toast.

Sort my shit out.

I don't know where to start.

And now there's more shit to sort.

I start by going to my suite and showering as instructed. Then more coffee. I go to one of the cabinets and pull the drawer open to get some clean boxers. Freeze.

Her bra stares back at me.

I slam the drawer and fetch some jeans.

More coffee.

Get a black shirt from my wardrobe.

More coffee.

Then I stand, wondering . . . what now? Leave. Get out of here. My best move right now would be to get my arse out of The Manor. I grab my keys and escape, driving to Lusso in a haze.

Of course, everything in my penthouse has Ava's mark all over it. There's no escaping her. Not from my mind, my eyes, my fucking cracking heart. I pace the place ten times, unpack a few more boxes, watch as time drags by painfully slowly. It's lonely here on my own.

By evening, I'm going certifiably crazy. I don't want to go back to The Manor. I don't want to be here alone. I've thought endlessly about calling Ava, hoping she'll answer and let me explain myself. Yet I know the gods won't be that kind to me. In the end, I settle on calling Sam.

"Where are you two girls having that coffee?" I ask, and he laughs.

"The little place at the corner of Burlington. I'll be there in half an hour."

"On my way."

By some unexplained miracle, I find a parking space a few hundred yards up the road from the café. Drew and Sam are sitting at a table outside, chatting, though they shut up when they spot me approaching. "My ears are burning," I quip, knowing Sam would have been filling Drew in on what he found in my office this morning. I take a seat and nod my thanks when Sam pushes a coffee across the table to me.

"How you doing?" Drew asks, and I smile over my cup at him, knowing he finds it hard to ask such simple questions. His usually impassive face breaks into an awkward smile.

"I'm fine," I reply. He won't know what to do with me if I offload what I offloaded on Sam this morning, so I keep it simple. I raise a brow at Sam when he scoffs. "Really," I add. "Tell me what's happening." I need to divert the subject from me. Try to find some kind of normality. Hilarious. We definitely don't *normally* meet for a coffee and a chat. More like a drink and a fuck.

Both of my mates are silent, and I look between them a few times. "You've got nothing to tell me?" I ask. Nothing at all? Sam shrugs and Drew stirs his coffee. "We do coffee meets in style," I mutter, just as Sam's phone dings on the table. His arm shoots out like lightning, swiping it up. Jesus, I've never seen him move so fast. Unless he's got rope in his hands. "Urgent?" I ask, watching as he shifts in his chair awkwardly.

"Nope."

Drew chuckles, and I turn my eyes onto him. He straightens his face immediately. "What's going on?" I ask.

"Nothing."

"Nothing."

"For fuck's sake." I slam my coffee down and stand. "You two were supposed to be a better option than kicking my fucking heels around my penthouse. Think I'll go watch some crappy TV alone."

Sam sags, flicking his gaze to Drew, who shrugs. "It's Kate." Sam flashes the screen of his phone at me. "She's out with Ava."

I freeze with my hands on the back of the chair, ready to push it under the table. My throat clogs up. My skin prickles. "That's nice." I strain the words, my mind off on a tangent. She's out drinking. Socializing. Getting attention from men probably closer to her age. So while I've been slowly dying on the inside, she's been living it up? It feels like someone's just plunged a dagger in my heart and twisted the fucker. When did I become such a dramatic wanker?

"Sit down," Drew orders shortly, leaning over and pushing the chair out again. I practically fall onto it, in absolute agony. "Drink." He physically places a bottle of opened water in my hand. "What are you thinking?" he asks.

"You don't want to know," I reply, taking a needed swig of

cold liquid. I'm thinking I want to find her, toss her over my shoulder like a barbarian, and cart her back to my cave. And kill anyone who tries to stop me.

"Yes, actually, I do." Drew turns in toward me, his head tilted in question. "What is it about this woman?"

I laugh, and it's unstoppable. Why does everyone keep asking me that obtuse question? And why the fuck did I ask myself that? It's a perfectly reasonable enquiry to the man who's *never* shown any interest in a woman unless he's half-cut and wants to put his dick inside her.

"Well?" he presses, and I frown.

How did I explain it again? "Drink makes me forget everything," I say, slowly spinning my bottle of water on the table, studying it. "It numbs the pain." I take a deep breath and exhale, sinking into my chair. "But I don't want to forget her, and I like the feelings she provokes."

Drew gives Sam surprised eyes. "Even that temper of yours that's come out to play lately?"

I laugh. "She's frustrating, yes." I smile, thinking about all the times she's fought me and lost. "Unreasonable, and that drives me crazy, yes." I look up at him. "But it still feels good. Fucked up, right?"

"It feels good to feel crazy?"

"She challenges me. I like it. She sets my insides alight, and I really like that. But most of all, I love the feeling of my heart beating for the first time in forever." *As if it deserves to.*

Drew sits back, alarmed, and Sam smiles across the table at me.

For fuck's sake. Apparently, she's also turned me into a girl. I scowl at my water, recalling what Sam said to me earlier. Ava's moping. But now I've heard she's out drinking. *Drinking makes people forget, Ward.* And that's a good thing for her. She needs to forget about me.

No, she doesn't.

Yes, she fucking does.

My teeth start to grind. How many men will she need to fuck to get me out of her head? Am I already out? I can't be because Kate said she's moping. *She doesn't want to forget you, Ward. Pull your head out of your arse. Do something about this.* I frown, looking across the street when I hear a commotion, seeing a man staggering out of a pub, pinballing off people, parked cars, walls. Erratic. Out of control. *Constrained.* And suddenly it's not a man I don't know. It's me.

"What's up there?" I ask as we round the gallery landing, Uncle Carmichael up front, John behind me, as if they're guarding me. I stop by the stained-glass window and look up to the wooden doors at the top of the second flight of stairs, hearing soft, erotic music playing. It's the first time I've been allowed past Carmichael's private apartment.

"Let's get a drink," he suggests, leading us back to the bar. I wander in and Carmichael motions to the Italian man waiting to serve me. "You're eighteen now, kid. All is not lost. You still have some wins ahead of you."

I step forward and scan the top shelf, wondering if he's right. Will I ever feel as though I can win at life again? Probably not.

I've never needed to be eighteen to drink, but I haven't touched a drop since Lauren produced that bottle of vodka. The haze was nice, the numbness, and I feel like I need to be numb now. I look around me, to the bar, where endless people sit, chat, laugh. No Lauren. Thank fuck. I'm safe. And that's Carmichael's point. Safe. Free. Away from the nightmare. "A vodka, please," I say, perching on one of the stools, feeling my body lighten and the ball of anxiety clogging my throat shrinking. A woman approaches. She's mature. Attractive. Smiling in delight.

In approval.

In acceptance.

I neck my drink and order another.

"Jesse?"

I blink and cast my eyes between my two mates, still thinking about Carmichael's words from nearly twenty years ago.

All is not lost. You still have some wins ahead of you.

Ava is my fucking win.

Win her back. Win her back. Win her back.

"Are you meeting Kate?" I ask, and Sam's head starts to shake. I roll my eyes. This isn't a case of not wanting to leave me alone while I'm behaving like a lovesick puppy, it's about taking me to within licking distance of alcohol. I stand up. "Call her."

"No."

"Do it," I growl, hearing Drew sigh. "You're going to meet Kate," I declare, walking off toward my car. "And I'm coming." I hear my friends scrambling up, the metal chairs clanging loudly.

"Wait, what?" Sam asks, chasing my heels. "What are you going to do?"

"Talk to Ava."

"Oh boy," he breathes. "Reasonably?"

I stop, turning an incredulous glare onto him. "I'm always reasonable." For fuck's sake. "Are you two girls coming or not?"

It's time to start fixing my wrongs, because I've tried to live without her, not think about her, forget about her. And failed. I need to fix this. And I especially need to learn how to manage the moods she spikes.

· · ·

Outside the bar, my phone rings. I ignore John's call. "She's in this bar?" I ask Sam, my teeth going to town on my bottom lip, thinking, wondering, hoping.

"Yeah, you know, maybe we should go," he says, taking my arm, undoubtedly feeling my anxiety. "Call her tomorrow."

I roll my shoulder, shrugging him off, my eyes like lasers on the entrance. "I'm fine," I insist, hearing Sam's phone start ringing. I look at him, not liking his worried expression. "Kate?" I ask.

"No, John."

"Don't answer," I order, nodding a hello at Jay, the doorman.

"Fuck you." Sam laughs. "He might hesitate to sock you one to the chops, but he wouldn't me. I'm not getting on the wrong side of that man for anyone."

Drew laughs under his breath. "Pussy."

"Meow," Sam says, taking his phone to his ear. "Big man." He starts pacing up and down, and I make a gesture to suggest I'll break his neck if he so much as mentions where we are and why. "Yeah, he's with me." Sam takes a hand to his forehead, wiping away the stressed sweat. "Sober," he confirms. "Sure will." He hangs up and stuffs his phone in his pocket. "Promise me you'll be cool."

"What do you think I'm going to do?" I ask, insulted. "I'm just going to talk to her." I stride into the bar, shaking Jay's hand as I pass. "Busy?" I ask.

"Packed," he confirms, and it sure is. The bar is ten deep, the dance floor crammed, the Saturday night crowd out in force.

But all of the chaos disappears when I spot her.

I'm forced to take a nearby ledge to steady myself, heart palpitations rendering me unable to squeeze any air out.

Look at her.

Just . . . look at her.

How the fuck did I walk away? *Why* the fuck did I walk away?

Because if I hadn't, I wouldn't currently be torn up inside with guilt and shame. Or, at least, more.

"You okay, man?" Sam asks, but my eyes don't stray from Ava, and he follows my line of sight. "Okay," he breathes. "Remember what I said?"

I remember fuck all.

She's placing some drinks on a ledge, smiling at someone on the dance floor. Why is she on her own? Where are her friends? She turns and heads toward the bar, and I definitely detect a drunken sway. She's had too much to drink, and she's alone. A sitting duck. What the fuck is she playing at?

"Drink?" Drew asks, his voice distant.

"Get him a water," Sam answers, seeing I'm in no position to form words. "Come on." He tugs me toward a table near the front, and I let him lead me, my stare trained on Ava. She makes it to the bar where I see Kate talking to a guy. They say hello. Kate moves back, her attention on the guy, leaving Ava alone. *Alone. Vulnerable.* I don't have a second to wonder what Sam might be making of this.

"You okay?" he asks, putting himself in front of me, trying to hamper my view.

I crane my neck to look past him. "Yeah." My eyes widen when a man moves in on Ava, taking her in a hug. *The fuck?* It's too much of a friendly hug for him to be a stranger. So who the fuck is he?

My feet are moving before I can convince them otherwise. "Whoa." Sam laughs, somehow managing to hold me back. "You said you'd be cool."

The guy kisses her cheek, and I growl, fighting against Sam to get free. "I'm cool," I bark, struggling in his hold. "Let me the fuck go."

"No way," Sam argues, knuckling down, tightening his grip. "She's just talking to him."

Just talking? I'm watching, and I can see the way he's looking at her. Fuck me, the rage. "I'm fine," I say as Drew arrives and holds out a bottle of water. "So fine." Sam's right. I can't steam on in there and cause a scene. That would go down about as well as a bottle of vodka right now. I'd kill all hopes of making amends. *Be cool. Be cool. Be cool.* The guy reaches for her arm and strokes it. *Be cool.*

"Oh boy," Drew murmurs, and I'm gone, charging through the crowds like a rhino, my rage irrepressible. *Get him. Kill him. Claim Ava.* My hand is out in front of me of its own volition, and his neck is soon in my palm. I slam him into the nearest wall and get up in his face, snarling like a rabid dog.

I have no words. Can't talk through the unbridled violence consuming me. All I'm capable of is constricting my hand. He touched her. He can't touch her. No one can touch her. Only I can touch her. *No one will take this piece of heaven from me.* I search for some self-control. None. "Keep your fucking hands to yourself," I hiss.

I can hear Ava's voice, yet it's a muffled white noise. Fuzzy. Unclear. But then I feel her on my skin, her small, smooth palm stroking my bicep. Touch. I blink my vision clear, realigning my attention on the fucker currently held in my grip.

"Who the fuck are you?" I demand, not easing up, not appreciating that he probably can't talk with me squeezing his throat. "Who?" I yell.

"Matt," he squeaks. "Ava's ex."

My snarl is lethal. Judging by the way he was looking at her, he doesn't want to be an ex. I hear more voices. More white noise. I can't make sense of any of it. It's just me and this dizzying rage.

"Jesse, my man, come on." A hand takes my wrist, trying to ease me away. "Let go of him, for fuck's sake."

"Jesse," Drew says, joining the party to calm me down.

I shake my head, frowning to myself, flexing my fingers and pulling away. The guy is gone like a shot, stumbling his way through the bar.

"Jesus," Sam breathes. "I knew this was a bad idea."

Drew scoffs, placing a bottle of water in my hand, giving me disappointed eyes. "What the fuck?"

"He was all over her," I growl, turning to find *her*. "Where is she?" I scan the crowds, searching for Ava, my anger disappearing, being replaced with a panic of equal strength. *Fuck, what have I done?*

"Let's take a timeout, shall we?" Sam sighs, taking one arm, Drew the other. They both lead me to the end of the bar, flanking me, and take up position, barricading me in.

"Drink," Drew orders, pushing the bottle to my mouth. "And calm the fuck down before Jay throws us out."

At the mention of his name, the man appears, assessing us all. "A disturbance has been reported. Nothing to do with you three, right?"

Sam turns on his charm, giving Jay a friendly slap on the shoulder. "Nothing but love, Jay. Nothing but love."

"Good. Keep it that way." He leaves, and my eyes go back to scanning the crowd, my hand slipping into my pocket to get my phone. What if she left? Has she left? Drew swoops in and plucks my mobile from my grasp. "What are you doing?" I ask, incredulous.

"Stopping you from doing something stupid."

"Too late," Sam mutters, swigging back his beer, clearly regretting coming here. "Sit your arse down." He pulls a stool over and pushes me onto it. "You think that's going to help your cause?" he asks, remaining before me, blocking my view and my escape.

I pout like a sullen schoolboy, dropping my eyes to my knees. What did they expect me to do? Watch while another man moves in on her? Not a chance.

"I'm no expert in the language of wooing, but I'd say you've royally fucked that up." Drew gives me a consolation pat on my back, and I look up at him, irritated.

"Shut the fuck up," I hiss, and he just smiles, shaking his head. "I thought you said she'd been moping?" I turn my attention to Sam, whose bottle pauses at his lips. "She doesn't look like she's moping to me." In fact, she looked like she was having a whale of a fucking time, and doesn't that just piss me off more? *Drink. Forget. Do stupid shit.* This time her, not me.

"Don't shoot the messenger."

My lip curls, and I stand, needing to stretch my tight muscles. Both men move in fast, blocking me, worry plastered all over their faces. "Where are you going?" Drew asks.

"Nowhere." For fuck's sake. "I need to stretch." And get a better view.

They relax and ease off, giving me space to breathe, and I search every corner of the bar. Nothing. "I need the men's," I say, taking only a few paces, my self-appointed guards following, but I come to an abrupt stop when I see her on the dance floor.

My dying anger bubbles again as I watch her shimmying around invitingly. Flirting without flirting. Giving out messages to men far and wide that she's up for a good time. My cheeks blow out. I've been there—am *very* familiar with how this sexual dance works.

"I thought you needed a piss?" Drew says.

"Changed my mind." I rest a shoulder on the pillar and settle in, and the boys start to talk between themselves, leaving me in peace to monitor her every move. And I don't like her moves.

And what the fuck is she wearing? Or *not* wearing, more like. Her dress is fucking outrageous. Gorgeous on her. Absolutely stunning. And as I glance around the bar, I conclude that every other guy in here thinks so too. I shift against the pillar, uncomfortable, beating back the urge to rip out the eyes of every male within a ten-mile radius. She's tipsy. People don't think straight when they're under the influence. They do stupid shit. And she is doing stupid shit.

I need to get her off that dance floor before some other prick moves in and I'm up for murder. "Where's my phone?" I hold out my hand to Drew, who happily returns it.

"Cool?" he asks.

"Cool," I confirm, forcing a smile, satisfying them both. They go back to talking, and I go back to drilling holes into Ava. Once again, she leaves Kate on the floor, heading for the bar alone. More alcohol? Alone? She has absolutely no regard for her safety. None at all. We'll be having a little chat about that. And the ridiculous dress. And the drinking.

She leans over the bar to order, and I watch as she visibly tenses, freezing in position, her eyes slowly turning this way. She sensed me. Knew I was watching.

She stares at me, and I try so fucking hard to soften my expression. I can't. There's just too much bothering me in this moment.

She quickly turns back to the bar, pays, and takes her drinks, and when I expect her to scurry off, she doesn't. She faces me, and our eyes immediately latch. Her eyes shimmer. I see her chest pump. Her swallows are hard. She absolutely cannot control her reactions to me. And my anger? It's gone in a single crash of my heartbeat. I push my weight off the pillar and start toward her, jolting when something grabs my arm and tries to haul me back.

"Jesse, no."

I shrug Sam off with ease, my determination helping, and

stalk across the bar. "Don't run, don't run," I whisper, seeing her body engaging, her eyes becoming worried. She discards her drink on the bar, and she's off, like a horse bolting, running away from me.

"Ava!" I yell, muscling someone out of my way and going after her. I make it to the entrance, but not through the door. Because Sam's blocking it. "I'm just going to talk," I assure him, physically moving him out of my way and charging out onto the street. I see her up the road, her arm waving in the air frantically, the fucking ridiculous dress looking even shorter. And she's alone again. "Ava," I yell, breaking into a run. She whirls around, sees me charging toward her, and makes off. "Fucking hell. Ava!" She'll break her fucking neck in those shoes. I increase my pace, gaining on her fast, and seize her around her waist, tossing her onto my shoulder like the animal I've become. Her protests are instant, as I knew they would be, but they stand for shit. She better not even think we're going back to that infuriating sway of acceptance and denial. No way. I saw the look in her eyes as she stared at me. I felt the bullets of desire hit me. She's not over me at all. I can feel it now, her body touching mine, burning, and anger is only half the reason. For both of us.

I carry her into a quiet side street as she smashes her fists into my lower back, screaming her objection. Lowering her to her feet, I move in, crowding her, making it impossible for her to escape. But she refuses to look me in the eye. I know why. And it only spurs me on. "Ava, look at me."

She tries to move past me, forcing me to physically stop her.

"Goddamn it, Ava."

She starts grappling with my hands, trying to pry my hold away. "Go away, please."

Go away? I refuse and curse, breathing in and calling on some calm, searching for some guidance. "Ava."

She tries again to escape, and I become more desperate,

forcing her back against the wall. *What am I doing? For fuck's sake, Ward!*

I release her, and her eyes drop like stones to her feet. "Ava, look at me," I grate. She covers her ears and slides down the wall, crouching. Making herself small. "Ava, why are you doing this?" I ask, taking her small wrists and trying to pull her hands away. "I don't want to do this here."

"Then don't." She fights with my hold. "Please, just let me walk away."

I sink to the ground with her. "Never," I murmur. I've tried. It nearly killed me, and seeing her like this now, tears pouring, knowing what I know, seeing what I've seen, I'm sure she's been in hell too. She was drinking to forget, and I'm all too familiar with that tactic.

"Why are you doing this to me?" she asks on a sob, and my heart squeezes. I surrender one of her wrists in favor of her jaw, forcing her to look at me.

"Doing what?" Trying to win her back? Trying to make her see? Trying to show her how deeply under my skin she is?

Because I've fallen in fucking love with you!

She swipes a hand angrily over the dampness of her cheeks. "You persistently pursued me, bombarded me with calls and texts, fucked me into oblivion, and then stormed off for four days." She inhales sharply, searching for air, and I shrink on the inside. "I don't even know why!"

God, baby, you don't want to know why.

"Now you turn up, trampling all over my night."

"Watch your mouth," I whisper, swallowing the tennis ball-sized lump in my throat. How can I possibly begin to explain? I'm gripped by guilt. "You asked for space," I murmur feebly.

"But you weren't prepared to give it to me," she yells, her voice rising. "What changed so suddenly?"

Everything.

Just remembering that moment on the street—the bruises on her arms, the fact she canceled our meeting, fobbed me off—brings back a barrage of stress. How easily she can go from all in, to not in. And, God help me, she's like that without the knowledge of who she's dealing with.

I would give anything in this moment to change things. I'd give anything to be rid of this crippling guilt and save her the hurt I'm going to cause. She cocks her head, waiting for me to answer, and I scowl at myself, unable to give her one. But I can show her, if only she'll let me.

She stands, leaving me crouched before her, and my hands take on a mind of their own, sliding onto the backs of her bare legs. She stills in a second. It's no wonder. Sparks are flying. Touch her. Remind her. It's all I have. Our crazy chemistry. My devotion.

"Let me go, Jesse," she begs, soft but firm, and I gaze up at her.

"No."

"You seemed to manage just fine on Tuesday."

I flinch, rising, making sure I don't break our contact. "I was mad." *Mad with you, mad with me, mad with everything.*

She swallows, every inch of her tense. "You're still mad."

"I just found your ex-boyfriend dribbling all over you."

"He wasn't dribbling," she argues, and it's all I can do not to laugh in her face, the rage creeping back up on me. "And how do you know who he is?"

"Because I strangled it out of him," I bark, blinking back the red. *Control it, Ward!* "You won't see him again, Ava." *That's it. Make demands of her, you stupid fuck. That'll get you everywhere.*

"Did you know I would be here?"

I remain quiet. It's a moot point, anyway. I'm here, and it's a fucking good job I was.

"You knew I would be here, didn't you?"

"Sam."

"Sam?"

"He rang Kate." *Because I forced him to.*

I'm done with the pointless whys and wherefores of how I came to be here. I'm here, and even though I can't confess my crimes, I want to—*need to*—hold her. Kiss her. *Feel her peace.* "I'm going to kiss you now," I whisper, my eyes on her lips, desperate to be there again. Desperate to remind her. Desperate for so much more than just her mouth on mine. "You're lucky," I go on, unable to stop myself, knowing I'm stooping to unfair lows. But it's the only way. My only option in this moment. "Because if I had you anywhere else, you would be getting a reminder . . . right . . . about . . . now." I close the space between us. "I like your dress." It's too short, too tight, too revealing, too Manor-ish, but God, she looks amazing in it.

I reach for her arm and trace the length with a light fingertip. More sparks. More heat. "It's too short, but I like it." I sink my face into her neck, taking an intoxicating hit of her scent, and she turns her face into me on a wonderfully accepting hitch of breath. *Please don't fight this.*

I dip and lift her from her feet, finding her eyes. They sparkle wildly. Speak a million words she isn't prepared to say. But I'll wait for them. I'll wait forever for them. "Do you have any idea what you do to me?" I ask, my voice straining with the effort to speak. Honestly, I could break at any moment. Cry on her. "I'm a fucking mess, Ava." She needs to know that. I ease my hold, and she slips down my body, her mouth meeting mine, and my insides twist, my skin blazes, and my thoughts straighten out.

I feel . . . stable again.

Her hands delve into my hair, every part of her responding. Accepting. I moan my satisfaction, deepening our connection, wishing us away from here. God, I need to cuff her to my bed and never release her. Have this sense of serenity constantly. Be glued to her. *Impossible*.

I hiss and pull away, breathless, resting my forehead on hers. "There she is," I whisper raggedly. My Ava.

"You've got me again."

I can't help but smile, loving her easy acquiescence. "I've missed you, baby." So fucking much.

"Why did you go then?"

"I've no idea." I really don't. Regret turns my stomach. How will I tell her what I've done? How will I make her understand the level of remorse plaguing me? I don't know. But I do know I'll make it up to her. I do know I'll right my wrongs. I do know I will never touch drink or another woman ever again. I'll prove myself. It's all I *can* do. And I will because I can be more than a fuck-up.

I can be what this gorgeous woman deserves.

I force my miserable thoughts into a box at the very back of my mind, vowing to deal with them. But not now. Not here. Call me low, but I've got to prove myself before I can even think about trying to explain, because explaining opens up a whole new can of worms that I just can't face right now. Right now, I just need to be here. With her. Showing her.

I kiss her, holding my lips on hers. The second her body brushes over my groin, my dick surges, and she looks up at me, surprised. Yes, just like that. *Ping!* "I should force you to sort this out." I grab her hand and rest it on my raging hard-on. "But I'm not having you on your knees out here." I give her a dark smile. "We'll make friends properly later." And every day for the rest of my life.

I hold out a hand, and she accepts with ease, letting me lead her back into the bar. How tiny she feels beside me. Her hand in mine. Tiny and fragile. "What do you want to drink?" I pull her in close, a sign of sorts. *Mine*.

"Zinfandel, please."

Wine? Hasn't she had enough? I look down at her face smiling up at me, pouting in thought. My instinct is yelling at me to refuse her. But, regrettably, I know that won't go down all too well. I've just won her back. Keep the peace. We'll address the drinking issue another time when I know she can't run away from me. Besides, she's with me. She's safe. "Your friends?"

"Oh, Kate's a wine, vodka and tonic for Victoria, and a piña colada for Tom."

"Tom?" I ask, alarmed. *Who the fuck is Tom?*

"You met him at Lusso," she reminds me. Oh yes. The touchy feely one. I instantly relax, turning back to the barman and ordering their drinks as I scan the bar for Sam and Drew, spotting them at the end, both of them looking this way. I shrug when they smile, lifting their beers. Drinks all round, then? Except for me, and I absolutely do not care. I don't need one. Not with Ava beside me.

I grab two of the drinks off the bar and turn, handing them to Ava's work friend and Kate, who dives on me and kisses my cheek. The woman is a fruitcake, but it's quite satisfying to know she's clearly glad I'm here. Which means Ava is glad too.

I dip and get close to her ear so Ava can't hear me. "She's staying with me tonight," I tell her, saving the trouble of Ava doing it later. The rest of my night is meticulously planned. And the rest of my life, for that matter. *You sure, Ward? Because after she's found out what you've done . . .*

I shy away from my conscience like the coward I am, handing Ava her wine and pulling her back into me. I can only manage a meek smile when she looks up at me, part questioning, part adoring.

I'm offered some respite from my consistent, taunting thoughts when Sam bursts through the crowds, Drew tailing him at a more leisurely pace. "Hey, my man."

I pass over their beers and smile as he presents his face to Ava. "Ava, where's the love?"

She humors him, and I roll my eyes as she comes in closer to me. I bend a little to ease the strain of her reaching up. "I'm going to join the others," she says, and I pout to myself. But if there's anything I can be, it's reasonable. So I relent for the greater good, and the greater good right now is remaining on her good side.

"I'll be watching," I warn, taking her earlobe in my mouth and giving her arse a small smack. I'll be watching *very* closely. I smile when she narrows her eyes, flipping her a playful wink. God help any man who so much as looks in her direction.

She shimmies away, and I watch her every move until she finds Kate on the dance floor, her friends greeting her excitedly.

"So," Drew says, moving into my side and chinking his beer with my water. "When's the wedding?"

Sam laughs, backing away toward the dance floor, his shoulders jigging in time with the beat. "So long, fellas. I'm about to get me a fine redhead."

"You're a whore," I call after him, laughing, but my amusement dries up when I catch Ava necking her wine. The whole fucking glass. Christ alive, she doesn't half know how to push my buttons. "Did you see that?" I ask Drew, gesturing with my bottle.

"I saw," he sighs. "She's out with her friends. Give the woman a break."

Nevertheless, the whole glass? It's irresponsible. She needs some water. "Watch her a second," I order, taking only two steps towards the bar before I stop dead in my tracks. My ears prick up.

"Oh no," Drew says over a laugh. "Don't do it. You'll scare her away and *never* get her back."

I pout as Justin Timberlake fills the bar and, damn, if it isn't my favorite track. "What are you talking about? I'm an amazing dancer." Scare her away? Fair enough, I'm usually ten sheets to the wind whenever I take to the dance floor, but since everyone keeps calling me uptight these days, perhaps I should flatten that stupid claim once and for all. I am not uptight. I'm in love.

I divert toward the dance floor as Sam, grinning, takes Ava's shoulders and turns her toward me. When she spots me, she looks wary, her body slowing until she's motionless. That dress. Fucking hell, that dress. I loathe it and love it.

I get up close to her, hauling her up my body. "You're going to get a lot of men dropped if you keep dancing like that," I tell her, forcing myself to keep my eyes on her and not the endless men appreciating what's mine. "You like a bit of JT?"

"Yes." She can hardly get her words out, and it makes me smile, wide and bright.

"Me too." I slam my mouth on hers, making a point to all watching, before releasing her and spinning her on the spot. Her face is a picture. *Yes, I'm doing this. In public.* I haul her back into me and drop my mouth to her ear. "And it's the extended version."

She has no idea what to make of this, looking between me and Sam, as if he will confirm what's about to go down. She'd never guess. But before I can demonstrate how fucking amazing I am on the dance floor, she's trumped me, throwing the surprise back at me, slipping down my body to the point I'm pretty sure that fucking dress is riding up her arse. But it's easy to disregard when she's looking up at me like she is, sex written all over her face. Looking at *me*. I'm going to take her in every way imaginable, fuck her until she promises to never leave me. This look. I want it every day. Minus the drink.

She starts slowly rising, and I fold at the waist when her nose traces the fly of my jeans. *Shit.* What's she playing at? I grab her and drag her up before I relent to my mind's demand to fuck her here and now with an audience. "I should bend you over here and fuck you until you scream." My body is alive, my mind clear, my heart pounding. "That dress is absurd." I spin her out and do the unthinkable. I dance. Sober. In a fucking bar in central London, I dance. What is she doing to me?

Ava, shocked, mouth hanging open, watches as her friends cheer, Sam laughs and Drew, fucking Drew, joins us too.

Go on, call me uptight now, I dare you. I yank her close as she laughs, grinding into her, doing myself no favors. I'm solid and, frankly, it's fucking uncomfortable. And when she notices my condition, she cups me. *Lord above, don't do that, woman.* I shake my head in warning, taking her hips and lowering to my knees. It's symbolic. If only she knew. The way she's looking down at me now, it's with adoration. Love? She glances around us for a few seconds, taking in the scene, maybe looking to her friends for guidance. She doesn't need it. I'll guide her wherever she needs to go, hold her hand all the way, support her, hug her, worship her. I want to be this woman's be-all and end-all. Can I have that? Will she let me?

Ava returns her gaze to me, half smiling, half unsure, her dark eyes shining. I'll make her sure. I clasp her hips and kiss her stomach, looking up at her, making a million silent promises to her as I do. I'll fulfil each and every one. It's my mission objective.

I get up fast and reinforce every one of my silent promises with a hard kiss, and she sighs, taking me in her arms and hugging me.

"It seems I have competition," I mumble into her mouth, the slippery friction of her tongue on mine dizzying.

"No," she says quietly. "You win."

I lean back, getting her in my sights. "I've won all right, lady." The fucking jackpot. Life-changing stuff. Now I have to show her I'm worthy of the prize.

But first, we dance.

I let her go and she flicks her hair over her shoulder sassily, ready for me. She's not ready. The thought runs on repeat until I bat it away.

Back to the here. Back to the now.

We dance together and it is, without a doubt, one of the most enjoyable things I've ever done. So simple, but so much fun. Me? Uptight? Give me a fucking break. Dancing with Ava is one of my new favorite things, and we'll be doing a lot of it. Closeness. Focus. A room full of people, and yet there is only us.

The beat slows, and with it, so do we. She's out of breath, her cheeks pink. I pull her close and move us together, singing quietly as she gazes into my eyes. Like . . . she could love me. I can only pray. Because make no mistake, I am head over fucking heels for her.

Ava instigates the next kiss, and I fall deeply into it, being taken off to a faraway land where pain and regret no longer exist. I feel her pulling away. No. I'm not done yet. So I bend with her, refusing to surrender her mouth, growling deeply in warning. She doesn't fight me.

This woman.

She's knocked me sideways, and she needs to know.

I forfeit her mouth for her eyes. It's no loss, because her eyes are always so alive, and that life is passing over to me. "You've got me, baby." Forever from now.

She gazes up at me, and I will her drunken mind to absorb that statement. She *has* to understand I am wholeheartedly committed to this. To her. But she's quiet, just watching me, thinking, and I begrudgingly accept she's had way too much to drink to make sense of this.

So I give her a small smile and a tender kiss. "Come on." I return her upright and cover her lower back with my hand, guiding her through the crowd to a table, having to encourage people aside to make way. She's definitely unsteady on her feet, and all I can think is . . . what if I wasn't here?

I scan the area for a spare stool, finding nothing. God damn it. I can't drag her around the bar until I find one. I position her at the table, checking her stability before releasing her. "Wait here," I order, dropping a kiss on her forehead. "Don't move." I back away, my eyes watching carefully for a stumble as she places her purse on the table. No stumble, but I don't feel any better about leaving her. I'm just about to return to her when I spy her friends joining her at the table. It gives me a few moments to hunt down a stool.

I find one at the end of the bar and grab it. "Hey, dude, I'm sitting there," a guy calls, making his way over.

I look at the stool. Then to him. "Looks empty to me," I say, lifting it and raising it over my head to clear the crowds.

"Hey, put the stool down."

I stop in my tracks, turning toward him, my jaw twitching. "Want it over your head?" I ask, and he backs away, hands up in surrender. "It's for a woman. You going to insist on keeping it?"

"You should have just said."

"I'm saying now. So, do you want the stool over your head?" I tilt my head in question, wondering what the fucking hell has gotten into me.

"Take the stool."

"Thought so."

I make it back to the table and set it down. "Sit," I order, physically placing Ava on the seat. I scan her, up and down, dying to declare our departure. At this rate, there will be no reminding her of anything. She looks fit to drop. *Fucking alcohol.* It's robbed me of so much, and now it's robbing me of Ava. "Drinks?" I'll get a round in, and then we're leaving. I'm hit with a splurge of requests that knocks me back a few paces.

"I'll give you a hand," Sam says as I head to the bar, him following hastily.

I smile to myself. "If I'd said I was going to take a piss, would you have come there too?" I ask. We've broken the girlie scale today. Coffee. Congregating to discuss women. What next? I muscle my way to the bar and throw my order at the barman.

"Shut up," Sam spits, just as Drew joins us. "I take it the talk went well."

There wasn't exactly much talking. "Yeah," I say, throwing a couple of notes down and turning into him. "What's the deal with you and Kate?"

Sam frowns. Opens his mouth. Shuts it. Then he turns to Drew. "What's the deal with you and Victoria?"

Drew frowns. Opens his mouth. Shuts it.

I laugh and slide some drinks over to Sam when they land on the bar. "Just remember one thing," I say, trying my hardest not to sound too serious, even though I am very serious.

"What?" they say in unison.

"Ava doesn't know about The Manor, which means Kate doesn't know, which means Victoria doesn't know."

"Yeah, I know," Sam sighs tiredly. "And when do you plan on telling Ava about your seedy little sex club?"

"Seedy?" I ask, insulted. "Little?"

"Okay, classy and fucking massive."

I look between my mates, both of their interested attention on me. "I don't know," I admit. The Manor has taken a backseat to the other shit I'm having to deal with. Like winning her back.

"Well, let us know, won't you?" Drew says, knocking back his beer. "Wouldn't want to drop you in it."

My hackles rise. "Only you can make sure that doesn't happen," I hiss threateningly, and he smiles around the rim of his bottle.

"So laid-back," he murmurs, mocking the hell out of me.

I throw him a scowl and return my attention to the barman while they claim the drinks and join the others. The Manor. I should start by telling her about The Manor. I look up to the ceiling of the bar, exhaling. "This is your fault, Carmichael," I say quietly.

I take the remaining drinks and head back to the table, arriving to find everyone laughing. *Yes, my situation is quite hilarious, I agree.* "What's so funny?" I ask, placing Ava's *small* wine on the table and her *large* water next to it. She's falling apart on her stool, laughing uncontrollably.

"We've just found Tom's Achilles heel," Kate says, and I frown.

"Sam," Ava splutters.

"Sam?"

"Tom fancies Sam!" Ava's blonde work friend—Victoria, I assume—sings, and it falls into place. I take Ava's water and unscrew the cap, having a quick swig before thrusting it at her. "Here, have some." She accepts without argument, lucky for her, but no sooner has she swallowed it down, she claims the wine and necks it. All of it. I should shove my fingers down her throat and make her throw it all back up. This is getting ridiculous, and it doesn't bode well for our future together. If she thinks I'm going to let her out with friends after what I've seen tonight, she can think again. She's plastered. It doesn't suit her.

I lean on the table, watching her, while the rest all chat, Drew getting interestingly close to that Victoria woman. What's his game? She's so far away from his type, she may as well be a bloke. And Sam with Kate? I like her, and I can only imagine the headache I'll get from Ava if my free-spirited mate messes her around. I shake my head to myself. *Yes, because you haven't got enough problems of your own to deal with, huh?*

I return my attention to Ava. *My Ava.* My very drunk Ava. For the love of God, she's going to fall off that stool soon. I round the table and place myself behind her, holding the base of her neck. "What's your plan?" I ask Sam, my eyebrow arched.

His smirk is filthy. "I might take a leaf out of your book and woo her. Take her for dinner or something, since I can't take her to The Manor."

I give him wide eyes, looking down at Ava. I've nothing to worry about. She's barely awake. Enough is enough—I've been more than reasonable. I claim her bag and crouch in front of her, waiting for her to open her eyes. It takes forever, and when she does, she's forced to close one in order to focus on me. What a state. "Come on, lady. I'm taking you home." I lift her off the stool and walk her to everyone in turn to say goodbye. "Can you get home okay?" I ask Kate, just as Sam swoops into her side and throws an arm around her shoulder.

"She can get home just fine."

"Is that so?" Kate asks, turning her eyes onto my grinning mate.

I laugh lightly. "What is it with you women trying to play hard to get?" I ask, leading Ava out of the bar. I get her onto the street, and she loses her footing, staggering a few paces. "For fuck's sake," I grumble, gathering her up and carrying her. I've never seen anyone so drunk in my life. Except, perhaps, me.

I look at her nestled into my chest, her eyes closed, her face peaceful. "You're not going to throw up on me, are you?"

She snorts. "No."

I laugh at her indignation. "Are you sure?"

"I'm fine."

Totally fine. I roll my eyes as we approach my Aston, making a vow to myself to never let her get in this state again. It's reckless. Dangerous. It's me. And it certainly isn't Ava. "Okay, a few seconds' warning would be nice, though." I unlock my car and negotiate her body in my arms to get the door open. "I'm putting you in my car now."

"I'm not going to throw up."

I sigh and place her on the seat, watching carefully for any signs that she's going to spill her guts. The harsh light inside my car shines bright, and my eyes fall to the top of her arm. The bruises. They've faded, but they're still there, marring her beautiful olive skin. I swallow and pull the belt across her body, fastening it as she drags her eyes open, squinting.

"You're adorable, even when you're legless." I drop a chaste kiss on her lips. "You're coming home with me."

"You're bossy."

No, Ava, I'm a man on the edge, and since you put me there, you've got to stop me from falling. Which means compliance. "Get used to it." I round the car and jump in. She begins circling her stomach with her palm when I start the engine, the deep rumble not helping. I laugh lightly, thinking this is not what I had hoped tonight would entail. But she's with me. That's the most important thing.

"Jesse?" she slurs, and I look up at her heavy eyes.

I smile a little, not that she'd know. She probably can't even see me now, and that's another reason why she won't be drinking anymore. I need her to see me as clearly as I see her. "Yes, Ava?"

She gives in and closes her eyes. "How old are you?"

I breathe out. Swallow. "Twenty–five."

"It doesn't matter how old you are," she says, and I cock my head, somewhat surprised. Then why does she keep asking?

"It doesn't?"

"No, it doesn't." She settles farther into her seat. "Nothing matters—I still love you."

I nearly choke on my tongue. "What?" I reach for her hand, taking it, threading our fingers together. "Ava?"

She's sparko. Unconscious.

And though it's been mentioned, suggested, and I've thought it a hundred times, I'm in shock.

She loves me?

I slide my hand into her hair, leaning over the console, and press my lips into her cheek, praying this isn't just the drink talking. Praying she remembers this.

"I hope you can love me, baby," I whisper, closing my eyes and ignoring the smell of so much alcohol on her, polluting her. "Because I'm madly, crazily in love with you."

I sigh, feeling despondent, and recline the seat to get her comfortable. I'll never forget this moment. But just in case . . .

I lift my arse from my seat, rootling through my pocket for my phone. And I take a picture of her, the only one I'll ever take of her plastered, but hopefully not the only one I'll take after she's told me she loves me.

The drive back to Lusso is long, with only my tormenting thoughts for company. I feel like I'm on a runaway train, coasting toward a disaster, and there is nothing I can do to stop it. But perhaps I can slow it down. Give myself time to figure some of this shit out.

"Fuck," I breathe, wedging my elbow into the door and resting my heavy head on it. And as if my car feels it's appropriate, *Angel* comes on, low and soft in the background. I look at her sleeping form.

Do whatever it takes to keep her.

Simple.

It's like trying to handle a slippery dead fish. She's floppy, a dead weight, could even be dribbling as I wrestle her out of the passenger seat. And the smell. Christ, the smell. I nudge the door of my Aston closed with my hip and stride into Lusso with her draped across my arms, lifeless. The concierge is propped in a chair behind the desk, napping. He must hear my footsteps because the old bugger startles and shoots up in a panic.

"Mr. Ward," he blurts, straightening his hat, his sleepy eyes on the drunk woman in my arms. He rushes to the elevator and punches in the code.

"Thanks," I grunt, and he backs away as I try in vain to tug Ava's dress down.

"Good evening," he says, returning to his desk.

"Fucking dress is fucking ridiculous," I grumble, boarding the lift and leaning down, stretching a finger to find the buttons while keeping hold of her. The doors close, and I look at her. She's dead to the world. "You're never drinking again, just so you know." My eyes drag down her dress. "And I'll be having a thorough check of your wardrobe." And throwing away any unsuitable dresses. I nod agreeably to myself and leave the lift, struggling to get the door open.

I drop my keys and phone on the table as I pass, heading straight for the stairs. As I enter the bedroom, I lose grip of her purse, and it hits the floor with a thud. I leave it and lower her to the bed, rolling her onto her side to access the zipper on her dress. She moans and murmurs as I peel the non-existent fabric down her body, revealing lace. Lace knickers, lace bra. Lots and lots of lace. I smile. Then pout. *Torture.*

I gather up her dress, getting a waft of wine. Did she tip it all over herself, as well as down her throat? I shake my head and take it downstairs, tossing it in the washer and frowning at the dials on the front. I have not one fucking clue what I'm doing, and after pushing and pressing, twisting and pulling, I give up and go back upstairs.

I walk into the bedroom and tread on something. My eyes fall to her purse on the floor. It's open, the contents scattered everywhere. I slowly dip and collect up her things. Her phone. Keys. A lipstick. My hand reaches for a thin strip of pills, my lip receiving a punishing chew as I turn them over in my hand, noticing only one has been taken. A new packet. *Do what it takes to keep her.* I shake my head. *What the fuck are you on, Ward?*

Stuffing the packet back inside her purse, I rise and toss it on the dresser, then slowly strip as I watch her sleeping. I round the bed and crawl in beside her, brushing her hair from her face. So peaceful. So unaware of the craziness running amok in my mind.

All is not lost. You still have some wins ahead of you.

Ava will make me a victor, not a failure. With her, I win.

Keep her. Do whatever it takes to keep her. Surely I can't—

My eyes fall to her purse on the dresser. I see the pills inside. And before I know what I'm doing, I'm out of bed and raiding her purse, digging out the small packet. I stare at them. For a long, long time, I just stare at them. *Crazy!* I quickly slip them back in and walk away. And stop halfway across my bedroom, my eyes darting at my feet. I've been trapped. I can't even believe I'm thinking this shit. But I didn't want to be kept. I wasn't in love.

Ava is.

I look at her on the bed. Oblivious. Oblivious now, drunk and sleeping, and oblivious tomorrow, awake and sober. She won't remember what she said. She won't remember a thing.

I reverse my steps, taking her purse and leaving the room. When I reach the kitchen, I stop by the island, swallowing hard, considering her clutch bag in my grasp. I throw it on the counter and pace back into the lounge, like I could be trying to escape a ticking time bomb. "Fuck." I find a wall and lean face-forward into it. "Stop," I growl, reaching up and smacking the side of my head, bashing away the madness. Someone needs to have a serious word with me because I'm trying myself and getting nowhere.

Desperate, I track my phone down to the table by the door and call John. He answers in a heartbeat.

"I'm about to do something monumentally stupid," I say when

he answers, letting myself out onto the terrace, hoping some fresh air might help clear the fog of craziness.

"Where are you?"

"Lusso."

"Does it involve alcohol?"

"Depends who's drinking," I reply, perching on the edge of a lounger and taking some deep breaths. John's silence spells confusion, so I elaborate. "Ava's here. Pissed as a fart."

"You plan on joining her?"

"No."

"Then what's the problem?"

"The problem is, I fear what I'm about to do would be worse than me cracking open a bottle of vodka." I'm speaking without thinking, my motor mouth working faster than my twisted mind in this mayhem.

"What the fuck are you going to do?"

I fall to my back on the lounger and stare at the black sky. What can I say? The truth? He'll have me sectioned. I deserve to be sectioned. And Ava would be well within her rights to walk away. Should I be giving her another reason to do that? Fuck me, I'm losing it. And before I confirm that to John beyond all doubt, I need to think quickly. "I roughed up her ex-boyfriend tonight," I say quietly.

His sigh is loud and exasperated. "What is with you lately?" he asks. I wonder that myself. "How bad?"

"Well, he won't be touching Ava again."

"How bad?" he growls.

"He might have a few bruises around his neck." He's lucky I didn't break his fucking legs.

"You said you're *about* to do something monumentally stupid."

"I want to find him and finish the job." That's not a lie; I do, but Ava's dickhead ex is the least of my problems at this precise moment. The fresh air must have worked because now I'm wondering what the fuck I'm doing calling John.

"Get some sleep," John sighs. "And for the record, nothing could be worse than you turning to the bottle again." He hangs up, and I laugh under my breath. If only he knew.

I drag myself up and plod back to my bedroom, crawling into bed next to Ava. She's moved from her back to her belly, her hair a beautiful mess over the pillow. I get as close as I can to her, my nose nearly touching hers. Her eyelids are flickering. She's dreaming. I smile and stroke her flawless cheek. "What are you dreaming about, baby?" I whisper, hoping it's me. "Tell me what you're dreaming about."

She murmurs something inaudible, her nose wrinkling as she turns her face into the pillow, smearing her makeup all over it before settling again. I resume tracing the contours of her face. "Don't fight him," she croaks, her hand coming up and taking mine, pulling it away from her face. I lean back slightly. She's frowning. "Accept him."

I swallow, remaining still and silent, waiting for more. *Accept him.* Fucking hell. Even drunk and unconscious she's still trying to convince herself to stick around. I roll to my back and cover my face with the crook of my arm, her words bringing on a barrage of memories, each one a good enough reason all on its own for her to reject me. A reason for her to run.

Drink. The Manor. Tuesday Night. Uncle Carmichael. Lauren. Rosie. Sarah.

I squeeze my eyes closed, trying to dull the sting at the backs of my eyes. I've never felt so hopeless yet so full of hope. Leaning over, I place a soft kiss on her lips. "I can't let you leave me," I whisper, stroking down her arm and taking her hand. "I'm sorry."

I get up and head to the kitchen, snatching up the pill packet on the counter. I go to the sink, popping each pill out of the foil,

ignoring my conscience—which is currently asking me what the
fuck I'm doing. I don't know. I have no clue. Yet . . . I can't stop.
I can't let her ever leave me again. I can't go back to those dark,
purposeless days. I need purpose. Ava is a purpose. She's also a
flight risk.

I look at the pills in my palm, hovering over the sink. Being a
father was the best thing that ever happened to me. How it
happened wasn't, but those three years I had with Rosie are the
only three years of my life that I've been alive. I won't fuck it up
this time. I swear, she'll never be replaced. Not ever. But I can
love like that again. I look over my shoulder. I'm already loving
like that again. Yet Ava isn't guaranteed. I have to ensure she is. I
inhale and tip my hand, sending the pills scattering in the bowl,
and I run the tap, washing them away, watching each one disappear down the plughole one by one. "God forgive me," I murmur,
discarding the packet in the bin, tugging out the liner and tying it.

Then I stand in the middle of the kitchen, looking around me,
searching for the sense I need to take back this craziness.

No sense.

Just more craziness.

Keep her.

I drop my head in my hands, gripping my hair harshly. I've
officially gone too far. And yet, I know I will go further. As far as
I need to. As much as it takes.

I won't lose her, because despite this craziness, it's respite too.
It's light where there has only ever been darkness. It's genuine
smiles when there have only ever been false ones.

It's love when there has only ever been loathing.

This is the beginning of my life.

And there can never be an end.

19

I WATCHED her all night long. Apologized a million times. Tried to convince myself to take back what I'd done. But I can't. Short of crawling down the plughole and somehow miraculously retrieving those pills, there's no going back.

I leave Ava in bed and take myself downstairs. My first port of call is the fridge. I grab a jar of Sun-Pat and sit myself on the worktop, taking solace in my vice as I check my phone. Three missed calls. Two from Sarah, one from John. I ignore Sarah, I'm not speaking to her, and call John, holding my phone to my ear by my shoulder so I can continue eating my breakfast.

"You had a visitor late last night," he says when he answers. "Mike."

"What did he want?"

"To talk."

"There's nothing to talk about."

"I don't think he agrees."

I look at the jar in my hand, grimacing and screwing the lid back on, my appetite gone. "I've made it clear to Coral." I move my phone to my other ear, sliding down off the counter and putting the jar back in the fridge.

"Perhaps you need to make it clear to Mike."

I slam the door a little too harshly, accepting what needs to be done. "Fine. Tell him I'll call him. I'll be over soon. Ava's got some work to do on the extension." She doesn't know it yet, but she will, when she comes back from the land of the dead.

"Is that wise?"

"It's Sunday." The Manor is notoriously quiet on a Sunday daytime after a Saturday night.

"You could just tell her and save yourself this stress."

Stress? I didn't know the meaning of the word until recently. "I'll tell her," I assure him. "Just not today." I hang up and spin my phone in my hand, thinking. I'm thinking so much lately, I've got a constant headache. A non-alcohol related headache. *Just tell her*. After all, she did declare her love last night. Or, again and very troubling, was it the drink talking? My eyes divert to the sink. My mind sees the pills swirling around the bowl. Instinct told me to do it.

And instinct might have fucked you over, Ward.

I go back upstairs and enter the master suite to find Ava slowly edging her way out of bed, her face a picture. Beautiful, even with her smudged eye makeup and tangled hair. I smile and rest my shoulder on the doorframe, every troubling thought forgotten. And there is the reason I took those pills. She's distraction incarnate. Heaven wrapped up in a body to die for. My greedy gaze journeys down her neat, tight little body, my hungry cock yelling its approval. But it's my heart I hear the loudest. Beat after beat.

She takes a moment, concentrating on not falling flat on her face, frowning deeply. I hope she swears to never drink again. I hope her head is hurting so much, she won't even be able to look at alcohol.

She peeks up at me, and I see with perfect clarity that she feels like death. I smile and make my way over, certain she's going to topple at any second. "And how is my lady lush this morning?"

"Terrible," she mumbles, and I laugh, delighted.

I take her in my arms, ignoring the stale stench of wine. "Do you want some breakfast?" She immediately convulses against me, and I chuckle. "Just some water then?"

"Please."

God love her. What a mess. "Come here." I dip and lift her, and her head goes straight onto my chest. I carry her downstairs, and it's an effort to release her. I place her on the worktop like I could be handling a priceless china doll.

She yelps, stiffening when the cold marble meets her arse. I laugh again. They just keep coming. I leave her when I know she's stable, trying to remember which cupboard Cathy put the glasses in. I open one. No glasses. The next. No glasses. The next. *Ah. Glasses.*

I snatch one down and pull open a drawer, riffling through for my faithful Alka-Seltzer.

"You don't know where you keep your own glasses?"

"I'm learning," I give the sachet a little shake. "My house-keeper tried to tell me, but I was a little distracted." *By you*, I add in my head, mixing the powder in the glass with some water and taking it to her. I shouldn't be offering a cure. I should be leaving her to suffer all day to increase the chances of her swearing off drink. She frowns at the glass. "Alka-Seltzer. It'll sort you out within half an hour. Drink."

She accepts willingly, closing one eye to focus on the glass, her hand shaking terribly. I know how that feels. Hate how that feels. I claim the glass and move in, lifting it to her lips, now keen to take away her pain. She downs it like she's not hydrated for weeks.

"More?" I ask, and she shakes her head. I set the glass aside.

"I'm never drinking again." She plummets forward, colliding

with my chest, and I smile mildly as I caress her back, hoping for both our sakes she doesn't.

"That would please me to no end. Promise me you won't get in that state when I'm not around to look after you." *Or ever at all.*

"Did we argue?"

"No, I submitted power temporarily."

"That must have been a challenge."

I smile at her sass and ping her bra strap. "It was"—she has no idea how challenging—"but you're worth the effort." And the stress, and the headache, and the whole heap of crazy she brings into my life. Burying my face in her hair, I silently beg her to forgive me for . . . everything.

Then on a deep breath, I lean back to get her in my sights, brushing a finger across the top of her lace knickers. "I love you in lace." Something so simple but so sexy. So pure. And, apparently, so *me*. Her useless body reacts as always. So pleasing, even hungover. "Shower?" I ask, wanting to wash the toxic aftermath of her reckless drinking away once and for all.

She curls every limb around me, and it's perfect. I take her to the bathroom and set her gently down, anticipation building within. It's time to make up for last night. It's time to bring her back to life. I quickly flip on the shower and return to her swaying form. She falls into me again and supporting her is so natural. "You *are* feeling sorry for yourself, aren't you?" I lift her and place her on the vanity unit. "I have fond memories of you sat exactly here." And now she's back, exactly where she should be.

She lifts her heavy eyes up. "You finally got me where you wanted me, didn't you?"

And where you *wanted to be, lady.* I stroke down her cheek, unable to keep my hands off her. "It was always going to happen, Ava." I pluck my toothbrush out of the holder and load it with paste, leaning past her to wet it under the tap. "Open," I say, and her lips part as she watches me, happy to let me take care of her. She's learning. I'm ignoring the possibility that she simply hasn't the energy to challenge me.

I meticulously brush her teeth, wondering what's running through her clouded mind as she watches me. Is she remembering her confession? Has it come back to her? Should I remind her? Questions circle as I work the brush, but I stop when I feel her palm lay over my cheek, my eyes falling to hers. She's staring at me with such intensity, it almost has me demanding an answer to some of my questions. But I don't. Let it come back to her naturally. Don't push her. So instead, I turn my mouth into her hand, my eyes on hers, and kiss it tenderly. If that kiss doesn't tell her how I feel, then she's more hungover than I thought. "Spit," I whisper, and she pulls her hand away, leaning over the sink.

"Thank you," she says quietly, thoughtfully, sitting back up.

"It's just as much for my benefit as it is for yours." I finally claim her mouth, kissing her deeply but softly. Fuck, I've missed her. So much. "You're rubbish at hangovers. Is there anything I can do to make it better?" There is only one right answer to my question, and if she doesn't get it, I'll happily, very happily, show her. I tug her down and reach around, grabbing her arse, giving her a little hint.

"Have you got a gun?"

I laugh loudly. Yes, I know how that feels too. "That bad, huh?"

She frowns, annoyed by my amusement. "Yes; why is it so funny?"

"It's not. I'm sorry. I'm going to make it all better now." Her eyes light up, and I smile on the inside as I reach behind her and unfasten the clasp of her bra, pulling it down her arms. I toss it into the nearby wash basket, watching as her nipples harden invitingly before my eyes. My mouth homes in, tasting each one in turn. Jesus, I'm home. I have to wrestle with the urgency inside to claim her hard, slowing myself down. She doesn't help my cause when her fingers slip into my hair and grip, her tongue circling mine perfectly. "You're addictive," I say, speaking my thoughts. I crave her more than I've craved alcohol, *need* her more than I need alcohol. "We're going to make friends properly now."

She exhales shakily. "Are we not friends?"

"Not properly, but we will be soon, baby." I plant a kiss on her nose and sink to my knees before her, slipping my thumbs past the seam of her lace knickers, anticipation killing me. And yet, I don't rip them off. I don't hurry this. Truthfully, I can't believe she's here.

I close my eyes and let my forehead fall forward, the weight of my thoughts too much. She loads me with strength, and yet makes me weak. She makes me see clearly, and yet distorts everything. She makes me crazy, and yet stabilizes me. The conflict is a burden. But also a blessing.

The sensation of her stroking my hair is hypnotizing, and I spend an age trying to straighten out my mind, trying to justify what I have done. I can't excuse it. I pull back on an inhale and stare at her stomach, apologizing over and over, leaning in and placing a lingering kiss there as I take the sides of her knickers and peel them down her legs. She lifts a foot in turn, and I cast them aside, fighting my mind from straying too far from this moment.

She tugs my hair and I look up at her questioning face. She's sensed my despondency. Would she understand why I've done what I've done? Does she realize she's saving me? I cup her arse and press my mouth into her stomach again. She has to understand. *Has* to.

"What's wrong?" she asks, and I face her. *I will make you understand.*

"Nothing." *Everything.* "Nothing's wrong." I need to distract her. Stop her questions until I've figured out how the fuck I can answer them. I yank her onto my mouth and plunge my tongue deep into the walls of her pussy. I'm instantly drunk on her, ravenous for more. I kiss her, bite her, suck, circle, plunge, lick.

"Ohhhhh!" she moans, yanking at my hair as I feast on her. "I need a shower."

"I need you," I mumble, and my need trumps all others. I need to sate it. And at the same time, send her delirious to the point she wonders what she ever did without me. She needs to be as addicted to me as I am to her. This needs to be even ground.

"You taste incredible," I mumble, her walls pulsing against my mouth incessantly. "Tell me when you're close."

"I'm close," she yells desperately.

"Someone's keen this morning." I introduce my fingers, enduring her vicious yanking of my hair.

"Oh, shit. Please."

"Watch," I growl, increasing my pace, "your," I circle my tongue firmly, her vibrations sinking into me, "fucking," I seethe, "mouth." I sink my finger deep, circling wide, my tongue making long, firm licks.

"Jesse," she yells, and then I see the torment on her face, her expression strained. *Oh yes, she's remembering.* And she tips the edge on an epic moan, her body folding to sustain the intensity as she comes all over my face, her grip finally loosening in my hair, my scalp tingling.

"You're the best hangover cure," she pants as I bring her back down to earth, drinking up her pleasure and swallowing it down.

"You're the best *everything* cure." I trail my tongue up her body, from her pussy to her throat until I'm on my feet again. "Hmmm." I kiss her jawline. "I'm going to fuck you in the shower." I pull her flushed face down and share her release, spreading it across her lips. "Deal?"

"Deal," she says, no hesitation, her hands and eyes drifting down my torso. I feel my muscles tighten the closer she gets to my scar.

"Don't even ask," I say without thought, knowing what's coming. "How's your head?"

She startles, her hands freezing just shy of my wound. God damn me, I need to think before I speak, manage my fucking tone. I fight to get my scowl under control as she looks up at me.

"Better," she says quietly, unsure, and I kick my stupid moth-erfucking arse all over the bathroom. But being defensive comes naturally, always has, and I need to kick that habit with Ava. I offer a small, apologetic smile, and move things along, glancing down at my boxers.

She reaches forward tentatively, as if bracing herself, and the second her touch meets my skin, I take a long, steadying breath, watching her concentrate, her eyes shooting to mine when she meets my solid cock. She moves in closer, my eyes close, and I lower my forehead to hers for a few relaxing moments, her hands drifting to my arse.

"I love this," she whispers, and I open my eyes.

"It's all yours, baby." *All of me is yours.* The good, the bad, and the downright fucking ugly.

She smiles, satisfied, and grabs my dick. I gulp. "I really love this."

Fuck me. I smash our mouths together, kissing her hard, possessively, tugging her close, absolutely loving her greediness. She's desperate. I'm desperate. We're going at each other like we might not live if we don't ravish each other, all tongues and teeth, moans and gasps. My head is spinning. Fucking hell, get me inside her. She must be on the same page because she's suddenly missing from my mouth, wrestling my boxers down my legs. I help her along, and as soon as I'm free, I grab her, hauling her into my chest. "Get your thighs around my waist," I demand, unable to control my tone, attacking her throat, getting my mouth anywhere I can as she circles my hips with her long, slender legs. I choke on nothing when my cock brushes her soaked pussy.

"Oh God," she yelps. I kiss her again, blindly walking into the shower and trapping her against the wall with my body, my hands wedged into the tile to hold me up. "This is going to be hard, Ava." I'll never be able to hold myself back. I'm too desperate. Too starved. "You can scream." Scream so loud, make my ears hear only that. I've missed it.

The water rains over us, and I rear back, mentally bracing myself for what's to come. Exquisiteness. That's what's coming. Perfection. I take hold of my cock, blinking the water from my eyes, watching her panting into my face. She's mentally bracing herself too.

"You and me," I whisper calmly, feeling anything but, and my kiss is proof. "Let's not fight it anymore." I buck and slip past her hot walls, and I'm swiftly out of my mind on pleasure, my fist hitting the wall, my bellow deafening. *Fucking hell.*

"God," she screams.

"No, baby," I murmur, hardly able to talk, my hips thrusting with no guidance. "That's me." *Let me be your god.* "Feels good, doesn't it?" *So fucking good.* And her fingernails going at my back like she's digging for fucking gold says she agrees.

"Ava?" I bark, smashing into her ferociously, her boobs slapping against my chest, my jaw about ready to snap. My eyes fall to her neck, the slippery skin glistening, sparkling. I move in, lapping and sucking at her hot throat.

"Yes!"

"You feel so fucking perfect," I mumble, powering on, my dick expanding by the second, my pace chaotic. "Remember yet?" What the fuck is with all this talking? Shut the fuck up and fuck her. And yet, I love hearing her pleasure. Seeing her face when she's full to the brim with me. Sex has never been about a connection. It's been about shooting my load. Forgetting. I'll never forget this, and neither will she.

"Ava, have you remembered yet?"

"I never forgot," she screams, prying her nails from my back and grabbing my face, sweeping through the water and sweat that's pouring from me. "I never forgot," she reiterates, her face serious, her body jolting with each smash I deliver. I honestly don't know how she's coping with my incessant need to pound her to death, but she is. I love her more.

I exhale shakily, kissing her madly as she holds my cheeks. I should slow down. I should take a moment to appreciate what she's just said. But I'm on autopilot, and when her thighs constrict harshly, I've no hope of slowing. "Jesus," I murmur around her tongue. "God, woman, I'm a slave to you." I can't take this anymore. My legs are going to give. I look to the sky, praying for more strength to keep me upright until the end. "Jesus fucking Christ."

"Jesse, please."

Hearing her beg injects me with more energy, more life, more purpose. I look her square in the eye. "Harder, Ava?" I ask, not relenting, keeping the pace, sending us both crazy. "Answer the question." I want to hear her say it. I want to hear how bad she wants it.

"Yes!"

That word. My drives get deeper, harder, and faster. Deep, hard, fast. Deep, hard, fast. My eyes are crossing, the steam of the shower suffocating me.

Pull out of her, you arsehole!

"Jesse!"

My name is but a squeak before she finds more air and screams, her body spasming, the walls of her pussy grabbing on and squeezing the fucking life out of my cock, dragging my orgasm out. *Jesus.* I groan and shake, trembling like a leaf, hissing at the sensitivity as I come in powerful, consistent bursts. "Ava," I yell, dropping my pace, bringing my relentless hips down to a calm thrust. I can hardly breathe, my heart galloping. My arm resting against the wall is the only thing holding us up.

"Holy shit," I murmur, rolling us so I'm against the wall, sliding down to my arse, Ava still curled around me. If I could reach the dial or be bothered to get up, I'd turn the water to freezing. But I can't. I drop my head back and close my eyes, my palms working circles across her blazing back. "Lady," I whisper, so fucking tranquil in this moment, "you're mine forever."

I know she's opened her eyes because I feel her lashes tickle my pec. What does she think to that? Of being mine forever? Am I going to give her a choice? I laugh to myself. Of course I am. But I won't need to because she wants to be mine. She loves me.

Say it!

But she doesn't. "Are we friends?" she asks instead, her face turning into my skin, peppering me with kisses. It's not what I wanted to hear, but I can wait because it will come.

"We're friends, baby."

"I'm glad." She sounds so content.

"Me too. So glad."

"Where have you been?"

I still. My lungs still. My mind stills. Not this. She can't spoil this beautiful moment with questions. Or, more accurately, I can't spoil this moment with the answers. "It doesn't matter, Ava." *Please, don't ask me. Please, just let me figure out how the fuck I'm going to tell you what I've done.*

"It matters to me."

"You asked for space." *Deplorable.* "I'm back." *And I don't deserve to be.* "That's all that matters." It isn't, I know that, but I need to get us to a point where she will think twice about leaving. And that point isn't now. My serenity is gone, and I can't help feeling pissed off that she's done that. I have no right. None at all,

I'm reasonable enough to accept that. But the feelings are there, and I'll be damned if I can stop them. I'm just one huge fuck-up, making mistake after mistake. I scowl to myself and feel for her arse, getting a good grip and tugging her closer, my soft, *bare* cock still warm and snug inside her.

She eventually sighs. Peeks up at me. She looks exhausted. I *feel* exhausted. Not physically, though. Physically, I could go on forever. Mentally, I don't know how much more I can sustain before I crack. It's an ironic notion. Physical well-being has always been an underlying concern. The drink, the sex. The true state of my mental well-being was masked. Now, I feel like I'm on a runaway roller coaster going one hundred miles an hour, no end in sight, and not a hope of getting off the fucker. And this woman? She's the reason why.

"I need to wash my hair," she whispers, and I reach up to push the wet locks from her face, giving her a tender kiss. "Are you hungry yet?"

"Very." She peels her body from mine, and I can't lie, it feels wrong. I'm lost without her all over me. I watch her as she scans the sparse shelf and plucks out a bottle. "Is this it?" She turns her eyes down to me, where I'm still on my dead arse recovering. "No conditioner?"

"No, sorry." I make a mental note to get some for her. A big bottle, so when she's showering every day here, she won't run out. On a sigh, I find some strength to pull myself up and claim the bottle. "I want to do it." I want to look after her. Feed her. Wash her. Do all the things to the point she forgets how to do them herself and has to depend on me.

She gives up the task easily, and I turn her away, smoothing some shampoo through the length of her hair and making sure I do a good job of massaging it in, smiling when she hums happily, her head falling back on her shoulders. My height gives me the perfect view of her face, her eyes closed, her lips slightly parted.

She looks like she could be walking on air, and I know I feel like I am. For the most part, anyway.

I take her shoulders and move her under the spray.

And my peace goes up in smoke, my shocked eyes nailed to her arse. Or the big fucking bruises covering it. "What the fuck are they?" Lord above, what happened?

She looks over her shoulder, copping a load of my wide eyes, and frowns, turning to find out what's got my feathers all ruffled. "What?"

I grab her when I lose sight of them and turn her back "Them!"

She frowns over her shoulder. "I fell over in the back of Margo."

"What?"

"I was holding up the cake in the back of Margo," she says on a condescending sigh. "I got chucked about a bit."

Yes, I knew she was holding up a fucking cake, but I didn't know this was the extent of the damage. "A bit?" She looks like she's been struck repeatedly with a fucking hammer. My face screws up as I dip and gently stroke the fading bruises. What was she thinking? Her irresponsibility and neglect for herself is leading to one thing: me wrapping her up in cotton wool, and something tells me Ava won't like that. Well, she'd better start fucking looking after herself. It's not beyond me. I'll bubble wrap her if I have to. What if a car had of ploughed into the van? I flinch harshly, blinking back the memories that thought spikes. She wouldn't have stood a chance. "Ava, you look like you've been used as a rugby ball."

She laughs. It makes me want to sew her mouth shut. This is about as funny as John's temper. "It doesn't hurt," she says, blasé.

It doesn't hurt? I beg to differ. I'm in fucking agony. "No more cake propping." I'll be having a word with her friend. "I mean it."

"You're overreacting."

Overreacting? Many would probably agree. I don't give a fuck. Those bruises shouldn't be tarnishing her flawless skin. Nothing should be tarnishing her. Alcohol. Blemishes.

What about you, Ward. Should you be tarnishing her?

"Probably not," I grumble in answer to my own silent question, falling to my knees and kissing her better. "I'll be having a word with Kate too," I warn, just to be clear, just so there are no surprises when I declare the demise of Margo. Fucking Margo. I need to call the dealership and see if they've found a replacement yet.

I rise, every muscle pulling, and turn her back to me, struggling to remove my fierce glare as I wipe the water from her face. Doesn't she realize how precious she is? She needs to look after herself, and if she's going to be difficult about it, I don't mind taking on that role.

When she opens her eyes, I dip and kiss her collarbone. Gently. Softly. Showing her. She quivers when I draw a perfect line with my tongue to her ear. "Later," I promise, smiling when she grumbles unhappily. There it is. Want. Greed. It's a leap in the right direction. The first step on the path that'll be her only route to what keeps her surviving. I'm much farther down that path. "Out," I order, finding it unbelievably hard to refuse her. But refuse her I must. I lack control in so many elements of my life, even more now. Controlling what I can is a necessity. A compulsion.

I guide her from the shower and dry her off, wrapping her up, snug and cozy in a towel. "All done."

I see her eyes roam the vast planes of my torso, see her delight. Irresistible. She finds me irresistible. Taking her hand, I lead her into the bedroom. I find my jeans and tug them on, depriving her. Increasing her want.

"No boxers?" she asks.

I'm careful as I fasten the fly, smiling. "No, I don't want any unnecessary obstructions."

"Obstructions?"

I yank a T-shirt over my head, feeling her burning gaze all over my front. *Yeah, I'm a tad older. But in incredible shape.* "Yes, obstructions," I say as I tug it down my body, watching in amusement as she tries to get her lax jaw under control. She's adorable. I walk over and take her neck, pulling her close, aware I'm being unfair. And I'm not sorry. "Get ready," I murmur lowly, sealing our mouths.

"Where's my dress?"

"I don't know," I say before I can stop myself, my mind working overtime. Use it as a bargaining chip. Ammo. I nod to myself as I stride out of my room. I'm all for give and take.

I make it to the kitchen and find my peanut butter, settling at the island and thinking while dipping, mentally making our plans. I haven't told her she's technically working today. How will that go down? I pull my finger from my mouth slowly, my eyes narrowing, my cunning mind off on a tangent. I'll convince her it's a great idea. Just watch me.

I turn on my stool when I hear her coming down the stairs, bracing myself for the vision of her naked in my kitchen. She may as well get used to it. I don't plan on letting her wear any clothes when she's here, and if I have my way, which I will, she'll be here a lot.

I look up, grinning like an idiot as I suck my finger clean. She's not naked. But she still looks like a dream in one of my dress shirts. My dick buzzes. My body calls for her. "Come here."

Her face falls into a frown. "No."

No? What does she mean, no? She can't stand there like that and then refuse me. "Come . . . here," I say slowly, my face twitching with the effort to hold back my filthy look.

"Tell me where my dress is." She looks at me with pure defiance. It doesn't bode well for the plans I've made and of which she is yet privy to. The battle to hold back that filthy look becomes too much, and I slowly rid my hands of my favorite thing, preparing to replace it with another one of my favorite things. Actually, my absolute preferred thing. She's challenging me. Somewhere between the shower and the kitchen, she's found her spunk. She's trying to claw back some control. Call the shots. I thought we'd reached an understanding. Apparently not. I actually love her spirit . . . but not all the time.

Hmmmm. What to do, what to do?

I should give her a chance to rethink because one thing becoming glaringly obvious to me is that she's more agreeable when she's in my arms and mindless on this insane chemistry we produce. So I have to ensure she's in my arms as much as possible. "You have three seconds," I say, surprising myself. Yet it's all I have, short of getting up and physically dragging her over. I need her to come to me willingly. Each time she does, it's a brick stronger in the structure that will be us.

"Three seconds for what?"

"To get your arse over here." Simple. Keep it simple. Simple but effective. I hope. We'll soon find out. "Three . . ." I say quietly, my face deadpan, though on the inside I'm laughing my fucking arse off. Not at her. At me. The fucking countdown?

"What happens if you make it to zero?" she asks, her face a picture of uncertainty.

I eradicate that sass and defiance you've found with a reminder of how good we are together, that's what. "Do you want to find out?" I ask, because I'm more than willing to show her. "Two . . ."

She's shifting from foot to foot, her eyes darting. Come to me. Don't come to me. Either way, she will be in my arms in . . .

"One . . ."

She shoots across the kitchen fast, and I welcome her with an open embrace, of course, deeply satisfied. She's learning well. My body relaxes immediately, and I rest my head on hers as she strokes my back. See? Perfect. Why ever would she play silly games and starve us of this? And speaking of starving us, has she remembered what she told me last night? I pout to myself. It doesn't hurt to ask.

I shift and lift her onto the worktop, moving between her thighs, smiling at my shirt drowning her as I skate my palms over the smooth skin. "I like your shirt," I muse, pulling my hand back from the brink of meeting the apex of her thighs.

"Is it expensive?" she asks casually.

I raise my eyebrows, smiling darkly at her cheek. She knows it's expensive. "Very." But fuck the shirt. Let's get down to business. "What do you remember about last night?"

She definitely withdraws, and it's far too long of a delay before I get an answer. "You're a good dancer."

Talk about stating the obvious. But it's not what I'm looking for. "What can I say? I'm a sucker for JT." Moving on. "What else do you remember?" *Come on, Ava. Give it to me. Don't make me squeeze it out of you.*

"Why?" she asks, looking at me in question. It makes me pause for thought. She really doesn't remember?

I deflate. Well, that sucks balls. Okay, let's try and clear something else up. "Do you remember seeing your ex?"

"Yes," she virtually snarls, though I can't be sure if it's at me or him.

"Do you remember my request?"

"Yes."

That's good. It's one less thing for me to worry about. But . . . back to the original matter. "And at what point do you draw a blank?"

Her body tightens in my hold. "I don't remember getting home, if that's what you're getting at." She's defensive. *Very* defensive. "I do realize I was stupidly drunk and highly irre-sponsible."

I couldn't agree more. So I'll take that as an indirect guarantee she won't be drinking again. Glad we've cleared that up. It's dangerous. And on top of that, she told me something ground-breaking and can't fucking recall. "You don't remember anything after the bar?" I ask, digging deeper, willing her to try hard and remember.

"No," she sighs, glancing away. She's not avoiding me. She's embarrassed.

"That's a shame." So I guess I have to wait until she has that revelation when she's sober. That's another solid reason to not let her drink again. There are too many to ignore. I take her cheeks and drop a kiss on her lips. *Dig deep, baby. Find those words.* Because I really need to hear them again.

"How old are you?" she asks.

For the love of all things old. Age is but a number. *So tell her, you colossal tit.* Yet I can't ignore the cautious part of my brain warning me to hold back on all the things that could potentially end this. So I do what I'm learning works for us. Kiss her. Consume her. Show her that nothing matters except how smitten I am. "Twenty-six," I murmur, gently biting her lip, smothering her with my mouth and relishing her immediate softness.

"You missed twenty–five."

"No, I didn't. You just can't remember asking me." *Right before you told me you love me.*

"Oh. After the bar?"

I touch her nose with mine. "Yes, after the bar." Her lips part, and I smile thoughtfully as I wipe the remnants of my kiss away. "You feeling better?"

"Yes, but you need to feed me."

I laugh. "Are you making demands?"

"Yes. Get me my clothes."

And now she's gone too far. I make a play for her hip and squeeze, making her jerk on a gasp. "Who has the power, Ava?"

She laughs, squirming, wriggling, generally increasing her torture all by herself. My grip is solid. "What are you talking about?"

"I'm talking about how much easier we'll get along if you accept who holds the power."

"You do," she screeches, and I smile, satisfied.

"Good girl." I haul her forward and reinforce it with a kiss. "Don't forget it." I break our connection, leaving her panting on the worktop, wanting more. Granted, I'm pretty pent-up myself, but depriving her is a tactic I'll exercise when necessary. I head upstairs, adjusting my dick behind my jeans as I go, and retrieve her underwear from the wash basket in the bathroom, her shoes from the floor, before heading back down to fetch her dress from the washing machine.

When I arrive back in the kitchen, she's still on the worktop, her cheeks still wonderfully flushed. Even if she's got narrowed eyes pointing at me.

I scoff. "Don't look at me like that, lady," I warn, handing over her things, giving the dress a filthy look as I do. "You won't be wearing that dress again, I can assure you." I'll cut it up to guarantee it. "Put the shirt over it." My phone rings, and I leave her with the facts as I take Sarah's call, wandering out onto the terrace.

"Morning," I chirp happily.

"So he's alive," she quips.

More alive than ever. But I quickly remember that I'm not talking to her. "What do you want?"

"Where are you?"

I roll my eyes. She knows exactly where I am, and who I'm with. "Why are you asking questions to which you know the answers?"

"With her," she sighs, as if it's a massive problem. "I'm surprised she's given you the time of day after—"

"Don't," I warn. "And had you not wanted to *help* me unwind, I wouldn't have to worry about being given the time of day."

She's silent for a few moments, and then she inhales, realization falling. "She still doesn't know about The Manor, does she?"

I glare at the beautiful view.

"And what about your Tuesday evening indiscretions?"

"Sarah . . ." I'm growling, hate rising, mostly hate for me. "I'll talk to you when I get there." I need to tell her the score, and she needs to stop fucking interfering. "Ava's coming with me to work on the extension."

"Risky."

"It's Sunday. It's quiet. See you soon." I hang up and rub at my forehead, ensuring all signs of stress and guilt are gone before I make it back to the kitchen. Except, when I arrive, I find Ava frantically rummaging through her purse, and that stress and guilt returns tenfold. *Fuck.* She's looking for her pills. "You ready?" I ask.

"Two seconds." She shakes her head, clearly casting her mind back, trying to remember the moment she *didn't* put her pills in her purse. I bite my lip as she approaches and takes my hand. It's easy to be distracted from my wrongs by that little black dress. She's put the shirt over it—good girl—but what use is that if it's flapping open?

"It's a good job Cathy isn't here. You would give her a heart attack in that dress."

"Cathy?" she asks, confused, as I set about fastening the buttons from top to bottom.

"My housekeeper." I nod my head approvingly. "Better." I take her hand and lead her out, looking at her as we board the lift. She looks thoroughly fucked. It suits her.

The doors close, and my head is quickly invaded with a

barrage of wicked ideas, all involving Ava, me, and this lift. Against the wall. On her knees. I shift on the spot, the rough material of my jeans rubbing against my bulging cock. I should have put some boxers on. I have a one-track mind lately and that one track always leads to Ava.

"Morning, Mr. Ward," the concierge says as we pass, smiling brightly at Ava. "You look better this morning, Ava."

I feel Ava's intention to stop and chat with the old boy. Not today. Our time together is precious. No sharing. Pulling her on, we make it outside, and I open the car and get her in, fastening her seatbelt for her. She doesn't bat an eyelid, just smiles up at me.

Acceptance. It's stunning on her.

Today is going to be a good day.

20

I SPEND the whole journey to Ava's detailing my plan to get her to The Manor with me this afternoon. It's simple. I'm going to tell her.

She slips out of my car when I park and rounds the front, joining me on the pavement. The way she's looking up at me tells me I could just ask and she'd agree.

She walks into my chest, tilting her head back, and I remain where I am, my hands restrained in my pockets. I could take what she's silently offering, but there's so much more pleasure to be had when she gives it to me willingly. She comes closer, closing the space between our lips, and when they meet, I'm done for. I give in to the power and seize her, tumbling into my newfound euphoria, working her mouth firm and steady, the world as I know it disappearing around me. I don't want this kiss to end, but I tear myself away, and she whimpers, her hands limply sliding from my shoulders. I've never seen a woman so deeply and obviously breathless. It's fuel to my fire of need. She doesn't want to leave me.

She walks up the path to the front door, unsteady on her feet, and I follow with a small smile.

She turns and finds me close behind. "What are you doing?" she asks.

"I'm coming in to wait for you."

"Where am I going?"

"You're coming to work with me," I tell her candidly, and her sweet frown deepens.

"You just kissed me goodbye."

"No, Ava." I reach up and sweep aside the lock of hair falling across her brow. "I just kissed you." She should get used to it. "Get ready."

"Okay."

Her easy agreement is promising. Let's keep that up. She opens the front door, and I follow her into the lounge, my eyebrows jumping up when I find Sam looking a bit cozy with Kate. He stayed here? All night? I throw him a questioning look.

"Hey, my man." He doesn't seem to give two fucks about the fact he's naked, hardly covered by the sheets. I cast a look across to Ava to see if she's at all affected by my well-formed, *younger* mate.

"How are you feeling, Ava?" he asks with a cheeky smile, and Ava's cheeks turn a fetching shade of pink. Embarrassed?

"Good." She looks away from my exhibitionist friend and finds Kate, tilting her head. It's a silent message. She wants to talk like girls talk. Good. Because I need to talk to Sam like a girl too. "I'll be as quick as I can." She dips out of the lounge, and Kate makes no attempt to untwine her body from Sam's.

"I think you're wanted," I say, subtly hinting for her to exit so I can pick Sam's brain. He must have talked about me with Kate. Ava's friend must have divulged *something*.

Kate lifts the sheets and peeks under them before returning her eyes to me. "Want to turn around?"

Realization dawns and Sam laughs as I quickly pivot, giving them my back while Kate dresses.

"Thanks," she says, moving past me, now decent. I make sure she's gone before I turn and find Sam shoveling cornflakes in his gob.

"Good night?" I ask, interested. I don't think I can ever recall him not being at The Manor on a Saturday night. What gives?

He peers up at me, smiling around his spoon. "Surprisingly yes, considering it was rather vanilla. You?"

The best. I look over my shoulder. "Very."

"You cleared the air?"

"Not exactly." Not in the sense he's talking about, anyway. But I do feel like I've moved mountains in the understanding department. It's a start.

"You haven't told her about The Manor?"

"No."

"About what happened on Tuesday?"

"No."

"Your drinking problem?"

I scowl. "I don't have a drinking problem." I need to remove my head from my arse.

Sam drops the spoon in the bowl, and it clangs loudly. "Have you told her anything?"

I feel my bottom lip jut out sulkily, my hands sinking into my jean pockets. "I don't know where to fucking start, Sam."

"How about with The Manor?" he asks, sitting up and pulling a cushion over his lap. "Then maybe I can stop biting my fucking tongue when your *hotel* comes up in conversation."

"Why, you planning on having lots of conversations?" I ask with a laugh. This time, Sam scowls, and it's quite a sight.

"She's a cool chick."

The fuck? Sam doesn't see chicks as cool. He sees them as playthings. "Wow," I blurt.

"Wow, what?" Kate asks as she saunters back in and drops to the couch next to my mate. She looks between us, and Sam gives me a look to suggest I need to pull my finger out and start spilling some truths.

"Nothing," I mumble, throwing him a look to suggest I'll do it in my own good time. Like when? When she's legally bound to me? What with? Marriage? A kid?

Both?

My eyes drop to the floor. I can't believe the things I'm thinking. She'll say no. Probably now, and definitely after discovering everything there is to know about me. Uncomfortable, I back out of the room to find Ava, needing to stabilize. Only she can do that. I hear the buzz of a hairdryer and approach the room, and when I open the door, she's bent over, her dark waves being blasted hurriedly. She looks like she's in a rush. To get back to me?

Taking myself to her bed, I climb on, bouncing, testing the mattress. Then I settle back and enjoy my view. She's definitely rushing. I pull my phone out and take a picture of her roughly running her fingers through the strands, and gaze around at her room. Her *temporary* accommodation. So where is she going to live when she leaves here? I ponder that, spying some trainers in the corner. Old trainers. She runs?

The hairdryer stops, and her hair wafts through the air. She finds me and takes in my reclined, relaxed form. Shudders. "Hey, baby." My gaze takes a lazy jaunt down her incredible body.

"Hey, yourself." Her smile is everything. "Comfortable?"

I pout, shuffling. "No." This bed isn't at all comfortable. Regardless . . . "I'm only comfortable with one thing under me these days." *You.* I get up, making my way to her, savoring the vision of her heightening craving the nearer I get. That's what I can do to her. Some might call it manipulation in a sense. I call it security.

I reach her, and I know she's expecting me to ravish her. I don't. I take her shoulders and turn her to face her wardrobe. I get as close as I can to her back, leaning past to browse the dresses. All lovely dresses. Some way too short. I find the perfect one. It's cream, will look beautiful against her skin tone and dark hair. "Put this on," I whisper, feeling her body stiffen. "And make sure there's lace underneath it." Lots and lots of lace.

Her shaky hand extends and accepts the dress without question, and I make sure when I release it that my touch falls precisely and softly over her naked breast. She shivers. I'm not without a reaction myself, my cock hammering against my jeans. *Take her.* I roll into her. Work her up.

Then step away, slapping her peachy arse. "Be quick." Turning, I leave, too fucking happy with myself.

I find Sam and Kate still on the couch all over each other, and I cough to get their attention. Kate shoots back, wiping her mouth, and Sam grins. "Tea?" Kate asks, jumping up.

"One sugar," Sam calls, chuckling and grabbing the remote control. "You know, vanilla ain't so bad." He looks across the room to me. "You heading to The Manor?"

"Yeah. I'm taking Ava."

"Risky," he says, flicking through the channels as I roll my eyes.

"There's hardly anyone around on a Sunday."

He exhales, tilting his head my way. "When are you going to tell her, mate? You can't go on dodging bullets. And you definitely don't want her to figure it out on her own."

I know he's right. "I'm working on it." I need to make a list of all the things I need to share and what order I need to share them in. I'll start there. In the meantime, I'll focus on helping Ava reach the same conclusion she reached last night. I need that. "Enjoy the rest of your day," I say sardonically. "Will I be seeing a request to pause your membership?"

He laughs loudly. "Calm down," he says. "Unlike you, I'm

not planning on stalking a woman until she agrees to be at my beck and call twenty-four/seven."

"You haven't got as many demons as me to restrain," I grumble, leaving Sam to go find Ava. I pass Kate in the hallway and she smirks. I stop and follow her with my eyes. "What's that look for?" I ask, raging with curiosity.

"No look."

"Where's Ava?"

"Looking for her pills in the kitchen."

My eyes shoot so fast toward the kitchen door, I nearly lose them in the back of my head. Looking for her pills? More pills? How many does she keep? I approach the doorway quietly, finding her scratching through a drawer, muttering and cursing under her breath.

She stops. Frowns at the contents of the drawer. Then slams it shut. "I always keep them in my makeup bag."

Oh? Good to know. "Problem?"

She startles. "I can't find my pills."

Good. I shake my head to myself. I'm deplorable. There's time for this little fuckup of mine to be rectified; she can't fall pregnant after missing one pill. Can she?

But . . . "Find them later," I say. This is a sign. An omen. The fates are speaking. They don't want her taking those pills either.

"Come on." I offer my hand, taking in the lovely cream dress. I have good taste. She should let me dress her every day. It'll be a win-win. She gets to look out of this world without so much as thinking about it, and I'll avoid unnecessary heart attacks. Perfect. The dynamics of our relationship are starting to figure themselves out, and I really like where it's heading. More peace. More Ava. "I like your dress," I tell her quietly, hoping she appreciates how much. She gives me a doubtful pout as she nears, her eyes narrowing suspiciously. *Oh, give me a break.* I can see by the look on her face she's going to try and play the cool card. Pointless. I reach under the cream material, smiling darkly when she gulps. *Nice try, baby.* She grabs me for support as I breach the edge of her knickers—lace, of course—and delve gently into her saturated pussy. "Wet," I whisper, circling slowly. So fucking wet. "Later." I have no idea how I manage it, but I remove my touch. My consolation prize is licking up her condition from my finger.

"You have to stop doing that." She's completely exasperated.

"Never," I promise, leading her out of the kitchen.

It's like a second nature to me to buckle her up, and it seems it's like second nature for her to let me. I slip into the driver's seat and roar off down the road, my hand automatically falling to her knee and remaining there. Constant contact. It's all I need. Not too much to ask.

I steal glimpses of her often, watching as she gazes out of the window, deep in thought. Is she thinking how amazing this is? Me and her? Natural? Easy together when we're on the same page? She looks across the car and catches me admiring her. I smile. She smiles. Even our smiles are perfect together.

The road to The Manor is dense with trees, the light wind rustling the leaves above, the sun bursting in the sky. It's a beautiful day.

"How long have you owned The Manor?" she asks out of the blue, cluing me in on what she's been thinking.

Now's the perfect opportunity to start slowly breaking some of my silence. "Since I was twenty–one."

I smile when those gorgeous eyes widen. It's quite surprising, I agree. And she thinks it's only a hotel. "That young?"

"I inherited The Manor from my uncle Carmichael."

"He died?"

I swallow. "Yes."

The compassion on her face hurts. Perhaps she wouldn't feel so sorry for me if she knew the circumstances. "I'm so sorry," she says quietly, clearly struggling for anything else to say.

"Me too." So sorry.

She leans across and rests a hand on my knee. I appreciate her sentiment, even if it's wasted. I push back the imminent onslaught of memories and flash her a smile. I don't deserve sympathy. I deserve reprisal. I've done a fine job of punishing myself over the years, all an act of self-preservation in a fucked-up sense. Hurt myself, lose myself, to escape the constant pain of my reality. To keep my past at bay. Being out of control was something I could control. With Ava, I still feel out of control, except now I have a cure. It feels like a double-edged sword. For the first time in as long as I can remember, there's hope. I never imagined I could feel happiness again. Never dared dream I could feel alive or have a worthwhile purpose. And the one thing that gives me that is the only thing that can take it away. How the fuck do I navigate these murky, unfamiliar waters and get to the other side with my sanity intact?

"How old are you, Jesse?"

"Twenty–seven," I reply without thought, and she sighs.

"Why won't you tell me how old you are?"

"Because you might think I'm too old for you and run a mile."

"Do *you* think you're too old for me?"

"No, I don't." *I'm perfect for you.* "My issue is your issue."

"I don't have an issue."

She doesn't? I narrow my eyes a fraction and turn them onto her. "Then stop asking me." My lips quirk when her face screws up in displeasure.

"What about your parents?"

The question comes from left field, and I am far from prepared for it. Then again, am I really prepared for anything where Ava's concerned? "I don't see them," I reply frankly, hoping that'll be that.

My hopes are answered. She leans back in her seat, falling silent, and I feel like an arsehole once again. It doesn't prompt me to correct myself though, and the rest of the journey is cloaked in an awkward silence that isn't perfect and doesn't suit us. I can't expect anything less. I was short with her, and if I'm not careful she'll be leaving me for being so fucking cagey.

As I rumble down the driveway slowly, I see John's Range Rover up ahead, the big guy slipping out. I don't know why he doesn't just move into The Manor. He only goes home to trim his bonsai trees.

I park next to him and claim Ava. "What's happening, John?"

"'S'all good," he grunts, extending his hand for me to slap as we pass. All good. Quiet as I'd expected, but I needed to check. I take Ava into the bar and find my staff washing glasses. Pete, understandably, is surprised to see me.

"Mr. Ward," he says, tilting his head in question.

"We'll take breakfast in my office." I reach across the bar for a menu. "What do you fancy, baby?" I ask, looking down at her. It might be me, but she looks pensive. "Except me, of course," I add, trying to loosen her up a little.

She smiles. "Do you serve eggs Benedict here?"

"We do," I confirm, and if we didn't, I'd have Pete fix that. Anything for her. "Coffee?"

"Cappuccino, no chocolate or sugar."

"And a flat white for me," I say, passing the menu to Pete. He's looking at me like I might have a colossal zit on the end of my nose. It's warranted. It's ten on a Sunday morning. I don't think I've ever been around at this time on a Sunday. And with a woman? A woman whom I'm calling *baby*, looking at adoringly, and feeding? "Pete?"

"Yes, of course."

"Thanks." I look at Ava and notice her wary gaze around the bar. She's definitely uneasy. Perhaps she's remembering the last time she was standing in this very spot after I'd cornered her in my suite. Or is she still stung from my snappy reply in the car?

I swipe up her hand and pull her along, my pace urgent, Ava practically jogging to keep up with me. I reach my office, swing the door open, tug her inside, throw it shut, and push her against it.

Fix it.

I grab the hem of her cream dress and pull it to her waist, planting my face in her neck.

I'm sorry.

I just need some time to figure this out.

My plan works just as I'd hoped. She's mine in a heartbeat, grappling at my T-shirt, her breath diminishing. I kiss her hard, molding her boobs, my despondency fading, quickly replaced with hunger. Starvation. Need. "Are you wet?"

"Yes." She yanks at my T-shirt, and her urgency spurs my own. Her desperation is like a shot of adrenalin. She wants our normal back too, and our normal is this unrestrained wildness. We can't get enough of each other, and I'm banking on that to carry us through.

My hand journeys from her breast to her knickers, and I unfasten my fly and let my weeping cock fall into it. I yank her lacy knickers aside, pull her thigh to my waist, and ram into her unforgivingly on a yell, my desperation getting the better of me. She screams.

"Quiet," I order, knowing Sarah could be lurking around, and the last thing I need is her coming to investigate and interrupting me.

I smash into her hard, the weight of my torment provoking me. Her head drops onto my shoulder. "Do you feel me, Ava?" *Do you feel how vital you are to me in maintaining my sanity?* "Answer the question!"

"Yes," she screams. "I feel you."

I smash on, pushing her higher up the door and me further into delirium. She's lost, her mind empty except for me. Me and the pleasure I give her. "Does it feel good?"

"Oh God, yes!"

I kiss her with unjustified vigor, sweating hard. "I said, quiet."

Her nails sink deeper into my shoulders, and I hiss, the pressure in my cock becoming painful. I'm going to come so fucking hard, and I need her there with me.

Her body jacks, she shudders violently, she screams, and it's like rocket fuel to my dick. I explode inside her, smashing my fist into the door by her head, every muscle tightening to stem the sensitivity.

Fuck.

Fuck, fuck, fuck.

I gasp for air, my lungs on fire, feeling her walls gripping me mercilessly. My face slips against the wet skin of her neck, her pores leaking pure sex. "I might bring you to work every day," I whisper through my labored breathing, clenching my eyes shut as I slowly ease out of her. She looks dazed. Lifeless. "Are you okay?"

She stays where she is, leaning on me for support. Always. I hope. "Don't let go of me."

I laugh lightly. Never. I lean back with a small smile as she locates some air to puff her damp hair from her wet face.

"Hi," she squeaks.

"She's back." I kiss her affectionately and pick her up, knowing she's not capable of walking. And I like carrying her. I place her on the couch and sort myself out, relishing the smile she's holding back. She's happy. But as I consider this room—and the shit that has gone down in here over the last two weeks—it makes me want to get rid of every item of furniture and start again. Fresh slate. *No erroneous, unforgivable mistakes.* But for now, I'll focus on the good, and that is Ava. She's been out of my arms for a matter of seconds, and I already miss her. So I put myself on the couch and drag her onto my lap. "I thought you could go up to the extension and start drafting some ideas." And while she's there, I'm going to write that list of things we need to talk about.

She looks taken aback, and for a moment I wonder if I said that out loud. "You still want me to design?" she asks.

"Of course I do."

"I thought you just wanted me for my body." Her eyebrows rise, and I wrinkle my nose, reaching for her nipple and giving it a little flick.

I want her for many things. Peace, purpose, distraction, and because I'm absolutely infatuated with her. Her body is just a bonus. "I want you for a lot more than your body, lady." Let's make that clear. I'm about to reinforce that with a smoldering kiss, but there's a knock at the door, and she's off my lap quickly.

"Come in," I order grumpily, and Pete wanders in with our breakfast. All I can think is . . . how can she sit on me while eating it? "Thanks, Pete."

"Sir." He leaves, and I pull the dome off the plate, pushing the tray toward her. "Eat your eggs, baby." And be quick about it.

And she is. I've never seen a woman tuck food away so fast, and it makes me wonder if she's eaten in the past week. I don't like that thought. Did she lose her appetite? Was she as lovesick as me?

I cough my throat clear, and she looks up, her next forkful hovering in midair. I drop my mouth open, remaining relaxed back on the couch. Eggs Benedict is her favorite. Will she share? I couldn't possibly challenge her if she refuses me. She's my favorite, and I wouldn't dream of sharing her.

She smiles and inches closer, diverting the fork to my mouth, and I keep hold of her eyes as I seal my lips around the egg and she slowly pulls the fork out. And just like that, I want her again. What am I talking about? I want her every second of every day.

She takes her last mouthful and I reach over, pulling her to my side and getting her under my body.

"I want to devour you." And I can see from the glistening of her eyes that she's so up for that. "But I have to fucking work." Or get to writing a list. Plus, the sooner she's done what she needs to do in the extension to move the project forward, I can get her home. I might not let her leave, either. It's Monday tomorrow. A workday. Can she work from home? *My* home? I'd promise to leave her alone so she could.

It's a promise I'd never be able to keep.

I kiss her and rip myself away, going to my desk and collecting a pad and a pencil and holding them out to her.

"I'll head up to the extension." She gets up and accepts, and my sulky bones just can't bear to see her go. So I make a play for her, grabbing her waist, and she laughs, trying to wrestle free.

"Kiss me," I order.

"I just did."

Wrong. I kissed her. Big difference. "Don't make me ask again, Ava," I warn, deadly serious. She should do everything I suggest. *You're not suggesting, you idiot. You're demanding.* I cock my head in expectation, and she smiles, giving in to me. She's learning. And there's something about receiving a kiss rather than giving one.

When she opens the door, my trusty John is waiting.

"I know where I'm going, John," Ava says, sounding tired. She might do. But I'm covering all bases.

"'S'all good, girl," he grunts.

I close the door and look across to the cabinet. All of the bottles I broke in my rage have been replaced. And I feel nothing. No hate for the bottles. No desire to grab one and sink it. But I would love to wring Sarah's fucking neck. She's quite happy for me to fuck my way through The Manor because I'll be close. Unattached. The same man I've been for sixteen years—not in love with her, but not in love with anyone else. Ava is a woman who could take me away from this life, therefore take me away from Sarah. She wants me to fail? Surely not. And yet, I know Sarah. She's as broken as I am, but she handles her guilt differently.

I sigh and sit down at my desk, checking through my emails quickly. Nothing important. Good. I pull out a pad and pen and write at the top, *The Path to Redemption. Number one: Ava O'Shea*. I smile and sit back, tapping the end of the pen on my bottom lip as I stare at her name for a long, long time, my mind speeding. I tilt my head. Pout. Then lean forward and cross out her surname, replacing it with mine. "Ava Ward," I say to myself, chewing my bottom lip.

The door swings open, John marches in, and I quickly pull the cover of the pad over the first page. He looks stressed. John doesn't do stressed.

"You need to tell her, motherfucker," he says, slamming the door on a deafening thwack.

I recoil. "Yes, I know that. I wish people would stop stating the fucking obvious."

"A member just stumbled out of a room, his dick practically hanging out."

I sit up straight in my chair. "Did Ava see?"

"Yes, she fucking saw." He drops into the chair opposite me. "Poor thing didn't know where to look." He leans forward threateningly. "And she seemed rather curious about the doors to the communal room."

Bollocks. I rub at my forehead, getting a heavy dose of John's stress. "I'll sort it," I assure him. "Where's Sarah?"

"I don't know. Probably having something pumped, sucked, or tucked. She said she'd be here by noon." He gets up and rounds the desk, helping himself to my laptop. "Am I going to be blessed with your presence for long?"

I huff to myself as he unlocks the screen and his fat fingers tap clumsily across the keys. "Long enough."

"Anyone would think you don't like being here."

"Why would I want to be here and be stressed when I can lock myself away in Lusso with Ava and be happy?"

"That's because when you're with Ava, you're living a fucking lie, moron."

Moron? "I prefer motherfucker," I grumble.

He turns his face to me, removing his wraparounds. "Tell her."

"Okay," I bark, flicking my hand out in my annoyance, sending the pad to the floor. And isn't it just typical that it falls in such a way that when John dips to pick it up, the words "Ava O'Shea Ward" stare up at him.

Silence.

Fuck.

I die a million times, cringing my arse off, shifting in my chair. Caught red-handed. He slowly rises with the pad in his hands, staring at it. "I was just fucking about," I say, mortified. "I was bored." I look away, feeling my face flame. I can literally hear him mentally calling me out as a crazy fucker. I can't bear his quiet judgments.

I look out the corner of my eye at him as he tosses the pad down. It lands with a slap. "Tell her."

Tell her what? That I want to marry her? Have babies with her? Keep my dick inside her twenty-four/seven? "Is it possible to fall in love so fast?" I ask. That's it. I can't possibly get any lamer. All or nothing. Besides, John's the only person on this planet I could ever speak to so honestly, and despite the stress I'm clearly causing him, I know deep down he's full of hope too. I've lost count of the number of times he's had me in a chokehold against a wall and threatened to rip me a new arsehole if I don't sort out my life. Well, I'm sorting it. And it's all a bit unexpected, to be honest, so he needs to be patient with me while I navigate this unchartered territory.

"Yes," John says, simple as that, surprising me.

"It is?"

He takes himself back to the other side of my desk and sits. He's getting comfortable. It's the kind of comfortable he gets when I'm about to have some hard home truths thrown my way. "Carmichael fell pretty hard for Sarah back in the day."

I laugh. "Bad comparison, John." My uncle might have fallen hard, but he also shared her. There will be none of that, I can assure him.

"A comparison nonetheless."

"Then why weren't they exclusive?" I ask. I've always wondered, but never asked. Historically, I've shied away from talking about my uncle. It always brought too much self-hatred, but as I sit here now, I feel none of that. It's . . . odd. Odd but nice.

"Your uncle knew if he wanted to keep her, he had to bend. Besides, he couldn't have let go of his old ways even if he'd wanted to."

"So he continued to spread the love."

"But it was always Sarah in his bed at the end of the day." His head lowers. "If you love someone, you bend."

I'm bending so much, I'm becoming a yoga pro. "What are you saying?"

"I'm saying don't crowd her. You'll push her away if you're too needy."

"I am needy," I mumble. I never knew it, but I am. And I don't mind so long as Ava feeds my neediness.

"And talking of need, you *need* to tell her."

"John," I say, getting up from my chair and starting to pace, "in the hopes of making you understand my predicament, I'm going to tell you a few secrets."

He laughs, and for once I don't appreciate the deep, rumbling sound. "What are they?"

"I'm scared," I say seriously, and his face straightens in a nanosecond, back to the usual impassive, scary expression. "She has run from me more than once with no justifiable reason." I approach him and crouch down by his chair. "So if she can walk away from me with no good cause, why the fuck would I offer up plenty of valid, *good* reasons for her to turn her back on me?"

"You're living a lie," he says quietly. "And it will eventually bite you on the arse and sting like a motherfucker."

"I *will* tell her," I assure him. "Just as soon as I know she won't run."

He points to the desk where the pad is. "What, like after you've put a ring on her finger?"

I don't tell him I'm actually considering it. That would confirm the kind of crazy I am these days. "I'm not completely loo-la." *Not at all, Ward. Stealing her pills last night was a dream, huh?*

He sighs and blindly points at the computer. "Since you're here, I need you to look at that."

I'll take his intention to change the subject as acceptance. Good. Hopefully now he'll stop nagging me. "What is it?"

"Proposed financials for the next year. We've soaked up the price hikes for the past few years. Time to increase membership fees."

I settle back at my desk and get to it, John joining me and walking me through his proposals. It all looks good, and a while later, my eyes are crossed with all the numbers on my screen. "Are we done?' I ask, getting irritable.

"All done."

"Good." I look at my watch. Shit, where did that time go? I get up and stretch. "I'm going to get Ava."

Sarah walks in, and I scan her face for puncture holes. "Why are you looking at me like that?" she asks, reaching up to her cheeks. I hear John laugh behind me, and she turns her questioning expression on him. "What's so funny?"

"Nothing," I say, passing her. I know I said I'd talk to her, but I'm done talking for the day. Now I just want to go home and talk to Ava in that way we do.

"Where's Ava?" she calls, and I freeze by the door.

"Why?"

Sarah passes me and closes the door, stalling my escape. I frown at her as she looks up at me, her face confusingly . . . what? What is that?

"I'm sorry I've been a total bitch," she says, pouting minutely. It's her lips. She's had her lips done, I can see some faint bruising she's tried to hide with a thick layer of makeup.

"Don't worry, I'm used to you being a bitch." I open the door, jumping back when it's slammed shut again. It's all I can do not to growl at her. I want to leave.

"It's just strange. It's always been you, John, and me."

"The three musketeers," John mutters sarcastically behind me, and Sarah tosses him a look that could kill.

I chuckle and motion to the door. "Apology accepted. Can I go now?"

"Oh, one more thing," John calls, reaching over and pulling my laptop across. "I need you to approve the proposal for the update of the CCTV system."

"Why?"

"Because it's expensive and I'm not comfortable spending that amount of money without your approval."

"I'm wanted in the spa," Sarah says, leaving us to it.

I stomp my way back to the desk and scan the itemized proposal. "When can they start?"

"Six weeks."

"Great." I get on my way again. Time is ticking on. Members will start filling the place soon.

"Oi, motherfucker," John growls, and I look over my shoulder. "Look at the fucking figures."

"God, you're demanding today," I say, reversing and doing as I'm told. "How much?" I blurt. "To update it? We could get a whole new fucking system for that."

"We'd have to. The security firm aren't willing to hand over the equipment. We'd need to replace it all."

"Do it," I order. The cheeky fuckers think they can back me into a corner? "See you later."

I hurry out of my office and fly up the stairs to the extension, bursting into the last room, my hands itching to get hold of her. I smile when I find her on her arse on the floor, the pad on her lap. But my smile drops when I register her expression. Then I find Sarah across the room. Oh. "All right?" I ask, cocking my head. She better be playing nice.

Sarah smiles, and I wince as her lips stretch, straining. That must fucking hurt. "Yes, sweetie," she purrs, joining me and rubbing my shoulder. I frown at her hand there. What's gotten into her? "Ava and I were just discussing the new rooms," she says. "She has some fabulous ideas."

They were talking? Like friends? "She's good." I flick a fond smile to Ava.

"Yes, very talented," Sarah replies. *Oh, you have no idea, Sarah.* But I appreciate her being nice for once. "I'll leave you to it." She drops a kiss on my cheek. "Ava, it was lovely to see you again."

"And you, Sarah." She smiles, and I watch, stunned, as Sarah leaves. Did they inject some reason into her when they plumped her lips?

"Let's have a look then, lady." I join Ava on the floor, taking the drawings. She did all this in a few hours? "Wow," I blurt, taking in the intricately detailed bed. "I love that bed."

"So do I."

"What's all this?" I ask, indicating the cover above.

"It's a lattice design. All the wooden beams overlap to form a grid-like effect."

"So you can hang things from them?" Interesting. Like handcuffs or people. This will go down a storm, but where the fuck did she come up with this?

"Yes, like material, or lights, maybe." She shrugs

Of course. "What colors did you have in mind?"

"Black and gold."

Perfect. Sexy but tasteful. "I love it. When can we start?"

"It's only a draft," she says. "I have to do some mood boards, scale drawings, lighting plans, that sort of thing. Will you take me home?"

I crick my neck when I look at her sharply. Home? Something tells me she doesn't mean *my* home. "Are you okay?"

She doesn't want to spend the rest of the day with me? She gets up, smiling. "I'm fine," she says. "I've got some work stuff to sort out for tomorrow."

Don't crowd her. *Fuck you, John.* I sigh, feeling lost. "Okay," I say reluctantly, begrudgingly accepting. "Are you sure you're okay?" Why do I sense something is amiss?

"I'm fine. Why wouldn't I be?"

I eye her suspiciously. Is her hand twitching? Is that smile fake? And why's my stomach turning? "Come on then." I collect her bag and her hand and take her downstairs, realizing halfway that I haven't got my keys.

We reach the entrance hall, and I make a quick scope of the space, hearing people in the bar. "Wait here," I say, but quickly rethink my plan. "Actually, go get in the car." I guide her to the door. "It's open." I leave her and rush to my office, bursting in and snatching my keys off my desk. I exit sharpish, jogging back through The Manor, but slow down when I reach the summer room, looking at Ava's bag in my grasp. I smile and pull out her phone, changing the ring tone before replacing it and picking up my pace, nearly taking Sarah off her heels when she appears from the bar, colliding with my charging form.

"Shit!" she yelps, and I grab her before she falls flat on her face and bursts her lips. She gathers herself, looking dazed. "Are we burning down?" she asks, following me to the door, laughing.

"Sorry." I stop at the top of the steps, seeing Ava by my car. "I'll see you tomorrow."

"Okay, sweetie." Sarah joins me and leans in, kissing my cheek. "See you later."

I break away and make my way to Ava, handing over her bag and opening the door.

"Hope to see you again, Ava." Sarah calls. I look over my shoulder. Her smile is dazzling, and I cock her a questioning look. She rolls her eyes and heads back inside. *Yes, too much.*

But I can't moan. She seems to be taking it on the chin, and I know this drastic change in the dynamics of our relationship will be hard for her. She's not wrong. It has been the three of us for a long time.

I round my car and slip in beside Ava, starting the engine and reaching for her leg, giving it a gentle squeeze, silently getting her attention. She seems . . . distant. "Okay?"

She offers a small smile that goes nowhere near her eyes, resting her hand on mine and returning my squeeze. "Yes. Just thinking of all the things I need to prep for my week."

So she has a busy week at work. I inwardly pout. Does that mean we won't get to spend any time with each other? I'm desperate to ask, just so I have all my ducks in a row—and so I can prepare myself for how long it'll be before I can see her again. *Don't crowd her.* I can already feel my mood dipping.

It's uncomfortably quiet on the way to her place. My thoughts chase around in circles, conjuring up reason after reason to keep her for the night. There's none except, of course, that I simply don't want to spend the night without her. *Just tell her that.*

I pull up outside Kate's, and I'm about to show my hand, tell her I want her to stay with me, when she quickly leans across and presses a fleeting kiss to my cheek before jumping out of my car at lightning speed. "I'll call you."

My frown follows her up the path until she shuts the door behind her. *What was that?* I drum the steering wheel with my fingertips. Then open the door, set to go find out what's going on. *Don't crowd her.*

"Fuck," I mutter, slamming it again and zooming off, my foot naturally heavy on the accelerator. What the fuck am I going to do until tomorrow?

21

GO CRAZY. That's what I did. Walked circles around my apartment, typed out a dozen texts, deleted them, went to bed, and tossed and turned all night.

I woke at five, ran ten miles, paced some more, and spent most of Monday trying to reason with myself, constantly hearing John telling me not to crowd her. Calling her wouldn't be crowding her. Texting her wouldn't be crowding her. Dropping in to see her at work wouldn't be crowding her.

But here's my problem: I don't have the mental capacity or energy to convince myself I'm being irrational. All I know is that when she's with me, I'm fine, and when she's not, I'm far from fine.

After calling and texting twice and getting no answer or replies, I try to convince myself she's just busy. But after trying again and again and again, I realize she isn't busy.

She's avoiding me.

Again.

~

On Tuesday, I'm wide awake at five again, and with nothing else to do but drive myself insane with my thought process and worries, I go for *another* run. I have another mental argument with myself. Another minor meltdown.

My drive to The Manor passes in a blur, and because I still haven't heard back from Ava, I text Sam, asking for Kate's number. Surely she'll tell me the truth. Kate's that kind of woman —shoots as straight as an arrow. I walk into my office and find Sarah at my desk pouring over some spreadsheets. "What did you say to Ava on Sunday?" I ask, my persona aggressive, my stance threatening.

She takes in my tall frame, probably frowning, though you'd never know it. "We chatted. About the designs. Is something wrong?"

I growl and toss my keys and phone on the coffee table, dropping onto the couch. "She's not taking my calls."

"Perhaps she's been busy."

Too busy to answer her phone or texts? I scoff, my foot tapping as fast as my mind is spinning. Chatted? I am ninety-nine percent sure Sarah is lying about what she did or didn't say to Ava, and I know with absolute certainty that even if I ask her, she won't be honest. And I hate that I can't trust someone who has been part of my life for the last twenty years. But it's fact. Ava has been back in this groove since spending time with Sarah.

I grab my phone when it chimes and deflate when I see it's John. I ignore him. Then I inhale when it chimes again and deflate, again, when I see it's Sam. But he's given me Kate's number, no questions. Before I dial it or text her, I try Ava again. Nothing. And after trying Kate then Sam and getting no answer from them either, I toss my phone on the opposite couch in a temper. "Why the fuck won't anyone answer their fucking phones?" *And fuck, I need to get rid of these couches.* I'm just about to demand Sarah to do that when my mobile starts ringing.

"It's mine," Sarah says, holding up her phone as I'm about to dive across the coffee table toward the couch. "He's here," she says, looking at me. "I'll send him."

"What's going on?"

"Leak in the plant room."

My shoulders drop, and I drag myself up, claiming my phone and leaving. This day. This *fucking* day. I grumble and mutter as I pace through The Manor, ignoring anyone who speaks to me.

When I arrive in the plant room, John's on his hands and knees, his suit jacket removed, a towel bunched up by the dehumidifier. "Motherfucker," he grumbles, twisting at something.

At least he's not calling *me* the motherfucker for once. "How bad?" I ask, joining him, seeing his face straining as he tries to unscrew one of the joints on the outlet pipe.

"Bad enough," he grunts and then gasps, dropping his hold and wiping his brow. "Bastard thing is jammed."

I wrestle off my jacket and nudge John out of the way. "Have you isolated the water supply?" I ask, and he grunts his reply, so I get a good grip of the joint and twist. It doesn't budge.

"Told you," John says, keeping an eye on the pressure gage. "Jammed."

I adjust my grip, getting a better angle, straining to loosen the thread. Nothing. "Fuck," I snap, kicking a pipe in anger. I growl and take hold of the joint again, twisting on a yell, straining hard.

Ping.

It pops right off, and the O-ring falls to the tile. I pick it up and inspect the corroded piece of rubber. "Seal's knackered," I say, tossing it at John and collecting my jacket.

"Where are you going now, you moody motherfucker? I've got shit for you to deal with in the office."

"I'll do it later. I'll be in the gym." I need to seriously work off some of this pent-up anger before I find Ava and bulldoze her.

That won't go down well. Gently does it. "Answer my fucking calls, then," I snap to myself, dialing her again.

By two o'clock, I'm no less stressed but I'm fucking beat after killing myself in the gym for hours in between calling Sam, Kate, and Ava. And then like a bolt of lightning when I'm in the shower, I realize something must have happened to her. She's been in an accident. Been hurt. That's why she's not answering my calls or messages, because she physically can't. And that's why Kate isn't getting back to me too. *She's with Ava.* My blood runs cold. My heart goes from zero to sixty in a nanosecond. I hear my phone ring, and I jump out of the stall in a mad panic.

And fall straight on my naked arse. "Fuck!" I yelp, slipping and sliding all over the tiles, trying to get to my phone. I stretch to reach it on the bench and flop down to my back, getting the screen in my view. "Sam," I blurt. "I can't get hold of Ava. I've been calling and messaging since yesterday. Have you—"

"Whoa, my man, cool it."

My jaw grinds harshly. "Don't tell me to cool it. She could be lying in a gutter for all I know. Have you spoken to Kate?"

"She's here. At my place," he says, somewhat gingerly. "Sorry, we just found all your missed calls."

I balk, fighting my slippery body up onto the bench, unable to give Sam's statement—a woman is at his place—the attention it deserves. "So she's not seen Ava either?" I ask, my damn heart pounding painfully. "She doesn't know if she's okay?"

"I'll get her to call her now."

"Yes, do," I growl. "And call me straight fucking back." I look up when John breezes in, giving my naked, soapy form the once-over, looking over his glasses. "Don't say a word," I warn. "And pass me a towel."

John silently reaches for a towel and tosses it at me, and I start rubbing myself down, ridding my body of the suds, my eyes on the screen of my phone, willing it to ring.

"Tell me why the fuck you look about ready to hit something?" he rumbles.

"Ava's missing." I stand and get my boxers on, mentally calculating how many hospitals I need to search and which one first. "No one can get hold of her." I flick John a worried look. There's no mistaking his own concern. Yes. Yes, it's like that. "I thought she was just avoiding me again." I grab my trousers and yank them on. "But, now I'm thinking about it, that doesn't make any sense. We made friends and everything was fine." I want to put a bullet in my head for letting all this time pass. I want to slowly torture myself for not insisting she spend Sunday night with me. Then I wouldn't be slowly dying now.

My phone rings, and I dive on it. "Sam," I breathe, my face screwing up in dread. *Please tell me they've found her.*

"She's fine," he says, and my hand freezes on my shirt. "She answered one of Kate's messages, so she's alive."

"What?"

"Listen, my man, don't lose your shit, but Kate mentioned something about Ava not seeing you again."

I stand stock-still. "What?"

"I said don't lose your shit."

"I'm not losing my shit."

"You sure?"

The burning sensation starts in my toes and spreads through my body like wildfire. "I'm not losing my shit," I grate, looking up at John, who's silently observing me.

Losing my shit.

I've been going out of my mind with worry, and she really is just avoiding me? Why?

"Jesse?" Sam asks quietly. Concerned. "Be cool."

"Be fucking cool?" I bellow, catching John's flinch in my

peripheral vision. "I've been going fucking crazy." I slam my phone down and fight my way into my clothes, barging past John.

"Don't crowd her," he calls after me.

"Fuck off!"

I throw myself in my car and roar off down the driveway, splitting my attention between the road and my phone, searching for the number for Rococo Union's office.

I dial and bark my order when a woman answers. "I want to talk to Ava."

"Yes, sir. Who's calling?"

"It's private."

"Oh. Okay, just a moment, please." The line goes quiet, and I scowl at the road. If she dares comes back and says—

"I'm sorry, sir. Ava is out of the offi—"

"Put her on the fucking phone," I roar, punching my steering wheel, unable to control my temper. I've gone from worry to anxiety to worry to fear to worry to fury.

There's a collection of bangs and cracks, no doubt the result of the poor woman dropping the phone in shock. "I . . . I . . . I'm . . . I'm . . . sor . . . sorry, sir—"

"Don't be sorry, just put her on the phone."

"Sir, please . . . I . . . I assure you . . . she's . . . she's not here."

My God, that woman will be the death of me. "Fine," I yell, smashing my finger repeatedly on the button to end the call. "Have it your way, Ava," I mutter, putting my foot down.

I pull up outside her office, double park, and march to the door, trying to wrestle myself into shape. I push my way in, giving no thought to what I will say and how I will handle this. I scan the space, seeing a desk up ahead, the chair empty. But where is she?

"Can I help you, sir?" a lady at the first desk asks.

"Where's Ava?" I growl, and she blanches, blinking rapidly. She looks brittle, but I'll be damned if I can get a hold of myself and this burning rage. The woman, I'm assuming the same lady I bellowed at on the phone, stares at me blankly, mute. "Where?" I yell.

"She left a while ago, sir."

I stalk back out, getting in my car and wheel-spinning down the street, calling Ava repeatedly. And with each one of my calls she ignores, my anger amplifies. She doesn't get to do this again. I send her a string of messages, and each time I click send, I think of something else to add.

I have been going out of my fucking mind.

Thinking unthinkable things.

I thought something terrible had happened!

But no. You've just got cold feet again?

No. You don't get to do this again. I won't let you, and you'd better get used to that and start rethinking how you handle what's happening between us.

Not surprisingly, she doesn't respond, and also not surprisingly, that only serves to piss me off even more. I screech up outside her flat and dial again as I stalk toward her front door.

"Hello."

I stop in the middle of the road, caught off guard. She answered? "Ava?"

"Jesse," she says, sounding rather calm. That's nice. Here I am, hanging off the edge of a fucking cliff, and she's all composed. Good for her. For fuck's sake. "I can't see you again," she says nonchalantly.

Oh no. Oh, no, no, no. "No," I say, trying to cool the burn inside. "Ava, listen to me—"

She hangs up. She fucking hangs up, and it's infuriating for more than one reason. Because she's scared. She's scared to talk to me, to see me, because if she does, she won't be able to deny our perfection.

I reach her front door and smash my fist into it. "Ava," I shout, hammering at the wood. "Ava!" I reverse my steps and look up at the window, dialing her again. "Pick up, pick up, pick up." My hand goes into my hair, pulling at the mess of blond. It goes to voicemail, and I stare at my phone in astonishment. "Ava! Answer the fucking door!" Why is she doing this? It's exhausting. Enraging. Confusing.

Through my fog of despair, I hear the roar of an engine, and I turn to see Sam swinging into a parking space behind my car. He gets out, Kate in tow, and approaches cautiously. I throw my hands into the air. "She's driving me fucking nuts," I yell, pointing up at the window. "Will someone please explain what the fuck is going through her head, because the last time I saw her things were pretty fucking amazing?"

Kate throws Sam a nervous look, moving in, bravely rubbing my arm. "Calm down."

I roll my shoulder to shrug her off. "What has she said?" I ask, pinning Kate in place with expectant eyes. "When she got home on Sunday, what did she say?" I can see she's torn. "Kate," I push, feeling fraught, moving in to make sure she can see my desperation. "I need to see her. I know she's scared, but if I could just see her"—and touch her— "I can show her there's nothing to be scared of. Please."

She visibly deflates. "Fine," she says, pulling her keys out and heading for the door. I follow keenly, using the time it takes Kate to let me in to talk myself down. I don't wait for a second to figure out if I've succeeded. As soon as my path to Ava is open,

I'm through the door and charging up the stairs. I can smell her, and I follow that head-spinning scent to the lounge, bursting in. And there she is, standing in the middle of the room in some skimpy shorts and a vest. I relax for the first time in days. She looks unimaginably beautiful, even with that look of alarm splattered all over her face. And, most importantly, she's in one piece.

Unlike my heart, which is currently in a thousand shards of trauma. She's okay. I'm not. My relief is quickly diluted by anger.

"Where the *fuck* have you been?" I yell, knocking her back a step. I can't stop myself. She needs to know where I'm at. Panicked. Stressed. Frightened. I'm being pushed to the brink of . . . what? Drink? "I've been pulling my fucking hair out!"

She says nothing, just stares at me for the longest time, somewhere between shock and disbelief. What the fuck did she expect? I hear Sam and Kate approach behind me, and Ava looks past me to her friend in disappointment.

"We're just gonna pop down to The Cock for a drink," Sam says, hauling Kate out of the way and out of my line of fire.

I take in air, controlled and calm, my head tilting back. *Calm the fuck down, Ward. You're not helping matters.* She's silent, waiting, and I drop my head to find her eyes. "Does someone need a reminder?"

Her mouth falls open. She's surprised? Shocked? Good. "No," she yells, pushing me out of the way and stomping to the kitchen. I follow, watching as she viciously swipes up a bottle of wine and tips half the bottle into a huge glass. "You're a complete bastard!" She tosses me a look that would hurt if I wasn't already in fucking agony. I still flinch, though. I'm a bastard? I'm not the one who's left her frantic with fucking worry these past few days. Where the hell does she get off doing this? What's her fucking point? "You've got what you wanted," she yells, and I frown. "So have I. Let's not fuck about."

I recoil. Swearing, drinking. Is she hell-bent on having me

sectioned? "Watch your fucking mouth," I bellow. "What are you talking about? I haven't got what I wanted." Nowhere near.

"You want more?" she asks, necking some wine. My jaw ticks as I watch her downing it like water, reckless and irresponsible. "Well, I don't," she yells. "So stop hounding me, Jesse. And stop shouting at me!" She takes another massive swig of wine. She's pushed me too far. She has a habit of doing this. It's like she's found my buttons and can't resist fucking pressing them.

I move forward fast, seizing the glass and tossing it in the sink, smashing it to smithereens.

"You don't have to drink like a fucking fifteen-year-old," I shout, and she glares at me, her hands balling into tight fists. She's mad? I laugh on the inside. *Welcome to my world, lady.*

"Get out!"

The pressure becomes too much, and I explode, swinging around and throwing my fist into the door, smashing a giant hole in the wood.

I turn, shaking my hand, nailing her in place with my eyes. She doesn't shy away. She can't. I close the space between us as she pushes herself into the worktop, and when we're front to front, she looks up at me, almost with challenge in her eyes. My breathing is shot. I'm damp with a stressed sweat. So fucking angry that she sways from all in to all out on a daily basis. And everyone thinks it's a good idea to spill every dirty secret I have? This, here, now, has only reinforced my decision. I'm telling her nothing until we're over this infuriating cat and mouse game.

I place my hands on hers on the edge of the worktop. Get my face close. Scan her eyes. My insides light up. This. This feeling.

Touch her and she'll be yours again.

I growl and push my mouth to hers, and she starts to wriggle and wrestle against me, so I harden my kiss, my hands tightening over hers. She refuses to open up to me, stands her ground. It's absurd. Her body is firing off spark after spark, her heart bashing against my chest. She can't hide that. I lick her sealed lips, tasting her want. It's embedded in her skin, and yet she still denies me, still refuses to open up. I ease my hold of one hand, and she grabs my arm. I don't move an inch. An earthquake wouldn't shift me. I take her hip and she jolts on a shallow cry. I growl, not giving up. I will *never* give up.

She turns her head away, leaving me breathing raggedly in her ear. I can smell her conflict. "Stubborn woman," I whisper, moving my attention to her neck, giving every inch a kiss or a lick or a gentle bite. *Come on, Ava. I'm tired of these games.* I feel like I've been through hell and back to get us both to a place of acceptance, and I'll be dead before I allow her to rob that contentment from us both. *Dead.*

I work my mouth up to her ear and bite down on her lobe, then feel her nails sink into my flesh through my jacket. She's caving. She's fighting to maintain this futile resistance. My cock sings its agreement, willing me on. I reach for her stomach and gently stroke from side to side.

"Please. Please, stop."

"You stop, Ava," I murmur, nuzzling her hot cheek. "Just stop." I dip a finger past the waistband of her shorts and softly skim her tummy, my tongue wetting her neck. She goes lax against me, her body wracking, and I laugh lightly at her willfulness.

She wedges a hand in my chest and tries to force me away. I'm unmoving. And she is getting desperate because she knows I'm winning. The feelings are winning. The chemistry is winning. She's outnumbered by a ton of raw passion.

I go in for the kill, push my fingers into her knickers, and gasp when I meet the fire there. *Jesus.*

She jolts violently. "Oh God."

I move fast, smashing my mouth on hers, working her clit

gently as I invade her mouth. And when I feel her tongue meet mine, I thank the heavens.

"Let my hand go," she orders, and I groan, freeing her, moving my hold to her neck as she encases me in her arms, going at my mouth like a madwoman, holding me tighter than she's ever held me before.

Peace overcomes me as I finger her slowly, relishing the consistent feeling of her throbbing around my touch. It doesn't take me long to get her to climax. Her cry is broken, her body stiff, as she comes all over my hand on endless whimpers.

"Remember yet?" I ask quietly, and she sighs, forcing her eyes open. Our stares meet. It tells me everything I need. I drop a light kiss onto her lips and pick her up, placing her on the edge of the counter and crowding her. Because crowding her works. *So fuck you, John.* "Why do you keep running away from me?" I ask, needing to know, desperately needing to know, so I can fix it and ensure it never happens again.

She looks away and shrugs. A shrug? *Come on, Ava.* I take her chin and direct her face to mine. "Talk to me, baby." *Please. Tell me everything that's on your mind. Let me help you figure this out.*

"You're distracting me," she says on a long exhale. "I don't want to get hurt."

There it is. And, fuck, I am guaranteed to hurt her. But . . . "I'm a distraction?"

"Yes."

"What am I distracting you from?" I ask quickly. She distracts me too, but whereas it's a good thing for me, it's mighty obvious Ava doesn't think it's a good thing for her.

"Being sensible," she says, looking awkward. Her answer throws me. Being sensible would be to stop incessantly challenging this incredible thing we have and accept it. Why can't she do that? It seems the second I don't crowd her, she talks herself out of it.

"Ava, know one thing." It's the only thing she needs to know right now. "I'll do anything to avoid hurting you." *Anything*. I'm yet to figure out how I can make that happen, but my good intentions are there. It's the very reason I'm holding on to my secrets. I don't want to hurt her, and in the process hurt myself. I'm done with hurting myself. "Please don't run away from me." I kiss her gently, resorting to my ace card. "I'm going to distract you some more now. We need to make friends." I pull her off the counter, and she wraps herself around me in that way she does. Like she doesn't want to let go. And I know deep down she doesn't, which makes the whole thing so frustrating. *What did Sarah say to her that made her run from someone she loves?*

I'm about to ask but think better of it. Not now. She's attached to me, and I can't risk changing that.

I walk us to her bedroom and kick the door closed behind me, setting her on the end of the bed. We both need this, but mostly Ava needs to know that whatever it is that spooked her, I won't let it take her away from me. I won't give up on her or us. But I will have more words with Sarah. Because when she hurts my girl, she's hurting me. She needs to realize that.

I stand over her and lift her vest up her body, marveling at the perfection of her boobs when they're revealed. My smile is unstoppable, my hunger moving into the realms of starvation. I toss her vest aside and dip to take the tops of her shorts. She obliges, of course, lifting so I can rid her of everything in my way.

"Stay there." Despite my urgency to be inside her again, I undress at a lazy pace, taking untold pleasure from her watching me, her hands twitching, ready to help me get naked. Her eyes jaunt leisurely across my bare skin, settling on my scar.

"Look at me, Ava," I say, sounding harder than I meant to as I push my boxers down my thighs. Her eyes glimmer excitedly when my dick is revealed, and she looks up at me, almost for permission.

"I'm desperate to be inside you," I whisper hoarsely. "I'll look forward to fucking your mouth later. You owe me." I loop an arm around her tiny waist and move her up the bed as I crawl on, settling between her warm thighs and caging her in. I need to keep reminding myself to take this slow, when all I want to do is smash into her like an animal. Sate my need. But no. Give it to her slowly. Every drive meticulous, every kiss gentle, every look deep. Don't blank her mind with a brutal fuck of ownership. Blank it with something else.

Love.

"We don't run anymore, Ava." I lift my hips and inhale as I sink into her. Her moan's loud, her hold of my shoulder fierce, and I still, needing to take a moment. I could shoot my load any second. I talk my dick down, closing my eyes, concentrating on breathing, as she strokes my arms softly. It takes me a good few minutes before I brave moving. I open my eyes and find her gazing at me. It's a look so penetrating. It's more than a look. It is *so* much more than a look. If I'm not staring into the eyes of a woman in love, I'll give up now. She *does* love me.

Shit, woman, I'm madly in love with you too. Even though you drive me to distraction. Even though you keep running. And once she stops running, I will entrust her with my truths, because I want more than anything to have this woman forever. For her to accept me in my entirety.

I prop myself up on my arms, inhale, and rear back, driving forward slowly, withdrawing slowly, slipping back in slowly. "Ava, when you're tempted to run again, think about how you feel right now," I say, barely able to talk through the pleasure but needing to say it. "Think about me."

She nods, swallowing. "Yes," she replies, low and husky, rolling her hips to meet my advances. I gulp and dip, catching her lips, our tongues falling into the same lazy pace as our lovemaking. "Does that feel good?" I ask, my heart frantic but peaceful.

"Too good."

"It does." Fuck, it does. "Are you there, lady?" She's tightening around me, squeezing my dick.

"I'm there," she confirms, biting at my tongue, her hands all over my back.

"I've got you, baby." She starts to stiffen. "Let it go."

She cries out, the sound incredible, her face twisting, her body vibrating. The vision is like nothing else, her moan long, and it's the end of me. It doesn't take any effort on my part to join her in her release, my body naturally following hers. I come quietly, maintaining our kiss as I close my eyes and struggle through the sensitivity. She's wringing me for everything I have. More than she'll ever know. "God, I've missed you." I plant my face in her neck and inhale her hot, wet skin, lifting my hips to slip out of her and falling to my back. I raise an arm in silent order, and she quickly tucks herself into me.

"I love sleepy sex with you," she says quietly, and I smile, brushing away some hair that's sticking to her cheek.

"That wasn't sleepy sex, baby."

"What was it, then?"

I lean down and place my mouth on her forehead. "That was catching-up sex."

"I like catching-up sex, then."

"Don't like it too much. It won't happen very often."

"Why?"

"Because, lady, you won't be running away from me again, and I don't plan on being away from you very often either." Let's be clear. "If ever."

Her leg is tossed over mine and I take her knee, trying to ignore where she's stroking me on my abdomen. *Don't ask, don't ask, don't ask.*

"How did this happen?"

"How did what happen, Ava?" I sound short, but it's hard not to resent anything that could pop our bubble. How that scar came to be could definitely pop our bubble.

"Nothing," she says quietly, sounding stung.

Guilt flares. *Change the subject.* My thumb works circles around her knee. "What are you doing tomorrow?"

"It's Wednesday," she replies, sounding confused. "I'm working."

"Take the day off."

"What, just like that?"

"Yes; you owe me two days."

"I have too much to do," she argues, and I pout. That's horseshit. And if it isn't, it sucks, because The Manor can practically run itself with John and Sarah around, leaving me twiddling my thumbs most of the time. "Besides, you abandoned me for four days," she says out of the blue, and I still. I owe her four days. So she needs to give me the opportunity to repay my debt, and I will. Tenfold. For the rest of my life.

"Come with me now, then."

"Where?"

"I've got to shoot over to The Manor, sort a few things out with John. You can have some dinner while you wait for me." I'll call ahead. Make sure it's not too busy. Walk her straight through to my office. It'll be fine.

She stills against me. "I think I'll stay here," she says as I look down at her, seeing the corner of her lip lost past her teeth. "I don't want to get in your way."

Get in my way? That's exactly what I want. Her, in my way, every minute of every hour. I seize her wrists and take her to her back. "You won't ever be in my way." I peek down at her breasts. Smile to myself. And drop my face, working my mouth over each nipple. She's immediately taut beneath me, her nipples like stones, her breathing shot. My smile widens. "You'll come."

"I'll see you tomorrow." She strains the words, and I bite down on one of her boobs, peeking up at her. "Hmm, sense fuck?"

A loud bang, followed by laughs, seeps into the bedroom. *Noooooooo.* I pout through my mouthful of boob, and Ava grins. "I don't suppose you can keep your mouth shut while I fuck some sense into you?" What sort of stupid question is that? "For fuck's sake." I force myself up, tactically brushing my knee against her center, catching her soaking pussy. She's restraining herself. She's so cute. I smash my lips on hers and kiss the living daylights out of her. "I've got to go. When I call you tomorrow, you'll answer."

"I will," she agrees without question and, God, the peace inside is incredible. See? All she has to do is agree and I'm calm. Even though she's obviously humoring me. Mocking me.

I smile wolfishly and make a play for her ticklish hip, grabbing it, and she screams, bursting my eardrums. She bucks, landing on her front. It's too good of an opportunity to pass up. I bring my palm down on her arse hard.

"Ouch!"

"Sarcasm doesn't suit you, lady." I jump up and grab my crumpled shirt.

"Will Sarah be at The Manor?" she asks, settling on her back.

Oh? I frown, reaching for my boxers. "I hope so. She works for me."

Her face is nothing short of shock. "You said she was a friend."

"Yes, she's a friend, and she works for me." A friend. What the fuck else should I call Sarah? Except, perhaps, a bitch.

I watch as Ava pulls on her shorts and vest angrily. Her clear surprise that Sarah works for me isn't what's taking up all my thinking space, though.

"Are you going to put some clothes on?" It's out before I can think how better to word it, and she frowns at her scantily clad form.

"I'm at home."

"Yes, and Sam's out there." I point to the door. She's practically naked. No bra. Boobs clearly visible through the thin, stretchy material of her top. Shorts skimming her arse cheeks. Legs for days on full display. Forgive me, but I'm not all too keen for my mate to cop the perfection of it all. Call me unreasonable. On this occasion, I don't care.

"Sam doesn't seem to think anything of walking around in his boxers," Ava quite rightly points out. "At least I'm covered."

I inwardly snort. Barely. "Sam's an exhibitionist." Like most members of The Manor. I go to her wardrobe and find something suitable. Ava is not an exhibitionist. It's one of the reasons I love her so much. She is *nothing* like the women of The Manor. "Here, put this on," I say, pulling out a massive cream jumper and passing it to her.

"No." She's looking at me like I've lost my mind. I haven't. But if she doesn't wear this jumper, I might. There's no way I can leave here while she's looking like that. No way. I push it forward with a warning look that I know she'll ignore. "Put the jumper on."

"No." She swipes it from my hand and chucks it on the bed, and I watch as it lands, munching on my lip, wondering how the fuck I'll get her in that jumper. It doesn't even need to be the jumper. A robe will do, but since she's being so fucking unreasonable about it, it has to be the jumper.

I turn my narrowed eyes onto her, and the face on her, the challenging, defiant, annoyed face, only makes me more determined. She'll learn, just as I'm learning. It's time for us to find out what happens on zero.

"Three," I say, loud and proud, watching in nothing but delight as her mouth falls open.

"Are you winding me up?"

No, baby. Not at all. "Two."

"I'm not putting the jumper on." She laughs, though it's nervous. Because she knows what's coming.

"One." I've never met such a willful, difficult woman in all my life, and I doubt I ever will. But she's *my* willful, difficult woman. And I love her.

"Do what you like, Jesse," she goads. "I'm not putting that jumper on."

Wrong. "Zero."

She stares at me, straining to appear strong, but she's unable to conceal her uncertainty. *Oh, this is fun.* I shake my head at her, breathing in, and I watch as her body engages, ready to bolt. I move fast, and she's off on a yelp, diving across the bed. I laugh and grab her ankle, dragging her back to me.

"Jesse," she yells as I spin her over, climbing on top of her and pinning her down. "Get off." Her hair is in her face, hampering her view, and I just manage to wipe my shit-eating grin away when she blows it away, using her last scrap of breath.

"Let's clear something up." I shrug myself out of my jacket, giving me more unrestricted movement in preparation. It takes everything in me to keep my amusement at bay. She looks like she could punch me in the face and take the greatest of pleasure from it. I grab the cream jumper and hold it up. "If you do what you're told, our lives will be a lot easier." Her jaw is about ready to snap. "All of this"—I squeeze each nipple in turn, but she doesn't flinch or buck or yell— "is for my eyes only." She's playing a dangerous game, because the more she tries to demonstrate power, the more I'll prove otherwise. But, make no mistake, she holds all the cards here. Not that I'll ever admit it. I grab her hip and dig my fingers in.

"No! Please, no." Her yells turn into laughter, and it's such a sight to behold. It's also an opportunity. I use my free hand to start feeding her arms through the jumper, constantly tickling her, using her flailing limbs and uncoordinated moves to my advantage. She throws her arm out, I get one sleeve on. She tries to hit me with the other, I seize her hand and get the other sleeve on. I have another dig of her hip, and her head flies up on a cry. I slip the neck of the jumper over her head and yank it down her body.

Done.

"That's better." I admire my work. She looks adorable in wool. I lean down and move her hair from her face, waiting for her to find me. She's knackered. Out of breath and sweaty. *Beautiful.* I give her a hard kiss. "You could have saved us both a lot of trouble if you'd have just put . . . the . . . fucking . . . jumper . . . on." But I can't deny how much fun that was. And how much I needed to simply laugh. *Wonderful, infuriating woman.*

I get up and slip my jacket on while she searches for breath, pulling herself up. She looks down her body. Growls like a tiger. A death stare. How I manage to restrain my smile, I'll never know.

"I'll just take it off," she declares fiercely.

My amusement can no longer be hidden. "No, you won't." She'll sleep in it all night and remember our amazing lovemaking, how the jumper got on her body, and who has the power. She stamps out of the room as I fix my tie, my smiling eyes following her.

"You're an unreasonable arse." The door to the bathroom is slammed with such force, the house shakes. Me? Unreasonable? After everything she's put me through, I'm the unreasonable one? I laugh but stop the moment my eyes land on her mobile, wondering what ringtone I'll give myself today. I smile as I change it and make my way to the kitchen, finding Kate and Sam all over each other.

"You look significantly happier," Kate muses, leaving Sam by the sink to fetch a mug.

"Ava and I have reached an understanding."

"Oh, good." Sam seems genuinely happy for me. Good. I'm happy too. "What's that?" He takes a chair, but I'm distracted from answering him when Ava stomps in. She's still in the jumper. And a filthy look is still marring her gorgeous face. She goes straight to the bottle of wine and pours a large glass as if to make a point. Oh, she's walking a very fine line. Next time, I won't force her into a jumper. It'll be a fucking cage. I glower at her as she settles against the worktop, wine in hand. Has she forgotten about the monster hangover she had? Has she forgotten that she swore to never drink again? She's doing this to rile me. To get one back.

"Made up?" Kate asks, crossing the kitchen and lowering to Sam's lap. He accepts with ease, doesn't bat an eyelid, even jokes about dropping her through his spread thighs. It's unusual to see him so wrapped up in a woman. I can't deny it suits him.

"No," Ava spits, and I pout. Well, that's not true. Why does she talk such nonsense? "And if you'd like to know who has put a hole in your kitchen door," she goes on, motioning to the wood I buried my fist in not so long ago, "look no further. He also smashed your wine glass."

"Let me know if it's any more." I nail Ava in place, daring her to continue with the childish games, as I toss a pile of notes on the table.

"That should cover it," Kate says.

I approach Ava, slowly and casually. "I like your jumper," I whisper.

Her head tilts, her eyes now slits. "Fuck off," she mouths, then follows up one transgression with another, necking a stupidly ridiculous amount of wine.

Let it go, Ward.

But she is quite funny. I kiss her nose. "Mouth." And grab the back of her head, pulling her into me. "Don't drink too much," I warn, and I kiss her. Hard. Like I own her. Because while I'm consuming her like this, I do.

The jumper is forgotten. Her sulk is forgotten. The wine and the bad language are forgotten. She's putty in my hands, and I am no longer pissed off with her.

"You might need to remind me of that," she says, and I laugh, a proper laugh, one full of happiness. I'll remind her of all the things for all the days.

She watches me as she takes another sip, waiting for my reaction. I don't give her one. Only because she's home and, actually, I don't want to leave her on bad terms. I want to leave her with a potent reminder of our chemistry. I've done what I came to do. "My work here is done." I turn and leave, starting to count down the minutes to tomorrow.

My phone rings as I pace to my car, John's name flashing up at me. "I'm coming," I say on a sigh.

"Good. There's someone here to see you."

"Who?"

"Freja Van Der Haus."

I stop in the middle of the road, looking back at Kate's place. Fuck me, never have I been so glad to lose a battle with Ava. "I'm popular these days, huh?" I quip, but John doesn't agree or even disagree. He hangs up on me and my shoulders drop, my palm running a long, slow stroke over my face. It's one step forward, ten steps back.

22

MY CAR ROLLS down the drive toward The Manor, seeming as reluctant as I am to be here. It's busy, cars filling the vast expanse of driveway, the double doors open.

Once parked, I notice the state of my gray suit. It looks like I've been wrestling in it. My hidden smile is huge, visions of Ava squirming on the bed beneath me running rampant in my mind. I reach down and adjust my dick, the damn thing swelling. I don't want to be here.

I stomp moodily up the steps, and when I walk in, I'm more than relieved I relented to Ava's refusal to come, not only because Freja is here somewhere. It seems *everyone* is here.

The foyer is a mass of people zigzagging past each other, coming to and from the bar, heading up the stairs, coming back down. It's the busiest *hotel* I've ever seen. On a colossal frown, I head into the bar. It's just as busy. Mario is frantic, serving, shaking, pouring. It's Tuesday night, a notoriously quiet evening. What gives?

I wander around the back of the bar and help myself to a water. "Mr. Jesse," Mario sings, ever happy, even when he's run off his Italian feet.

"What's going on, Mario?" I ask, motioning to the crowd.

"I not know," he says, getting back to the masses of people waiting to be served.

John strides in, scanning the chaos, finding me tucked away behind the bar. He jerks his head and leaves. "On my way," I mutter, stealing a glimpse of the top shelf, starting to feel clammy under the pressure of my impending confrontation with Freja. I shake my thoughts clear and follow him to my office. "Where is she?" I ask his wide back, but he doesn't answer, just opens the door for me when he arrives, standing back like a gentleman and sweeping an arm out in an over-the-top, sarcastic gesture. "Thanks," I grumble, seeing her sat on the other side of my desk. I'm wondering whether it's wise to be in a room alone with her. Not because I'm worried about what I might do, but what Freja will do. I've been on the receiving end of a desperate woman one too many times recently.

But I conclude very quickly my office is my only option, especially with The Manor so busy. I don't need a scene.

I go to my desk and plant myself in the chair, putting a huge chunk of wood between us. "Freja." My eyes fall to the back of the couch where last time I saw her, she was bent over it. I cringe those thoughts away. "What can I do for you?" Why the fuck would I ask such a stupid question?

Her head cocks in question as if she's surprised. It doesn't sit well. "I thought—"

"Oh, no," I say before I can engage my brain and consider a more diplomatic approach. "Well, *I* thought we'd reached an understanding."

"Yes. Then last week happened."

The dormant guilt rises and engulfs me. "It was a mistake." She can't have missed the moment I lost my baggage and threw them out. I was a mess. She's being very selective with her memories. "Freja, what happened on—"

"There's word that you're seeing someone."

I bolt back in my chair like I've been shot, my eyes regarding her warily. That felt like a backward threat. What's the word, and who the fuck has been speaking? I'm struck dumb, unable to unravel my tangled thoughts.

"Does that mean you're off the market?"

"I was never *on* the market, Freja."

"But available, yes?"

"You mean to fuck?" I ask, keeping it factual, pushing myself farther back in my chair. "Available to fuck."

"And now you're not." She smiles, and I one hundred percent hate it. Fucking hell, this isn't good.

"How's the divorce going?" I ask.

"We're locking horns."

"Over what?" *Please say money.*

"Over blame."

I glance away, not liking the satisfied glint in her eyes. I'm not being intuitive. I'm being real. Freya told me her husband didn't know she'd been in my bed. Now she has again, has that changed? "Have you told your husband about what happened last week?" I ask, getting fucked off with dancing around her need to stretch this out. I need to know what I'm dealing with.

"No," she says, and my eyes shoot to hers, surprised. I don't know why I'm feeling so relieved. I can see there's a catch coming. "But I'm curious. Why are you so worried about my husband finding out, Jesse?"

I close my eyes on an inhale. "Like I said before, I don't want my manor being dragged into your mud-slinging match in court." I can't tell her about Ava and give her the ammunition she's looking for. Of all the people who shouldn't know about Ava, it's Freja. I can't risk her telling Mikael. Because if he finds out Freja has been in my bed, he'll take the sickest pleasure in trying to exact his revenge. He's already got his eye on Ava, without me in the equation, that was obvious at the Lusso launch.

"Really?" she asks, and I ball my fists, feeling the pressure building.

"Freja, I'll ask you again. Why are you here?"

She gets up and rounds my desk, unraveling the belt of her trench coat as she does. I'm out of my chair like a rocket, averting my stare before I get an eyeful of what's beneath, or, more to the point, what's *not* beneath. Namely, clothes. "Don't make me spell it out, Jesse."

"Cover yourself up, Freja," I warn. What the fuck is wrong with her? I threw her out of this office mere days ago. Why would she even consider coming—?

"Don't you want to keep our secret?"

Ah. There it is. That's why she's here.

I remain with my back to her, looking across the grounds of The Manor. Beautiful grounds. Trees bursting with lush green, every blade of grass in place, the beds spilling over with spring blooms. Everything is so perfect. Except for the woman behind me, whose talons are encroaching.

I feel her hand on my bicep, and I look down at it, my nostrils flaring, my temper rising. Not perfect. I move away and turn around, making sure I keep my eyes up. "Are you saying, if I indulge your every pleasure, my establishment and I will never be mentioned where your husband and divorce battle is concerned?" Let's see how far she thinks she can get. Let's see if I really do need to remind her of the contract.

She smiles. God have mercy on my soul, it makes me want to slap it off her face. I didn't think Coral could be beaten in the underhanded stakes, but Freja is going lower than a snake's belly. "Well, I wouldn't put it like that, but . . ." She shrugs, rolling her shoulders and sending her coat to the floor. My eyes remain on her face. "In a nutshell, yes."

I nod, my lips straight, and I approach her, watching as her body starts to tighten with anticipation. I get as close as I can without touching her. Breathe in her face. Start lowering slowly, my eyes never leaving hers. She's trembling. I fucking hate it.

I snatch her coat up from the floor, rise, and shove it into her chest. "I'll take my chances," I say flatly, backing away, giving her a look that spells out exactly what I think of her. Scum. We have an iron-clad contract that prohibits her talking about The Manor in a court environment, and if she's forgotten that, she will be completely screwed. *Blackmail me?* That is not happening. "Now get the fuck out."

Her eyes are wide and surprised. It's an insult. "Have it your way." She fights her way into her coat, roughly tying the belt, and I laugh under my breath. If I truly had things my way, I wouldn't be such a monumental fuck-up. I wouldn't be in this fucking situation.

"Goodbye, Freja," I say with a finality she can't question. "And for the record, I had you pinned as a classy, dignified woman," I add, watching her face fall. "I'm sorry to be proven wrong." I stride to the door and swing it open, not being a gentleman, but just wanting her gone. Again.

The moment her heels are over the threshold, I slam it shut, kick it hard, and dump myself on the couch, closing my eyes, suddenly exhausted.

Fuck everything, but especially fuck *me*.

I come around to the sound of my mobile squawking, and I pat around my arse, feeling it vibrating against me. I hold it up. Frown at the number. "Hello?" I answer groggily, swinging my legs off the couch and rising on a halfhearted stretch.

"Mr. Ward, it's Victor from the Volkswagen dealership. I think I may have found just what you're looking for."

"What am I looking for?" I ask, my brain still asleep.

"A pink van?' he says on a question, following it up with a chuckle.

Fuck. The van. "Yes, a pink van," I confirm, looking at the window. It's daylight. *What the fuck?* I glance at my watch and balk, then swing around when the door to my office opens. Sarah stutters to a stop when she sees me, understandable confusion in her eyes. "Email me the details." I hang up and show the ceiling my palms. "What day is it?" I ask, disorientated.

"Wednesday. Have you been there all night?"

Shit, I must have conked out. I've never slept so long. I shake my head clear, trying to get a grasp of where I should be and what I should be doing.

"Coffee?" Sarah asks, obviously seeing my muddle.

Yes, coffee. "Please." I drop to my arse, my head in my hands, willing myself to wake up.

"And then perhaps a shower?"

"Please," I say again, just as the big guy strides in.

"Morning, Sleeping Beauty."

"Morning." My arms go into the air, my stretch now epic, and I yawn like a lion. Fucking hell, that felt good. I stand and face my audience with a smile. I get to see Ava today. I'll take her to dinner. Devour her for dessert. "What's on the agenda?"

There's no hiding their bewildered expressions. "The pool guy will be here at ten to fit a new seal."

"Do I need to be here?" I ask.

"No."

"Good." I get on my way, passing between the middle of them. "I'm going for a run."

"What about your coffee?" Sarah calls, tailing me.

"I'll have one when I'm back." My phone dings and I find an

email from the dealership. The images of the pink van that greet me when I open the attachment make me blink back the vividness. It's fucking hideous. And perfect. I call him straight back. "I'll take it," I say, rounding the corner to the stairs. "I'll have the money transferred within the hour. Can you deliver it today?"

"No problem."

"Excellent. I'll email you a note that I want delivered with it, along with the address and other information you'll need. Good doing business with you." I hang up and take the stairs three at a time.

"Deliver what today?" Sarah calls after me.

"I need you to transfer forty grand to the bank details I'm forwarding to you."

"What for?"

I stop halfway around the gallery landing, leaning on the balustrade. She's halfway up the stairs, looking indignant. I smile. "What is it with your incessant need to know the ins and outs of a cat's arsehole?"

She recoils, her indignation growing. "Fuck off," she spits, turning and marching down the stairs. "Have a nice day."

"Oh, I will," I murmur, heading for my suite, arranging flowers for Ava and her work friend on my way.

23

I TRY to lose myself in some work. *Try* being the operative word. I'm absolutely *itching* to break free of The Manor by two o'clock, my eyes constantly dropping to my wrist to check the time. Has a day ever passed by so slowly? I'm restless. Impatient.

I stare at the spreadsheet detailing the next delivery of toys, one line blurring into the next. All I can see is lace. "Fuck it." I slam my laptop shut. My head's not in it. Grabbing my phone and keys, I head out, meeting Sam on the driveway. My mate always has a certain spring in his step, but today it's particularly . . . springy.

"My man," he sings, giving me a playful slap of my shoulder.

"What's going on with you and Kate?" I ask. He was with her Saturday night, Sunday, Monday, *and* yesterday. It's unheard of. Unless, of course, he's lost in one of the rooms of The Manor.

He shrugs it off like it's nothing, when I know it is anything but. "Where are you going?"

"Don't change the subject. What's going on with you and Kate? And don't tell me she's cool."

"She's cool," he says over a laugh, and I roll my eyes, jumping in my car.

I leave the door open and start her up. "If she's so cool, what are you doing here?"

"Lunch."

"What?"

"I'm meeting Drew for lunch. Did you know he's got a date with Ava's work friend? What's her name?" He looks to the sky. "Victoria."

I laugh, grabbing the handle of my door. "Drew doesn't date."

"I'm telling you. A date. I got it from the horse's mouth."

I still, my door halfway closed. I don't like this. All of my mates are getting way too close to all of Ava's friends. Which means it's more likely someone will drop something they shouldn't, therefore drop me in the shit with Ava.

"Seriously, dude. When are you going to tell Ava about this place?" he asks, motioning to The Manor.

"She knows about this place," I mutter, slamming my door. Sam's up against the glass in a second, his usually cheerful face cut with impatience. I sigh and let the window down. "Maybe tonight. I'm taking her for dinner."

"Good."

"What's it to you, anyway?"

He straightens and wanders off. "I'm fucking *dying* to get that redhead in the communal room," he calls over his shoulder, and my head falls back against the headrest. I'm imagining Ava's reaction to The Manor. It's not good. I'm imagining her reaction to her friend partaking in some play with Sam. It's not good.

"Hey, Sam," I yell, leaning out of the window. He stops at the top of the steps, looking back. "I bought Kate a van," I declare proudly.

"What?" The poor bloke looks as confused as he should be. "Why?"

"Have you seen that old jalopy she chugs round in?"

"Yeah. It's cute."

"It's also a death trap."

His jaw tightens. It makes me smile. "Are you saying I don't know how to look after a woman?"

I slowly lift my eyebrows. *That redhead.* "Do you want to look after a woman?"

"I want to fuck her black and blue. That's what I want to do."

Now *that's* more like the Sam I know. I flash him my signature, dashing smile and slip my shades on, razzing off down the driveway.

I shower and change at Lusso, kill *more* time tidying up around my apartment, all the time wishing Cathy back soon.

Finally at five, I'm calling Ava to advise her that I'm on my way and to be ready. Except she doesn't answer. Not the first time, and not the eighth fucking time, by which point I'm pulling into her street. "Answer the fucking phone. Is it too much to ask?" I park up and jog across the road, feeling that god-awful dread creeping up on me. I knock the door gently. It takes everything out of me. Nothing. "God damn you, woman," I mutter, dropping my forehead to the wood, hoping to God we're not back at square one again. I walk down the path, turn, walk back, turn, walk back, dialing her again.

"Hello?" she says, sounding perfectly unruffled and calm. Unlike me. This woman is the beginning and end of my stress.

"Where the hell are you?" I snap, unable to hold back the anxiety.

"Where are you?"

Surely this apprehension is not unreasonable. *She promised she'd pick up when I called.* No, it's not unreasonable. Every fear, dread, and worry I have is perfectly reasonable. "I'm outside Kate's, kicking the door down." I march to the front door, set on actually kicking it down. "Is it too much to ask that you answer your phone the first time I call you?"

"I was in the shower."

"Take your phone with you," I bark, flopping against the wall in relief. She was in the shower. She wasn't avoiding me. She answered the phone. *Finally*. We need to have a serious conversation about her phone etiquette.

"You don't need to shout at me," she fires, and I pout. *Then stop driving me fucking crazy.*

"I'm sorry," I murmur. "You make me crazy." So fucking crazy. Crazy good. Crazy bad. Crazy sad. Crazy. "Where are you?" My knees give, and I slip down the wall to my arse, exhausted by my crazy. Her fault.

The front door opens.

"Here."

I look up, finding Ava in the doorway wrapped in a towel. My God, just look at her. My heart twists and turns, yelling at me. I'm crazy in love too. At least I'm consistent and she owns all of my crazies.

She smiles lightly and joins me, sliding down the opposite wall, struggling to keep her towel in place. She's naked under that towel. Beautifully naked. Easily accessible. My hand reaches for her knee and the moment our skin meets, there are tingles. Tingles everywhere. And heat. And sheer, unstoppable contentment. "I thought—"

"I'd run again," she says, reading my mind and state. She knows, and I deem it a good thing. Perhaps now she appreciates the level of need in me. "I was in the shower," she says softly, reassuringly, taking my hand in hers.

"Where are your clothes?" What do I care?

"In my wardrobe."

My lips straighten, and I make a play for her hip, giving it a warning squeeze. "Sarcasm doesn't suit you, lady."

She squirms, laughing her apology, loosening the towel. I ease up on my torture and she sighs, relaxing. "Sally loved her flowers."

"Did you love yours?"

"I did," she says around her smile. "Thank you."

They're just flowers. I want to give her so much more, and I pray she'll let me. I pray she'll listen to my confessions and listen to her heart. She belongs with me. We both know it.

"My man!" Sam's voice infiltrates our moment, and I look down the path to see him approaching.

Ava's naked.

My eyes only.

I'm up in a heartbeat, working fast but carefully to ensure I keep her covered. The thought of another man's eyes taking pleasure in what I adore seems wrong on so many levels. I can't hack it. Friend or not, *this* woman I'm keeping to myself.

"Sam, don't fucking move," I bellow, darting through the door with Ava in my arms. He laughs, the fucker. He knows what I'm thinking. He knows how I feel. Jesse Ward is possessive? It's unheard of. "I'll rip their prying eyes out," I grumble, taking the stairs fast.

I burst through the door of her bedroom and drop her to the bed. "Get dressed," I order. "We're going out."

She looks startled for a moment. Then she crawls off the bed, minus one towel, and sashays across to her wardrobe. Fuck me, those legs. That arse. The skin of her back. "Where?"

Where what? I'm rapt, my eyes greedy for her. Where are we going? Oh, yes. "Well, it occurred to me when I was out running that I've not taken you for dinner yet. You have the most incredible legs. Get dressed." I motion to the wardrobe with a flick of my head. How I'm going to endure dinner I don't know. My dick is dancing. My heart is singing. My skin is awash with goosebumps.

And then she starts massaging cream into that skin, and my eyes cross as she bends to reach her ankles. Dinner is seeming like a terrible idea. "Where?" she asks.

"A little Italian place I know." It's close by and the service is super fast. Ideal. Feed her. Then make mad love with her. "Get dressed before I collect on my debt." I am seriously holding myself back from chucking her on the bed and ravishing her.

She straightens, and her boobs, so fucking perfect, send me cross-eyed. "Debt?" She's being coy. It's cute . . . and totally wasted. She wants me to spell it out? No problem.

"You owe me."

"I do?"

"Oh, you do." And I'm going to cash in big time. But until then, I need to remove myself before I give the whole neighborhood a screaming show. *Get her back to Lusso. Never let her leave.* "I'll wait outside at the risk of cashing in sooner." I grin like an idiot. "I wouldn't want you to think this was *all* about sex," I say quietly, but I know she can't possibly think that. Not after my recent performances.

I leave her to get ready and find Sam in the kitchen making himself a cup of tea. Fucking hell, who is this man? I rest my arse against the counter and watch him with a secret smile.

"Don't say a word," he warns.

What, like question why he's here? "What are you up to tonight?"

"Well," he muses, adding milk and stirring, "what I would like to do as soon as the spitfire redhead is back from test driving her new wheels is take her to The Manor and play with her."

Oh, the van. I forgot about that in the midst of my brief panic attack.

Sam collects his cup and takes a sip, looking at me over the rim. "But I can't do that, can I?"

My eyes narrow to slits. "You're assuming she'd be fine with it."

"I have a feeling in my bones."

"No, you don't. You have a feeling in your cock."

"Same thing. So how are you going to break it to her?"

Not a fucking clue. "I'll find a way." *I hope.*

He nods, thoughtful as he watches me. "Well, you ne—"

"Thank you!" Kate screeches, flinging herself into my arms. I just manage to catch her. "She's perfect."

Sam rolls his eyes. "Let go of him," he grumbles. "He's got somewhere he needs to be." His head tilts, his eyes telling me to start confessing some truths.

Luigi's place is the kind of restaurant London is short of. Traditional, authentic, and cozy. It's been here forever and will be here forevermore. The moment he spots me, his face lights up, but I can see the questions in his eyes when he notices Ava's hand in mine. In all the times I've eaten here, I've never been with a woman. Not even Sarah. It's always with the boys.

He weaves through the tables and greets me in his usually happy way, shaking my hand.

"Luigi, good to see you too."

"Come, come." He guides us to a table for two at the back, and I make the introductions, killing his curiosity. "Ah, a beautiful name for a beautiful lady, yes?" he says, and I mentally agree as we take our seats. "What would Sir Jesse like?"

I'd like to eat fast and leave. "May I?" I ask Ava, reaching for my gentlemanly manners.

"You usually do," she quips sarcastically, and I throw her a playful, warning look. Yes, I do, and I'm glad she accepts that.

"Okay, Luigi," I say, ready to reel off our order fast, hoping he'll take it fast, have it cooked fast, served fast, and cleared fast once we're done. My dick is aching like fuck. "We'll have two of the fettuccine, with yellow squash, parmesan, and lemon cream sauce, a bottle of the *Famiglia Anselma Barolo 2000*, and some water." It all rolls off my tongue automatically, and I frown to myself as Luigi writes it down. Wine? I don't drink anymore.

"Yes, yes, Sir Jesse."

I'm about to cancel the wine but Luigi backs away, and I quickly reason with my intention. She can have a glass. She'll think it's odd if I don't order wine. Besides, she's with me.

"Thank you, Luigi."

Ava gazes around the space as I admire her across the table. "You come here often?" she says, and I crack a smile.

"Are you trying to chat me up?"

"Of course."

She eyes me as I shuffle in my seat. She knows what's going on down below. *Talk.* "Mario, the head barman at The Manor, insisted I try it, so I did. Luigi's his brother."

"Luigi and Mario?" She laughs, and I watch, happy but stumped. "I'm sorry, that really tickled me."

"I can see that." I accept the drinks when Luigi returns, filling Ava's glass halfway and pouring some water into my own. I don't think I've ever eaten Italian without my favorite wine, and oddly, I'm not the least bit bothered.

Ava looks from her wine to the water. "You didn't get a whole bottle for me? Are you not having any?"

Think fast, Ward. "No. I'm driving."

"And I'm allowed?" she asks, an ironic smile on her face. A glass, yes. She can forget it if she thinks she's sinking the whole bottle.

"You may."

She dives in, and I watch as she takes that first sip. "You bought Kate a van."

I rest back in my chair, gauging her reaction. "I did." I can see she's got a pile of questions locked, loaded, and ready to fire. I'm beginning to think this was a bad idea for more reasons than delaying getting my hands all over her.

"Why?"

"Because I don't want you being tossed around in the back of that jalopy."

She seems to accept my reasoning, which is good. Yet, I should stop and ask myself what lengths I'll go to in order to maintain the calm inside I'm coming to depend on and, worryingly, what only she can supply. I seem dead set on eliminating all things that could tip me over the edge of the cliff I've recently found myself on. It's paramount. Impossible?

"I want to know how old you are."

"Twenty-eight," I say, ignoring my conscience. Holding back is natural, and if it comes naturally, I'm going with it. "Tell me about your family," I say, and she looks at me in disbelief.

"I asked first."

"And I answered. Tell me about your family."

Her shoulders drop, defeated, and she takes another sip of wine. Sips. Sips are good. "They retired to Newquay a few years back." There's a certain edge of sadness in her tone. She misses them. "Dad ran a construction firm, Mum was a housewife. My dad had a heart attack scare so they took early retirement to Cornwall. My brother is living the dream in Australia." *Oh, she has a brother?* "Why do you not speak to your parents?" she adds, and it's a bolt out of the blue. I swallow hard, yelling at myself to give her something. Start the process. Build the picture.

"They live in Marbella," I tell her, delving deep to find the strength required to speak of my past, even if the information is relatively inconsequential. It's a start. A step in the right direction. "My sister's there too. I've not spoken to them for years." I still don't understand why Amalie continues trying to reach me. Why bother? Why does she still want to know me? "They didn't approve when Carmichael left me The Manor and all of his estate." Hated him was more apt and, subsequently, hated me for accepting and embracing it. For falling into the lifestyle. For not listening to them.

Her surprise is warranted. "He left it all to you?"

"He did." I never expected it. Had no idea he'd put me in his will as sole heir. "We were close." A stab of guilt grabs me. "And my parents didn't talk to him. They didn't approve."

"They didn't approve of your relationship?"

I look up at her, bullying my mouth into speaking the words. "No, they didn't." I hate the curiosity emblazoned across her face. She has no idea. No idea of the demons I harbor. Of the sins I've committed. Or the losses I've faced.

"What was not to approve of?"

Everything. But, ironically, they would approve of Ava. She's not what my lifestyle represents historically, not what I've sought, which begs the question why the fuck I'm so attached to her. It's unexplainable. And yet I am, and here she is asking questions I desperately want to give her the answers to. Except, it's ugly. All of it is hideous, and the possibility of having it snatched away— by Ava herself, or by an outside force—is a risk I'm not yet prepared to take. "As soon as I left college," I begin, stretching the truth somewhat—there was no college—and scraping the barrel of strength while restraining my pain, "I spent all of my time with Carmichael. Mum, Dad, and Amalie moved to Spain, and I refused to go. I was eighteen and having the time of my life." *With a baby on the way.* How did it all go so horribly wrong? *Because you're a fuck-up. And you'll fuck this up too.*

I gulp back my self-loathing. "I stayed with Carmichael when they left. They weren't happy about it. Three years later, Carmichael died"—*entirely my fault*—"and I was left to run The Manor." And left to spiral into my own form of hell. Which I rightly deserved. After all, everyone I cared about back then was dead. *Because of fucking me.* I stare at the wine on the table. There's peace in that bottle. Escape. I grab my water and gulp it down. "The relationship was strained after that. They demanded I sell The Manor, but I couldn't." Wouldn't. *I should have sold the fucking Manor.* "It was Carmichael's baby." *And I'd already let him down enough.*

Her eyes are wide, a little glazed, and I shift in my chair uncomfortably, praying she doesn't push for more. I'm drained. Does she sense my increasing despondency? My grief?

"What do you do for fun?" she asks. It's all I can do not to spit out my water in surprise. Fun? There's been nothing fun about my life. Not until she breezed into it. But even amid the fun element of our relationship, which is basically me bending her to my will in the bedroom, there's stress and mood swings and a whole pile of other unexpected feelings. But there's also a heartbeat inside of me. There's a purpose. I would question if it's too soon to share that with her.

If I hadn't heard her drunkenly confess her love.

Has she thought more about it? Has she concluded she *does* love me, and more importantly, while she's sober?

I consider the glass of wine in her hold. What do I do for fun? I peek up, finding her waiting patiently for a reply. *It seems, Miss O'Shea, that for fun, I stalk my interior designer and bend her to my will.* "Fuck you."

She can't contain her shock. "You like power in the bedroom."

Not at all. I like power over you. It'll keep the insanity you spike in check. "I do."

"Are you a dominant?" She rushes over her words, and I cough with a mouthful of water, having to grab the napkin and wipe my chin. A dominant? What does she know of dominants? Where the fuck did that come from? I've no clue, but surely it's a lead into something that needs addressing.

Like the fact I have a mammoth building full of dominants. I'm not one of them. Truthfully, I'm always too under the influence to play like that. It requires control and trust, and it would be too much to expect a woman to trust me when I'm ten sheets to the wind. Fuck, how do I approach this?

"Ava, I don't need that sort of arrangement to get a woman to do what I want her to do in the bedroom." I'm full of shit. Because, ironically, I need that kind of arrangement with Ava to get her to do *anything*. One touch, and she's mine to bend, whether it's her body or her mind.

"You're very controlling," she says coolly, but her eyes betray her, and she glances away.

"Look at me," I order, and she does. Immediately. I need to be crystal clear with her. I want her to know this kind of behavior from me is unheard of. She's special. Unique. The only thing in this world who seems to be able to control *me*, and she is blissfully unaware of that. "Only with you."

Is that a pleased glint in her eye? "Why?"

"I don't know," I whisper, wondering how I could ever explain. "You make me crazy," I add, putting that out there too, though she'd have to be deaf and blind not to have noticed that. I look past her, seeing Luigi dancing through the tables with plates balanced on his arms. Thank God. "Here's your pasta."

"Lovely people," he sings, sliding his dishes before us proudly. "*Buon appetito!*"

"Thank you, Luigi," I say, also quietly thanking him for his perfect timing as Ava picks and pokes at the dish, lost in thought. I don't think I can take any more questions, and I definitely can't handle more halfhearted confessions. She deserves more than the scraps of information I'm giving. More than the twisted answers. I've got to somehow find it in myself to do the right thing by her. *Even if it means the wrong thing by me?* And who's to say it's the right thing by her? Ignorance is bliss. Does she even need to know?

Fucking hell. The weight of it all is too much. This could be a new start for me. A fresh one. No past, no sins. No chance of her leaving me so I have to face life alone again.

I think I could literally talk myself in circles over this.

"Good?" I ask when she finally takes a bite.

She swallows. "When did you buy the penthouse?"

My fork falters on its way to my mouth. She's not done. "March."

"You never told me why you requested me personally to work on the extension of The Manor." She drops her fork and pushes the plate away, and I stare at the barely touched pasta.

"I bought the penthouse and loved what you did with it." Yet nothing prepared me for the face behind the project. The face gazing at me now. "I can assure you," I say quietly, "I didn't expect you to come rocking up, with your perfect figure"—fuck, that figure—"olive skin"—that's wonderfully soft—"and big brown eyes." *That I get lost in each time I look at you.*

"You weren't exactly the Lord of the Manor I was expecting, either," she says, her lips stretching. Is she remembering our first encounter? The chemistry? The intensity? I catch a slight roll of her shoulders. She's remembering. "How did you know where I was on that Monday lunchtime when I *bumped* into you at the bar?"

"Lucky guess." *I didn't follow you there at all.*

"Of course," she huffs. She knows. It makes me smile.

"I couldn't think of anything else after you left The Manor. I had to have you."

"Do you always take what you want?"

Give it to her straight. Eliminate any room for doubt, just in case you haven't already. "I can't answer that, Ava, because I've never wanted anything enough to pursue it so relentlessly. Not like I wanted you."

"And now you have me," she whispers, her eyes moving to my lips. She wants to kiss me. "So," she goes on, lifting her gaze to mine, "with the chase over, do you still? Want me, I mean."

"More than anything."

"Then I'm yours."

Mine. Never has anything sounded so right, and when her eyes drop back to my mouth, I lazily lick my lip. She will beg for me. "Ava, you've been mine since you turned up at The Manor."

"Have I?"

"Yes." She knows it. I know it. The fates know it. "Will you spend the night with me?"

"Are you asking or demanding?"

"I'm asking," *Make the most of it.* "But if you give me the wrong answer, I'm sure I can think of something to change your mind." I'm rolling over all the ways right now, listing and filing them for future reference. Something tells me I'm going to need them.

"I'll spend the night with you."

Of course she's spending the night with me, I can literally taste her want, and since she's being so acquiescent, let's see how far I can push this. "Tomorrow night?"

"Yes."

Oh, she is making me a very happy man. She won't regret it. "Take the day off."

"No," she fires quickly. I've reached my limit. Too bad for her, there is no limit. But for the sake of my sanity . . .

"What about Friday evening?" I need clear and concise arrangements between us.

"I've arranged to go out with Kate on Friday night."

"Cancel." It's out of my big fat gob before I can hold it back, and she balks at my abruptness. I can't abide the thought of her out drinking. *That's your problem, Ward. Not hers.*

"I'm going out to have a few drinks," she says with a pretty formidable glare. "You can't stop me from seeing my friends, Jesse."

Out for a few drinks? I've seen Ava after a few drinks. "How many is 'a few drinks'?" I've said I'll have a *few drinks* before. Next minute, I'm unconscious after fucking my way through The Manor. *But she's not you.*

"I don't know." She looks so bloody confused by my twenty questions. "That depends on how I feel."

She should take a leaf out of my book. Go T-total. It's liberating. Refreshing. Knowing what I'm doing every second—even losing my fucking mind—is oddly nice. Shit, how do I deal with this? "I don't want you out drinking without me," I grate. Her safety is a good enough reason. The other reasons are of no consequence.

"That's a bit of bad luck, isn't it?"

Not really, baby, because you won't be drinking. "We'll see." Is she smiling? She finds this funny? I stare her down, intent on maintaining the displeasure but, in truth, her sass drives me wild in more ways than one. It turns me on. How she tries to fight me. How she invites the inevitable, almost as if she *wants* me to take charge. Fine by me.

"You like?" I hear Luigi say, but nothing would make me look away from the challenge in Ava's eyes.

"Great, Luigi." I can barely talk with the lust clogging my throat. "Thank you." I narrow my eyes further as Ava melts me with her blazing stare. She's egging me on. And fuck, I'm game.

"The bill, please, Luigi." Get her home. Get her naked. Get her in bed.

Luigi, God love that man, is back in a flash. I stuff my hand in my pocket and toss a pile of cash down, then claim her.

"We're going." My dick is beginning to weep, my heart is bashing relentlessly. I've never been so desperate to be inside a woman. Kissing her. Showing her.

"Are you in a hurry?" she asks, her feet moving fast as I guide her out of the restaurant.

"Yes." I spin her and thrust her up against the side of my Aston, rolling my groin into her, demonstrating my rock-hard situation. My forehead on hers, I pant, and she's right there with me. "I'm going to fuck you until you're seeing stars, Ava." I thrust forward, and she moans. "You won't be going to work tomorrow because you won't be able to walk." That's a promise. "Get in the car." She doesn't move, can't move. She's useless. Needs me to help her.

I open the door and deposit her in my car, and as I'm rounding the back to get in, my mobile rings. I laugh sardonically, leaving it in my pocket. It'll be John or Sarah, or someone else that'll beckon me away. No. Wild horses won't get me away. Whatever it is, whoever it is, can wait.

Tonight, I'm all hers, and she is all mine.

24

I'M SO INTOLERANT of the other drivers on the road. Throbbing behind my jeans. Impatient to get her back to Lusso. It's a short journey, but the longest fucking drive ever. My Aston is bursting at the seams with sexual tension, so much so, I'm forced to crank the aircon up to circulate some air.

I glance across to Ava. I shouldn't have. She's rigid, her fingers clawing at the seat by her thighs, her chest expanding on every inhale. Not in all my time frequenting the rooms of The Manor have I seen a woman so hungry for me. And that's a feat on her part. I'm not being a conceited twat. I'm being real. She's so into me, desperate for me, set to beg for me, this beautiful, *normal,* pure, real, *young* woman, and that turns me on like nothing else.

I reach up and wipe my upper lip, puffing out my cheeks, part in disbelief, part in awe. She's the impossible. The unthinkable. The cure. And tonight, I'm going to speak to her in a way she'll understand because, fuck knows, she could never comprehend the actual words.

The gates to Lusso come into view, and I tap my steering wheel constantly as I wait for them to open. She looks across the car at me. "You're going to have a seizure if you don't calm down."

My hands stop tapping, and I meet her hungry gaze. "Ava, I've had a fucking seizure every day since I've met you." Whether caused by pleasure or stress.

The gates finally grant me access, and I put my foot down.

"You're swearing a lot," she muses.

"And you're going to be screaming a lot. Out." I eject myself from my car fast, joining her on the other side. She's not even got one leg out of my Aston by the time I make it to her. When the hell did she turn into a fucking tortoise? Can't she see my urgency? And where the fuck has hers gone? "What are you doing?"

She pouts, taking a lazy gaze around the docks. "Do you fancy a walk?"

A walk? What does she think this is, a 1920s romance novel? I couldn't have heard her right. "Do I fancy a walk?"

"Yes," she says, cool, casual, but I can see the slight lift of her mouth. She's playing. "It's a lovely evening."

It is. But it will be even lovelier when I get her naked. "No, Ava." I move in. "I fancy fucking you until you beg me to stop." Dipping, I seize her and haul her over my shoulder, loving her exhale of surprise. One day, she'll be so used to me picking her up, she'll stop being surprised. *Do I fancy a walk?* I scoff and do the unthinkable. I kick my car door closed. My two-hundred-grand car. That's how desperate I am. That's what she does to me.

"Jesse," she yelps as I pace into Lusso. "I'll walk!"

"Not fast enough. Good evening, Clive."

"I'm not drunk," she blurts, and I frown, catching the concierge's look of alarm. Yes, I'm a caveman. Confirmed. But she'll learn. Don't deprive me. Don't play games. I smack the code into the panel in the elevator and look over my shoulder, smiling. It drops the moment the minx slips her hands past my jeans. The heat spreads like wildfire. Uncontrollable. Uncontained.

I'm one stroke away from dropping her and taking her here and now. Jesus. My teeth press together, and I close my eyes, willing myself to hold on just a little while longer. I open my eyes and watch as the dial ticks painfully slowly through the floors. *Come on.*

The doors open, and I'm out fast, struggling to walk with the bulge I'm packing. "No fucking about." Let's be clear. She needs to lose whatever sassy streak she's found and give me what I need before I combust. "I want inside you now. You fuck about, I swear to God—"

"You're so romantic," she says, close to a giggle.

"We've got all the time in the world for romance, lady."

I make it to the kitchen—I don't know how—and let her slip down my front slowly, my body folding, a suppressed moan vibrating at the back of my throat. She's clinging to me for support, can hardly stand on her own two feet, and I've not even started yet. "You know," I say, sounding in control but feeling anything but, "you're really not going to be in a fit state to work tomorrow. Strip, now."

Her surprise is endearing. She thought I'd rip off her clothes. No. I'm starving for her, but this won't be rushed. Every moment will be slow, giving her mind space to process it. This will be the loudest I've ever spoken, and I pray she hears me.

I take her hands from my shoulders and guide them to her blouse. She needs help. Needs *me*. "Start with the shirt."

Her head tilts, her hands still. "So, am I in charge?"

I could laugh. *Oh, lady, you are so in charge.* She rules me. Eases me. Strips me of reason. I'm incapable of thinking straight around her, and I'm constantly fighting with my conscience and my instinct. Instinct always wins. "If it makes you happy." I watch her as I remove my watch, her eyes clouding, her shaky hands starting to unfasten the buttons. The first one reveals her smooth décolletage. I gulp. The second her breastbone. The third, her bra. Fuck me, if this isn't fucking about, I don't know what is. But watching her giving herself to me, albeit slow as fuck, is satisfaction personified.

She releases the final button, exposing her front to me. I'm vibrating. Rapt.

Lace.

She pushes her chest out as she shrugs it off, but she doesn't let it fall to the floor. She holds it out to the side in a loose grip, as my eyes travel over every inch of her skin, eventually making it to her face. Her eyes sparkle like priceless diamonds as she releases the blouse.

"I love you in lace," I whisper.

She says nothing and starts on her trousers, my body temperature rising fast, my hands sweating, itching to grab her. *Ava O'Shea, oh what you do to me.* Take her. *No, give her this time.* Take her, she's yours. *No, let her have this moment.*

Her hands pause in the tops of her trousers, and I look at her. She's loving my condition. *I'm* loving my condition. *Make her promise to never leave you.*

I'm on fire, and never has being burned felt so good. I peek up through my lashes, finding nothing but pure, justified satisfaction plastered all over her face. "I could rip them off in two seconds flat."

"But you won't," she says confidently. "You'll wait." She kicks her shoes off with a little too much force, and they land with a thud across the room.

I smile on the inside. She's making the most of this. "Taking this a bit far, aren't you?" It's me who's taking this too far, and I'm suddenly regretting it. I'm setting a rod for my own back, giving her a false perception of what our relationship will be like.

The control in our bed has to stay with me, no question, because I feel like there is little control elsewhere.

She smiles and shimmies out of her trousers, and I'm hit between the eyes by more lace. That's it. I'm done. I'm taking the control back. I reach for her.

"No," she warns, and I halt, looking at her in surprise. No?

"Fuck you," I growl.

Her smile is demure. "Please do."

Oh? I grin darkly on the inside. And there it is. She doesn't want the control. She just wants *me*. And, like she's done to me, I will make her sweat. I grab her and place her on the worktop, my mind spinning, conjuring up a plan, putting myself between her legs. Her warm, slender, long legs. Legs that were made the perfect length and shape to wrap around my waist. I don't think I could have crafted a woman so perfect. I take her waist and pull her snuggly into me. Perfect. I roll my hips into her. Perfect. She breathes in, releasing the air on a shallow moan. Perfect. She holds me around my neck. Fucking perfect.

"I thought I was in charge," she whispers, hoarse and low. Perfect.

"Wrong." I remove myself from her space and strip down, not making a meal of it like she did. I'll make her sweat in another way.

I stand before her, naked, ready, and admire her admiring me. "It's rude to stare," I whisper when her eyes falter on my abdomen, making her shoot those huge pools of diamonds to my face.

I have her attention again. I need to keep it. Stop her questions building. I put myself back between her legs, leaning past her, my chest meeting hers. Our skin melds, sticks, slides as I unhook her bra and cast it aside, my nose invaded by her glorious scent. My ears invaded by her rushed breathing. Pulling back, I take some support from the edge of the counter, wedging my hands there, keeping her eyes as I lower my mouth to her chest.

She bucks, then sighs, her head falling back, and she slides her hands into my hair, holding me lightly so I can pass from boob to boob, nipple to nipple, rolling my tongue slowly as she makes the most incredible sounds. I lick the length of her torso and slip my fingers into the side of her knickers. "Lift," I say quietly, dropping a kiss on her chin. She complies immediately, making my task easy. "I'll be back." I drop her knickers to the floor and take a moment to drink in the perfection of her naked body on my kitchen counter. "I'm a bit peckish." I head to the fridge and collect my tools, feeling her eyes on my back. I turn, my hands full. She's in a trance. "Enjoying the scenery?"

She blinks herself back to life and diverts her stare as I shake the can of squirty cream, taking it to my mouth and releasing some.

"And that's a staple food in your world?"

This should be a staple in everyone's world. Along with peanut butter. And chocolate spread. "Absolutely." She'll agree with me when I'm done with her. Putting myself back where I should be, I shake the can and tap her chin. "Open."

The sight of her pink, wet tongue nearly has me abandoning my plan. Nearly. This is going to be heaven. I lift the can to her lips and squirt cream into her mouth, smiling when she licks it up. She slowly leans back. I lazily skate my eyes over her flesh.

"Do your worst, Mr. Ward," she says, happy with my plan.

I grin. Heaven. "This might be a little cold." I give her no time to prepare, releasing the cream, starting just shy of her chin and finishing at the apex of her thighs, relishing the expansion of her chest. Perfect. I squirt a little more on her pussy. So perfect. I lick my lips, stand back, and take in my handy work.

"It's a bit of a cliché, isn't it?" she says on a playful grin.

Yes, yes, it is but, fuck me, this cliché looks pretty fucking perfect to me. I have another quick hit of cream, thinking how much better it'll taste when I'm licking it from her flesh. "The old ones are the best." *Old.* Like me. I kick that ridiculous thought away and focus on the woman before me.

The woman who finds me irresistible.

Now, time for part two of my plan. I go to the cupboard and rummage. "Here it is." I eye up the jar of chocolate spread, my mouth watering. This has got to be up there with the greatest of desserts. I grab a spatula and casually hit the top of the jar with it, delighting in the satisfaction growing on her face.

I get rid of the lid, mirroring Ava's curious, raised brow as I plunge the spatula inside, loading it with as much chocolate as I can get.

And smack it on her boob.

"Ouch!"

My grin is irrepressible as I spread it far and wide, coating her everywhere, her hums as constant as the throbs in my cock.

She's covered. I'm done. And a fucking amazing job it is too. "My very own Ava éclair."

She peeks down at her coated body. "I guess now you've had your fun," she says, her arms wedging onto the counter. "I should go take a shower."

What? I'm on her like a wolf, locking her to me, the slap of our chests deafening. She laughs, squirming against me, making sure I'm as covered as she is.

"Sneak," I grumble, looking between us as I peel myself away, pouting. It's all ruined, like a squished, melted, chewed-up eclair. Damn her.

Time to sweat, baby.

I lower her to the counter. "I've not even started with the fun part, lady."

"I'm filthy," she says around a dizzying grin.

"Oh, I love that grin." It's light, it's happy, and I put it there. It's fucking life. "You won't be filthy for long." I bend over her, my cock getting a torturous rub in the right spot. *Control!* I'm a joke. My finger must be vibrating against her skin as I drag it through the mess on her body. She's regarding me with nothing less than adoration. That in itself is addictive. I pass over her erect nipple, watching her stiffen, her eyes shimmering with want. I make a meal, literally, of licking my finger clean. "Hmm," I hum. "Chocolate, cream, and sweat." And it is divine.

She's growing more impatient, struggling to contain herself, reaching for me. I can't bring myself to deny her. I'm done for, a slave to her demand, a fool in love. I take her mouth, and she kisses me to the clouds where I float for a while, consumed by our inexplicable connection, but the inferno inside is roaring loudly. I moan, she writhes. I can't hold back anymore.

I pull her up, never leaving her mouth, her hands moving frantically through my hair, and tear my lips away, moving up her cheek to her ear, biting down when she forces her hips forward into my gyrating groin.

"Jesse." It's a plea, her body bowing.

"I know." *Fuck, I know.* "You want me to take care of it?" *Take care of you? Because, baby, need sounds good on you, and it feels pretty fucking amazing on me.*

"Yes!"

She doesn't know you, Ward.

I close my eyes tightly, pushing away my bullying, hounding conscience. *Listen to her. Hear her. She loves you. Wants you. Needs you. She won't leave you.* I grit my teeth and place a tender kiss below her ear, bracing myself to face her. To tell her. I lower her to her back again, and she looks up at me with so much reverence, it physically hurts. *Tell her.* But tell her what? Which part? What horror do I begin with? I push a lock of hair away from her face, my gaze rooted on her adoring expression. Her face now, looking at me, waiting, watching me tear myself up inside. She has no idea.

I can't do it.

I can't take that look away. I can't be the reason for her hurt. I've hurt too many people, and I'll be dead before I add Ava to that list. She's redemption for me and, selfishly, I can't take that away from myself either. "Everything is so much more bearable with you around, Ava," I whisper. That much she *can* know. I'll be lost without her. I know it to be true, because during the times we're apart, I feel like I'm slowly dying again. Counting down the minutes until she takes me to the clouds. Talking myself in circles if she so much as misses a call. Beating myself up, constantly worrying about what the future holds. I don't know what it holds, and it's fucking scary. So, no matter what, to preserve this crazy kind of wonderful, I must do what I need to do. And she has to find it in herself to accept that.

I gaze down her body. Look into her eyes. My mind yells. But my heart screams.

I can see her intention to speak, to push for more. I hate myself for it, but I can't give it to her, and I question in this moment whether I ever will.

Distract her.

My mouth falls to her breast, feasting on her, instantly driving her wild.

"Feel good?" I ask, knowing the answer, feeling anger festering. I'm a true, total fuck-up.

"Yes!"

"You want more of my mouth?" I goad, wanting her need confirmed, demanding to hear it again.

"Jesus, Jesse!"

There it is. All for me. I divide the attention of my tongue between her boobs, allowing her increasing impatience and breathy gasps to ease me back down to stable. Will I ever be stable? I hiss when she sinks her nails into my scalp, willing on the punishment until I've no more mess to lick up.

"All clean." I stand, wiping my mouth. "But she wants more of my mouth." This isn't about what she wants, despite her wanting it. This is all about me. Easing my insecurities. Easing my pain. Easing my conscience. I place a hand on each of her thighs and spread her legs, dragging in air at the mere vision of her. "Fuck, Ava. You're weeping." I cast my eyes to hers as I lower my head, her smell potent, her heat sizzling. Every muscle she has locks tightly, preparing for me.

Am *I* prepared?

Never.

I plunge my tongue deep into her, flattening it and dragging it firmly up her center.

"Oh . . . God!" She bucks, and I drive two fingers inside, pinning her down with my forearm.

"You want me to stop?" I ask, licking her, kissing her, pumping hard with my fingers. I smile wickedly, maintaining my cruel combination of tongue thrashes and drives, savoring the sight of her falling apart. She's coming. I can taste it. Feel it. Smell it.

Her clit pounds against my tongue and her body bends violently, her head tossing from side to side as she explodes on a yell, vibrating manically. Then she flops back down to the counter, gasping for breath, wet through. I should give her time to recover. Should. I can't. She's dripping, and my cock wants part of that. "You're amazing. I need to be inside you." I haul her hips up and hammer forward as I yank her down. "My turn." There's no space for consideration. No room for accommodation.

My hips piston, and I bang into her, out of control. It doesn't take her long to find my sway. Her arms are flung back, she yells, and she accepts my power. I'm tight everywhere, my arms, my grip, my jaw. The friction is sublime, her face a picture. "Does that feel good, Ava?"

"God, yes."

"You won't run away from me again, will you?" I grunt through my pounds.

"No!"

It's exactly what I needed to hear. Yet it doesn't slow my thundering hips, doesn't make me take my time. I drag her up and swing her around, slamming her into the wall, my urgency, my conscience, getting the better of me. But can I stop? Never.

Her yells are persistent and loud, like fuel to my engine. I don't know how she's sustaining this. I'm close to collapsing myself. My cock is becoming tender, my balls ache, my muscles scream.

I'm close. I look at the ceiling, my jaw set to snap, then her teeth sink into my shoulder. *Fuck!* My head collides with the wall, and she screams a scream I'm sure could reach The Manor.

I still, feel her pussy squeeze me, and I'm a goner.

I slam forward, my dick lunges, explodes, and I groan my way through my orgasm, feeling lightheaded and absolutely wrecked. "Jesus," I choke, having to stop moving, the sensitivity too much, my whole frame shaking manically. I'm dazed. Confused. Out of breath. And out of my fucking mind in love.

She hugs me, gasping against my shoulder, both of us drenched, sticky, and useless. It takes me a few moments to find the required energy to get her back on the counter, and as soon as she's on her back again, I collapse onto her. Spent. That was fucking brutal.

I dot kisses across her hot cheeks as she lies still and quiet, her eyes closed. What is she thinking? Is she wondering how she ever existed without this? Without *me*?

Her eyelids flicker, and she gazes sleepily up at me.

"You and me," I say quietly, scanning her eyes, seeing life in their depths.

She doesn't say a word. Doesn't need to.

When she hides herself in my neck, I know what she's telling me, but I may have to accept that she will never speak the words. I can do that, because Ava and I will always do our talking this way.

I don't want to move her. Don't want to separate our bodies. "We need a shower," I say reluctantly, dragging both of us up, every one of her limbs remaining curled around me tightly.

"Let's stay," she pleads groggily, and I laugh.

"Just hold on." *Always hold on to me.* "I'll do all the work."

She doesn't protest. I hope she never will. I carry her to the bathroom and place her on the vanity unit. She looks magical on that unit.

"You're sticky, I'm sticky." And I want to show her how good I am at taking care of her. Let her become accustomed to my devoted attention. Expect it. Get shitty with me if she doesn't get it. "Let me wash us both, then we can get in bed and snuggle. Deal?"

She pouts, barely able to keep her eyes open. I've literally fucked her to sleep. "No, put me in bed."

"You're adorable when you're sleepy." And sassy. I pick her up and carry her into the stall, and she clings to me in that amazing way she does. "I'm going to put you down." She increases her hold. It's thrilling. "I can't wash you without any free hands," I say over a laugh.

"I want to stay stuck to you."

Oh God. More of that, please. All of that. Bring it on, I'm ready. I show my appreciation with a gentle peck on her forehead. I can flex. So I maneuver her in my hold, supporting her under the bum with a knee, and reach for the products I need, dropping them to the floor. Then I take us down together until she's cradled in my lap, curled in snuggly. The water pouring down on us is peaceful, but my head is screaming. It's relentless, and none of the thoughts welcome.

Tell her.

I can't, and that makes me hate myself even more.

I grab the soap and start working it over her skin where I can, given her arms are locked around my neck. I have no desire to remove them. None at all. I do the best I can on her hair, working through some shampoo and then some conditioner, and as I'm rubbing her scalp, rinsing it from her hair, my movements falter, my eyes stuck on her dozing form. So unaware. So in the dark. I lean in and kiss her temple, squeezing my eyes closed. "I want to look after you forever," I murmur, silently begging she lets me do that. Devote myself entirely to her. It'll make me feel better about deceiving her so terribly. For betraying her. *Please forgive me for all of my past sins.* Please complete me.

My eyes fly open when I feel her hand loosen from around my neck, sliding over my shoulder to my front and slipping down to my tummy. She's awake.

"Okay," she whispers.

My fucking heart cracks for her, but for me, it beats faster. *Life.*

Okay.

"Come on," I say, my voice thick. "Let's get you out."

She kills me some more when she kisses my chest gently, and I blink back the sting in my eyes. Hopeless. I swallow and drop my gaze, and she smiles, hesitant and unsure. I try my hardest to give her a sincere one in return. "What's wrong?" she asks.

What's right amid this pile of wrongness?

Only her. She's right.

"Nothing's wrong," I lie. "Everything is right." I clench her cheeks, trying again with that smile, absorbing every inch of her. Just to check she's real. Just to check she's really here.

I'm only half assured.

I reach behind me and flip the shower off, helping her up, and I wrap myself in a towel quickly then spend an age taking immense pleasure from rubbing her down and squeezing the water from her hair. *Look after her.* She's welcoming right now, but what about tomorrow when she's not immersed in my physical attention and my body? "You want me to carry you?"

She nods, and she's back in my arms in a heartbeat. I put her in bed and smile as she crawls under the sheets. I join her, and I've barely come to rest before she's smothering me completely, spreading herself all over me. I'm completely swathed in her. And it's the most soothing place in the world.

"Go to sleep, baby." I kiss her sweetly, pulling her closer.

And I lie there all night trying to figure out how the fuck I get to keep this woman, and at the same time save her from me.

25

IT'S BEEN a long time since I've been awake so early and wanted to be. It's a new day, and after the perfection of last night, I'm excited for it. I'm also terrified. If I could just make the entire world disappear, except for us, that would be ideal. Keep us in a bubble. One that could never pop, let alone explode. Because it will. It has to.

And the shards of devastation could be scattered for miles.

She's dead to the world, her breathing light, her lips parted just so. She looks so cozy. Comfortable. Like she should never leave my bed. I've only ever watched one other person in my life sleep. Sit there for hours, just making sure her chest was moving up and down, every so often placing a palm there to feel her heartbeat. To feel her warmth. The only warmth that was in my life.

I swallow and reach for Ava's chest, laying my hand between her breasts. The feel of the beats pulsing into my touch makes me smile sadly, uncomfortable with the life seeping into me. Because if there is one thing in the world I know for sure, it's that life isn't guaranteed. It can be stolen. Ripped away. I can't allow that to happen again. I'll never survive it.

My touch moves to her face. Her skin is glowing. Her lashes are incomprehensibly long. Her lips are beautifully swollen and pink. *You need this.* "Do whatever it takes," I whisper, my eyes traveling across her peaceful face. "You want to be here," I tell her quietly. "And I will absolutely ensure it's the best decision you'll ever make." I lean in and drop a kiss on her lips, and she murmurs sleepily, her hand lifting and falling onto my nape. I pull back a little, studying her. "Save me, Ava," I whisper. "You're the only one who can." My eyes close, and I sink my face into her neck as she skates her hand back and forth across my nape for a few hypnotic moments, before her moves slow to nothing again. I remain still against her. Rested, despite my restlessness. Calm, despite the swirl of torment inside. Happy, despite the misery shrouding my existence.

I tear myself from her body and tuck her in, then pad quietly out of the bedroom, taking myself down to the kitchen for some water. As I'm downing the glass, my eyes land on her purse. I wipe my mouth with the back of my hand and approach with caution, my eyes flicking to the doorway, my mind seeing her snuggled up safely in my bed. Unconscious. Unaware. This huge, sprawling penthouse feels somehow homelier with Ava here. My life is somehow more tolerable.

I reach into her purse gingerly and shift a few things aside. A pack of pills lays at the bottom. *Take them.*

I retract my hand, stepping back, getting a safe distance away. "Stop it," I say to my wayward mind. "Just—" My foot catches something on the floor, and I glance down. Her shoe. I look across the kitchen and spy the rest of her clothes, scattered all over the place. Without a second thought, and perhaps to get me away from her purse, I gather her things and place them on the island. And stare at them.

Keep her.

I scoop the pile up and go to the fridge—the fucking fridge?

—and stuff them all inside. I close the door. Stare at it. "Call the fucking shrink, Ward," I say, and yet I don't rectify my move. Instead, I collect my clothes from the floor and pace out of the kitchen, refusing to look at her purse, my face bunching up as I fight off the devil on my shoulder yelling at me to secure the deal. *For fuck's sake.*

Distraction.

I take the stairs two at a time, already feeling like it's been too long since I've seen her, touched her, kissed her. I find her sprawled on her back, her hair wild and fanning the pillows, the sheets skimming her waist. Her skin tone against the crisp white is utter perfection. I take my phone out of the pocket of my trousers before I toss them in the washing basket, and I check the screen as I go back to the bed. I stop at the edge. Stare down at my sister's name. *Fuck.* I clear her missed call and file that problem away to deal with another time.

Then gently pull the covers down Ava's body, exposing her completely, and crawl onto the bed, putting myself between her legs, my chest blanketing hers. Peace is mine again. The feel of her boobs squished against me? Pure bliss. Her breaths warming my face? Total gratification. The feeling inside of me? Absolute, complete, earth-shifting, universe-shaking love.

I cradle her head with my arms, nuzzle her nose, shift my hips a fraction to make room for my instant morning glory, and it falls perfectly to the soft, warm place between her thighs. Complete heaven.

Her eyes blink their way open, and I see her mind slowly figure out where she is and with who.

"Morning, lady," I whisper, feeling her body tighten beneath mine, every limb stretching as best it can with me restraining her.

"Morning, yourself." Her voice is rough and throaty, and the steady beats of her heart against my chest increase. Instant want. Instant need.

One roll of my hips puts me inside her, and I drop my head for a moment, my teeth gritting, the feeling . . . out of this world. This. Every morning, this.

I force some life into my muscles and lift my heavy head, retreating and driving forward again slowly, watching her immediately coming undone. She holds on to my arms tightly, gazing up at me.

"I love sleepy sex with you." Unwilling to break our connection, I secure her against me and roll to my back, and she hisses as she settles above me, straddling my waist. Her chin drops to her chest. She's struggling with the position. Struggling to accept me. Not for long. Soon, I'll have had her in every way and position known to man, and that sweet place of hers will know nothing but me. It will accept nothing but me.

"Ride me, Ava."

Her hands meld to the muscles of my chest. "I'm in charge?" she asks, a certain level of delight in her tone. She is one hundred percent in charge. On the odd occasion that I'm not.

She senses that, and I feel she gets a kick out of me holding the power. But I also know she'll fight me on it. "Do your worst, baby." And, fuck, she could do some damage.

I egg her on with a jolt of my hips, sending my dick plunging deep and hard. Her jaw tightens, and she slowly rises, hovering above me, the tip of me skimming her delicious heat. She'll milk this for all it's worth, make me beg, send me wild, and I am fine with that. My current view is unmatchable, her expression a mix of determination and craving. The craving I understand. Appreciate. Love. The determination? She's wasting her fucking time. I'm already hooked. Already at her mercy, and I'm at peace with the fact that I always will be. *So do your worst, Miss O'Shea.*

And she does.

She lowers carefully, watching me acutely, so obviously

relishing the strain on my face. And she grinds down beautifully, rendering me incapable of holding back my sounds of pleasure.

"Again?" she asks, and I curse, the tips of my fingers sinking deeper into the flesh of her thighs, anchoring me. "Mind your language, please." She starts rising lazily again, and I have not one fucking clue how she's maintaining her controlled moves, because I already feel set to bounce around the room on constant yells. Up. Down. A precise grind. Over and over, each move sending my mind and body further into bedlam. I moan, my head thrown back, my hands reaching for her boobs.

She stops moving, her thigh muscles tense as she holds her position. I swallow hard.

"Down?"

I've never seen such a sight, and I mumble my plea for her to indulge me, my hands clawing into her perfectly formed, perfectly sized breasts. She catches me by surprise when she suddenly changes her tactic, smashing down hard. "Jesus fucking Christ!" She doesn't relent, crashing up and down, and I'm quickly catapulted to the edge. "Fuck, fuck, fuck." I'm going to explode. See stars. "Ava, I'm going to come!" I'm completely dumfounded when she tells me to wait. She does this, makes me lose control, and then expects me to have control? I'd admonish her, if I could string a sentence together. Lucky for Ava, I'm incapable of nothing except fighting back the imminent detonation of my dick.

She continues to roll, lift, lower, grind, moan. "Ava, I can't," I mumble, feeling my limit come and go. There's nothing I could do to hold myself in check now. Not when she's looking like that. Not when she's doing this to me.

"Shit!" she gasps "Wait."

"Watch your mouth," I shout, frustration joining the barrage of feelings holding me hostage.

"Fuck off, Jesse."

What the fuck? I choke on my shock, outraged and disappointed, though I'm incapable of voicing it. All I can do is glare at her with all the threat I can muster, the vision of her riding me with so much purpose making my eyes cross.

Then she screams, "Now," and pounds down, and all thoughts of swearing and punishments disappear amid a fog of pleasure. My vision fails me. My hearing distorts. I am absolutely and completely out of my mind, being seized from every direction by an unconquerable force. My cock rolls relentlessly, my groans sound distant. I can't control my breathing. My heart is working overtime. My body overheating.

She splatters onto my front, her breathing erratic, and I hold her to me while we recover. "I love sleepy sex with you," she rasps, her throat undoubtedly sore after her screams. Sleepy sex? The only thing sleepy about that sex is the sleep I'll need to recover.

"Except for your filthy mouth," I murmur. Her face appears, her chuckle sweet, even if I'm unamused. She strokes my cheek, and I smile at the tender gesture. "I don't think we can call that sleepy sex, baby," I whisper.

"No?"

"No," I sigh. "We'll think of a new name for that one." Something like, *Kill-Jesse-Sex.*

She agrees, flopping onto my chest again. "How old are you, Jesse?"

I look down at the precise circles she's drawing around my nipple. "Twenty–nine," I answer, and she huffs. I roll my eyes, insulted. Clearly, I look older, which should be fine because I am. By a considerable amount.

"What's the time?"

I don't know why she's asking. She's not going anywhere. "I left my watch downstairs." I start to peel us apart, and she grumbles. She doesn't want to leave, so it should be fine that I won't let her. "I'll go take a look."

"You need a clock in here."

"I'll put in a complaint to the designer." I get up and go downstairs, finding my Rolex on the island. "Seven thirty," I call, slipping it on, focusing on my wrist and not her purse a few feet away. Hiding her clothes is a short-term fix. I need a long-term fix.

You have one!

I clear my throat and push her purse away without looking, focusing my attention on the fridge as I approach it. I hear the urgent pounds of her feet flying down the stairs, and I smile at the piles of clothes as I take a jar of my vice from the shelf and settle on a stool, waiting for it.

She lands in the kitchen as I take my first mouthful. Naked. Sexed up. She looks incredible after mind-blowing sex, but I sense my contentment ends now. She looks in a rush.

"You'll have to drop me at home."

Have to? Wrong. "I'm a bit busy this morning." I dip and sweep, pouting at my finger as I pull it from the jar.

"Where are my clothes, Jesse?"

I plunge and suck the good stuff off, closing my eyes, savoring the taste, before slowly dragging it past my lips. "I've no idea." I lick my lips and re-dip, hearing her snort and stamp out of the kitchen. I smirk and continue with my breakfast, looking up at the doorway every now and then when I hear a door close or a drawer shut.

I have a childish little chuckle.

"Where are my fucking clothes?" she yells, appearing at the doorway as I startle, nearly biting off my fucking finger. For the love of *God*.

"Watch your fucking mouth," I bellow, my appetite gone. What is it with this woman? *What is it with* you, *Ward?* But look

at her. Things so vulgar shouldn't fall from the mouth of something so beautiful. And she has the nerve to look at me in disapproval? She is so far past unreasonable, she really could be the
death of me. Going from naught to one hundred miles an hour in a
fraction of a second can't be good for my heart.

"Jesse." Her head tilts, and it's condescending as fuck. She
thinks I'm the unreasonable one. She's a case. I'll show her
unreasonable. Happily. "I never swore out loud before I met you."
Her eyebrows raise slowly. "Funny, huh?" She smiles sweetly,
and I snarl. Not funny at all, actually. "I need to get home so I can
get ready for work."

Work. Fucking work. Why does she have to have a job? Or
anything that takes priority over me? Because she is sure as shit
my priority. "I know you do." I moodily shove my finger back in
the jar.

"So, where are my clothes?"

"They are . . . somewhere." I look up, and the repulsion on her
face strangely makes me smile. She doesn't like my vice of
choice? Maybe she would if she knew of my previous vices.

"Where is somewhere?" she asks.

I swallow down my peanut butter, the voices in my head
talking non-stop. *You can't keep her prisoner. How will that help
you? Don't crowd her.* I pout. She likes being crowded. "If I tell
you," I say, reluctantly accepting the voices in my head are right.
Yet the notion that my time in bliss will soon be temporarily
suspended isn't resting well. "You have to give me something in
return."

Her nostrils flare. "What?"

"Don't drink tomorrow night." I blurt it out quickly and brace
myself for the blowback. But, and I will fight her on it, I am not
prepared to accept that level of drunkenness, especially when I'm
not around.

"Fine."

Huh? Just like that? I'm elated. She's getting good at this. "That was easier than I thought. What about lunch later?"

"Okay. Get my clothes."

"Who holds the power, Ava?"

"You do. Get my clothes."

I slide my jar onto the counter, satisfied. "Correct." That's a good day's work done. Until lunchtime when I suspect she'll challenge me all over again. But I'm ready. Armed.

I go to the fridge and pull out her pile of things, presenting them to her. "Here you are, lady."

She frowns, glancing past me to the fridge. And I beam at her. *Aren't I a clever boy?* Then she scowls an epic scowl, but I let it slide. I've won.

She grabs her things viciously. She just can't help herself.

"Have I got time for a shower?" I ask as she dances around the kitchen, struggling into her clothes, gasping and hissing at the cold material on her skin.

"No."

She turns, and her arse is quickly all I can focus on. For cursing like a sailor, I give it a firm slap as I laugh my way out of the kitchen and sing my way up the stairs, humming as I brush my teeth, and whistling as I throw on my running kit.

"Hurry up," she yells as I wander out of my bedroom to the top of the stairs, looking down as she paces, her face engrossed in her mobile. What the heck am I going to do until lunchtime? There's only so far and so long I can run, and I'm quite envious—and annoyed—that she'll soon be distracted by work because nothing can distract me from her.

She looks up at me standing motionless at the top of the stairs, gesturing impatiently for me to get my arse in gear. "You're very demanding this morning,' I grumble, ignoring her huff of laughter. How many hours until lunchtime?

"Going for a run?" she asks as I collect her and move us

toward the door. She can't hide her delight, her eyes taking a greedy jaunt up and down my physique.

"Unless you have something better for me to do?" I open the door, and she rolls her eyes, passing through.

"Right now, all you need to do is get me home sharpish."

"Yes, so you keep saying." Stupid work. "Ever thought of setting up your own business?" I ask as we board the lift. She's more than capable, then at least she's not answerable to anyone except me. I smile on the inside. Perfect solution. I'd make a double appointment every single day.

"Maybe one day." She goes to her bag and rootles through, and a few things spill over the top, falling to the floor. A lipstick. And her pills. "Shit," she curses, and I slap a palm on my forehead, closing my eyes, gritting my teeth. "Sorry." She looks anything but sorry. I dip and pick up the bits, my hand faltering on the pill packet. There's one less than there was an hour ago.

"Okay?" she asks as I hover in my crouched position. I look up, and she tilts her head in question. I force a smile and hand them to her.

"Never better," I murmur, raising and guiding her out of the elevator. She's taken a pill. That's a good thing.

But what about the plan to keep her, Ward?

Fuck off!

Once she's in my car, I make quick work of getting behind the wheel and revving the engine hard.

Anything to drown out the voices in my head.

Yet when we pull up outside Ava's, the voices haven't fucked off, and I can't say I heard a word she said on the drive to Kate's. Did she even speak?

"Are you okay?" she asks when I pull up outside, her curious eyes boring holes into my profile. Am I okay? No, I'm pretty sure

I'm ready to be assessed. I turn and force a smile, reaching for her cheek. My smile turns from forced to natural when she inhales, closing her eyes and leaning into my touch.

"I'm not sure how I'll survive until lunch." I'm being honest with her. Telling her the truth. Although not talking about my past and my demons isn't technically lying.

"Think of me," she says, taking my hand from her cheek and blinking her eyes open. I look at her with all the adoration I'm feeling and hope she sees it. "Won't be long." She hops out and dashes up the path to the door, rummaging through her bag as she goes. Her hair swishes across her back, and I settle back in my seat, watching as she faffs and fiddles to find her keys. She drops them, and I shake my head around my smile. Then nearly swallow my tongue when she bends to pick them up. "Jesus, Lord above," I breathe, my hand resting over my shorts, my arse shifting in my seat. She disappears through the door, and I drop my head back against the seat, looking up at the roof of my car. This morning is going to drag painfully. I know it.

I pull my phone out to text Sam.

Run?

I click send and startle when my phone starts buzzing in my hand. I drop it like a hot potato into my lap, looking blankly out of the windscreen. *Not today, Amalie.* The constant rings are like a foghorn, going on forever. She's not giving up. My forehead drops onto the steering wheel, the sound of my mobile cutting through me.

Then answer her call, you coward. Take the first step.

My phone goes quiet, but not for long. She tries me again. I feel blindly around in my lap and pull it out, my thumb hovering over the screen. *Do it.*

I hit the red icon. I can't. Reaching for the stereo, I crank up the volume, closing my eyes, trying to get myself back to a relatively peaceful place. This conflict makes no sense. Amalie often tries to get in touch, and it never hits me this hard. Right now, I feel guilty. I feel like a bastard. Blocking her from my mind and my life has always been easy. Casting thoughts of my parents aside was instinctive. Why now am I finding it so hard?

The only thing that's changed is the lack of alcohol.

Why is everything—emotions, actions, thoughts—all related to the fucking bottle?

Because drink masked everything.

I look up at Kate's house. *She's* why. For her, I don't want to be a bastard. "Fuck," I breathe, resting my head on the window, trying to muster the courage to call my sister back.

Ten minutes later, I still haven't. I drag my hands down my face and try to realign myself, ready for Ava because, obviously, she sees when something is on my mind, when I'm unsettled, when I'm sad, and she presses me.

Knock, knock, knock.

My head nearly hits the roof of my car when I jump. Disorientated, I look out of the window, seeing a man's face pushed up close to the glass. I back up a bit. Then his uniform registers. "For fuck's sake." I roll my eyes, looking at the rearview mirror. It's a quiet residential street, there's no traffic, and I'm not blocking the road. I let the passenger window down. "I'm waiting for someone," I say, immediately clicking the button to put the window back up, taking away his opportunity to challenge me. I'm in no mood. I hope he senses that.

Knock, knock, knock.

I grind my teeth and slowly turn warning eyes onto him. He doesn't heed the caution, motioning up and down the road to the non-existent traffic. "Fuck off," I grunt, looking past him when Ava comes flying out of the door. The fact that she looks crazy gorgeous is superseded by the speed at which she's running, looking into her bag as she stuffs things into it. For Christ's sake, she'll trip.

I give the warden my middle finger when he knocks again, glancing at my phone when it starts ringing. My sister's name on the screen makes my mood plummet further. *I don't know what to say to you, Amalie.* I let the window down again, and the drone of the warden's voice becomes clearer. "I'm just doing my job. Abuse will not be tolerated."

I look past him, seeing Ava hovering beyond, constantly moving from side to side, trying to find a way around him. "Move so the lady can get in the car," I order. He ignores me. Stupid fuck.

"Excuse me," I hear Ava say sweetly, and yet the eejit blabbers on at me to the point I could quite easily reach across my car, grab him by the scruff of the neck, and yank him in before smashing his face against the steering wheel. But I can't do that.

"For fuck's sake." I get out and stomp around the front of my Aston, pleased to see him finally backing off when I meet him on the pavement. That's better. I open the door and help a quiet Ava into the seat. "Have a good fucking day," I mutter as I pass him, falling back behind the wheel and roaring away.

"They're just doing a job, you know," Ava says quietly, and I laugh on the inside. So was I. And this morning my job is to get her to work on time.

"Power-hungry failures who didn't make cops," I reply, peeking across at her, finally getting my moment to absorb her. Her face is fresh and free from makeup, although that looks like it's going to change. She's pulled the sun visor down to get to the mirror. She doesn't need makeup. She doesn't need clothes. She doesn't need work. "You look lovely."

"Watch the road," she says over a laugh, dabbing at her face. "Oh, Sam said he can't make your run."

"Lazy bastard," I mutter, returning my attention to the road. I pull around a slowing cab, frowning. "He's still there, then?"

"He's got Kate tied to the bed," she says, and I recoil, flicking my eyes across the car. She sounds completely unfazed by that as she applies some eye makeup. I slow down a little while she's holding a stick so close to her eyes.

"Probably," I muse, grimacing, wondering where that word came from. I look out the corner of my eye, seeing Ava frozen, her mouth agape. I quickly look away.

"You don't sound shocked."

"That's because I'm not." What the fuck is wrong with my mouth right now? Why am I feeding her curiosity?

Her teeth sink into her lip, her mind clearly racing. Lord, if she's struggling to get her head around a bit of rope play, her mind might explode if I share more. "I don't want to know," she eventually says, returning to the mirror to finish her makeup.

"No, you don't."

"What?"

"Nothing." I reach for her knee and take hold, siphoning off some willpower and strength to get me through my morning. "So what have you planned for the day?"

"Work," she answers dryly, flipping the mirror back up. I give her knee a squeeze in warning, and she laughs over a yelp, grabbing my hand.

"Sarcasm," I say, and she sighs, settling back. "Well?"

"I'm catching up on all my projects and making sure I'm up to date on all the things. I'm busy . . . ish."

I smile, and her lips twist from trying to prevent her own smile. "Is that why you've had me drive like a loon to get you to work on time? Because you're busy . . . ish? Because I can think of many ways to keep you *very* busy *all* the time."

She laughs. "I'm sure you can."

"Yes, I can."

"Your current perks aren't enough?"

Actually, no, they're not. The perks should be constant, and until they are, I'll never feel quite complete or content. "I'll take everything you're willing to give, Ava," I say seriously, and she withdraws slightly. How much is she willing to give?

She doesn't answer, and the rest of the journey is quiet until we pull off Piccadilly.

"Pull up around the corner," she instructs, probably thinking she was lucky the day I literally picked her up and carried her out of the office. Has anyone asked her about that?

I zip into a space and turn in my seat to face her, taking her knee again. She's instantly stiff. I'm not so soft myself. "What time's your lunch?"

"One," she says, a little high-pitched as I tilt my head, moving my touch up her leg. She leans back in the seat.

"I'll be here at one then," I whisper, stroking my way to between her thighs.

"Right here?"

"Yes, right here."

"Jesse, stop," she begs. Stop? Why ever would I do such a stupid thing?

"I can't keep my hands off you, and you're not going to stop me, are you?"

I move in and pull her lips to my mouth, humming as I work her over her trousers, getting a balance of pressure and friction just right, building her slowly, feeling her shift in her seat, her lips getting harder on mine.

"Let it go, Ava," I order, increasing my strokes, nibbling her lip. "I want you in that office thinking of what I can do to you."

She releases a suppressed yelp, her body going lax, and I kiss her through her orgasm, slowing my rubs.

"Better?" My mouth works from one side of her flushed face to the other, dotting kisses on my way.

"I can work in peace."

"Well." I chuckle. "I'm going home to think of you and sort this out." My cock's standing to attention. I can't run with this. She leans across the car and drops a light kiss on my lips, a cheeky smile forming. I raise my eyebrows. Don't tell me she's going to offer?

"I could do that for you." Her hand is in my shorts before I can blink and, naturally, I'm fucking delighted.

"Oh, fuck, Ava." My torso folds as she wraps her hand around me, and my head loses all strength, falling back. "That feels so good." She works me perfectly, slowly, not seeming in such a rush all of a sudden. And I am here for it. I close my eyes and savor the feel of her warm palm pumping me, my groans constant, my veins hot. Yes. *Oh yes.* Blood surges into my dick, my hand shooting out to grab the door. Then the steering wheel.

Fucking hell. My legs extend, trying to straighten in the confines of my car. I'm getting hotter. Stiffer. Harder.

And then I feel a dash of contact from her slippery tongue, and I curse, my arse leaving the seat, my knuckles white around the steering wheel. My eyes spring open, finding her head in my lap. "Oh Jesus," I breathe, watching her start to bob up and down.

"That's it, baby. Take it all the way." She pauses a beat, then moves again. "Keep going, just like that." My hand falls into her hair and guides her, my skin starting to tingle. Fuck me, that mouth was made for me in every way. To give me sass. To kiss me. To smile at me. For my dick to fuck.

But very quickly, my dick is suddenly cold, and my hand naturally falls over it to protect it. I open my eyes. She's grinning, swiping the back of her hand across her face. I don't like that grin. It's crafty.

"I'd love to," she purrs, and I slowly grasp what is about to happen, "but you've already made me late for work." She moves fast, and lost in shock for a few seconds, all I can do is watch her escape.

"What the fuck? Ava!" I dive across the car, just missing her wrist. "Fucking hell." I quickly tuck myself away and jump out, astounded, pissed off, shocked. I have to commend her on her bravery, though. "Jesus," I groan, wincing. She's made it to the other side of the road by the time I've straightened my crossed eyes, and she looks all too pleased with herself. I can't help but let her have this win. Just look at her delight.

"How old are you, Jesse?" she calls, backing away.

Good question. How old am I, because I feel like a lovesick teenager right now. "Thirty," I yell around my smile, and she shakes her head but doesn't argue. I'm not foolish enough to think if I promise her my real age, she'll finish what she started. "That wasn't very nice, you little temptress." I'm already planning my revenge. But I'm also smiling, because my girl just felt relaxed enough to have some fun, and I can't say I'm sorry I'm the victim of that fun.

She blows me a kiss and performs an elaborate curtsy, then dances off. I just manage to snap a picture of her before she disappears around the corner, and I look down at the screen she's filling. "And this was the day you blew me to distraction," I murmur, tucking my phone in my pocket. I rest my arse on the bonnet of my car, folding my arms over my chest. "Oh, Miss O'Shea, you're walking on dangerous ground," I say quietly, though she'll never comprehend just how dangerous.

I glance across the street, seeing a bakery opening up. I smile to myself, heading over, and I find the biggest éclair there is. I scribble a note while they box it up. "Would you deliver this to the Rococo Union Office around the corner sometime this morning?" I ask, putting down a twenty. "Keep the change." I dazzle the server with a wicked smile and she slowly pulls the note toward her.

"Sure."

"Thanks." I grab a water and step out into the sunshine, swigging it back. It's just a few hours until one. I toss the bottle in a nearby bin, readjust my now tame dick, and start running toward Green Park, dodging the pedestrians, focusing forward.

My legs are soon numb and my body drenched. And despite the gorgeous scenery, I see only her.

I run for two hours, circling all the parks, nearly making it back to Lusso at one point. I head back to my car but detour down Bruton Street, just to catch a glimpse of her. She's at her desk, relaxed back in her chair, twiddling a pen as she looks over some papers in her grasp. She still looks perfectly flushed. Perfectly engrossed. Perfectly mine.

I could stand here and watch her all day, but I won't. Because that would be weird. So I force myself back to my car and race over to The Manor to get my bike, stopping by Lusso to pick up my helmet. It's the perfect day to ride and, shit, do I need to feel the peace that can be found while speeding through the country-side on my Ducati.

I hear Jake in my mind yelling at me to take it easy. I smile. "Just because you would have ridden like a Nancy," I say, reaching for the stereo. Placebo joins me, and I slip my shades on, cocking my arm on the window. I'm thinking. I'm thinking what an amazing track this is to make love to. I play it on repeat for the entire journey.

The second I cut the engine, my phone sings, and I huff a sardonic puff of laughter as I answer, taking the steps up to the entrance fast. "You need to stop saying stupid shit to Ava," I warn Sam.

"What's classified as stupid shit?"

"Anything relating to kinky sex."

He laughs, and I scan the entrance hall as I pace to my office, hoping no one is going to hinder my speedy visit. "But she *was* tied up," he goes on. "And you know what?"

"What?"

"She fucking loved it."

"I'm happy for you."

"You know, I think Kate will be totally cool when I tell her."

I'm ground to a stop. "You're not fucking telling her," I practically growl, making Sam laugh.

"Not yet. Not until you open your big gob and enlighten this woman, whom you're apparently in love with, on what you do for a living. But in the meantime, I'm having fun priming Kate. Where are you?"

I get moving again. "At The Manor collecting my bike."

"Which one?"

I smile. Sam's a petrol head too, his Porsche giving him multiple orgasms daily. "The Ducati."

He whistles. "Why won't you let me ride that thing?"

Because that thing is precious. Jake's dream. "You couldn't handle it."

"Fuck you."

I laugh and hang up, arriving at my office and swapping my keys before making a sharp exit to the garages. Sarah catches me in the lobby, just as I'm a few feet from freedom. I carry on walking, and she follows. "Going for a ride?"

"Yep." Opening the garage door, I scan my rows of bikes before I put on my helmet.

"You only ride when something is on your mind," she says. By *something*, she means Jake. It's my way to feel close to him without being able to *be* close. I fucking hate that Sarah knows everything there is to know about me. I hate even more that Ava doesn't. *The woman I love should know my soul.* I swallow hard and throw my leg over the saddle. But today, I don't only want to feel close. My rides are soothing when nothing else soothes, but they're also a glorious time killer. I need that now.

"I'll see you tomorrow." I start the engine, tingling everywhere when the exhilarating sound travels through me. I would give anything to have seen Jake ride just once. Anything. For me, as an adrenalin junkie, it even gets *my* pulse kicking. Jake would have creamed his boxers. I kick the stand up and rev a few times, and Sarah appears in front of me, her mouth moving. She looks irritated, but I can't hear a damn word she's saying. It's a blessing. I snap down my visor and skid off, kicking up clouds of dust that's probably left her coughing all over the driveway. I shouldn't laugh. I know I shouldn't laugh.

But I do.

As I approach the gates, I start to slow, seeing they're already opening. John's Range Rover pulls in, and I lift a hand as I pass. As soon as I hit a clear road, I open her up.

I thought I told you to take it easy.

My adrenalin surges.

You'll get yourself killed.

The world racing by is a total blur.

I don't want to see your annoyingly good-looking face just yet. What the fuck?

Jake's voice, his words, charge through my head like a stampeding heard of elephants, and I yank the accelerator, frowning. The pull of my bike beneath me as I max out the last but one gear is as fierce as first gear. Fucking wicked.

You have something to live for now.

I jerk, only a fraction, but at this speed, a fraction is all it takes. "Fuck," I curse, fighting with the handlebars, trying to regain control and get myself back in a straight line, automatically easing my grip of the accelerator. I manage to claw back some control and let the bike slow until I'm chugging along at a pathetic forty, getting honked at by cars overtaking me. I blink, shaking my head. "If I have something to live for, why the fuck are you trying to kill me, Jake?" Jesus, that was close.

And get some fucking leathers.

"Fuck off," I mutter, pulling into a layby to gather myself. "Since when has it been acceptable to talk to me like that?"

Since I'm dead and you're a fuck-up. And you can't swing at me.

It's actually quite a relief to hear my brother and not my bastard conscience. I don't know what comes over me. I pull off my helmet, and I laugh, leaning forward and using the bars to hold myself up. What the ever-loving fuck is wrong with me? My eyes are streaming. My body out of control, jerking with my hysterics. I'm gone. Take me to the fucking loony bin.

I glance around the countryside, and all I see is Jake's smiling face. He's happy. Because I'm happy. Where the hell has he been all this time? I dream of him. Think of him. But never has the fucker ever really spoken to me. And he chooses now? Of course he does. Because . . . Ava. "You proud of me, bro?" I ask, pushing my fingertips into my eye sockets. "I've found *the* woman I want to spend eternity with. A good woman." Okay, a little younger than everyone probably expected, but still. "You'd love her. She's smart, like you. Ambitious, like you. Sarcastic as fuck and absolutely does not suit swearing." I smile. "Yeah, you'd love her."

Great. But twenty-six, Jesse?

I laugh. "Yes, twenty-six." *God, I miss you, Jake. Still.* Scrubbing my hands down my cheeks, I look over my shoulder when I hear a car on the gravel behind me. A car I recognize. "Oh, no," I say quietly, putting my helmet back on with haste. By the time I'm ready to pull off, Freja has parked her Maserati conveniently in front of me.

I start pushing my way back to gain enough space to swing out. "I thought it was you," she calls, holding the top of the door, smiling at me like I didn't send her packing the other night with a few home truths. She starts to wander over, and I seriously dislike the cocky swagger she's got going on. "I thought you should know," she says, the triumph in her voice heightening my worry. She knows she has my attention, because her smile's just widened. She thought I should know what? I don't want to ask. I pull my helmet back off, waiting for her to hit me with whatever it is that's going to fuck up my day and my mood. "Mikael has hired a designer for his new project." She pouts. "I think you might know her."

Dread. It's like a pile of bricks falling onto me. I don't have the capacity to wonder how the hell Freja knows about Ava. All I can think is . . . *hell to the fuck, no.* Ava is *definitely* not working with Mikael Van Der Haus. The smarmy fuck. He had little to do with the development of Lusso, his partner overseeing the works. Now? Now he's met Ava? I bet he'll insist on more briefing sessions than necessary. More calls. Perhaps a few dinner meetings. Lunch meetings. *Fuck, no.* "Do you want to keep playing at The Manor, Freja?" I ask, going into immediate damage control. Her fading smile gives me my answer. "You'll keep your mouth shut, or I will give your husband everything he needs to wipe the floor with you in court, do you hear me? I don't give a fuck if my Manor is brought up."

Her face is a picture. Didn't she think this through? I push my helmet on roughly, pumped up on anger, and zoom off fast, cursing. Why can't the world just fuck off?

26

FREJA'S MADE ME LATE. Jesus, hell hath no fury. I see Ava up ahead, walking to the end of the road. It could be me, but she looks a little heavy-footed. Annoyed?

I whizz past and pull up at the curb, slipping off my helmet and resting it on my lap, and I watch as she leans against a wall, her attention on her mobile phone. She looks up, sees me, and smiles. My beautiful girl. My fingers tingle at the thought of touching her.

Pushing herself off the wall, she struts over, her eyes getting their own fill of me. The satisfaction never gets old. "Good afternoon, lady."

"You're a menace."

Truth. A menace who's head over heels. "Did I scare you?"

"Yes," she huffs, motioning to my bike. "That thing needs a noise risk assessment."

Thing? "This *thing* is a Ducati 1098." I slip my helmet on the handlebars and make a grab for her. "Kiss me," I order quietly, leaning her back and moving in, not giving her the opportunity to comply. I can't wait. And neither can she. She holds me tightly, and I'm a slave to what she does to me, the feelings she evokes.

So when she starts trying to break free, I'm indignant, natu-rally. I've only just got her in my arms again, so I hold tighter, kiss her harder, feeling her hands on my chest, trying to pry us apart. What the fuck is she playing at? I release her mouth, but not her body. "What do you think you're doing?"

She continues to squirm. "Let me go."

Never. "Hey. Let's get one thing straight, lady," I say, sounding as outraged as I'm feeling. "You don't dictate when and where I kiss you, or for how long." That's my call.

"Jesse," she huffs, out of breath from her struggling. "If Patrick sees me with you, I'm in all kinds of shit. Let me go."

My instinctive flinch as a result of her foul mouth gives her the break she needs, and she's gone from my arms, putting way too much space between us. "What the fuck are you talking about?" I yell, feeling immediately lost without her close, adding to my grievance. "And watch your mouth!"

She snorts and glares at me, a glare fierce enough to sever my dick. "*You* have not paid your bill, and now I'm supposed to be giving you a polite reminder," she says, straightening herself out. A polite reminder? She's not sounding very polite right now. In fact, she's being plain rude. "I was forced to give some spiel about you being away."

"Consider me reminded," I grunt, reaching for her. "Now get your arse here."

"No."

I'm stunned. Because I didn't pay my bill? Truth be told, I totally forgot about the bill. That's her fault, anyway, and now she's punishing *me*? I don't think so. Let's get some things straight before she sends me off the deep end.

Too late, Ward.

I get off my bike, clawing through my head for the right words, words that'll cool the heated situation. "Three . . ." Perfect. I'm such a cock. Seems Ava's shocked by my choice of word too, because her chin just hit the pavement. But I'm committed now. I'm not backing down. Oh no. "Two . . ."

Wide eyes join her gaping mouth. Then she huffs. "I'm not getting into a row with you in the middle of Berkeley Square. You're a child sometimes." She's gone faster than I can think of a comeback, marching away. *Child?* "One," I bellow, going after her.

"Fuck off," she yells over her shoulder, the sharp curse hitting me like electricity, making me twitch as I stalk after her. She's absolutely begging for it. *Begging!* "You're being unreasonable and unfair," she calls.

I'm being unfair? I'm not the one depriving her of everything wonderful because her boss has got the hump. "Mouth!" I shout. "What's so unreasonable about wanting to kiss you?"

"You know damn well what's unreasonable about it. And it's unfair because you're trying to make me feel shitty about it." She suddenly disappears through the door of a shop, leaving me on the pavement outside, astounded. How did we go from smiles and kisses to fucks and fury?

I need to calm the hell down. Easier said than done when she's being so difficult. I get my face up close to the window, spotting her by a rail with a shop assistant. My eyes narrow naturally. She thinks she's safe from dealing with me in there, does she? Wrong.

I push the door open, just as Ava pulls out a ridiculously skimpy cream dress. "You're not wearing that," I snap, staring at the scrap of material dangling from her hand. Over my dead fucking body. Never. Jesus, she'll floor every man in a ten-mile radius, and if she doesn't happen to drop them, I absolutely will.

I lift my eyes to Ava. Disgust is emblazoned all over her face. Good. Then she knows how I'm feeling. But it's soon *my* jaw sweeping the floor when she mouths, "Fuck off," before dismissing me and turning to the assistant. She did not just do that.

"Have you anything shorter?" she asks.

Is she for fucking real? "Ava," I growl, twitching like I'm being tasered. "Don't push me."

"No, I don't think so," the assistant says, sounding hesitant.

"Okay, I'll take this one." Ava hands the dress to the lady.

"Urh . . . is this the correct size for you?" she asks.

No, it's fifty sizes too fucking small.

"It's a ten?"

"It is, but I would recommend you try it on as we don't offer refunds."

That's not a problem because she's not buying the dress, but before I can advise the young woman, she's shown Ava into the dressing room. My feet are itching to steam in there and rip that dress to shreds, and my hands are flexing, preparing to wring her fucking neck. I pace the store for a few minutes, searching for my lost control. It's gone, mislaid, and I fear it may never be found.

The assistant appears from the fitting room, her lips straight as she slinks behind the cash desk, avoiding my accusing glare. Okay, I can pull this back. Play reasonable. Get her on side, and then think about how to deal with the dress once we're friends again. I take a needed hit of air as I pass the cash desk, looking out the corner of my eye to the assistant, who's fiddling with some tissue paper. "I want you to tell her it doesn't suit her," I say, and she swings a startled look my way. "And in return, I'll buy all your stock."

"Seriously?" she questions.

"Deadly."

I leave her with that and enter the fitting room, and my eyes cross the second I clap eyes on Ava in front of the mirror, the cream silk clinging to every curve it touches, and it doesn't touch much. "Oh, Jesus, Mary, and Joseph," I murmur, my eyes glued to her long, willowy legs. My hands go to my hair. Tugs. She looks fucking incredible. A deity. My fucking savior and, dressed like this, my downfall. I take a few steps, fighting to reason with myself. She's mine. She wants to be mine. This young, fresh beauty in a showstopper dress is in love with me. Me. Not so young. Not so fresh. Although, admittedly, I'm feeling younger and fresher these days. All her.

I look at her amused face. She's mine, yes, and wants to be, but that won't stop people trying to take her away from me. And in this dress, those chances are multiplied by a million.

"You're not . . ." I murmur, waving a finger up and down her body, "you . . . you can't . . ." It's too short. *Way* too short. I'll be up for murder. I need to make her understand, but as I look at her, defiance and willfulness etched across her beautiful face, I just know reasoning isn't going to work. "Ava . . . baby . . ." I take another look down the dress, and my cock, the traitor, swells. "Oh, I can't look at you." I remove myself from the dressing room before I pass out. Or jump her. I'm hot. Suffocating.

I pass the sales assistant and glare at her, dropping my hand from the front of my jeans. "Remember?" I ask, as she disappears into the changing room to join Ava.

"The dress looks incredible," I hear her sing, and I slap my forehead as I head for the door, needing air. But I'm slowed to a stop by a wall of shoes, in particular a pair of skyscraper stilettos. How on God's green earth do women walk in those ankle breakers? I pluck one from the shelf and study it, mentally measuring the height of the heel. Seven inches. Seven inches! Nearly as long as my cock.

My bewilderment is interrupted when I hear activity, and I look over my shoulder. Ava's there, half grinning at me. Glad she's finding this funny. I shove the shoe back on the shelf on an epic scowl that goes way over her head as she pulls her wallet from her handbag and the assistant wraps the dress, taking a long-arse time about it too.

"Enjoy the dress, madam," she finally says, handing the bag to Ava once she's paid. "It really did look lovely on you." She looks at me, and I roll my eyes.

"Thank you." Ava slowly pivots, and I quickly find my scowl again. This isn't over. That dress is not making it onto her body. Unless we're at home. Alone. And it'll be quickly removed again. This woman is impossible, just trying to prove a point. "Excuse me," she says, stopping before my imposing frame, looking at me expectantly.

"You've just wasted hundreds of pounds," I say, motioning to the bag. "You're not wearing that dress." I'm so mad. But equally hard. I can't cope with the conflict. My dick and my sensibility are at war.

"Excuse me, *please*," she says slowly.

I take one step to the side, and she scoots past, leaving the store. I'm quickly on her heels, breathing down her neck. "Zero." I pull her into an alley and push her against the wall, and I kiss her like a man deprived. And, of course, she is with me after just a moment of quite pathetic resistance.

"I'm not going to let you wear that dress," I gabble between the thrashes of our tongues.

"You can't tell me what I can and can't wear."

"Stop me."

"It's just a dress."

"It's not just a dress on you, Ava. You're not wearing it." I pepper kisses over every inch of her face, and she breathes out tiredly, bored with the argument. At least we can agree on that. I can see she's exasperated, her sigh heavy and meant to be heard. But, like me, I know she doesn't want to fight. And I sense she's becoming aware of my fear of losing her. Of the need to pacify me. Calm me. Soon, she'll start demanding to know why.

"Thank you for the cake," she finally whispers.

"You're welcome. Did you eat it?"

"Yes, it was delicious." She nuzzles my cheek, and peace blankets me. "I'm not supposed to be spending any more time on you until you've settled your bill." She constricts her hold of me as I bite at her ear. In each other's arms, calm is ours again.

"I'll trample anyone who tries to stop me." She's seen what I'm capable of.

"Why are you so unreasonable?" she asks, and I frown, visions of the cream dress invading my mind. The very *unreasonable* cream dress.

"Can I ask you the same question?"

She looks at me tiredly, shaking her head. "I'd better get back to the office."

"I'll walk you," I say, resigning myself to not getting an answer. But I want one later when we'll be having a very frank conversation about her stubbornness.

"Halfway. I can't be seen to be entertaining clients for lunch without Patrick knowing, especially ones in debt. Pay your bill."

Oh for the love of God. How long does she plan on hiding our relationship from her boss? *Perhaps as long as you plan on hiding your secrets from her.* I grimace. "God forbid Patrick should find out that you're having your brain fucked out by a non-paying client."

Her gasp of shock makes me smile. She loves me fucking her stupid. I plan on fucking her very stupid later. I feel out the small of her back and lead her on, reaching for her hand, but she denies me, pulling it away. She just can't help but be difficult. I grunt and make another play for it.

And miss again.

She walks on, focused forward, silent. Is she moody? I leave it a few moments, knowing she's waiting for me to try and claim her again, and when I see she's relaxed a little, I swoop in and win her hand, and I make sure I keep hold of it. Better. Much better.

Just before her office, I stop us and walk us to a wall, needing to see her. This was not how I planned on spending her lunch break. "Why are you sulking?"

"No reason," she replies quickly and quietly, her hand twiddling her hair wildly.

I pull it away. "Tell me the truth," I order, but she remains mute, refusing to look at me. "Answer me, Ava."

She doesn't, and I start to get impatient. "Is this over a dress?" I ask. "Because you'd better get used to that. My eyes only, Ava."

She muscles her way past me. "What do you care?" she asks, wrestling her bag onto her shoulder. "After all, you're just fucking me." She disappears through the door, and I blink rapidly, standing motionless on the pavement, unable to unravel my confusion. *I'm just fucking her?*

What planet is she on? Does she think I behave like this with the women I've *just fucked*? She'll put me in an early grave, way earlier than alcohol at this rate. So she wants me to spell it out? I'm certain I have already, but for the avoidance of doubt . . .

I push my way through the door of her office—*fuck her boss* —and I'm pulled to an abrupt stop on the threshold when I see her on her phone, her hands sifting through various papers on her desk.

"Yes, I received your email too," she says, and a nasty feeling lands in my gut. "I'll have some schemes ready for you." She nods, picking up a board and scanning it. "Yes, of course. Any particular day?" Another nod. "Okay, Mr. Van Der Haus."

My back goes ramrod straight, and Ava stalls in her faffing, her eyes darting across her desk. "Goodbye, Mikael."

And there it is. Mikael. First-name terms is the beginning. It's also the end.

She's engrossed now, her hands moving across designs,

files, her mind whirling with ideas. I reach back for the door
and open it again, closing it loudly. She still doesn't look up,
but her work colleague does, and his eyes glimmer with
happiness.

"Ava." He taps his pen on his mouse mat, his head tilting. "It's
someone for you-hoo."

She looks up.

And flies back in her chair.

Her alarmed eyes get wider the closer I get to her desk. "Miss
O'Shea," I say calmly.

"Mr. Ward," she breathes, glancing around cautiously.

"Aren't you going to ask if I would like a seat?"

"Please." She points a shaking hand to one of the chairs,
looking at me in question as I lower. "What are you doing?"

"I'm here to settle an invoice, Miss O'Shea," I say around a
smile.

"Oh." She doesn't appreciate my killer beam. "Sally, can you
deal with Mr. Ward, please?" Her eyes never move from mine.
"He would like to settle his outstanding account."

Unbelievable. She truly is.

"Of course," Sally replies from behind me.

"Sally will look after you, Mr. Ward," Ava says coolly,
seeming to have located her poise.

"Only you," I confirm, frowning when she closes her eyes and
inhales deeply, like she needs the extra air. Then I clock her boss
approaching from behind, and her actions make sense.

"Ava?" he asks, giving me the once-over.

"Patrick." She forces a smile as she points a pencil at me.
"This is Mr. Ward. He owns The Manor." Her eyes speak to me,
and I see the message there. She's begging, and for the first time,
I consider why she's so worried. Is Patrick Peterson a dick?
Would he fire her for getting involved with a client? "Mr. Ward,"
she says. "Meet Patrick Peterson, my boss."

"Ah, Mr. Ward," Peterson sings. "I know your face." He offers a hand, and I stand, accepting it.

"We met briefly at Lusso."

"Yes, you bought the penthouse," he chimes happily. I've dealt with many businessmen in my time. Some cool, playing their hands close to their chests, others transparent as fuck. This one here is as transparent as fuck. He wants in on my fortunes.

Sally approaches and her feet nearly leave the floor when Peterson grabs the papers in her hand. "Have you offered Mr. Ward a drink?" he asks her, and I see the panic on her face. Poor thing. She's obviously of a nervous disposition. My guilt for yelling at her is back with a vengeance.

"I'm fine, thank you," I rush to say. I don't want a drink. I want to clear up a small matter with my girl. "I've just come to settle my account."

"You shouldn't have rushed in just for this." He laughs, Ava scoffs, and I smile.

"I've been away." Technically, that's true. I've been away with the fairies. "My staff overlooked it."

"I knew there would be a perfectly reasonable explanation," Peterson says, not seeming at all bothered by my outstanding payment. But it irks me no end to think he's given Ava a hard time about it and, as a result, I'm now sitting here having to fix a problem that shouldn't even be a fucking problem. "Was it business or pleasure?"

I can't help myself. I cast a dark look on Ava. "Oh, definitely pleasure."

She blushes terribly, and I'm left restraining my amusement.

"I'd like to make some appointments with Miss O'Shea while I'm here," I declare. "We need to get a quick turnaround on this."

"Absolutely. Are you looking for a design, or a design consultation and a project manage?"

Ava shakes her head. She knows what's coming. Who am I to

disappoint her? "The whole package," I confirm, and Patrick Peterson very nearly raises the dead with the sound of his excited clap.

"Super! I'll leave you with Ava." *Yes, please do.* "She'll take good care of you." He extends his hand, and I take it blindly, watching as Ava squirms all over her desk.

"I know she will," I say quietly, tearing my eyes away and looking at him, raising from my chair. "If you give me your company bank details, I'll arrange an immediate bank transfer. I'll also make an advanced payment on the next stage." *So you don't have to get on Ava's back.* "It will save any future delays." *And my sanity.*

"I'll get Sally to note them down for you." He heads back to his office, pleased as punch. Now, then. Back to the matter at hand.

I drop to the chair and give Ava my full attention. She's in a bit of a trance, but I'm quickly faced with pursed lips and a face to rival any filthy look I've seen before. "When are you free?" she asks.

Easy. Every second of every minute of every hour of every day. "When are you?"

"I'm not talking to you," she snaps.

"What about screaming for me?"

She recoils. "Neither."

Wrong. So wrong. "That may make business a little tricky," I muse, taking immense pleasure from her attempts to keep me in her bad books.

"Will it be business, Mr. Ward," she asks, "or pleasure?"

"Pleasure, all the way."

"You do realize that you're paying for me to have sex with you. That, in effect, makes me a hooker."

Why does she do it to me? All the fucking time, she ruins the moment with that mouth of hers. If I didn't want to kiss her so much, I'd sew it shut. I move forward, getting threateningly close. "Shut up, Ava. And just so you know, you will be screaming later"—I nod in approval, relaxing back—"when we make friends."

She looks utterly exasperated. And then she laughs.

"Is something funny?"

She starts going through her diary with a heavy hand. "Yes, my life. When shall I pencil you in?"

Pencil? I don't think so. I scan her desk and spot what I'm looking for, claiming it and holding it out to her. "I don't want to be penciled in anywhere," I say quietly. "Pencil can be erased." She looks up slowly, warily, her eyes on the black marker pen. *Just you try to erase me, Ava.* "Every day."

"Every day?" She laughs. "Don't be so stupid."

I've never been more serious. I remove the lid and slide her diary over to my side, making sure our hands skim as I do. She inhales. I smile.

I start working my way through, page after page, filling her diary with my name every day of the week. When I reach Friday, I smile. "You're mine then anyway."

Monday's page shows a ten o'clock appointment penciled in, and to prove my point, I reach for an eraser and rub out the name. Gone. Like it was never there. Let's see her try to rub out the marker pen.

I dip and blow across the page, smiling as Ava looks on, stuck for words. So I carry on to the next week.

"What are you doing?" she eventually asks, halting my writing.

I look up at her stunned face. "I'm making my appointments."

"You're not happy enough controlling the social aspects of my life?"

Controlling? I'm not controlling. There's absolutely no control anywhere to be found.

"I thought you didn't make appointments to fuck me?"

"Watch your mouth," I grate. "I've told you before, Ava. I'll do whatever it takes."

"For what?"

"To keep you," I answer frankly, and if that, this, doesn't spell it out, then I'm at a loss.

But, typical of Ava, she can't help but let her defiance loose. "What if I don't want to be kept?"

Listen to her. Who is she trying to convince? Herself? Me? Should I remind her of the words she murmured in the shower? Or the drunken words in the car? Nothing but complete candor will work here. "But you do," I say. "By me. This is why I'm having such a hard time trying to figure out why you keep fighting me off." I go back to her diary and finish penning in every single day for the rest of the year, and she remains silent the entire time.

When I'm done, I shut the book and stand, satisfied. My work here is done. "What time will you be finished work?"

"Six-ish," she whispers, looking somewhat dazed and muddled.

"Ish," I mimic, offering my hand. She stares at it for a time, psyching herself up. I'm doing the same, but all the time in the world wouldn't prepare me for the reaction I have to physical contact. I jerk. She jerks, her eyes shooting to mine. How could she even try to deny that? I gently pull away, dragging my touch across her skin, my body blazing. "See?" I say quietly, and she swallows. Yes. She sees. But if I don't get out of here sharpish, Ava's boss and colleagues are going to get quite the show.

I'm going to have to wait a few more hours to continue proving what I'm so sick of proving.

27

I KILL the rest of the afternoon drinking coffee in a nearby café after shooting to the bike store across town to pick up a few bits for Ava, as well as some new running shoes. And a few other essentials.

John has been persistently calling, and I've avoided him. He only calls when there's a problem these days. I've enough of my own, and one in particular is scratching at my mind like nails down a chalk board.

Mikael Van Der Haus.

If he even so much as *thinks* about making a move on Ava, I won't hold back. It'll be the last thing he does. God damn it, why does this world have to be so small?

Between five fifteen and five fifty, I watch as all of Ava's colleagues leave the office one by one. I look down at my watch, feeling impatience taking hold. Where the hell is she? A text lands from John.

Answer your motherfucking phone or I'll beat you hard, you ignorant motherfucker.

It immediately rings, and I immediately answer. I'm not stupid. "John," I sigh, and he growls down the line before he speaks.

"I'm working to a deadline. These contracts need to be signed, or else the new surveillance company can't order the equipment, and the installation will be delayed another month. I don't know about you, but I don't like the thought of The Manor with no security. And Sarah needs you to sign off the accounts so she can file the tax returns. So get your motherfucking arse over here and sign some motherfucking papers, boy."

"Good day?" I ask, throwing a twenty on the table and rising from my chair.

"Don't test me, Ward."

"But I have Ava with me," I whine, even if that's not technically true. Again, where the heck is she? "I'll do it in the morn—"

"Do. Not. Test. Me." The line goes dead, and the pure threat of John's words has my face screwing up, defeated. He's right. I can't risk leaving The Manor so vulnerable, nor the members. Our security is a huge reassurance to our people. "Fuck it," I mutter, wandering over to my bike, my eyes never moving from the door of Rococo Union. Did I miss her leaving already? Impossible. My stare has been so focused on her office, my eyeballs are sore.

Then I see the door open, and she backs out, pulling it closed behind her. My smile is instant. I push my helmet on and jump on my bike, starting her up and screeching across the road. Ava jumps like a startled cat, swinging around fast.

I remove my helmet and join her on the pavement. Her semi-scowl doesn't sit well. "Good day at work?"

"Not really." Her expression is pure, cock-slashing disdain. She's still cranky? And then I see the bag with the ridiculous dress hanging from her grasp.

Kill it.

I think for a few moments, sprinting through my options. There's only one. Distract her from her grievance.

I stroke her forearm, working my way down to her hand. My entire body lights up, despite her displeasure. "Can I make it better?"

"I don't know; can you?"

Silly question. She knows I can, and I know that both thrills her and pisses her off. "I think I definitely can." I beam at her, my knockout smile. She's softening. I can see it in her eyes, feel it on her skin, and judging by the way she looks to the heavens, she's willing herself not to fold under the power of our touching skin. "I'll always make it better." I'll fix everything. Always. "Remember that."

Her face is quickly incredulous. "But you made it shitty in the first place."

"I can't help it," I mutter, accepting that we'll never move on unless I bend a little. And I want to move on. On to The Manor, then on to my bed. We need to reconnect. Make friends properly. We need to close our bubble again, because in our bubble, there's no interference. The horrible feeling in my chest is non-existent. We're safe.

"Of course you can," she exclaims.

She's so wrong. Where Ava is concerned, I'm at the mercy of a power far stronger than any reason I could find if I had the energy or inclination to find it. Which I don't. I'm ruled by desperation. Driven by fear. I don't want to be. It just is, and she doesn't help the matter by fighting me on just about every-fucking-thing. "No, with you, I can't help it." But I might be able to if she relents and constantly feeds this odd, unrelenting hunger. Speaking of which . . . "Come here." I lead her over to my bike and she frowns at the bag as I open it.

"What's this?" she asks, definite worry lacing her tone.

"You'll need them." I pull out the rather fetching pair of

leather trousers and present them to her. Realization hits her like a brick. Literally.

She jumps back, shaking her head. "Jesse, I'm not getting on that thing."

Wrong. She's definitely getting on that thing, and I'm going to love every second of her pushed up close to my back. I drop to a knee and shake out the trousers. "On."

"No."

I look up, ready to wrestle her into them, but the genuine anxiousness blanketing her face stops me and has me rising, moving in close, feeling at her face.

"Listen to me, lady," I whisper softly. "Do you honestly think I would let anything happen to you?"

"They scare me," she murmurs, gazing at me, searching for the reassurance she wants. She's found it. I'm right here.

Getting my face close to hers, I smile on the inside, feeling her lean into me. Wanting to get close. "Do you trust me?"

"Yes."

You shouldn't.

I swallow and kick that thought away, planting a light kiss on her nose before crouching and removing her cute red pumps. Truth be told, I'm amazed at her answer. *She trusts me.* Even though my behavior with her is somewhat . . . intense.

Slowly covering her from head to toe in protective leathers, literally wrapping her in cotton wool, I ignore Jake's irritating whine in my ear asking me why the hell I didn't buy myself some while I was at the store. It didn't cost me a thought. Never does. Reckless, I know, but I lost any sense of self-care long ago. But now?

I should definitely get some leathers.

"Take the pins out of your hair," I say, stuffing her things away, waiting for her to chastise me for being so rough with her new dress. The dress that's conveniently going to go missing very soon.

"Where are *your* leathers?" she asks, her hands in her hair feeling around, pulling grips out here and there. My mind blanks, not only because of her question, but because I'm being blitzed by some pretty fucking incredible memories of me plucking millions of the things from her hair after the Lusso launch night.

"I don't need them," I say mindlessly.

"Why, are you indestructible?"

"No, lady, self-destructible."

Her frown is instant, and so is my regret. "What does that mean?" she asks.

"Nothing." I shove her helmet on quickly before she can challenge me, making sure it's snug and safe before lifting the visor. The second I have her eyes again, I know my hope of avoiding my cock-up is wasted.

"You should wear protective clothing," she grumbles, motioning down her front. "You're making me."

"I'm not prepared to take any risks with you." *Because you're precious, and I am not.* "Anyway . . ." I go on, keen to change the subject, giving her leather-clad arse a little slap, "you look fucking hot." *But hotter in lace.* I drape her bag across her body. "When I'm on, put your left foot on the peg and swing your right leg over, okay?" I say, slipping my helmet on and mounting my bike. She steps forward and, with a grace that's not at all surprising, she gets on the back.

"I feel too high."

"You're fine," I say, looking back at her. "Hold on around my waist, but not too tight. When I lean, gently lean with me and don't put your feet down when I stop. Keep them on the pegs. Clear?" She nods, and I smile, seeing excitement past the anxiousness. "Put your visor down," I say, knocking mine into place as she follows suit, settling into my back, her thighs framing me. This takes the thrill of riding to a whole new level.

I start the engine and push back into the road, checking for traffic before pulling off uncharacteristically slowly.

I don't question it. I don't need to. I'm carrying precious cargo.

It feels like the fastest journey ever. I relish every second of her clinging to me, and when the gates to The Manor appear, I feel resentment that the best ride of my life is coming to an end. But what about Ava? Did she enjoy it? Will she indulge me again?

"Off you get," I order gently when we come to a stop, lifting my visor and looking back. She springs off, and I kick the stand down and swing my leg over, setting my helmet aside.

My hand goes through my waves, not to sort out my mussed-up hair, but because I'm nervous. I want her to like riding with me, because I need to experience that kind of new peace again. Tentatively, I lift her helmet from her head, and her face slowly appears. It's expressionless, and my heart sinks. But then she grins, eyes sparkling, and dives into my arms, wrapping every limb around me, as if she already misses being stuck to me. I'm so fucking happy, I could cry.

"There's that grin," I say, reaching back to set her helmet on the seat of my bike so I can hold her with both hands. "Did you enjoy that?"

She pulls away, finding my eyes, and then she hits me with something I'm not expecting, *or* that I'm prepared for. "I want one."

What? No, wait, that wasn't part of my plan. "Forget it," I blurt without thought. "Not a fucking chance in hell." I'll be a nervous wreck, more than I am already. "Never, no way." Good God, what was I thinking? "Only ever with me."

She's amused. I am not. "I loved it," she declares, hauling me in, giving me a long, lingering, hot kiss. "Thank you."

I hum, resigning myself to a new way of riding from here on in. *With* leathers. And considering I'll likely buy some to protect myself as well says something. *She's changing me.* It makes me wonder if I could possibly like myself one day. Am I capable of that? She makes me want to be a better man, and even though there's a huge black cloud hanging over my head, waiting to rain all over my parade—that's the understatement of the century—it makes me hope. Maybe this fuck-up could finally find peace. Be happy. "You're more than welcome, baby," I whisper.

"Why are we here?"

"I've got a few things to sort out." Annoyingly. "You can have something to eat while we're here." I'm being tactical, reducing the need to waste time eating when we get back to Lusso. I may as well use this time wisely. "Then I'm taking you home, lady." I place her down and remove some strands of hair from her cheek.

"I've got nothing with me," she says, as if that's a problem. It isn't. Ava just doesn't know it yet.

I clear my throat and prepare for the backlash. "Sam's here," I tell her, taking the lead and pulling her along. "He brought some of your stuff from Kate's."

Surprisingly, I get no counter or challenge. It's refreshing. Are we finally having a breakthrough?

As we enter The Manor, I feel my body tensing, the noise a good indication of how busy it is this evening. I knew it would be —Thursdays always are. My eyes are peeled as I walk with pace to my office, ignoring the looks coming at us from every person and every direction. The cat's officially out of the bag. Yes, I'm seeing someone. Let's not make a big deal of it.

"Good evening," I mutter, my legs moving faster, keen to get us out of the spotlight. I don't like the sea of frowns coming from the women, and I positively *hate* the looks of interest on the male members' faces. My hold of Ava's hand tightens, my eyes narrowing, firing looks of warning far and wide.

"Jesse."

I glance up and see John at my office door, his eyebrows high past the tops of his wraparounds.

I get Ava into my office, safe, away from the members of my manor. "Any problems?" I ask, forgetting myself for a second.

"Small issue in the communal room, now resolved," he answers, clearly forgetting himself too. I throw him a look. "Someone got a bit excited," he goes on, and then I see the second his brain catches up. John flicks a look to Ava as I stare at him, stunned, feeling Ava's curious eyes on my profile.

"'S'all good," he rumbles. I laugh on the inside. Is it? "I'll be in the surveillance suite." He slides out quickly, leaving me to face the impending interrogation alone. Think.

Think, think, think.

"What's a communal room?"

Bollocks.

I grab the collar of her jacket and tug her into me, making fast work of removing her bag and attacking her mouth. "I like you in leather," I breathe, removing her jacket. She's mine in the blink of an eye and a crash of her hammering heart. "But I love you in lace." I reach for the waist of her trousers and work the zipper fast. "Always in lace."

"I thought you have work to do," she pants in my face.

Work? Do I? I can hardly remember to breathe when I'm with her, so remembering anything else is impossible. I need an Ava fix. Something to keep me going until I can get her home. I lift her and carry her to my desk, and the delight in her eyes only spurs me on. I pull off her boots and dip, getting close. Her eyes are swimming with anticipation. I'm certain mine must be swimming with love. "It can wait." Nothing is more important than she is. I wish she'd adopt the same theory where I'm concerned. Be all and end all.

I help her down to her back and take a moment to drink in the perfection of her spread across my desk. "You drive me crazy, lady." My voice is hoarse. I'm trembling, my fingers struggling with the buttons of her blouse.

"You drive *me* crazy."

My palm meets her chest, and I inhale, the heat of her body penetrating me. I drive *her* crazy? She's here, spread on my desk, bowing her spine, pushing her flesh into my touch, egging me on. And I drive *her* crazy?

My eyes fall to the beautiful lace cups covering her beautiful boobs. "So we're made for each other," I declare, pulling them out of my way. Her breathing escalates, and I look up at her, desperate to ask if she's ready to fight me on *this*? I know it's the only thing she won't contest. Because, like me, when there is us, there is nothing else.

"Probably," she whispers.

"There's no 'probably' about it." I curl an arm under her back and lift her, my mouth homing in on her neck, licking and biting, sucking and kissing. She sighs, the longest, most beautiful, contented sigh, as I lazily work my way up to her face, my tongue burning on the fire of her skin. My dick is crying. My heart singing. My skin blazing.

Fuck, woman, I'm mad for you. I need to be inside her, feeling her, kissing her, falling harder.

The office door swings open, and I flatten Ava against my chest, covering her. I turn my dazed eyes and find Sarah at the door, taking us in. *What the actual fuck?*

"Oh, sorry." She's not sorry at all. I can read her like a fucking book.

"For fuck's sake, Sarah," I grate, trying in vain to keep my anger locked down. "Knock!"

She isn't fazed. Never is. "Finally got her in leather, then?" she snipes, and I gape at the door as she slams it behind her. What the fuck is it with everyone and their runaway gobs today?

"What did she mean?" Ava says, shifting in my hold, obviously uncomfortable now. I can't blame her. So much for Sarah's sincerity. I should have known. She's a bitch, always has been, always will be. If I wasn't so committed to my redemption, I'd kick her out on her arse.

"Nothing," I grumble. "Ignore her, she's trying to be funny." Fucking hell, I just need to sit Ava down and confess.

I get her down from my desk, cover her boobs, fasten the buttons of her blouse, and remove the leather trousers. And the whole time, I'm speaking silent words of encouragement to myself. Where will I start? How will I explain? And, more importantly, how will she take it all?

I can feel her watching me as I dress her, and for the first time in the history of our relationship, I take no pleasure from her studying me. I leave her and retrieve her bag, getting her shoes and placing them at her feet. *Start talking, Ward.* And yet words fail me.

I round my desk and drop into the chair, my legs feeling unsteady. Have I ever been this afraid? Categorically, no. When I lost Jake, I wasn't afraid, I was too shocked. When I lost Rosie, I wasn't afraid, I was broken. When the knife pierced my abdomen, I wasn't afraid, I was numb. After all, I deserved that and more. Fear has never featured in my existence, and now it is here with a vengeance. Fear I'll lose like I've already lost. The darkness darkening. The pain intensifying. The guilt crippling.

I watch Ava intently as she tucks in her blouse, digging deep for some strength. "What?" she asks, her head tilting just a smidge.

"Nothing." It's out before I can stop it. That strength is nowhere to be found. "Are you hungry?"

"Ish," she says on a cute jump of her shoulders.

I can't help my smile, even if I'm feeling anything but happy right now. How can I ever be truly content when I'm deceiving her? "Ish," I whisper in return, and she smiles lightly. My heart splinters. Not only do I need so desperately to avoid what might be the end for us, I need to avoid the pain I know I will cause her. Fuck, I'm in a mess, and I have no idea how to right it. Except to show her how much I love her. Will that redeem me? I can only hope because I have nothing else to offer her. Just me, as I am, and I am mad for her. "The steak's good," I say, clearing my clogging throat. "Do you want that?" She nods, and I call in the order. "Ava would like the steak."

"Certainly," Pete says. "How would she like it cooked?"

"How do you like your steak?"

"Medium, please."

"Medium, with new potatoes and a salad." She nods her confirmation, and I smile on the inside. I know her so well. "In my office . . . and bring some wine . . . Zinfandel. That's all . . . yes . . . thank you." I make a few more quick calls to John and Sarah before hanging up. Ava is still standing, and I frown, pointing at the couch. "Sit."

"I can go if you're busy."

Go where, exactly? "No, sit."

She settles, and I get on with what I was forced here to do. Except everything on my desk is everywhere, and as I glance across the surface, papers strewn as a result of Ava squirming across the wood, I sigh. This will delay things considerably. I spot a pile of bound papers still piled, albeit messily. There's a Post-It note on top with John's messy handwriting ordering me to read it and sign. I gather it up and flick through, making sure the pages are in order, every so often glancing up. Each time I do, she's engrossed in whatever it is she's doing. It's quiet. Nice. Ava being here while I work is nice.

Pete arrives with Ava's steak, and I point to the couch, my eyes landing on the bottle of wine. A whole bottle. I obviously wasn't clear. I should have stated a glass rather than *some* wine.

I leave Pete to serve Ava's dinner, returning my attention to the surveillance contract and the proposed camera placements. All looks good. Timeframe? Great. Cost? Stupid but necessary. I grab a pen and scrawl across the final page before I stand and wander up behind Ava, smiling at the sounds she's making.

"Good?" I ask, placing my chin on her shoulder, her hair tickling my face.

"Very." She can hardly speak over her mouthful. "You want to try?"

I open my mouth in answer, and she shares, feeding me. If only she knew that it's not just food she's feeding me. "Hmmm, very good."

"More?"

I nod, and she cuts me another piece, holding out her fork. I move in slowly, open my mouth, pull off the steak slowly, and chew slowly. Her expression is a picture. My face plummets into her neck, my hands finding her shoulders.

"You taste better," I growl, biting my way to her lobe and latching on, making sure I breathe deeply, right into her ear. She shudders, pushing her head into me. "You eat," I order, kissing her head, working her shoulders. "You're tense. Why are you tense?"

She doesn't answer, just hums, soaking up the pressure of my hands, and I am fine with that.

There's a knock on the door. "Yes?"

Sarah wanders in, and I toss her a warning look, a look that tells her not to say anything smart. I don't know if she catches it. She's too focused on me massaging Ava.

"Your figures," she mutters like a petulant child, setting them on my desk, frowning at the mess.

I drop a kiss on Ava's cheek and take a long shot of her scent to see me through another half hour or so. "Thanks, Sarah. I have to work now, baby. Eat your dinner."

I leave Ava on the couch and face Sarah. She's smiling. Fuck me, her mood changes faster than the wind, and it's about to change again. I pull the envelope out of my back pocket and hand it over. "Have one hundred thousand transferred into this account ASAP."

"One hundred?"

"Yes. Now, please." *And do not question me.* I go back to my desk and focus on the figures and accounts. "That's all, Sarah," I say, feeling her moody presence like a knife dragging across my skin.

I only glance up when I hear the door open, relieved to see John is back. Although he better have his big trap under control now.

He joins me, also looking across my desk that was perfectly tidy when he left. I shrug and start scooping up the papers. Where the hell has that contract gone?

"Looking for this?" John reaches forward and drags it from beneath a file.

I curl my lip and pluck it from between his sausage fingers. "I knew that," I mutter, pulling the Post-it off the front. "All signed." I give him a cheesy smile as I slip the pages into a stapler and smack the top before cockily presenting them to him. His face is straight. Unamused. "Did you get out of the wrong side of the bed this morning?"

"Fuck you."

I laugh and find the accounts again, having a casual flick through. "You've seen these?"

"Yeah. Very healthy."

"Aren't they just," I muse, looking at the net profit, the only line I need to see.

"I'm expecting a healthy . . ." John fades off when Ava appears, placing a glass of wine in front of me. Both John and I stare at it for a few seconds as I shift in my chair. God love her. I swallow and reach for the glass, even the feel of it in my grasp feeling odd, and John watches me with an interest I don't like.

"I'm fine," I say to her, detesting her slightly injured state. I force a smile, my hand beginning to tremble the longer I'm holding the wine. I don't want to drink it. Not at all. But I also don't want it in my grasp. "Thank you, baby. I'm driving."

"Oh, sorry." She smiles awkwardly. I hate that too. Fuck, I hate myself right now.

"Don't be," I say. "You have it. I got the wine for you."

She nods, accepting the glass, and I feel like a ton of bricks has been removed from my shoulders the second it's out of my grasp. I flick John a look. His serious expression, despite being pretty serious permanently, forces me to look away. "Don't say it," I whisper, finding the accounts again. "What went down in the communal room?"

"A miscommunication between members. Nothing more."

"Good." I sign the accounts and rest back in my chair, as John lifts from his. He looks across my office to Ava, and I follow his eyes. She's reading a magazine she's found. Totally absorbed. Completely oblivious to what is going on upstairs.

"I'll leave you to it," he rumbles, leaning over my desk. "Do it."

"I've tried, John," I whisper. "Believe me, a million fucking times, I've tried."

"Try harder."

"I'm going fucking crazy." I move in closer, checking Ava is still distracted. "Do you know what I did today?" I don't give him time to ask. "I talked to Jake. I'm talking to my dead fucking brother. That's how crazy I feel right now." *A brother Ava knows nothing about.*

He lifts his shades, revealing eyes that are nothing less than alarmed. "And what did he say?"

I lean back, cautious, wondering if I should divulge more. Undoubtedly, I shouldn't, it'll only encourage John to remain on my case, but I need to share and John is my only outlet. "He told me to buy some leathers."

"Listen to him. And to me. Tell her." He turns on his big boots and strides out. Ava doesn't look up. She's in a world of her own, so I leave her, and use the time productively: beating myself up over and over until I physically hurt.

God damn me.

I lift my heavy body from the chair and creep up behind her, looking over her shoulder to what she's reading. Superbikes. I've bought every monthly edition since Jake died and added them to the collection he kept hidden from our father under his bed. My heart constricts. "I've started something, haven't I?" I ask, leaning down to kiss her.

"Why haven't you upgraded to the 1198?"

Christ, what have I done? "I have, but I prefer the 1098."

"Oh." Her eyes become saucers. "How many do you have?"

"Twelve," I reply, rather proudly. Every new model that's released is in my garage sharpish. They're more for Jake than me. I just wish he was here to ride them with me.

"Twelve?" she asks, alarmed. "Are they all superbikes?"

"Yes, Ava." God, love her. "They're all superbikes. Come on, I'm taking you home." I seriously need to get myself back on an even playing field, and I can think of only one way to achieve that.

"You know," she muses, getting up from the couch, "you should be wearing leathers."

"I know I should." Between Ava and Jake, I feel thoroughly nagged.

"So why don't you?" she asks as I lead her out of my office by her hand.

It's a good question, and one I've avoided answering myself for all the years I've indulged in the thrill of the ride. Because I'm reckless. It's the same reason I drive like a dick. Driving made me so angry for so many years after I lost Carmichael and Rosie. Just getting behind the wheel brought on a fury like no other. So I drove recklessly.

Maybe because I wanted to be dead too.

I flinch. Stop getting angry behind the wheel. "I've ridden bikes since I—" *Since I lost Jake.* "For many years."

"You're going to have to reveal an age at some point." She smiles, and my damn heart bleeds as I force one in return.

"Maybe."

I move quickly through the summer room, despite the fact the crowds have thinned out, members making their way upstairs. I hear Sam before I see him. "My man," he sings as I pull Ava into the bar. "Ava, I love your Little Miss knickers." He grins as he thrusts a bag forward, and I glare at him.

"Don't push your fucking luck, Sam," I seethe. What was I thinking having him rummage through Ava's drawers?

"There's a line, Sam," Drew pipes up.

"Hey, I'm sorry," he grumbles, though I hardly hear him, my attention on the bar and the members having a good gawp at Ava in my grasp.

I claim her bag. "I'm taking Ava home. Are you running tomorrow?"

"Nah, I might be tied up."

"Where's Kate?" Ava asks, her cheeks bright red.

"She had a few deliveries to do." Sam takes a swig of his beer, raising his eyebrows at me over his bottle. "She got all excited about taking Margo Junior out on her maiden voyage. I've been dumped for a pink van. I'm heading over when I'm done here."

"Done what?" Drew says, and Sam's happy eyes narrow.

"Fuck you."

It's time to go. "Bye, lads," I call, tugging Ava away before they drop me in the shit. "Tell Kate Ava's with me." I make a sharp exit, Ava pretty much jogging along behind me to keep up. I pull the door of my Aston open, and she pouts.

"I want to go on the bike."

"Right now, I want you in lace, not leather. Get in the car." I've been waiting all day for my medicine. I'm sure I'll keel over if I don't get it soon and, thankfully, Ava must appreciate that, because she's quickly in the passenger seat. I dive in the car and pull off like a bat out of hell, racing down the driveway. *It's time to stop driving like a dickhead.*

But I can feel the want coming off her skin like steam, and that is not helping my urgency.

"One hundred thousand pounds is a massive overpayment," she says casually, and I laugh. I was wondering when that might come up. What does she want me to say? That I want unlimited access to her?

I shrug. "Is it?"

"You know it is." She throws me a half-dirty look.

"You're underselling yourself," I say to the road. *I would've paid ten million.*

"I must be the most expensive hooker ever."

My smile falls. "Ava," I grate, irritated. "If you refer to yourself in that way again—"

"I was joking," she replies, chuckling.

"Do you see me laughing?"

"I have other clients to deal with."

Unfortunately, yes, she does, and I'll accept that so long as one of those clients isn't Van Der Haus. "I know," I say quietly, holding my tongue. I know Ava, and if I demand she removes him as a client, she'll fight me on it for the sake of it. And ask lots of questions I can't answer. "But I'm a special client." I grab her knee, and she laughs.

"You're special all right."

I move my hand to her hip and squeeze, relishing her sweet squeal, before turning up the music. She sighs, settling back. I know she's studying me. I know she's smiling. And I hope she's thinking about how much she loves me.

28

THE ROADS ARE KIND, which is a good fucking job because the closer I drive to Lusso—or, more to the point, my bed—the more impatient I'm becoming. It's been a long, mixed day of amazing, frustrating, and worrying. We need to get back to amazing. The zeal swirling inside is becoming excruciating, and I can only compare it to a craving I'm all too familiar with.

Alcohol.

Knowing it's close by.

Knowing that with one sip, every muscle will become loose and every thought will become clouded.

Escape. And yet I know in my heart of hearts, this craving for Ava is just as unhealthy as my dependence on drink. I also know Ava can't be readily available. Alcohol can be found anywhere. I can lay my hands on it in a heartbeat, and often did. With this new addiction, I'm depending on someone else to feed it, and that's far from ideal.

"Are you okay?" she asks as I stop at a red light, my thoughts bringing on a cold sweat. "You look troubled."

I flex my hand, loosening my grip on the steering wheel. My knuckles are bloodless. "Yeah." I look across the car, and as ever, the vision of her hits me like a sledgehammer to the gut. One corner of her mouth lifts, and she blinks slowly, making her lashes fan her high cheekbones. I feel like my only saving grace here is her equal, obvious craving for me. I need to maintain that. Build it. Nurture it.

She shifts in her seat, and the buttons of her blouse pull across her chest. It's like rocket fuel to my dick. I'm sure she does things like that on purpose. Goads me. She's a temptress, begging for it constantly, albeit subtly. Her face lights up when she sees me adjust myself. I'm going to burst out of my jeans soon.

The lights change, and I pull off quickly, taking the turn for Lusso, smacking the button to open the gates. They seem to take years to finally give me room to pass through.

I park, collect her, and lead her determinedly into the building. She greets the concierge as I tug her past his desk and, thank God, luck is on my side, the elevator doors open, waiting for us. I virtually toss her inside.

"Are you in a rush?" she asks.

Stupid question. "Yes." I enter the code, the doors close, and my restraint snaps. I have her up against the wall fast. "You owe me an apology fuck," I declare, ramming my tongue into her mouth, my kiss desperate and hungry. Her fault.

"What's an apology fuck?" she asks, breathless.

I spread her legs with my knee, kissing my way to her ear. "It involves your mouth." And it might kill me off, but all I can think of right now is owning her. Having her bend to my will. Indulging me. I rip myself away from her and lean back against the wall opposite, studying her shaking like a leaf, her breathing all over the place. Like mine. I pull my T-shirt up over my head, and her eyes drag down my torso to my jeans as I work the buttons. Her hands twitch by her sides, her eyes cloud, her lips part. This sight? Fucking magic. The way she's looking at me? It's a unique cocktail of everything amazing. My new drug. Her young, fresh face tells a thousand stories.

She's never experienced this before. This . . . ecstasy. And despite knowing without question my sex life has been far more colorful than Ava's, I'm one hundred percent with her in this unchartered territory. Because even though my sureness and experience in the bedroom hasn't changed, the feelings that accompany me have.

She likes my domination. Craves it. It's my only weapon in this relationship, and I will exercise it shamelessly.

My rigid cock falls into my palm, and I look down, seeing it weeping. I grit my teeth and circle my palm, hissing as I start to thrust slowly, calmly, sharp tingles rolling across my skin. I look up through my lashes, my sight distorted, but I see her. I see her clearly. She's plastered against the wall, her stare rooted to me working myself, her lips wet.

Ready.

She glances up, and I'm taken aback by the look in her eyes. I've never seen so much longing. And it's for me. "Come here," I order, my voice thick, and she obeys, looking at me with doe eyes, waiting for her next instruction. Her disposition, while recognizable, still floors me. How quickly she can go from pure fight to pure submission. How she bows to me like this. *Me*. A dark, fuck-up of a man pushing forty who can't get his head on straight. "On your knees."

Her hands meet my thighs, and my cheeks expand. Fucking hell. Whose bright idea was this, because I'm about to break? She must see the desperation in my eyes as she stares up at me, lowering to her knees as I continue stroking myself. I reach for her flushed cheek, struggling to push out air. "Open."

Her lips part. Her hands hold the backs of my thighs. Her eyes sparkle. This is, categorically, the most beautiful thing I've ever seen. I demonstrate my approval, stroking her face as I rest the tip of my cock on her bottom lip. "You'll take it all the way," I whisper, leaving a shimmering trail of cum on her mouth. "And I'm going to come in your mouth." Her tongue shoots out and licks, her eyes dancing. "You'll swallow." I push into her mouth on a suppressed growl, my stomach aching from tensing so much, my eyes closing as inch by inch she takes me. I fight to get hold of my control, my legs beginning to shake, my hand tightening around my shaft, restricting the pulsating veins. Fuck, I could come right now. I feel her hands tighten on my thighs, and then she pulls me onto her.

"Fuuuuuck," I breathe, feeling for her head in my darkness, too afraid to look at her for fear of ending this sooner than I want. I need to let go of my dick. I start panting, clenching every muscle, preparing, and I loosen my hold on a strangled breath, moving my hand to join my other on her head. That's it now. She has unlimited access.

She's taken the power.

I'm not given any time to brace myself. Her hand drifts between my thighs and cups me, and my shakes take on a new level, my moans coming thick and fast as her delicate touch draws paths of fire across my balls, her hot mouth motionless around my dick. She circles my girth at the root. Licks around the head. Drops a tender kiss on the very tip. My heavy eyes peel open, my limp head falling. What I find when my vision clears is nearly my undoing.

She's looking up at me like I'm a god as her tongue flattens and she drags it from tip to base. Jesus. Air hisses through my clenched teeth, my hips vibrating. Fucking hell, I'd endure her defiance every day if this is what I'll get in return. What I'm seeing now, how I'm feeling, it's biblical. Her mouth glides smoothly across my taut flesh, her eyes as starving as her mouth. She loves this. Loves rendering me this desperate. She pushes the tip of her tongue into the tip of my dick on a raised brow, like . . . *this? Do you like this, Jesse?* She'll never know. I smile at her sass, but then very nearly crumble when she unexpectedly yanks me into her mouth, taking me all the way.

"Oh Jesus, Ava!"

She withdraws, and my hips buck, plunging me back inside deeply. I groan, seeing stars. She's toyed with me for too long. It's time to take back the power. "You have a fucking incredible mouth, Ava." I hold her head firmly, driving in and out. "I've wanted to fuck it since I laid eyes on you."

Her teeth graze my flesh, dragging slowly down the length.

I yell out, not prepared to surrender. "Take it deep." I thrust forward wickedly, feeling her mouth fighting the invasion. "Relax your jaw," I order, losing my ability to keep it controlled, thrusting repeatedly, moaning constantly, feeling the telltale tingles engulf my dick, my balls becoming heavy, my heart racing.

I'm past the point of return. I retreat from her mouth a fraction, giving myself room to hold myself, and start working myself fast. Her eyes close as she licks and laps, a buzz so intense charging up my cock. "In your mouth, Ava," I bark, and she moves fast, encasing me.

I come hard, feeling her swallowing around me, and I look up at the ceiling on a gruff yell, my hips rolling, as I ride the waves of my orgasm, weak with pleasure. I feel crippled by the intensity, my legs numb. I drop my head and take her under her arms, lifting her to me, taking her mouth, tasting my salty essence. "You're amazing," I whisper. "I'm keeping you forever."

"That's nice to know."

"Don't try and pull a hurt with me, lady. You left me high and dry this morning." I roll my forehead across hers as she strokes my bare chest.

"I apologize," she murmurs, dotting kisses around my nipple. I sigh and let my heart return to a safe beat. Or as safe as it'll ever be when I'm around this woman.

"You have lace on. I love you in lace." *I love you, period. So fucking much.*

I pick her up and feel her legs circle my hips, her arms around my shoulders, and I collect our things and walk us out of the lift.

"Why lace?" she asks.

Because it's clean. Pretty. Pure. "I don't know, but always wear lace." I stop at the door. "Keys, back pocket."

She pulls them from my jeans and unlocks the door, and I drop everything to the floor and make my way up the stairs with her clinging to me like a baby chimp, snuggled in my neck. She's tired. Me too. But never too tired for more. I pull my phone out and load the music app, hitting shuffle before tossing it on the cabinet. And like an omen, Massive Attack's *Angel* plays.

Perfect. So fucking perfect.

I pry her from my body and set her on her feet. "I'm taking you to bed now." I start unbuttoning her blouse, seeing her visibly tense. It's not just me. It's the music. So fucking sexy, and so fucking apt. I gaze at her, my eyes soft, hers full of wonder. Or love.

"Why do you try to control me?"

Her question throws me for a loop. Control her? The chance would be a fine thing. And I wouldn't call it control, more asser-tion. But *try* is the operative word here. If she knew my story, she might understand. *So tell her*, Jake screams from the dead. "I don't know," I whisper, feeling my forehead go heavy. "It just feels like the right thing to do." It's all I'm capable of. Control has been non-existent in my life, and, clearly, I don't know how to handle it. I drop her blouse to the floor as she studies me, quiet, not challenging me, which is good because what the fuck would I say?

The truth.

It is far from appropriate for my brother to be here right now, taunting me, nagging me. *Fuck off.*

Fine. I can't watch this train crash anymore.

I jerk a little, like he could have just prodded me; I swallow hard, waiting for him to enhance my guilt some more. He doesn't. But he doesn't need to. I look at the woman before me and it's there with a vengeance.

Make love to her. Show her. Make her see. I'm doing it constantly in between the minor meltdowns, but I need to speak the words and hope she reciprocates.

Then, spill it all. Every unbearable, heartbreaking moment.

I shake my head clear and remove her trousers, feeling her watching me with a curious interest I don't like. I need to turn this around. I step back and kick off my shoes and jeans, and something in her eyes shifts. She's back. I'm back. I take in every inch of her, from her toes to her hair and lift an arm, reaching for her bra and pulling the cups down, tracing the stiff nub of her nipple with the back of my hand. Her chest expands. "You make me crazy," I whisper.

"No, you make *me* crazy." Her counter is laced with too much lust for me to take her seriously.

"Crazy," I mouth, lifting her and laying her down, blanketing her completely and lazily lowering my lips to hers. She opens up, her tongue meeting mine, sweeping in sync, rolling and stabbing gently.

Fuck, I love you.

Just. Spit. It. Out.

And yet although the words are hanging off my tongue constantly, they refuse to leave my mouth.

The reason why kills me.

Because the only people in my life whom I have loved this fiercely were taken from me. I feel like I'd be jinxing her. Poisoning her. Sentencing her. So where the fuck does that leave me?

I swallow and take her knickers, dragging them down her

legs, getting to my knees, and pulling her onto my lap. I don't know. *I don't fucking know.* "Lean back on your hands," I order, reaching for my erection as she leans back, her mouth open, her eyes drowning me. I position myself at her ready pussy and lazily, slowly, gently, push my way inside of her on a hiss, holding her under the small of her back.

Good Lord. I gulp, guiding her waist around, following the sway of my hips and the beat of the music. Gone. I'm gone. A slave to her, to this, to love. My skin is damp, Ava's cheeks perfectly tinged red, her nipples like stones. My pace is meticulous. It's calm, it's perfect, each drive steady, every retreat unrushed.

"Where have you been all my life, Ava?" I whisper, swiveling deliberately and firmly.

She inhales sharply, her eyes never leaving mine, and it's the sexiest thing imaginable. I lick my lips, swallow the lump in my throat, feeling a wash of emotion take hold. "Promise me something," I demand, executing another flawless grind, making her moan. She's struggling to keep her eyes open, but I see the question there. "You'll stay with me," I murmur, full of hope.

She stares at me, caught between the untold pleasure we're sharing, and bewilderment I just can't stand. And then she nods, and I groan as I pull her down and circle into her.

"I need to hear the words, Ava." I increase the pace and the friction, and she becomes frantic, her arms shaking, ready to buckle.

"Oh God, I will."

Fuck, yes. "You're going to come."

"Yes!"

"Jesus, I love looking at you when you're like this." I strain the words, my eyes on her sweating face. "Hold it, baby," I order, searching for my release. "Not yet." I move my hold, seeing she's going to break, and haul her into me, our skin colliding, sparks flying, my hips bucking. She cries out, my dick sinking deeper, her nails plunging into my back. *Fuck.*

I pump, grind, roll, our eyes glued. "You're painfully beautiful and all mine. Kiss me."

There's no objection. When we're together, connected, making each other feel like this, there is no other way for us. She encases my face with her palms, scans my eyes, swallows as I watch her, and drops her mouth to mine on a moan.

"Jesse," she mumbles. "I'm going—"

"Control it, baby."

"I can't." She bites my lip, and I yell, the pain hitting me hard in my cock.

And there it is. My release. I'm on my knees fast, rearing back and thundering into her, holding her against my chest as I explode on a yell that instantly makes my throat sore. "Jesus, Ava," I garble mindlessly, my eyes clenching shut. "What am I going to do with you?"

I'm useless, quaking, my body completely out of control. Weak. Helpless.

Alive.

In hell but in heaven.

She hugs me fiercely, as if she senses I need help to stop my violent shakes. I do. "You're shaking."

"You make me so happy," I whisper, my voice ragged, my heart hurting.

"I thought I made you crazy."

I smile sadly and face her. "You make me crazy happy." I push away the hair sticking to her perfectly wet face, kissing the tip of her perfect nose. "You also make me crazy mad." My eyebrows lift without instruction.

"I prefer you when you're crazy happy," she tells me. "You're scary when you're crazy mad."

Yes, I know. I scare myself, but . . . "Then stop doing things to make me crazy mad."

She has the nerve to appear outraged. Don't tell me she wanted that dress today. She didn't. Don't tell me she enjoyed downing that whole glass of wine the night I wrestled her into a jumper. She didn't. I'm all for her holding on to her free will, but not at the expense of my sanity. She'll learn. But, more importantly, will I learn to deal with my newfound intense reactions? Or better still, control them? I can try. Honestly, though, I don't have much faith in myself. Ava O'Shea brings out the best in me while bringing out the worst. Strangely, the worst is a side I never knew I had, and I'm fucked if I know how to handle it. A little like she doesn't know how to handle it. We're in this together. Navigating these foreign waters together.

"I would never hurt you intentionally, Ava," I say without much thought. I'm being provoked by the unknown. The unknown is how she'll deal with the truth.

"I know." She sighs, and it holds too much uncertainty for my liking, but I can't ask for much more. I turn and fall to my back, bringing Ava with me, and we settle, me staring at the ceiling as I weave my fingers through her hair, Ava tracing patterns across my stomach, slowing when she reaches my scar. It tingles under her fingertip.

"Were you in the army?" she asks quietly.

My hands still for a beat. I could say yes, end the mystery for her, but as my lie tickles my lips, giving me an out on this particular problem, I find other words materializing. "No. Leave it, Ava."

"Why did you disappear on me?"

"I told you," I say, swallowing, becoming hot for other reasons. "I was a mess"—that's the truth—"and you asked for space." That's a cop-out.

"Why?"

I close my eyes, praying for the end of this interrogation. I'm not prepared. Not ready. "You spark feelings in me."

"What sort of feelings?"

"All sorts, Ava." So many, I'm struggling to find the words to explain, but I'm trying. I'm trying so fucking hard.

"Is that a bad thing?" she presses.

"It is when you don't know how to deal with them." I sigh, and she stalls stroking my stomach for a few moments. She's thinking, and what this woman thinks is a constant fear.

"You think I belong to you."

Think? "No. I *know* you do."

Is she smiling against me? "When did you establish that?"

"When I spent four days trying to get you out of my head."

"It didn't work?"

"No. I was even crazier." I would move heaven and earth to change how I handled that particular meltdown. "Go to sleep."

"What were you doing to try and get me out of your head?"

Don't be mad, Jesse. You can't be mad with her. "It doesn't matter. It didn't work, end of. Go to sleep."

I know it's hard for her, but she relents, settling, making my skin heat under the friction of her repeated swirls. The silence screams. "Tell me how old you are."

"No," I say shortly, unable to muster the energy to remember where the fuck we got to in this ridiculous age game. There are more important matters to deal with. But while she's snuggled into me like this, quiet, her leg thrown over mine, her cheek squished to my chest, those issues are easy to disregard. Just hold her.

Her breathing becomes shallow, and I love the warmth of her breath spread across my skin. Asleep. I reach across to the night-stand, trying not to disturb her, feeling for my phone. I pull the camera up and turn it onto us, getting us both on the screen. I gaze at her. She looks peaceful. I move my eyes across to myself. I look peaceful too.

But I feel far from it.

I drop my nose into her hair and take a picture. Then scroll through all of the other snaps I've caught of her over the weeks. Each one brings on another level of dread until I'm at the very first image I took of her.

Running away from me.

Time is ticking.

29

THE SECOND I WAKE, I know I need to run. I don't feel rested. I don't feel settled. Sleep hasn't chased away my fears. The more time that passes, the more my contentment is fading. How long will it be until this bliss is gone completely?

My mind drifts to the upcoming anniversary at The Manor. It's only two weeks away.

I turn onto my side and gently push some hair out of Ava's face. She doesn't even stir. "Will you come with me?" I ask her sleeping form. I want her on my arm. I want her to accept The Manor and embrace it. I need her to understand meaningless nights of illicit pleasure are no longer on my agenda. I wince when a sudden stab of pain radiates through my lip, and I reach up to wipe the tiny drop of blood away. And yet I go back to biting it, thinking, wondering if I'll still have the pleasure of this view tomorrow, or the next day, or the next.

I ignore the hollowness that falls into my gut. I can't believe that everything is going to be anything but all right.

I pull the covers over her tummy and edge my way out of bed, scrubbing my hands down my face as I leave the bedroom. I make it to the kitchen and fall onto a stool, spinning my phone in my hand. Chewing my lip again. My elbows hit the counter, my face falling into my hands.

Feeling hopeless, bro?

I clench my eyes closed, willing Jake to stop taunting me.

Only you can fix this.

"I know," I murmur. "And I will."

Before or after she finds out for herself?

"What are we talking about?" I ask my darkness. "The Manor? My fuck-up last week? Rosie? You?"

All of it.

All of it. And, God, there is so much. I can't hit her with every detail in one sitting. The poor woman will probably pass out with shock.

Then start with The Manor. The rest will come.

But does the rest have to? The Manor is The Manor, and that isn't about to change. It's here, in the present, not going anywhere. But my past. That's gone.

Check your phone.

I frown and tap the screen of my phone. A message from Coral. And what it says tells me my past isn't going anywhere either. At least, some of it.

That's what you get for being such a stud.

There is really nothing amusing about this, but I still let out a bout of laughter. "I fucking hate that we're twins," I say, erasing the message. "Stop talking to me." I hit my temple with my phone, achieving nothing more than pain. "You're making me feel crazy."

You don't need me for that, brother.

I growl and stand, stalking out of the kitchen. I'm halted in my tracks by Ava's bags by the door. Her phone is goading me. I grab it without thought and scroll through her contacts, heading straight for V.

Van Der Haus's details greet me and, on an epic snarl, I

quickly copy his number to my mobile. I'm covering my bases. Making sure I can speak to him if I need to, and something tells me I will need to. Then I change Ava's ringtone and toss it back in her bag. The foil of her pill packet catches the light.

It sparkles.

Dares me.

Jesus, someone hold me back.

I reach forward and grab the pills, going to the sink in the kitchen and popping each one out as I run the tap, washing them away. And I watch as they disappear down the plug hole, my hands braced on the edge of the counter.

So you steal her contraceptive pills?

"Fuck off," I grunt, turning away and heading back upstairs. I need to run.

I need Ava.

I pull on my shorts, sitting on the chaise across the room to tie the laces of my trainers.

"What are you doing?" Her sleepy voice replaces the void in my stomach with relief. She's awake. It's a new day. A day for me to finally sort out my shit.

She loves me. *That's* my lifeline.

I peek up, finding her blinking her sleepy eyes, her arms stretching high over her head. "I'm going for a run." I finish tying my laces and stand. Her eyes are wide open now, and looking rather appreciative.

My gaze drops to her chest. "I'm quite enjoying the view too."

"What time is it?"

"Five."

Her face falls, and then her body, back to the mattress. She covers herself with the sheets, and I smile as I pace to the bed, whipping them back off and getting my face up in hers. Her pout is adorable as she slides her arms around my neck, applying force, trying to drag me down.

I have her on her feet quickly. "You're coming." I flip the cups of her bra back into place before I change my mind. "Come on."

"No, I'm bloody not. I run in the evenings," she calls as I head to the bathroom, smiling. I look over my shoulder and see her plummet back to the bed. *Oh no.* I hurry back over before she gets too comfortable, taking her ankle and tugging her to the bottom. A pillow covers her face, so I whip it off, leveling her with a serious face.

"Yes, you are. Mornings are better." I see her mouth engage to protest, so I quickly flip her onto her front and give her arse a swift slap. "Get ready," I order, swooping up the bag of women's sportswear from the chair.

"I don't have my running kit." Her smug face falls when I throw the bag and it lands precisely next to her. "You bought these for me?"

"I saw your trainers in your room. They're wrecked." She's not a serious runner if she runs in those things, but I'll soon change that. I can think of nothing better than starting my day off with Ava and a run. "You'll damage your knees if you keep running in them." She shows no signs that she's going to indulge me, so on a huff of displeasure, I start rummaging through the bag to find something suitable. I pull out a sports bra. Inspect it. Smile and hand it over. It's snatched from my hand on a scowl, and that scowl remains fixed as she puts it on. I pass her some shorts, *hers* to match my *his*, and finally a vest. She takes her time changing, delaying, sulking. "Sit," I order, and she drops to the bed heavily. "I'm ignoring you." I get her trainers on and pull her up, giving her a thorough inspection.

She looks hot as fuck.

"Come on, then, lady," I say, pulling her out of the bedroom before I push her onto the bed. "Let's start the day how we intend to finish it."

"I'm not running again today," she splutters, looking alarmed.

"That's not what I meant," I say over my laugh as we take the stairs.

"Oh. What did you mean?"

I can hear the hope in her voice. She knows exactly what I mean. Lucky for Ava, I'm in a giving mood today. I just hope she's in an accepting mood. "I mean by being out of breath and sweaty."

She straightens her shoulders. "You're not seeing me tonight," she says, almost smugly, like she's won something. I'm not seeing her? We'll see. "I need a hair tie." She tugs her hand free and goes to her bags, and I go to the kitchen to get some cash. She'll never make it around my route, and it would be highly unreasonable to expect her to. I'm not unreasonable. I stuff a note in the small zip pocket with my phone and fetch her.

The journey to the foyer in the elevator is excruciating. She constantly reaches for her ponytail, adjusting it, thrusting her boobs forward in that tight vest.

"Stretch," I order when we make it into the fresh morning air, extending my quadricep. The sky is clear, the sun low, the air crisp. Beautiful. I inhale, filling my lungs with air and my mind with positivity. *It'll be all right. She'll come around when she's got used to what I've told her.* I feel her watching me, and I peek out the corner of my eye. She's grinning. "Ava, stretch."

She huffs, puffs, and makes a meal of expressing her irritation, bending at the waist and pushing her gorgeous backside out. Right in my face. I scowl at the firm, lycra covered flesh and clamp my teeth into her right arse cheek, biting down. She yelps, startled. So I slap it too, and she swings around, outraged. Her look is pure filth. I tilt my head, daring her to challenge me. She doesn't, her face softening. She's learning.

"Where are we running?" she asks over a sigh, pulling her foot to her bum.

"The Royal Parks. Ready?"

She nods, seeming quite accepting, surprisingly. Then I see her walk to my car, and I laugh on the inside, going the opposite way to the gates.

"Where are you going?" she calls.

"For a run." My smile widens as I look back, seeing the penny drop. Her face. I have to stop myself fishing out my phone and capturing the sight.

"Urh . . ." She clears her throat. Straightens her back. "How far is it to the parks?"

"Four miles."

She starts coughing, and I start falling apart on the inside, my earlier troubles fading with each second I'm watching her failing to play it cool. She rearranges her top, and my eyes light up as she paces over.

"It's eleven, twenty-seven, fifteen," I say as I press the code for the gate. "For future reference."

She jogs off, and I grin at her arse as she goes. "I'll never remember that," she yells back. I roll my eyes, going after her. And there we have the proof, if ever I needed it, which I don't, that she purposely challenges me. She'll remember that number.

I fall into stride next to her, peeking down, checking for any early signs of how this is going to pan out. I won't tell her I'm one gear off a walk. That would be cruel. So instead of taking my calm from pounding the pavements, I take my calm from having her beside me. Constantly checking me out. Constantly smiling up at me.

It's another new form of bliss and, unlucky for Ava, I might decide I need this every morning. My mind is clearing, Jake is no longer haunting my thoughts, playing with my conscience, and my heart is beating steady and strong.

"Okay?" I ask, and she nods and instantly realigns her focus on the route ahead, not giving me nearly enough time of her bright eyes. But I still caught the flash of determination. She *is* struggling now. How long will she hold out? How long will she kill herself simply because she doesn't want to lose?

We pass through Green Park, and I drop my speed a little more, keeping by her side, waiting for her to break. I silently will her to stop being stubborn and admit defeat so I can ravage her on the grass, and yet she soldiers on, her cheeks red and wet, her breathing loud. It's doing me no favors, the sight of her like that, all hot and bothered. My dick is starting to fight for room in my shorts.

We approach Piccadilly, a good ten miles in, and I start to think she's actually prepared to do herself some serious damage to prove this point of hers. And then what? If she pulls a muscle, that's also going to do *me* damage. No sex.

Oh no.

But just as I'm about to call a halt on our run, she gasps and takes a sharp right back into the park and tumbles to the grass like a sack of shit. I smile at her splattered form, wandering over and getting the photo I've been dying to get all morning. Our first run together. I drop to my knees and crawl up her body. The heat emanating off her is burning through my shorts.

Her lashes flutter open, and she looks at me with a million pleas in her eyes. She's nothing to fear. I won't be making her run anymore. Only to the taxi so I can get her home pronto. "Baby, did I wear you out?" I rub my face into hers, spreading the sweat, kissing her everywhere. "Hmm, sweat and sex." I roll us, getting her on top of me. She's good for nothing. That needs to change sharpish.

I give her a few moments to find her depleted breath, content just for now, to lie here with her spread all over me. Eventually, she struggles up, straddling me. It's a vision and a half.

"Please don't make me run home."

This is a turn out for the books. She's begging. I should use this to my advantage. The Manor anniversary stamps its way across my mind. Two weeks.

"You did better than I expected."

"I prefer sleepy sex," she moans, plummeting to my chest. I smile. I can't argue with that.

"I prefer sleepy sex too." I agree quietly. I should have thought this through. "Come on, lady. We can't frolic in the grass all day; you have work to do." I can't wait to watch her all day. Seeing her mind whirl with ideas, her hand working fast across the page as she sketches. It'll make being at The Manor today far more tolerable.

She struggles to her feet, and I join her, pulling her into my side and walking us across the road. I spot a cab and wave it down.

"You brought money for a taxi?" she asks, sounding injured as I get us in the back. I pull her onto my lap and give her a taste of what's to come. Of course, she's all mine in a second, taking my mouth hungrily. The temptation to stop the cab, throw the driver out, and bomb it to Lusso is too much. *Put your foot down!* "Enough," I mumble around her frantic mouth, but she doesn't let up, rubbing into me in places she shouldn't be rubbing into me right now.

"Fuck," I growl, pushing her off me, trying to catch a breath. She flops into the seat beside me, equally as breathless. "You're seriously getting it when I get you home."

The corner of her lip lifts as she pulls her running top away, trying to circulate some air. "Can't wait," she pants, breathless.

"Don't goad me, lady."

"Don't torment me, then." She gazes out of the window, and I observe her with untold pleasure as she watches the world go by, my elbow wedged into the door, the inside of my finger brushing across my top lip. Torment? I smile, but it's sad. She knows nothing of true torment. The sun has always hovered on the horizon of my existence, tormenting me with hopeful light. Now, it feels like it could drop out of the sky at any moment and cloud me in darkness forever. Or, equally as frightening, rise and shine a light on all of my wrongs.

By the time we reach the penthouse, urgency is a vise around my cock, screaming to be relieved. Ava drops to a stool heavily, her breathing still labored, and that urgency throbbing inside subsides at the sight of her so shattered. She doesn't run like I run. She doesn't need to.

It would be easy to toss her on the counter and ravage her. Get my fix. Fuck away this unsettling feeling within. But I abstain. It takes everything in me, but I abstain. She looks good for nothing, except maybe a lovely hot bath. She can lie all over me. Catch her breath.

Agree to come to The Manor's anniversary party with me.

I fill a glass with water and pass it across the counter. "Here."

She chugs it down at an epic rate, not even coming up for air.

"I'll run a bath." I collect her from the stool, smiling when she engulfs me with every limb, finding just enough energy to cling to me.

I make my way slowly up the stairs and set her neatly on the bed. "I don't have time for a bath," she says. "I'll have a shower."

"You have plenty of time." All day, in fact, and I cannot wait to spend it with her. "We'll grab some breakfast and go to The Manor mid-morning. Now, stretch." I press my lips into her sweaty forehead and linger for a while, before I push myself up and head for the bathroom, naturally chewing on my bottom lip as I go, waiting for the fireworks to explode, my shoulders high in preparation. I flip on the taps and pour in some bath soak. Will she challenge me? Refuse? I swish the water, creating masses of bubbles.

"Jesse, I need to go to the office," she calls, sounding uncharacteristically timid. She's worried that I was serious when I hijacked her diary.

I was. "No, you don't," I call back. She will not win this one. Besides, I have an appointment. Doesn't she want to spend the day with me? And it's Friday. It'll get my weekend off to the best start. I smile, excited at the prospect of three whole days indulging in her. In us. "Stretch."

There's silence for a few beats, but just when I think—and hope—she's relented, she speaks up, albeit quietly. It's the voice of someone who knows they're fighting a losing battle. "All of my equipment is at the office. My computer programs, reference books, everything."

I wander to the door and lean against the frame, finding her looking small in my big bed. Small and nervous. "And you need all that stuff?" I ask.

"Yes." She shows the ceiling her hands, as if it's an obvious answer. Nothing is obvious to me these days, only one thing. How I feel about her. "To do my job," she adds.

Her job is to keep me in the light. "Okay, we'll stop by your office." Problem solved. I go back to the bathroom and check the bath, her sigh so loud I can hear it over the rushing water. I sit on the edge, gently gliding my hand through the bubbles, my eyes on the doorway, waiting for her to storm in and demand I stop being unreasonable. I'd like to think her lack of an appearance is because she's concluded that devoting her day to me is too appealing to turn down. But I know she's simply too exhausted to take me on.

I wait for the water to get halfway up and then turn off the taps before I make my way back into the bedroom, finding her spread-eagled on the bed. I dip and get close to her ear. "Bath's ready," I whisper, gathering her into my arms. She doesn't fight me. It's an encouraging sign.

"You were serious, weren't you?" she says as I set her down by the bath, taking the bottom of her running top.

"I was serious about what?" Her accusing eyes disappear for a split second when I pull the vest over her head, but they're soon back, and even more accusing. I'm serious about a lot of things when it comes to Ava. Her question is far too broad.

"About not sharing me."

Oh, that. "Yes." Deadly serious.

"What about my other clients?" she asks, studying me as I continue to strip her down. There's only one other client who is of particular interest to me, but by singling him out, I'll raise questions I don't want to answer. So I'll be comprehensive. For now.

"I said I don't want to share you." I lower to my haunches, taking her shorts with me, and she lifts a foot in turn for me to remove them.

She makes no attempt to get in the tub, still drilling holes into me as I rise. This doesn't bode well. Her breathing is no longer strained, and that's leaving space for vigor.

"I don't need to be at The Manor to collate designs, Jesse," she says as I pick her up and put her in the bath.

"Yes, you do."

"No, I don't," she argues as I strip, looking at me in the way she does when she's set for a win. Which means I'll lose. I'm not in a losing mood today.

She shifts forward in the tub, and I slip in behind her, settling back and positioning her just so, her back to my front. It's quite incredible really. We're kind of having a disagreement and yet we both still need to be touching each other. "If I let you go to the office," I say quietly, choosing my words *very* carefully, "you have to do something for me."

"Okay. What?"

My eyebrows jump up at her easy acceptance. Then I'm quickly and silently pointing out to myself that she doesn't yet know what the condition is. It also reminds me she doesn't know what The Manor is. But she will. That's the point. It'll set things in motion. Give me a timeframe to work to. "You'll come to The Manor's anniversary party."

She tenses. "What? Like a social event?"

"Yes." I nod. That's the perfect description. A social event. Where everyone gets naked, screws each other, and whips and bondage gear galore come out to play. After they've had an indulgent three-course meal, obviously. "Exactly like a social event," I add on a frown. I can see her face in my mind's eye. It's horrified.

"When?" she asks over a sigh.

I cage her in my arms and legs, clinging tightly, a silent message that I will never let her go, no matter her reaction. No matter her disgust. "Two weeks today."

Fourteen days and counting, brother.

"You'll come," I whisper, sucking her ear, licking the shell, smiling when she stiffens and wriggles, her skin gliding perfectly over mine.

She inhales. "Stop."

"No. Say you'll come." I've got her. Water is drenching the floor, her fruitless fighting doing nothing but making a mess.

"No." She laughs, and I increase my torture, breathing heavily into her ear, my hand slipping down her body to her tickle spot. "Stop," she yelps.

"Please," I whisper softly, kissing the soft, sweet spot below her lobe. She can't ruin my plans before they're even in motion. She just can't, and if that means begging and giving up today with her, I'm here for it.

She stills and thinks, just for a moment. "Okay, I'll come."

The pressure releases, just a little. That was supposed to be the easy part. I drop my face into her neck and take a hit of life. *Thank you. Thank you so, so much.*

Silence settles, and I rest my head back, cherishing this moment of peace. "I've never had a bath before."

"Never?" she replies, surprised.

"No, never." Baths leave too much time alone to do nothing but think. And, worse than that, they remind me of the times I used to give Rosie her bedtime bath. The water no deeper than a few inches. The bubbles overflowing. Her little body lost amid the puffs of white. Her laugh. Her smile. The way she looked at me like I *wasn't* a hopeless wanker. "I'm a shower man," I whisper, my throat tight. "But I think I might be a bath man now."

"I love having a bath."

"Me too," I breathe. "But only if you're in it with me." Never alone. "It's a good job the designer of this place anticipated the need for a big one."

She laughs, and it's golden. "I think she did well."

"I wonder if she ever considered being in it?"

"No, she didn't." Her words are wistful. Like me, she can't believe she's here either, although for entirely different reasons. I drop my chin and observe her wet hair covering every inch of my chest. Her legs rubbing against mine. Her hands lying across my forearms where they're holding her.

I have a nibble of her ear. "Well, I'm glad she is," I whisper, and she sighs, settling deeper into my body, closing her eyes. She looks so peaceful. So . . . mine.

I let her be, happy to watch her, happy to just soak in the warmth of the water and her body. It's something else to be added to my list of favorite things.

"You're going to be late for work," I say when I'm sure she's dozed off. "Just think . . . if you didn't go to the office, we could stay longer." I smile into her temple and rip my body from hers, hoping she feels the pain like I do. But it's for a greater good.

Fourteen days and counting.

I leave Ava in the bath, hopefully regretting refusing to work on The Manor today, and by the sound of her disgruntled moan when I tore myself away, my hopes have been answered.

When I make it to my dressing room, I pluck out a black shirt, a gray suit, and get dressed, planning my day by the hour in the hopes it'll pass quickly.

When I arrive in the kitchen, I call John and settle on the stool to eat my breakfast. He answers with a grunt. "So tell me who got too excited," I say before sliding my finger into my mouth.

"Ken Fraser. He's remorseful, of course."

"They always are." Especially when confronted with a pissed-off John. "What did he do and what was his excuse?"

"He videoed another member giving him head."

I nearly bite the end of my finger off. "He did what?"

"A moment of madness, he claims."

"Did you get the phone?"

"Yes."

I look up when I hear Ava coming down the stairs, her heels clinking the marble. She appears, and everything inside of me pouts. Damn her job. She looks me up and down with her own little pout in place. She's damning herself too. Wishing she hadn't been so unreasonable and given me what we both want.

"I'll be there after I've dropped Ava at work." I swivel to face her, throwing an order with my eyes.

"The kitchen has the final menu for the anniversary."

"Yes, tell Sarah I want it on my desk when I get there."

Ava wanders over when I pat my lap. "And what about Ken? What shall I do with him?"

"We revoke his membership," I say as Ava comes to rest on my lap, my mouth moving without instruction, my mind consumed in an instant. My face goes into her neck, my nose breathing her into me. "Simple."

"He won't be happy," John says. "It'll kick off."

"He can kick off all he likes," I ramble on, forgetting myself completely. "He's gone, end of. Get Sarah to cancel it."

"With immediate effect?"

"Yes."

"Done."

"Okay. See you in a bit."

I pull Ava into my chest, slamming my hungry mouth onto hers for a few mind-spinning moments. It's going to be a long, *long* day. "Breakfast?"

"I'll grab something at the office," she says, freeing herself of my clutches. "Can I have some water?" she asks, and I tense. I can't help it.

I turn away, cringing, warning Jake to keep quiet. "Knock yourself out, baby." I dip my peanut butter and shove my finger in my mouth, following her path to the fridge where she places her bag on the side and starts rummaging through. She huffs. Puffs. Sighs. Starts pulling everything out.

"What's up?"

"Nothing." She stills for a moment. I can practically hear her asking herself what she's done with them. "Fuck," she hisses, starting to dump everything back in her bag with heavy hands.

"Watch your mouth, Ava," I grumble, screwing the lid on the jar. I'm a disgrace. "Come on; you'll be late."

"Sorry," she says, making me feel even worse. "This is your fault, Ward."

"Mine?" I gawp at her, my mind telling me to shut the fuck up but my ego preventing me. *Don't ask. Don't ask. Do not ask.* "What's my fault and how?" *Twat.* Is she suspicious? God, I can't quite believe I've stooped to such a low myself. Does she think I'm capable of such an underhanded act? And if she does, why the fuck is she still here?

Because she loves you, you fool, and that may be the only thing that saves you.

"Nothing." She shakes her head to herself. "But it's your fault because you're distracting me."

Distracting her. Like, stopping her from thinking of anything else but me? That makes me a very, very happy man. "You love me distracting you," I say around a smile.

What the fuck am I playing at stealing her pills? It's betrayal of the worst kind. It's yet another lie I could get caught in. But I know the truth. Keeping this amazing woman isn't my only objective. A lost part of me would also do anything to right my wrongs as a father.

It's no excuse. Nothing would make this okay. I take little comfort in the fact that I'm aware of that.

My plan is a simple one. Get her to work fast, hope she gets all of her work done fast, get her back in my bed fast.

I dip and weave through the early morning traffic, my mind constantly wandering to crazy places. Crazy but wonderful. Crazy but amazing. Crazy but stable. I want to spend the rest of my life with this woman. I'm not being compulsive, I'm being a realist. This crazy can't end. I need it. More than I need redemption, because without it, I don't feel like I can ever have redemption, and despite there being many I need forgiveness from, Ava is the only person alive who can give me that forgiveness. With her mercy, I can move on. Build on my dreams. Forgive *myself*.

I pull up down the street from her office and shift in my seat to face her. Her smile is demure. Her eyes bottomless pits of possibilities. She can't be this close without me touching her.

Reaching for her full lips, I rub my thumb from one side to the other, and her mouth falls open a fraction. Just this simple, tiny touch. Explosions. "I love waking up with you." I hate the unstoppable thoughts haunting me but having her around makes them more bearable. She makes me think harder. Want better.

"I love waking up with you too," she replies softly, turning her face slightly into my touch. "But I don't like being run ragged at five in the morning."

"You would prefer to be fucked ragged?" I ask, my hand sliding down her front.

"No, I prefer sleepy sex." She leans across the car, dislodging my hand from her chest, and plants a fleeting kiss on my lips. I don't get a second to appreciate it or escalate it. She's out of the car quickly, leaving me a burning mess in front of the wheel, wondering where the fuck the rest of that kiss is. "I'll be seeing you tomorrow." She smiles sweetly, and my frown deepens. *Tomorrow?* Definitely not. "Thank you for exhausting me before work." The door shuts, and my brain doesn't work nearly fast enough to tell me to stop her. I sit, pouting, wrestling back my compulsion to dive out and pin her to the ground to convince her otherwise.

"Tomorrow?" I ask myself, seeing her disappear into her office. "Tomor . . . oh no." It's Friday. She thinks she's going out with Kate tonight. "Over my dead body." Visions of wine and a stumbling Ava is suddenly all I can see. Drunk Ava. Reckless Ava. Vulnerable Ava. "Not happening," I say to myself, starting my car and performing a quick three-point-turn in the road. I cruise past her office slowly, looking through the window. She's already at her desk. Head down. Pen in hand. I roll to a stop, trying to conjure up a viable excuse to stop her going out tonight.

You're being unreasonable, Ward.

"I don't think I am," I say quietly, drumming the steering wheel. The last time Ava was let loose with too much alcohol, her ex made a pass and she was in no fit state to fight him off.

She also told you she loves you.

That part was nice. A shocker, but nice.

She also promised you she wouldn't drink tonight.

I laugh out loud. I'm not stupid. I know a lie when I'm being told one. She was appeasing me.

Beep! "God damn it," I mutter, looking up at my rearview mirror, finding a dustbin wagon up my arse. I speed off down Bruton Street, trying to figure out how I can change her mind.

Sarah's coming down the steps when I pull up at The Manor. Does she have a fucking radar on me? Some papers are thrust against the window, and soon after, her indignant face. Fuck me, I'm pretty sure if those lips met the glass, they'd spread to each edge. "The chef wants approval today," she says, moving back when I open the door to get out. I take the menu. "And Ken wants to talk."

"Not interested."

"And you signed the wrong section of the accounts."

"I did?"

"And John's got a leak in the plant room again."

My shoulders drop.

"And Mario wants your approval on the anniversary cocktail."

Fuck this. I stuff the papers back into Sarah's chest and head for the garages.

"Where are you going?" she calls, tottering after me. "We have work to do."

"You have work to do. I'm taking the day off."

"Again?"

I don't entertain her, opening the doors of the garage with my fob and grabbing my helmet. Today is shit already. I need to rectify it.

"You're wearing a suit," she goes on, prompting me to shrug off my jacket and dump it on a nearby shelving unit. "Jesse, I can't do everything myself."

"I pay you good money to do all the things, Sarah. You always managed fine when I was in an alcohol-induced coma." I shove my helmet on and straddle my bike.

"That was different. You were incapable."

"I'm incapable now." I kick the stand up and start the engine, revving loudly. "Or was it because you knew where I was all the time and now you don't?"

"What?" she yells, scowling fiercely, her hands over her ears.

"Never mind." I speed away, the front of my shirt sticking to my chest, the back ballooning.

You should wear leathers too.

I twist the throttle harder.

I kill a couple of hours in the countryside before collecting my car and driving back into the city, and I only just manage to hold myself back until after lunch to call Ava.

The endless weight across my shoulders alleviates immediately when she answers. "I like," she says. The ringtone. She likes the ringtone I chose. And she hasn't given me a hard time for invading her phone.

"Me too," I say. "We'll make love to it later."

"You're not seeing me later." She sounds sure. She shouldn't be.

"I miss you," I say around my pout.

"You miss me?"

"I do." I sound like a sullen child. "I miss you." Something terrible. Days are no longer endless alcohol-induced hazes. They're just endless. I pull up across the road from her office and find her standing by her desk, one heel pulled up to her arse. I smile. "Don't go out tonight." My words were supposed to be soft. Pleading. Unfortunately, they sounded more demanding.

"Don't," she says slowly, falling heavily into her chair, her move displaying her exasperation. "I've made plans."

Yes, plans that don't involve me, and that's a problem. I hate that she can so easily resist me. Even if I know she really can't. It's ridiculous. She's cutting her nose off to spite her face. "You know, you may be at work, but don't think I won't come down there and fuck some sense into you."

There's a brief silence, and I know she's wondering if I'd actually do that. "Knock yourself out," she whispers, and I laugh.

"I was serious, lady."

"I know you were."

"Do your legs ache?"

"Ish."

"Ish," I whisper, relaxing in my seat, the stress draining. She's aching for all the wrong reasons. I should make her an offer she can't refuse. My hands working those sore muscles all night. All weekend.

Don't crowd her.

But I've already concluded that she likes being crowded. Especially by my body.

Does she like being told what to do?

Stupid fucking question. I've never met such a difficult woman. "Remember our deal?"

"No reminder fuck required." She's back out of her chair, stretching.

"Watch your mouth, Ava. And I'll decide when and if a reminder fuck is necessary." And one is definitely necessary now.

"Roger that."

I exhale, accepting that while I can't get my hands on her, I'll never win. "When will I see you?"

"Tomorrow?"

It pains me. Physically pains me. "I'll pick you up at eight."

"Noon," she fires in return.

"Eight."

"Eleven."

"Eight," I snap.

"You're supposed to meet me halfway!"

I'm slowly accepting that she's going out tonight, whether I like it or not. "I'll see you at eight." I end the call and watch as her foot drops from her arse and she looks down at the screen. I know what she's thinking. She's thinking I'm impossible.

She's a gem. As much as I love her to death, I do not understand her mentality sometimes. Not that I have any knowledge of relationships, but surely you don't always want to test the boundaries of your partner, right? I've never met a woman who can push for her own . . . opinions so consistently. Relentlessly.

I still love her, though.

One o'clock to seven is a blur of nothingness. As I walk up the path to Kate's front door, I meet Sam on the doorstep. My eyebrows shoot up as he buttons the fly of his jeans. "What are you doing here?" he asks. "The girls are going out."

"I know," I grunt, pushing past him.

"Have you told her yet?"

"Won't everyone just stop with that?"

"Easy." He laughs. "So, what are you doing here?"

I peek up the stairs, hearing the whir of a hairdryer. She's up there, making herself look even more celestial, ready to go out and dazzle every man in sight. And there's fuck all I can do about it without causing a monumental shitstorm. Right now, that seems more appealing than the alternative.

"Exacting damage control," I say to myself as Kate appears at the top of the stairs, her head a mass of Velcro round things.

She frowns. "Hey, what are you doing here? We're going out."

"Rub it in, why don't you," I mutter, taking the stairs two at a time, unfastening my jacket as I go. Kate moves back, allowing me to pass.

"Who's pissed you off?" she asks, making Sam chuckle downstairs.

"I'm not pissed off."

"You sure?"

"No." I push my way into Ava's room gingerly, finding her going through some drawers. Underwear. She's looking for underwear. Lace? My dick punches against my trousers, wanting out. My thirty-seven-year-old ego pouts at the thought of this gorgeous, mid-twenties goddess finding better than what I have to offer. Ten years plus, history, secrets.

I'm moving across the carpet like a gazelle before any sense or reason can find me. Take her. Mark her. Make her mine.

She's already yours.

"What—" Ava says over her shoulder as I grab her, tossing her onto the bed, relishing her gasps and yelps as I pin her down and seal our mouths. The sounds she's making are sounds of both surprise and lust, and I turn her over fast, pulling her hips up to meet my groin, my hand slipping between her thighs. Wet. Ready. I make fast work of releasing myself and leveling up, pushing my way inside her on a restrained roar. She squeals in shock at my ruthless invasion, and my hand quickly finds her mouth.

"Quiet," I order, powering into her mercilessly, every muscle of mine tense, every one of hers squeezing me beautifully. I stare down at her flawless back, my jaw tight, my vision clouded by a passion and lust that's beyond my control. When I'm inside her, there is nothing else. Nowhere my mind can wander. Only she exists—how she feels, how she looks, how she sounds. Her sodden, hot flesh blistering me. The shockwaves riding through me collect together and deliver one hell of a sucker punch to my heart.

I release my hand from her mouth, and she gasps, her head thrown back in ecstasy. "Jesse!"

"I said, quiet," I grate, my eyes dropping to her arse, seeing my cock entering and withdrawing, the sight dizzying. She's meeting every one of my punishing advances, her hands clutching at the bedding. I'm going to come so hard, it might knock me out. Good. Hopefully, I'll come around in the morning when she's home from her night out, because I am not winning this battle. I know that. I know *her*. But, make no mistake, I will win the fucking war. I'll be scarred. Beaten. Wounded. But I'll win.

My hands squeeze her hips as she blesses my hearing with the sounds of her pleasure, blood whooshing up my dick, my shaft becoming sore with the friction. She starts hitting the pillow, her yells suppressed. She's coming, and by the sound of it, as hard as I am.

Fuck! I plunge deep one last time, my climax catching me off guard, my body folding over Ava's collapsed form, my dick surging relentlessly, emptying inside of her. She groans. I pant. Holy fucking shit, if that doesn't convince her to come home to me, I have no fucking clue what will.

"Please, tell me that it's you," she wheezes, both of us a useless pile of breathlessness.

I smile. "It's me." Turning my face into her skin, I lap up the salt mixed with me and her. "Don't be having another shower," I whisper.

"Why?"

I hiss as I withdraw, my dick pleading to go back. Turning her over, I secure her to the bed and take a few moments admiring her flushed face and drowsy eyes. Perhaps she's too exhausted to go out. Wouldn't that be satisfying? "Because, I want *me* all over *you* when you're out." I kiss her softly, taking that little bit more life I need, floating away.

"Do men have an instinct for recently fucked women?"

And then she brings me back down to earth with her disgusting language. "Mouth." I lick my lips and flinch. Alcohol. I can taste alcohol. "You've had a drink."

"No."

Her arms tense in my hold. If I didn't have them secured to the bed, her fingers would be in her hair twiddling wildly. I have every right to be concerned about her night out. She's no intention of abstaining, only from me, and that's a kick in the teeth. "No more," I command in vain, indulging myself again in her mouth, ignoring the faint edge of wine on her tongue and focusing on tasting only her. Lucky for me, she's far more potent than wine. "I was hoping to find you in lace." My fingers trace a blazing trail down her body and drift in between her legs.

"You would have ruined it."

I slip my fingers inside of her, and she stiffens, gripping me fiercely. *Oh, you want more, baby? Can't get enough?* Me neither. Suddenly, I'm very much the one in control, and maybe, just maybe, I might win this battle after all.

"Probably." I would have torn that lace from her body without apology. "Don't be wearing anything ridiculous either." Alcohol, a sexy dress, her otherworldly beauty. It's a recipe for disaster. I scoop my fingers wide, staring down at her, waiting for her to find the right answer.

"I won't." She tosses her head from side to side, and I smile, her clitoris vibrating against the pad of my thumb.

"Are you going to come, Ava?"

"Yes." She becomes deranged, her legs tensing and kicking out, her eyes clouding. "Please!"

Got you, lady. I shrink the space between our faces, breathing across her skin, sweeping my fingers through her cruelly. "Hmm, that feel good, baby?"

"Oh God," she chokes, trying to catch my mouth. "Jesse, please."

"You want me?" I ask, pulling back. Denying her.

"Yes."

I smile on the inside. "Do you want to please me, Ava?"

"Yes. Jesse, please!"

I give her one last feel of my thumb circling her buzzing nerves and then pull away, getting up off the bed.

"What are you doing?" she gasps.

Not a fucking clue. "You want me to finish the job?"

"Yes!"

Me too. But . . . "Don't go out," I order, watching as realization descends and the red of her cheeks turns from flushed to hopping mad.

"No!"

So I don't win the battle after all. She's so fucking stubborn. If it was me on the receiving end of that kind of performance from her, I would do absolutely anything she asked. Sign my life away. I need to fuck that irritating streak of defiance out of her. "My work here is done," I whisper, regarding her closely as I kiss fresh air. She looks plain furious as I turn and walk away, pulling the door closed behind me harshly.

"I'll sort myself out then!" The force of her yell hits me in the back as I take the stairs.

"No, you won't," I whisper, leaving before I give in to my compulsion to physically restrain her.

"All right?" Sam asks when I reach the front door.

"Fine. What are you still doing here?"

"I thought you'd need some company while you stew for the next few hours."

"Good," I reply. "I do."

"She's in love with you, Jesse."

"That won't stop some young prick making a pass at her. Or her drinking. Or, apparently, her fighting me at every fucking turn." I pass him, stalking to my car. "Where are we going?"

"Your place?"

"I'll call Drew." I reach for my phone.

"Don't bother."

I frown. "Why?"

"He's taken that girl out. The one Ava works with."

"The one who looks like she's got a stick up her arse?"

"More like a tree trunk." Sam stops me from getting in my car, his hand on my shoulder. I know what's coming, so I get in first.

"I've asked her to the anniversary party," I say, and his head retracts. "Therefore, I have to tell her about The Manor in the next two weeks."

He nods. "You're doing the right thing."

"Am I?" I haven't a clue what I'm doing these days.

Sam shrugs. "What else *can* you do?"

"Keep my secrets."

He laughs. "The Manor is a pretty big fucking secret to keep."

The Manor has nothing on the rest of the surprises I have in store for Ava.

Nothing.

Sam completely bypasses the fridge when we enter the kitchen, heading for the kettle and flicking it on. I roll my eyes at his back as he goes about making tea, plonking myself on a stool, spinning my phone in my grasp.

"Chill the fuck out, will you?" he says without turning away from the worktop.

My hand stills. "I'm fine."

He laughs, squeezing the tea bags and dumping them in the bin. "Sure."

I get up, restless, and start pacing the kitchen, glancing at my Rolex. She'll be in a bar by now. Drinking. Being admired.

"How's Kate?" I ask out of nowhere. I need to distract myself or there's a high possibility of me tracking Ava down and making sure she's okay, and we all know that won't go down very well.

Sam turns, two mugs in his hands, his head slightly cocked. "Do you actually care?" His eyes follow me as I make another circuit of the island.

"Of course I care."

He huffs, slipping the tea onto the counter. "You're going to give yourself a heart attack at this rate, mate. Or, alternatively, royally fuck it up."

I halt pacing, chewing my lip incessantly. "Fuck it up how?" I need to stop asking dumb questions.

"I can see you're a heartbeat away from hunting her down."

"Would that be a bad thing?" Maybe she'll be pleased to see me? Maybe she'll make me finish off what I started in her bedroom.

Or maybe she'll punch me in my stupid face and swear like a trooper.

"Sit," Sam orders, pulling up a stool beside me, getting close, like he senses I'm a flight risk and needs to be nearby to tackle me to the floor when I try to escape. I drop to the stool on a sigh. Then get back up when the most brilliant idea comes to me. I start pacing again, pulling up my contacts. "What are you doing?" Sam asks tiredly.

"Making a call." I dial, putting the phone at my ear.

"I strongly advise against it. Don't suffocate her."

I dazzle him with a mammoth smile. "I'm not calling Ava." The call connects as Sam frowns. "Jay," I say, and realization catches Sam. His head goes straight into his hands in despair. I ignore him. This might be the only thing that gets me through the night.

"Ward? What can I do for you?" Jay asks.

"You working tonight?"

"I'm always working."

"Good. Have you seen two women? One dark-haired, beautiful, willowy. The other is a fiery redhead with a ton of attitude. Mid-twenties."

"Hey," Sam pipes up, his face appearing from its hiding place. "I love that attitude."

My eyebrows shoot up, and Sam frowns. *Thought so.* I'm not the only one who's spellbound around here but, and I don't mind admitting it, Sam's handling the stab of Cupid's bow a lot better than I am.

"Yeah, I know them," Jay says. "They arrived not long ago. Giggly little things, aren't they?"

She's having fun without me. Well, that sucks. "Keep an eye on them, yeah? Text me the consumption levels, and if any blokes sniff around, I want to know." I'm still mindful that Ava's ex is on the prowl trying to make amends.

Jay laughs deeply. "You're a fuck-up, Ward."

"Tell me something I don't know." I hang up, smiling down at the screen. "My work here is done," I murmur, slipping my mobile onto the counter and taking a seat. I reach for my tea and take a sip, happy with myself. I can feel Sam staring at me, and I look up over the rim of my mug. "What?"

He shakes his head. "Unbelievable."

"Or just creative?"

"No, just neurotic. And what's with this big age secret?"

My tea pauses on its way down to the counter. "What do you know about the big age secret?"

"That it's no fucking secret," he says over a laugh. "Only to Ava."

"Wait, did you tell Kate how old I am?"

"No. Although she's asked plenty." He rolls his shoulders, like trying to rid a weight there. "Truth be told, I dare not even talk about you to Kate. I don't know what I can say or can't say, what

Ava knows or doesn't know." He hits me with an accusing look, and I shy away from it. "This is getting a bit stupid."

His flippant comment riles me, and I stand, swinging away and stalking to the fridge to grab some comfort. It's that or swing at one of my closest friends. "It's not stupid, Sam. I have a list as long as my fucking arm of shit to share and I'm fucking terrified that sharing any one of those things will result in a swift return to nothingness." I yank the fridge open and snatch down my peanut butter, diving in without delay. He's quiet behind me as I work my way through half the jar, getting more worked up by the second. "There's only ever light when she's around. There's only ever hope when I'm with her."

"You can't glue her to you."

I laugh. Should I tell him that I've thought about it?

I'm still pondering that when my phone pings, and I quickly forsake my vice and rush across to the island to grab it. Opening Jay's message, I read, and every word I absorb seems to raise my temperature by a few more degrees.

"What?" Sam asks.

"She's on her second glass of wine." Second? She's not been there more than a half hour.

"Oh my God," Sam breathes, but not in despair for the level of alcohol being sunk in such a short space of time. No. His despair is directed solely at my reaction to the level of alcohol being sunk in such a short space of time.

"Is it necessary?" I ask my screen.

"What?" he questions over a sigh.

I shove my phone in his face, as if he's not getting the same message as me. "It's reckless."

His eyebrows blend with his hairline as he looks at me. "They're enjoying themselves."

What he means, but will not say, is they're not drinking for the sake of drinking. They're not drowning themselves. They're not escaping.

"I'm just going to say it how it is," he begins before I can counter. He's right. Of course he's right, and I have a feeling I'm about to be hit with some more home truths. "Sit," he orders, and like an obedient dog, I do. He leans in, my usually cheeky, fun, jokey friend as serious as I've ever seen him. "You have an unhealthy relationship with alcohol, Jesse."

"Had," I pipe up. "I *had* an unhealthy relationship with alcohol."

"You think because you haven't had a drink for a couple of weeks you're sober? The alcoholic is still there."

My jaw twitches. "I'm not a fucking alcoholic."

His eyes close, his palm stroking his forehead. "No, you're not an alcoholic," he sighs. It's as condescending as fuck. "You can't stop her drinking."

Does he wanna bet? "I'm—"

"Not everyone fucks anything in sight when they're inebriated, Jesse. Not everyone who drinks is drowning out misery."

I recoil. Swallow. Snap my mouth firmly shut.

"For fuck's sake," Sam says, softening his stare and reaching for my hand. "Please, just tell her your story. And at the same time, how fucking old you are and what The Manor is."

"All in one go?" I ask quietly, feeling the vise of terror squeezing me. "Everything?"

"Just let it all out. You can't carry on like this. And, frankly, neither can I."

My eyes drop to the counter, the prospect no less daunting no matter how much I ponder doing just that. "I will," I say for the sake of it.

"And then you can crack on with this thing you've got going on with Ava."

Thing? This isn't a thing. It's *every*thing. "What if she leaves me?"

"She won't leave you. She loves you. And when you love someone, you love them despite their flaws." He squeezes my hand, and I look up, smiling mildly. I wish I was as optimistic as Sam.

"Thanks."

He frowns, retracting his hand, clearing his throat. "How are you settling in?" His tone is purposely deep.

I laugh as my phone dings again, and I hit the open button on another message from Jay. My laughter stops. I start overheating, the calm Sam's helped me find vanishing.

"Oh no, what?" Sam asks.

I'm off my stool like a spring, snatching my car keys off the side and heading for the door, Sam on my tail. "Don't try to stop me," I warn, simmering dangerously.

"Don't worry, I'd like to keep my head."

30

THE TRAFFIC IS HORRENDOUS. I drive like a complete maniac, which is apt because I feel like one. A man. Talking to Ava. A man who sounds uncannily similar to her ex-boyfriend, going by Jay's description. A man who's had her. A man she loved. A man in his mid-twenties.

I glance at my rearview mirror, seeing Sam in the distance, his Porsche struggling to keep up with my Aston. My phone rings. "What?" I answer shortly.

"If I get a speeding fine, I'm sending it your way."

"Fine." I hang up, and my phone immediately rings again. "Jay," I answer, praying he doesn't feed me more information that could result in me getting locked up.

"Third bottle."

I gape at the windscreen. "What?"

"They're on their third bottle and getting . . . loud."

Third fucking bottle. I'm fuming. "And the man?"

"Can't see him."

"Be there soon." I hang up and put my foot down, a small part of me willing myself to calm the fuck down to avoid the explosions that are about to go off. It's no good. I cannot accept such recklessness. I cannot stand by and allow another man to worm his way back into her affections. She's a sitting fucking duck. Drunk. Vulnerable.

I park illegally outside the bar and dive out of my car, just as Sam screeches up behind me. "Fuck me, Jesse," he says, joining me on the pavement.

"What's up? Your pretty Porsche struggling to keep up with a real man's car?" I pull my jacket in and stalk into the bar, hearing Sam laughing behind me. I spot them in a nanosecond, laughing, staggering.

And then they clatter to the floor in a drunken mess.

And my temper goes from hot to burning, not only because she's fucking plastered.

The dress. She's wearing the fucking dress. The dress she didn't want to even fucking buy but did, solely to piss me off. The dress she probably didn't want to wear tonight but did, solely to piss me off.

"Keep your cool," Sam says quietly beside me, holding on to the sleeve of my jacket.

"Still think this is fine?" I ask, tugging myself from his hold and marching over as Kate pushes herself up a little. She clocks me. Her face drops. *Yes, be worried.*

Her head tilts farther back, keeping me in view as I get closer. "Oh shit," she breathes, prompting Ava to sit up, quickly but clumsily.

"What?" Her eyes climb my body to my face. I expect panic to find her. It doesn't. Her lips straighten. Is she restraining laughter? Leaning into Kate, she says something, and as a result, Kate snorts and Ava falls apart. She finds this funny? Side-splitting funny by the look of her rolling around on the floor.

I, however, could quite easily wring her fucking neck.

Sam appears at my side, and I glance out the corner of my eye at him. He, too, is restraining his amusement. So everyone finds this funny except me?

"Jesse, sort your woman out," Jay says tiredly, motioning to the pile of females littering the bar floor.

"Oh, don't worry," I say menacingly, giving Ava the death stare. "She'll be sorted out. Thanks for the call, Jay." Ava's eyes widen. *Yes, I've been keeping tabs. Yes, I'm fucking livid.*

Sam moves in and helps Kate to her feet. "Come on, you pest."

She falls into him, laughing. "Take me to bed, Samuel. You can tie me up again."

He gives me a wary gaze, still holding on to his laughter, as he's smothered by Kate's drunken mouth. I return my eyes to Ava. That ridiculous dress is practically around her waist, revealing a slither of the lace beneath it for all to see. "Up," I hiss. "Now."

"Oh, lighten up, you bore," she sighs, attempting to get herself off the floor. For fuck's sake. I find it in myself to help her, and once she's vertical, the dress sucker-punches me in the gut. Or, what there is of it, which isn't fucking much.

"Are you mad at me?" she asks, clinging to my suit to hold herself up.

Oh, she has no idea. "Crazy mad, Ava." I take her elbow and lead her out of the bar, where we find Sam negotiating Kate into his car. Ava bursts into fits of giggles again.

"Samuel, tonight is your lucky night," Kate declares.

I shake my head. We all know the only lucky thing that'll happen to Sam tonight will be avoiding the inevitable spewing session.

He nods his goodbye to me and gives Ava a kiss on her cheek before I pull my irresponsible girlfriend away, my mission to get her out of public view in that fucking dress my main objective. She's staggering. It makes me even madder. How was she planning on getting home?

I deposit her in my car and reach for the belt. "I can put a seat-belt on," she snipes, pushing my hands away. I glare at her and, wisely, she quits fighting me, shutting the hell up. It's evidence of the fury she's facing if, even drunk and feistier, she's backing down. I secure her, leaning across to fasten the belt. "You smell delicious," she whispers.

I turn my eyes to her. I can't even bring myself to relish in her appreciation. I slam the door and get behind the wheel, taking out my anger on the pedal.

"Kate's house is that way."

"And?" I ask, taking a right at the lights.

"And . . . it's where I live."

"You're staying at mine."

"No, that wasn't part of the deal. I have until eight in the morning before you distract me again."

"I've changed the deal."

"You can't change the deal."

I turn my incensed expression onto her, forcing back my growl. "You did," I say lowly, watching as her expression turns into pure filth.

But she doesn't murmur another word. What could she say? I'm right, and she knows it. She flops back in her seat, staring out of the window. She's sulking. She'll be sulking harder when I rip that dress off her, and not because I want at her body. She's gone too far. Every second from the boutique to now has been a mission on her part to create problems. I'm done with it. It's time to demonstrate some power.

31

A FEW TIMES on our way back to Lusso, I see her head bob slightly from where she's defiantly trying to keep her eyes open. Part of me hopes she'll doze off. Maybe confess her love for me again. Instead, she snaps awake and throws me a curled lip when she catches me fleetingly watching her. She's so fucking exasperating. She wouldn't be in this car if she didn't want to be. That much I do know. I never knew it was possible to love someone and want to throttle them in equal measure.

I don't offer her my hand when she slowly gets out of my Aston, concentrating hard. Offering help will only give her cause to refuse, which she will. Her steps are tentative and measured as I follow her through the foyer, and Clive, wisely, senses the spikey atmosphere and keeps his mouth closed.

She waits for me to join her in the lift, her eyes angry slits. "You need to get this code changed." She punches in the sequence of numbers with a heavy fingertip and focuses on the doors closing before us. The small space feels like a pressure pot. I glance down her body, getting a last good look at her in that dress. That fucking dress. Either the lame scrap of material takes the brunt of my rage, or Ava will.

She peeks up at me. Shifts on her heels. And for the first time since this morning when I dropped her at work, I'm amused. Even hopping mad, she's desperate for me. I can see desire crawling all over her exposed skin, and there's a lot of exposed skin. I could push her up against the wall. Take out this frustration on her body, and she would welcome it because she has some unwarranted frustration to be rid of herself. I'm smiling on the inside. Does she think she has the power?

She does.

But my displeasure is in control right now, and that will pave the way to what is going to be an epic showdown. I will take a lot, but I refuse to take her childish need to rub me up the wrong way. It's uncalled for. Especially when I already feel like I'm fighting against the current.

I step out of the elevator and let us into my penthouse, heading straight for the kitchen for some water. I have a few swigs to moisten my parched mouth before handing it to Ava, and I watch her as she obediently hydrates herself, emptying the rest of the bottle.

"Turn around," I say once she's set the empty aside. Her body stiffens before my eyes, her chest concaving on her inhale of anticipation. And she slowly turns away from me. No challenge. No defiance. I step in and rest my palms on her shoulders, feeling her burning up. I pull the zip down leisurely, my eyes falling with it, taking in her exposed skin, and she steps out and turns to face me. My mind is screaming a million questions as I consider her from my crouched position. But one is louder than the rest.

Why?

I rise, the dress in my grasp, drawing a path up her front with my nose, breathing in every inch of her. Smelling her yearning. "Do you want my mouth on you, Ava?" I ask into her neck, and she gulps, exhaling dreamily. "You need to say the word."

"Yes."

"Do you want me to fuck you, baby?" I slip my hand between her legs and brush lightly over her lace knickers.

"Jesse."

"I know," I whisper, deeply satisfied. "You want me." I nibble at her ear, breathing heavily, pushing her to her limit. She'll break soon. *I'll* break soon. Yet I can't let this go.

My dick is screaming as I back away, asking me what the fuck I'm playing at, but it's for the greater good. It has to be. "Stay there," I say, seeing the docile, compliant woman that resides beneath the temptress. The woman who cannot resist me. The woman who submits.

I collect what I need from the drawer and pace slowly back to her, and her heavy eyes follow me, her lips parted, her hands twitching, dying to grab me. I take that final step into her body. Meld our chests. Her heartbeats clash against mine. Whimpers of contentment come thick and fast as I coat her face with my lips.

I kiss my way to her mouth, but I don't allow her to progress it to tongues. I slowly crouch before her, studying her perfection as she finds my shoulders for support. Satisfaction. It feels so good. I stand and breathe down on her. "You're so affected by me."

She agrees. No doubt.

"I know you are." I kiss the hollow beneath her ear and absorb her violent shudder. "It . . . really . . . fucking . . . turns . . . me . . . on." What I'm about to do feels inhumane.

Almost.

I step back, and she blinks her surprise.

I hold up the dress.

And a pair of scissors.

I'll never forget the look on her face in this moment. It's somewhere between daring me, and fear that I'm about to do what she fears I'm about to do.

I won't disappoint.

I set the scissors at the bottom of the dress and cut my way straight through the middle of it. And then through the middle of those two pieces. And then through the middle of those smaller pieces. And do you know what? It feels good. Like the pressure inside releases slowly. Just like that, my problem is gone. She can no longer wear the dress. If only I could rid myself of all other issues so easily.

I set the pieces on the worktop, and I look at her. She's in a state of shock, dazed, and then she glances from what's left of the dress to me.

"I can't believe you just did that," she splutters, her limp hand indicating the scraps of material decorating the island. Honestly, neither can I. But if she thinks I'll leave that dress in her wardrobe to brandish like a weapon every time she's got the hump with me, she's wrong.

Which is crystal clear to her now the dress is no more.

"Don't play games with me, Ava," I say quietly but firmly.

Her mouth drops open, and I watch, slightly amused, as she searches for some words.

Eventually, her fuzzy mind gives her some instructions and she shoves a finger in my face. "You're crazy!"

Short and to the point. And she's not wrong, but she's got a fucking nerve to sound so accusing when it is her sending me that way. "I fucking feel it," I yell. I have so much more to say. So many words to shout. So many rules to lay down. But, fuck me, I'm exhausted by my anger. "Get your arse to bed."

She recoils, stunned, as I heave before her. "I'm not getting in bed with you." Her shoes are removed, and she stomps away, muttering as she goes. I hear the stairs shake under her angry feet, and then a door slam. I stare at the empty space before me, knowing I need to calm the fuck down before I go after her. "For fuck's sake," I mutter, swiping up the scraps of material and stuffing them in the bin. "The woman is impossible." I get more water, my throat feeling sore. Then I make my way to my room.

I sigh when I find she's not in our bed, rolling my eyes and backing out. She's in the last spare room I check, the one farthest from our bedroom. I scan all of the fancy dress cushions littering the carpet, the ones she's tossed around in a temper, as I pace to the bed and lift her into my arms, and there is not one word of complaint. In fact, she snuggles into my suit jacket. She's so fucking confusing. I put her where she should be—in our bed— and start stripping down as she buries her face in a pillow. I know I catch an exhale of contentment, and yet when I crawl in behind her, she finds that irritating defiant streak and pushes my hands away when I reach for her.

"Get off!"

"Ava," I growl.

"Tomorrow, I'm out of here." She breaks free and I laugh, so fucking amused. She's going nowhere. She knows it, I know it. For the love of God, she just cuddled me as I carried her here. Breathed me in on the sheets.

"We'll see." I seize her and yank her into my front, making sure she can't break free. She doesn't even try, and I'm certain it's because of the peace that is suddenly enveloping us. This is our bubble, and despite her being affronted, she settles in my arms. The arms that will protect her from everything.

I lie for a time, my eyes wide open, my heart rate stabilizing, but my crowded mind becomes busier. She's sound asleep. Peaceful. It's a stark contrast to the turmoil within me. But is it only inner turmoil? Of course it's not. My unrest must be plastered over every inch of my skin. It's obvious in all the things I do. This evening I shredded her dress. I would try to reassure myself it was a knee-jerk reaction, but I had plenty of time from the bar to Lusso to reason with myself. I chose not to. It wasn't a knee-jerk reaction. It was a demonstration of my desperation. Only, she doesn't know that, and I can't expect her compassion and understanding while she's so completely in the dark.

My sigh is long and tired as I break away from her body and sit up against the headboard, and with a lack of my chest supporting her sleeping form, she rolls onto her back. I stare down at her beautiful, sleeping face. "I love you," I whisper, hating myself for not being able to tell her that. And yet, I know I'm expressing my love in so many other ways. She must see that.

I lean over to my nightstand and grab my phone, going straight to the picture gallery. The grid of images that greet me is all Ava. I scroll back to the beginning of the album. To the day she walked into my office. The day my heart started beating again. The day she became mine.

I swallow and cast my eyes back to her, and still when she murmurs and turns, snuggling into my side, her hand resting over my scar. I point my phone down my torso and catch the moment. The moment I decided that tomorrow, I will start sharing my secrets little by little. My time swinging from ignorant bliss to stark, fearful reality is over. I dip and kiss the top of her head, my eyes squeezing closed. "Please don't leave me."

32

MY EYES SPRING open at the crack of dawn, and I immediately search for her, my speeding heart rate recovering the moment I find her curled up in my side. I drop my head back to the pillow relieved. Scared. Unsure.

Today.

Today I give Ava my truths and hope to fuck her love for me will allow her to accept me fully.

But before I wake her and set the wheels in motion, there's something I need to do. I peel her hands away from my torso and edge carefully to the side of the bed, not wanting to wake her. I don't think I have anything to worry about. She's dead to the world.

I pull on some shorts, stuff my feet into my running shoes, and throw on my T-shirt as I head downstairs and grab my keys. I close the door quietly behind me and then hurry to the elevator.

The fresh morning air sticks to my skin as I jog across the car park to my Aston, and I'm soon speeding across town, on a mission. The roads are clear, my journey quick. I park and run up the path, hammering on the door when I get there.

It swings open a few moments later, and Kate glares at me,

her look fierce as she knots the tie of her dressing gown. "Are you serious?"

"Deadly." I push my way past her and head upstairs, finding Sam standing in Kate's bedroom doorway, bollock naked, squinting.

"What the fuck are you doing here?"

"Collecting a few of Ava's things." I let myself into her room and get to packing.

"Does she know?" he asks, dropping to Ava's bed as I hurry around her room, grabbing anything and everything.

"What do you think?"

"I think she'll cut off your balls when she finds out you've taken it upon yourself to move her into your apartment."

I pull her top drawer open and nearly drop to my knees with the amount of lace that greets me. *Fucking hell.* "Ava will pretend she's opposed for the sake of it. I'm just moving the inevitable along." I scoop up a pile of lace, piles and piles of lace, and stuff it in the bag.

"Or perhaps you're making it as difficult as possible for her to leave when you tell her you're the Lord of the Sex Manor."

"Lord?" I laugh, going back to the drawer to close it, stalling when I see something in the bottom corner. *Look away from the pills.* I cast a look over my shoulder as Kate enters the room.

"That's what she calls you," she says, falling to the bed with Sam. "The Lord. I'd personally call you a fucking rhinoceros. What the fuck are you playing at?"

I grab the packet of pills and discreetly slip them into my pocket as I turn and face my audience. Lord of The Manor. That's what most women around there call me. Ava's no different . . . but so, so different. "Like I explained to your naked boyfriend, I'm just moving things along."

"He's not my boyfriend."

"What if he wanted to be?" Sam counters, and both Kate and I balk at him. Fuck, this is more serious than I thought.

"I'll leave you two to it." I slip out with Ava's things, and the moment I'm on the street, I pull the pills from my pocket and drop them down the drain.

Done.

Gone.

Once in my car, I crank the music up to drown out the sound of Jake and my conscience.

I creep around my bedroom and dressing room like a super sleuth, unpacking her things and setting her cosmetics in the bathroom just so. And it feels right. All of it feels right. If there's one thing I've learned about my girl, it's that she sometimes needs gentle persuasion to do what she really wants to do but won't do because she's a stubborn sod. I'm effectively eradicating the potential of a row. I'm doing us both a favor.

I back out of my dressing room, taking one last look at her dresses hanging next to my suits. "My work here is done," I say quietly, stripping down and going to the bed, crawling up to her, chuffed with myself and my work. I drop endless kisses onto her face, and she starts to stir. "Rise and shine, lady."

Her eyes open. She frowns up at me. I can see her mind giving her a sordid replay of last night, and I brace myself for the fireworks.

"I'm not talking to you," she grumbles groggily, shoving me away and flipping onto her side. I scowl at her lace-covered arse and slap it hard, pulling her back and pinning her down. "That hurt!"

I grin at her. She's confused, wondering why I'm smiling and not puffing like a raging bull. Not today. Today is going to be so perfect that leaving me will be unthinkable. "Now," I start, spelling it out for her. "Today can go one of two ways. You can stop being unreasonable and we'll have a lovely day together, or you can continue being a defiant little temptress and I'll be forced to handcuff you to the bed and dig you in your tickle spot until you lose consciousness." God, I'd love to tickle her stupid, just to hear her chuckles. But I'm hoping she'll opt for option one without fuss. "What's it to be, baby?" I dazzle her with my megawatt smile while she thinks, still clearly confused. Then she brings her face closer, and everything inside tingles. *Yes, I'll take a kiss in answer.*

"Fuck . . . off," she snarls, and my face drops like a rock.

"Watch your fucking mouth."

"No! What the hell are you doing having doormen advise you of my movements?"

I sigh and drop my head. I have to try and explain with words rather than actions. "Ava, I just want to make sure you're safe. I worry, that's all."

"I'm twenty-six years old, Jesse."

Yes, and that's part of my problem. I'm hot, I know I'm hot, but I'm far from in my mid-twenties anymore. There are plenty of eligible bachelors who are, though, all with clean pasts and no demons, and they're waiting on the sidelines ready to whisk her off her feet. And in that dress? "Why did you wear that dress?"

"To piss you off," she snarls, fighting my hold of her. And there we have it. Pure and utter irrational behavior.

"But you thought you weren't going to see me."

"It's the principle."

Principle? Fuck that. It's nothing but stupidity. I hope she realizes it now, and if she doesn't, I'll happily shred all ridiculous dresses until she does.

"You owe me a dress," she mutters, and I smile, knocking her back a little.

"We'll put it on our list of things to do today," I say. I'll buy her a million dresses, all beautiful, all expensive.

All below the knee.

But she'll be stunning in them, and I'll preserve my sanity.

The scowl that hits me is impressive. Then she rolls her hips up into my groin, and I fall apart on the inside. There she is. This mid-twenties woman who can't resist this man who's knocking on forty.

"What's all that about?" I ask. She will beg. Show me how crazy she is for me.

I know the moment she grasps my intentions because her face drops and her body goes lax beneath me. "You don't need to keep me safe." She wriggles free and heads for the bathroom, and I roll onto my back on a drained sigh.

"That's how much I care about you," I say to the ceiling. *Love! Love, you fool. You fucking love her.*

I hear the door close, and slap my palms over my face, scrubbing them down my bristles. *Idiot.* I roll onto my front and shove my face in the sheets, giving the pillow a few thumps. "I love you," I mumble. "So fucking much, I'm in constant agony because I'm not sure you should love me back."

The door opens. I still, listening hard. The sound of her feet pads the carpet past me. She's going into the dressing room. Oh, here we go. I have zero faith that my gesture will be taken well. Not after her performance this morning.

I creep off the bed slowly and take tentative steps to the doorway, chewing nervously on my lip. "Problem?" I ask when I find her gazing at her dresses.

She turns toward me, my toothbrush hanging from her mouth. I frown. She didn't see her own next to it? Her eyes fall down my torso. I consider distracting her further and giving her what she was asking for in bed a moment ago, but she speaks before I can act. Or, at least, she tries to. "Wh . . . hell . . . roths . . . ing . . . ere."

I can't restrain my smile completely, not when she's got tooth-paste dribbling down her face and she's looking at me with such outrage. "I'm sorry. Run that by me again." I need time to consider my answer, and it'll be something she can't argue with.

Her nostrils flare. *Oh boy. Keep it light, Ward.* Today *has* to be a good day.

She waffles on again, looking like she's foaming at the mouth. She kind of is. Exasperated, I collect her and carry her into the bathroom, setting her by the sink. "Spit."

She spits like a bloke and swings back to face me. "What's all this?"

I can't take her seriously when she looks like this, so I lean forward and rid her face of all toothpaste with my tongue. Distract her. Yes, I'll give her what she wants, and she'll agree to anything *I* want. That's how we work, and it suits me fine. "There," I whis-per, finishing at her lips. She breathes in, her body hardening. "What's what?" I work my way to her ear, reaching between her thighs.

"No!" She shoves me away. "You're not manipulating me with your delicious godliness."

My shoulders roll. My chest swells. "You think I'm a god?" Then she is my temptress. My defiant, little temptress.

Ava snorts and turns away, and I move in behind her, crowding her with my godly body as she stares at me in the reflection of the mirror.

I'm so fucking hard for her. "I don't mind being your god."

"Why is my stuff here?"

"I collected it from Kate's earlier. I thought you could stay here for a few days."

"Do I get a say?"

I thrust my groin forward, and she inhales sharply, her eyes sparkling. "Do you ever?"

Her head shakes mildly, her body alive, throbbing, glowing back at me through the mirror. I have her. But still, I will drag this out. It might kill me, but she needs to comprehend the sheer depth of our needs. I need her to comply. She needs me all over her. "Get yourself ready, lady. I'm taking you out. Where would you like to go?" I give her backside a swift slap, and she jolts forward.

"I get to choose?"

"I have to let you have your way some of the time." I'm not a complete control freak. And besides, I need her in a good mood today. "So, what would you like to do?"

"Let's go to Camden."

Camden? I inwardly groan. I'd rather pull my own teeth out, but for the sake of peace and because I'm fair . . . "Okay." I can make Camden work. I flash her another smile and hop in the shower, singing to myself as I wash my hair. I can feel her staring at me incredulously, probably still wondering where the raging bull is, and perhaps wondering why I've not dragged her in here.

She only has to beg.

But she remains on the other side of the glass, and I can sense her getting more and more worked up. Good. I step out, pull a towel off the rail, and dry myself slowly, ignoring her unmoving form before me. "All yours," I say, dropping the towel and passing her, feeling her eyes following my naked back to the sink. I smile to myself. Perhaps now she knows what it felt like all that time she denied me. Granted, I'm punishing myself too, but I've never known a greater satisfaction than this. Feeling her want, seeing her tenacity. But she won't just crack. She'll break clean in two for me, and then the power will be mine again.

I grab my shaver and trim down my stubble, brush my teeth, and leave Ava still standing outside the shower waiting for me to indulge her.

After throwing on some jeans and a polo shirt, I head to the kitchen to wait for her, and I've worked my way through a jar of peanut butter by the time I hear her feet padding down the stairs. My phone rings, and I eye it warily, hoping this call isn't going to put a dampener on my mood or ruin my plans for today. "John?"

"Just checking you're alive," he rumbles, and I smile. "And Ava, for that matter."

"Spoke to Sam?"

"Yes. It sounds like you're doing a fine job of getting that woman onside, you stupid motherfucker."

I roll my eyes. "We're both alive," I assure him. I can feel I'm under close observation, and I turn on my stool, finding Ava at the doorway admiring me. "I'll be in tomorrow." My eyes take a leisurely jaunt down her front. "Is everything okay?"

"'S'all good."

She's wearing a lovely dress and, blow me away, it's of an acceptable length. And there I was thinking reasonableness was like rocking horse shit where this woman's concerned. It seems she's cottoning on to how this game is played. "Thanks, John. Call me if you need me." I hang up and get comfortable on my stool. "I like your dress."

She takes a peek herself, like she hasn't seen it, and pulls a cute knit over her shoulders. Good Lord, she really is being compliant this morning. I'm suspicious. "Ready?" she asks.

No, not at all. I am, however, ready to spend all day with her. I'm ready for her to beg me for some contact. I'm ready to fall in love with her some more. But I'm not ready for the moment I find the courage to do what's right.

I get to my feet and wander across the kitchen to her, slipping my shades on and claiming her hand. I smile as I pull her on. She was expecting a kiss.

"You're not going to touch me all day, are you?" she asks as I lead us to the lifts.

"I'm touching you."

"You know what I mean." Her words are tight. Frustrated. "You're punishing me."

I get us into the elevator. "Why would I do that, Ava?"

"I want you to touch me."

I smile, pressing the button to take us down. "I know you do."

"But you won't?"

"Give me what I want, and I will."

"An apology?"

"I don't know, Ava." I don't look at her, but it doesn't lessen the burn of my skin under her pissed-off gaze. "Do you need to apologize?"

"I'm sorry," she grates, and I mentally dance in celebration. She craves me. Even when she's mad with me, she craves me. I feel like it's my only defense in the battles, and yet rather than accept her apology, I just can't help pushing my limits, my ego swelling.

"Now, if you're going to apologize, at least *sound* sorry," I say quietly, and she audibly breathes in some patience.

"I'm sorry."

I look at her reflection. "Are you?"

"Yes, I'm sorry."

She's not sorry. She's giving me lip service, but that's how much she wants me all over her skin. "You want me to touch you?"

"Yes."

I move in and crush her body against the wall. Breathless, she stares up at me. "You're beginning to understand, aren't you?"

"I understand," she agrees on a wheeze.

I kiss her hard, feeling her short nails sinking into my flesh, and I make up for the many kisses I deprived her of this morning. "Happy?" I ask, and she sighs, relaxing against the wall.

"Yes."

"Me too." I drop a gentle peck on her forehead and take her

hand as the doors slide open. "Let's go." I slip my shades back on, looking over my shoulder as we pass through the foyer. She's grinning. Fuck, I love that grin. I need to keep that smile on her face all day. Make this a date she'll never forget. I feel like I'm winning already.

I open the door of my Aston, sweep my arm out in gesture for her to get in, and bend to pull her seatbelt across. She doesn't murmur a word of protest, letting me do my thing. The clip locks in place, and I pull back, my face close to hers. She smiles demurely, and I return it, running my tongue across my bottom lip. She hears my silent demand, pushing her mouth onto mine. Another kiss. Slow, soft, calm, but full of purpose.

"You're a good kisser," she mumbles.

"I know." I move my mouth to her cheek and playfully bite, and she laughs, the sound dreamy.

My day is planned out meticulously. Breakfast at a place that serves the best of Ava's favorite, a stroll holding hands, and then home to make mad sweet love. It's a beautiful day. The sun is beaming down, the breeze mild, and I'm with my favorite person. I glance across the car at her when I've pulled up outside the bistro, and she gives me another smile. She's full of them since we made friends in the elevator. I never want to be the person who takes those smiles away.

I swallow and eject myself from my Aston, collecting her and guiding her toward the bistro. "You'll love it here," I say, offering her a chair. "We'll sit outside."

"Why will I love it?"

"They do the best Eggs Benedict."

The delight on her face is endearing, as is the waitress's when she approaches. I place our order and once we're alone again, I refocus all my attention on Ava. "How are your legs?"

"Fine. Do you run often?"

I get comfortable, seeing a million questions in her dark eyes. "It distracts me."

"Distracts you from what?"

"You." That's a lie. Nothing distracts me from her, but I can appreciate my infatuation isn't healthy—always wanting more time with her—and Ava's in full control of that side of our relationship.

She snorts. "Why do you need distracting from me?"

"Because, Ava . . ." My exhale is heavy. Tired. Doesn't she get it? "I can't seem to stay away from you and, even more of a worry, I don't want to."

I expect at least some shock in response, and yet she just stares at me. She *does* get it. So why does she constantly rebuff me? She dangles herself like a carrot, denying me even the smallest nibble, when what I actually need—and she knows it—is a huge fucking bite.

"Why would that be worrying?" She busies herself with something, and I look down seeing our coffees have been delivered to the table. And there's my point. I didn't even notice because . . . her. I scowl at myself when I bite too hard on my lip. She's waiting for an answer. What on earth do I say?

I have to look away from her for a moment, unable to face the concern on her face. It's a hint of what's to come. "It's worrying because I feel out of control," I blurt, giving her the truth. "Feeling out of control is not something I do well, Ava." Terribly, in fact. There's a part of me that copes so much better when she is around. And there's another part of me that completely sinks. I have to fight my compulsions. "Not where you're concerned."

"If you were more reasonable," she says, her voice quiet, as if she's afraid to speak up, "you wouldn't feel out of control." Her lashes flicker when she blinks at me, her fingers toying with the edge of her coffee cup. Reasonable. Yes, let's talk about being reasonable, but before I can open my mouth, she goes on. "Are you like this with all of your women?"

The fuck? All of my women? Does she actually think this is normal behavior for me?

Ah, so you're admitting to abnormal behavior?

I shake Jake's irritating voice from my mind. "I've never cared enough about anyone else to feel like this," I say, making that crystal clear. *All of my women?* I'm feeling strung. This is not how I planned the day to be.

Oh, so you thought it would be all sunshine and smiles, huh? No questions? No truths? And what the hell do you mean, you've never cared enough about anyone?

I grab my coffee and mentally beg Jake to leave me alone, just for today. This is going to be hard enough without him poking at my conscience. "It's just fucking typical that I would go and find the most defiant woman on the planet to—"

"Try and control?"

I shoot her a startled look. *No. To fall in fucking love with.* For Christ's sake. Doesn't she see it? And I don't try and control her. I try to control *myself*. And fail.

"What about other relationships?" she asks, clearly not seeing my silent plea for this to stop.

"I don't have relationships." Only with drink. "I'm not interested in getting involved." Except, clearly, with her. "Anyway, I don't have time." What the fuck am I saying? I'm being backed into a corner, completely caught off guard. I'm not prepared. This talk was supposed to happen later after our wonderful date.

"You've devoted enough time to trampling all over me," she says, almost laughing.

"You're different. I told you, Ava, I'll trample anyone who tries to get in my way. Even you."

She seems to take that news quite well, not scoffing or snorting her disgust. "Why am I so different?" she asks quietly, again distracting herself from looking at me. Breakfast is on the table. I missed that too.

"I don't know, Ava." I collect my cutlery and poke at my plate. My appetite is gone.

"You don't know much, do you?"

Oh, baby, I know too much. And I want to protect you from it all.

"I know that I've never wanted to fuck a woman more than once," I say quietly, my mouth speaking words I didn't tell it to. "You, though, I really do." Peeking up, I find Ava not just looking horrified, but hurt too. "That came out wrong." I drop my fork, giving up on breakfast. This isn't going well at all. "What I'm trying to say is that . . ." *I love you.* "Well . . ." *And for some fucking reason, I can't find those words.* "I've never cared about a woman enough to want more than sex. Not until I met you." My attempts to massage away my thumping headache are futile. "I can't explain it, but you felt it," I say, searching her eyes. "Didn't you? When we met, you felt it." I wasn't alone in that crazy. I'm still not, and I need her to tell me, at least only to prove I'm not going in-fucking-sane.

"Yes," she breathes, and I feel my shoulders lighten. "I felt it." Her smile is knowing, and I match it. That's it. No more. Let's end it on that high for now.

"Eat your breakfast," I order gently, and she begins to pick her way through her plate, quiet and thoughtful. I won't ask what those thoughts are, but I hope she's concluding what's true amid the unknown lies shrouding me. She's special. "We need to buy you a dress for The Manor's anniversary party."

She looks up at me, pulled from her daydreams. "I have plenty of dresses," she says tiredly, going back to her bagel.

I expect she does, but I'd like to buy her a new one. Something special. Like her. "You need a new one," I declare, and her shoulders drop. She's exasperated? "Anyway, I owe you one."

"Do I get to choose?" she asks, looking at me with a fixed glare as I move a piece of hair from her mouth.

"Of course. I'm not a complete control freak," I say in jest, because I know she thinks I am.

Her body jerks. "Jesse, you're really very special."

"Not as special as you." I smile cheekily, and she shakes her head. "Are you ready to hit Camden, baby?"

She goes to her bag, and I watch in disgust as she places some money on the table. *What is this?* I'm insulted. I stand and replace it with some cash, snatching her bag and stuffing her money inside. She's taking this whole independence thing too far now. Way too far. What has—

I'm distracted from my grievance when her mobile rings, *"Mum"* flashing up on the screen, and I grab it and answer. Don't ask me what the hell I'm playing at; I couldn't tell you. And Ava's jaw hitting the table is a clear sign she's wondering the same thing.

"Hello," her mum says, and I smile, thinking she sounds so similar to Ava. And, actually, quite young.

"Mrs. O'Shea?"

Ava's recovering jaw plummets again, and she swipes at me, trying to win her phone back.

"Oh, who's this?" her mother asks, as I dive out of Ava's reach.

"I have the pleasure of being with your beautiful daughter." I suddenly comprehend the reason why my instinct had me hijacking this call. Win her mother over. It's common knowledge that if a man can win a mother's approval, he's halfway to a happy ever after.

"How lovely. I'm Ava's mother."

"Yes, Ava has told me lots about you." I smile wickedly at my girl as she practically chases me around the small table. "I'll look forward to meeting you." I raise my brows, and Ava recoils. It doesn't sit well, and the reason stings like a bitch. My unknown age. She's worried her parents won't approve.

"You too," she says, sounding hesitant. "Is she there?"

"Yes," I murmur, my mood dipping. "I'll put her on. It was lovely to talk to you."

I pass Ava her mobile and throw her a warning look when she snatches it. *So* unnecessary. I was only trying to break the fucking ice. Isn't that the right thing to do? Introduce oneself to your girlfriend's mother? Not that I've ever had to do that before.

"Mum?" She turns away from me, and I pout, watching as she hunches over, like making herself small will lessen the chances of me hearing.

"He's just a friend, Mum," she says. It's my jaw's turn to scrape the ground. I'm raging, could quite easily claim that phone back and put Ava's mother right, but, instead, I plunge an imaginary knife through my heart. Ava rolls her eyes, then I see her visibly solidify, swinging away from me. What was that?

"Mum, can I call you back?" she asks, and my suspicions increase. "I'm in Camden; it's loud." She's being shifty. "Okay, I'll call you later." She hangs up and takes a few moments before facing me.

Her face is tight with anger. "Why did you do that?"

Keep your cool, Jesse. It's tough when I'm constantly trying to advance our relationship and she's constantly putting the brakes on it. "He's just a friend?" I say, not prepared to let that slide. "Do you often let friends fuck your brains out?"

I expect a slap, not that I deserve one, it's just that . . . well. Ava. But as I'm bracing myself, she seems to fold, and defeat looks utterly shit on her. "Is it your mission objective to make my life as difficult as possible?"

"No," I breathe. That hurt. "I'm sorry." It actually hurt.

"Forget about it." She whirls around and starts walking away, and I trudge after her, giving myself a thorough telling off. My age bothers her. Her parents' opinion bothers her.

Obstacles. Constant fucking obstacles.

I shouldn't be making this harder for her because in the process I'll be making it harder for me. Fuck everything.

I catch up and throw my arm around her shoulders, pulling her into my side, and she comes with ease, my stride dropping to her slow meander. Her head sits perfectly on my chest. Her arms fit perfectly around my back. Her hand rests perfectly on my stomach. She's mad with me but finding comfort in me. I drop my mouth to the back of her head and hold it there as we walk, and she answers by slipping her hand beneath my T-shirt, stroking over my stomach. Her tracing stops over my scar.

And I squeeze her into me that little bit harder.

I never knew wandering aimlessly could be so pleasurable. She moves so in sync with me, her steps following mine, as I weave our joined bodies through the crowds of Camden market. Every so often, she stops at a stall and pokes around, but never, not once, does she break her hold of me. For every second we're stuck together, I feel myself fusing to her even more. My heart blending with hers. My mind traveling in circles. My skin permanently buzzing.

My fears intensifying.

I'm a man tiptoeing on the edge of paradise and destruction, and this woman in my arms will dictate which way I fall. I look down at her tucked into me, mentally begging her to find strength to see this through, and when she breaks away from me, I think she might have heard my silent pleas. She starts wriggling out of her cardigan, huffing and puffing. My amusement can't be contained, my smile breaking. For the past few hours, I've been thinking she must be stifling. What took her so long?

She turns a full circle, her eyes down as she pulls her cardigan around her waist, and my smile plummets when her back comes into my view. Her *naked* back.

"Ava," I blurt, "your dress is missing a huge chunk." What the heck is she doing? My dick twitches behind my jeans at the gorgeous planes of smooth, delicious skin staring back at me, then I'm checking to see if anyone else has copped a load of my half-naked girlfriend. I spot a man walking past, looking back over his shoulder. I snarl at him, returning my attention to Ava as she pivots toward me. She's smiling. Why the fuck is she smiling?

"No, it's the design," she says, blasé, rolling her eyes. Another man wanders past, and my narrowed eyes follow his path, daring him to look back for another peek. He gets a good few paces before he does, and my nostrils flare dangerously. Lucky for him, he catches the growling wolf beside the beauty he's admiring and quickly gets his wandering eyes under control.

No. This isn't happening.

I huff and take the tops of her arms, turning her away from me and pulling the cardigan up her back, covering her up. "Will you stop?" She chuckles, batting my hands away and slipping from my reach. She might be laughing now. I guarantee she won't be when I get her home and cut up another dress.

"Do you do this on purpose?" I position my hand over the gaping hole in her dress, fanning my fingers to cover as much of her exposed flesh as possible. I don't want an argument. I need her in the best mood, loving me the most, when I drop my bombshells. I walk us on, my eyes scanning the crowds for potential pervs.

"If you want full-length skirts and polo-necked jumpers," she mutters, "then I suggest you find someone your own age."

My spare hand goes to her ribs, and she squeals on a jump. She's joking. *I think.* Is she? "How old do you think I am?"

"Well, I don't know, do I? Do you want to relieve me of my wondering?"

"No."

"No, I didn't think so." She's suddenly gone from my side, shimmying through the throngs of people.

"Ava," I call, my eyes like laser beams on her *naked* back as I hurry to catch up with her, knocking people out of my way as I go. I arrive at a stall and grimace, the stench of burning fragranced sticks dotted everywhere irritating my nose. She's reaching up for something on a shelf, but before I can make it to her to help, the stall owner—he's definitely the stall owner, all dreadlocks and baggy pants—is by her side doing my job for me, pulling a cloth bag down and handing it to her. I scowl at him too and move in, returning my hand to her back as she rummages through the bag and pulls out . . .

"What's that?" I ask, frowning as she flaps out a huge piece of material.

"These are Thai fisherman pants."

Now, I'm all for plenty of material to hide her precious body from roving eyes, but, even for me, this is going a bit too far. She could cloak the entire market in the things she's currently holding. "I think you need a smaller size."

"They're one size."

"Ava, you could get ten of you in those." And probably ten of me too. In fact, are they maternity pants? I tilt my head thoughtfully. She'd look good in maternity pants. She'd look good pregnant.

"You wrap them around. One size fits all."

"Here, let me show you." The hippy takes them from Ava's grasp and kneels before her. What the fuck is he doing?

"We'll take them," I blurt, his face way too close to Ava's legs.

"You need a demo," he says with a laugh, ignoring the threat on my face and continuing with his task of getting Ava in the giant maternity pants. Without instruction, my spare hand reaches for her arm and pulls her back, and she stumbles, throwing me a displeased look.

"You have great legs, miss," the stall owner says.

"Thanks."

Is he goading me? *Enough.* "Give me those." I swipe the pants from his hands and move Ava away from him, falling to my knee and unraveling the endless material. This is ridiculous. How do they even work?

Ava takes the pants and tucks and ties. "Like this, see?"

No, actually, I don't. Could she be pregnant? I don't see why any woman would wear these things otherwise. "Wonderful." I take my eyes to her face. Her beautiful, smiling face. *She could be pregnant.* I inhale, shaking my head at myself and the craziness. "Do you want them?"

"I'm paying," she says adamantly as she removes them.

I sigh, ignoring her and facing the hippy. "How much for the oversized trousers?"

"Just a tenner, my friend."

"Is that it?" I ask, ignoring Ava's protests. All that material, just a tenner? I shrug and slap a note in his outstretched hand, and he thanks me as I claim Ava and get us on our way.

"You didn't have to trample the poor man. And I wanted to pay for the pants."

"Shut up," I order gently, getting her close, distracting her from her grievance with a few kisses to her head.

"You're impossible."

I smile. *So* deluded. "You're beautiful," I counter. "Can I take you home now?"

"Yes," she answers without hesitation, and I smile but fold on the inside. The day is nearly over. My clock is ticking, and I've not even thought about where I might start when I sit her down at

Lusso. I should start with Jake, because, really, that's where the story that is my fucked-up, sad life begins.

My thoughts are interrupted by music, and I notice we're approaching the entrance to a renowned alternative store. Ava's pace slows. She's curious. And so am I. I know what's within these walls—I'm not curious about that, but her reaction to it?

"You want to see?" I ask, and she glances up.

"I thought you wanted to go home."

I do. I don't. "We can have a quick look." I divert us and lead her down the stairs into the darkness. The music is brutal, a stark contrast to the evocative, sexy tracks that play in the communal room at The Manor. I watch Ava with interest as she wanders aimlessly through the glowing space, her eyes high and low, hands reaching out and touching the clothing. She skims her fingers over some rare pieces.

"It's not lace, is it?" I ask quietly.

"Lace, it's not. Do people wear this stuff?"

I chuckle at her wonder and indicate a crowd of hardcore clubbers passing by. But, really, all this stuff that's got Ava's mouth hanging open is tame. I look past her as she walks on, seeing she's mindlessly heading toward the adult department. I'm too curious to stop her. She takes the steps, oblivious, and the moment she realizes what's surrounding her, she stops still.

I restrain my smile as I take it all in too, the dancers, the cabinets loaded with toys, the music booming. It's nothing like The Manor.

Ava looks up at me, and her face is a picture of astonishment that she's trying so hard to hide. "Shocked?" I ask.

"Ish."

I laugh inside. That was a big *ish*. But I need her to know, this isn't my idea of sexy. "It's a bit over the top, isn't it?" I take her hand and lead her to a cabinet.

"Wow," she gasps, and I smile at the huge dildo that has her attention, dipping to her ear.

"Don't get excited. You don't need one of those."

"I don't know," she muses. "It looks like it could be fun."

I bolt upright. No. I am *not* being sacrificed for a toy. "Ava, I'll die before you use one of those." I say it as it is, shuddering at the thought of something else, whether it be a man, woman, or a toy, giving her pleasure. That's my job, and I take it very seriously, especially since she's always so flexible during the throes of our passion. "I'm not sharing you with anyone or anything, even battery-operated devices."

She bursts into laughter, and the sound is heaven.

"I might stretch to some handcuffs, though," I say thoughtfully, and she smiles. Ava cuffed to my bed? It would be amazing.

"This doesn't turn you on, does it?" she says, finally asking what she's been desperate to ask since I let her stumble in here.

I take her in my hold and get us moving. "There's only one thing in this world that turns me on," I whisper into her hair. "And I love her in lace."

Love. I *love* her in lace. I *love* her in my bed. I *love* her full stop. Did she hear that?

"Take me home," she says, looking at me with aching eyes.

I kiss her, simply because I can't *not* kiss her. "Are you making demands?"

"Yes. You've not been inside me for too long. It's not acceptable."

Jesus, those words. Make love to her. Take her to paradise. Then talk to her.

"You're right; it's not acceptable." All of this is not acceptable. She needs the truth. She needs to know the real me. I hug her into my side and walk us back to the car, showering her head with kisses.

I'm no longer a man I recognize.

What I can't fathom is whether that's a good thing or not.

33

I'M AWASH WITH PURPOSE, although it's purpose of another kind. My plan has been shattered. All I can think about is getting her into my bed. Getting her under me. Worshipping every inch of her and more. My confessions are forgotten, my urgency growing the closer we get to the penthouse. She's fidgety. Flushed. Begging for me.

I'm about to blow her world apart. Sate her need. I don't think my heart has ever pounded so hard.

By the time we're in the elevator, I'm set to explode, and yet I don't get the chance to pounce. Ava beats me to it, pushing into my chest, catching me off guard. I stagger, my back slamming into the wall, and she's on me, her mouth and hands everywhere, leading the way. And, of course, I'm with her, my fingers gripping her neck, securing her, my mouth working hers with equal energy. It's crazy, clumsy passion, desperation embodied. This. I've never had this before. It's empowering. It's terrifying. Empowering because it gives me hope. Terrifying because I've lost the only people I've ever loved this fiercely.

"The doors," I mumble jaggedly as her tongue swirls and stabs with mine, her hands holding my face, her whimpers and moans endless. I push my back from the wall and start moving blindly forward, as Ava steps back, unwilling to detach herself. I fumble and feel my way to the door, struggling to unlock it. "Easy," I say, pushing at the handle. The door releases, and we fall over the threshold, a chaotic mess of bodies. It'll take too long to get upstairs at this rate, so I pick her up, win back some control, and walk us to the kitchen.

Music. I need music. I find the control and flick on the system, then make fast work of getting her to my bedroom as Placebo's *Running up that Hill* gradually builds.

"I want you in bed." But I also need to slow this down before it's over too quickly. I kick the bedroom door open, set her down by the bed, and instruct her to turn around. She slowly pivots, giving me her back. I reach forward, my hands shaking terribly, and start to unfasten the buttons on the back of her dress. "Please tell me you have lace on. I need you in lace." She doesn't have a chance to confirm. Her dress hits the floor, and my heart joins it. Jesus. I can only stare, mesmerized, as she returns to face me. My eyes fixed on her boobs, I extend a hand and pull one cup down, stroking across her nipple with the back of my hand. Her body concaves, like she's trying to escape my touch. Or more, struggling to deal with the contact. I remove my T-shirt and toss it aside, and her eyes fall onto my chest, her wonder obvious. It's somewhere close to mine.

"Have you had a nice day?" I dip and remove my shoes.

"I've had a lovely day." Her voice is pure hunger, her eyes pure awe.

"Me too." I swallow, kicking aside my conscience, which is currently reminding me of the vows I made. "Shall we make it even better?"

"Yes," she whispers, not moving, waiting for me to claim her.

"Come here," I order gently. She's pushed up against me in a heartbeat, her hands stroking my chest, looking at me with so much fucking love. It's love. Can't be anything else. She loves me.

I lift her, and her legs coil around my body, her touch moving to my head. My mouth finds hers again, except this time we both seem content to take it slowly, our moves, our kiss, matching the dull, slow beats of the music. I lower her to the bed and crowd her, settling her arms on the pillow before rising to my knees. And I watch her watching me, her eyes heavy, her gaze concentrated. *Say it. Tell her.* But what if she doesn't say it back? What if I'm completely mistaken? What if my instinct is playing tricks on me? What if it really was the alcohol talking for her that night? This uncertainty, the second-guessing, is driving me to distraction.

I extend a hand and roll my fingertip around her nipple, making her back bow subtly. "I could sit and watch you writhe under my touch all day." Watch her body respond so willingly. So naturally. "Stay where you are." I move down the bed, peeling her knickers off as I do, and her legs shift, exposing her entrance, her flesh glistening with her desire. I stand, swallow repeatedly, my eyes nailed just there as I remove my jeans and boxers. I bend, resting my weight on my fists, and crawl up her body, dragging my tongue across her pussy.

"Oh God, God, God!"

My greedy tongue dives into her, licking and lapping every inch I can reach, kissing her, sucking, making love to her with my mouth. I force my hand onto her hip, fighting to hold her still, her arse constantly leaving the mattress as she squirms. Lord, help me, I'm lost.

I send her wild, as well as myself, exploring her flesh like it's a new and wondrous thing. It kind of is. I've never paid much attention to pleasing a woman. Never cared much for leaving a lasting impression. I'm usually laced with alcohol, my mind foggy. With Ava, though, I get so much joy from hearing and seeing her desire. And for that, I need to be totally with it. Even if, technically, I'm far from with it. She fogs my mind in other ways. Distorts everything.

She's out of control under my ravenous tongue, throbbing violently. I can feel her release on the tip of my tongue, and it tastes out of this fucking world. I wince when she fists my hair, and she bellows to the ceiling, my hands now unable to hold her down, and I lock my lips around her and suck hard, easing off as I feel her body begin to soften. She's sweating and heaving. Seeing her like this, so crazed as she orgasms, so out of control, hits me hard in my cock. I could come right now.

I hum, licking her gently. "I can feel you throbbing against my tongue, baby." I nibble and kiss my way from her inner thighs to her mouth and spread her release across her lips, gazing at her in amazement, my dick like steel. She must see it in my eyes. The adoration. The conflict. She curls herself around me on a long exhale and holds me close, accepting my heavy weight upon her.

"You make me so crazy mad, lady," I whisper, flexing my hips and driving deep. I choke on the pleasure, my heart twisting, words falling from my mouth. "Please don't do that again." I lift her leg over my shoulder, wedging my fists into the mattress and raising my upper body, needing to see all of her.

"I'm sorry," she murmurs, but I can tell she really doesn't know what she's apologizing for. And, really, neither do I. The dress? The drink? For not hearing me when I tell her I love her? Who the fuck knows?

"Ava, everything I do, I do to keep you safe and to keep my sanity." The words are coming, instinct guiding me. "Please listen to me." I withdraw and sink carefully into her, and we both lose our breath.

"I will."

"I need you," I whisper, my eyes refusing to leave hers, begging her to understand me, pleading for mercy on my tortured soul. My throat clogs with warranted fear, my vision clouding. "I really need you, baby." My hips roll and thrust intermittently, keeping her on the edge.

She looks so confused by my words. "Why do you need me?"

"I just do." I'm a coward, talking in riddles, expecting her to understand me. "Please, don't ever leave me."

"Tell me."

"Just accept that I need you and kiss me." I grind hard and roll deep as she stares at me, bewildered. Caught between taking the pleasure or pressing me. I will her to take the pleasure. To ignore my cryptic words because I don't want this moment to end. Not ever. And yet I know I'm being unfair, asking her to agree to things without the full picture. "Ava, kiss me."

Her hands find my face, her mouth finds my lips, and with that submission, I increase my pace, so badly needing the release of pressure. She's already on the cusp of explosion again.

"Not yet, baby." I have to be there with her, because there is no greater pleasure than coming with Ava, our climaxes combining and our sounds blending. "Together," I command, and she nods, unable to speak, letting me control the pace and the rhythm. Fuck me, I can feel my dick expanding by the second, the friction growing, my blood burning. "Nearly there, baby." This is going to knock me out.

"Jesse!"

"Hold on," I whisper, sounding composed but feeling anything but. "Just hold on." I slip free of her and plunge back inside, hissing, "Now, Ava."

She stiffens under me, her kiss becoming firm, and my orgasm strikes hard, shredding me as she moans, accepting every drop of me, her mouth becoming lax, her kiss taking a different direction. Not firm but soft. Not frantic but calm.

And then I feel dampness meet my cheeks, making me withdraw abruptly. She's crying. "What's the matter?" I ask, slowing my drives.

"Nothing." She shakes her head, and I look at her in question, one part of me willing her to share, another part uncertain whether I want her to. "What is this?" she asks.

"What's what?" *What am I, stupid?*

"I mean me and you."

Her need for reassurance endears me. "This is just you and me," I say, when what I should actually do is seize this unexpected opportunity and spill. And yet, I don't. "Are you okay?" I ask, kissing her in apology.

"Fine," she snaps, and I recoil in surprise as she starts trying to squirm her way free from under me. Fine? She looks far from fine to me. I draw breath to push her, but clarity seems to hit me like a boulder to the face. She does. She really does love me.

"I need a wee," she grumbles.

She seers my skin with pure fury in her eyes. She's angry. Angry with herself because she's having the same hard time trying to explain her feelings. So, like me, she does it in another way. She expresses them through our connection and chemistry. We do our talking in a different way, and while it's amazing, it's also leaving room for gray space. It's time to fix that. But how? Beat it out of her? Or perhaps I can lead the way. Set the pace.

I pull my eyes from hers, slowly slipping free of her and letting her escape. She's gone like a shot, hurrying to the bathroom, yanking off her bra as she goes. We're both going crazy.

"Fuck," I hiss, getting up and pacing to the bathroom with purpose. I bowl in without knocking, finding her in front of the vanity unit. She looks up at the mirror and her eyes fix to mine as I approach her carefully and meld my front to her back. I rest my chin on her shoulder, regarding her as she regards me.

"I thought we made friends," I say quietly, breaking her in gently, bringing her around carefully rather than demanding a confession.

"We did."

"Then why are you sulking?"

"I'm not sulking," she protests, and I exhale my frustration, giving her a roll of my hips. If I have to, I'll fuck it out of her. She's always more agreeable when my dick is inside her.

"Ava," I breathe tiredly, "you're the most frustrating woman I've ever met." And I must be the most perverse arsehole. I suck on her neck, and she stills. It's time to talk and kicking things off with her confessing her love will pave the way. "Are you holding out on me for a reason, lady?"

"No," she replies huskily, making me smile into her flesh. She has no reason. I, however, do. Which makes this fair game. I slide my hand down her front and start massaging her, studying her in the mirror. Her head rolls back invitingly, and I take full advantage, licking a blazing trail to the bottom of her ear. "You want it again?"

"I need you," she admits.

"Baby, those words make me so happy." It's close, but I want more. "Always?"

"Always."

My cock reloads as a result of her admission. Fuck knows what'll happen when she finally confesses her love. I'll be permanently hard, so let's see if I really can fuck it out of her. "Fuck, I need to be inside you." I step back, bend her over, and smash into her like I haven't just had her, giving her no time to brace herself or prepare.

"Oh, shit, Jesse!"

"Watch . . ." *Bang.* ". . . your . . ." *Bang.* ". . . mouth!" Frustration fuels me, my hips like pistons. She's helpless to my merciless attack. "Look at me," I bark, slamming forward brutally. Her heavy eyes find me, her body soaking up the power of my hits perfectly.

"You'll never hold out on me, will you, Ava?"

"No," she screams.

"Because you're never leaving me, are you?"

"Where the fuck am I going?" she yells, going red in the face, but it's not from desire. It's frustration.

"Mouth!" I roar, flexing my fingers in her hips, feeling them going numb from the power of my grip. "Say it, Ava," I demand through gritted teeth.

"Oh God!" Her body folds, her orgasm hitting hard, and the sight of her so enraptured catapults me onto cloud nine with her.

"Jesus!" I bark, coming so fucking hard, my legs give and I collapse to the floor, Ava tumbling down with me.

Our labored breathing is loud and chaotic. My pulse booming. My chest heaving. "I'm fu—" She just catches her tongue.

I'm out of breath, unable to speak, so I feel around blindly for her hip and squeeze, making her yelp. "You didn't say it," I gasp. Then I'm hugging her. Hugging her as hard as I just climaxed.

"What?" she questions. "That I won't leave you? I won't leave you. Happy?"

"Yes, I am, but that's not what I meant." My teeth sink into my lip, chewing madly as I wait for her to reply.

"What did you mean?"

Oh, for the love of God. It's like trying to get blood out of a fucking stone. "Never mind," I sigh, too tired to battle with her. What the hell will it take? "Want to go again?"

She chokes, and I laugh to myself.

"Absolutely," she says. "I can't get enough of you."

"I'm glad," I reply. "I feel exactly the same, but my heart has been through enough in the last twenty-four hours, what with your defiance and lack of obedience. I don't know how much more it can take."

"It must be your age," she murmurs sarcastically.

"Hey, lady." I move fast, getting her face down on the floor, gnawing at her ear. "My age has nothing to do with it." I squeeze her hip, and she squeaks. "It's you."

"No." She laughs, bucking like a donkey. "Okay, I give in!"

I laugh hysterically on the inside. Wouldn't that be nice? "I wish you fucking would." I free her and get up.

"Old man."

Oh, too far, Ava. I grab her and thrust her against the wall. Old? "I prefer god." I tackle her mouth with the force of a man who most definitely isn't old. "I really can't get enough of you, lady," I say, splashing her face with kisses. "You're my ultimate temptress." And my complete and utter obsession. "Are you hungry?"

"Yes."

"Good."

She grins at me, and I grin right back. "I've fucked you, and now I'm going to feed you." *And then talk to you, I promise.* It seems that if I wait for her love confession, I'll be waiting a long fucking time.

I leave her in the bedroom with instructions to wear lace and meet me in the kitchen, before heading downstairs. I open the fridge. "Well, that didn't go exactly as I planned," I say to the peanut butter.

"I can't find my stuff."

I look back at the door. She's in a towel.

"I'll take naked." I grab my jar and wander casually on over, my greedy eyes starting at her feet and dragging all the way to her face. "Cathy's off and the fridge is empty. I'll order in. What do you fancy?"

"You," she quips around a cheeky smirk.

I pull the towel from her body and pout at the naked flesh before me. "Your god needs to feed his temptress. The rest of your stuff is in that dirty, great big wooden trunk that you had dumped in my bedroom. What do you want to eat?"

"I'm easy."

"I know, but what do you want to eat?"

"I'm only easy with you."

"You fucking better be," I say, almost laughing. "Now, tell me, what do you want to eat?"

"I like anything. You choose. What time is it, anyway?"

"Seven. Go and take a shower before I abandon dinner and take you again." I send her on her way with a slap on her arse, and she jumps a little as she goes. The sight is too good to give up, so I follow her, unscrewing the cap of my peanut butter, resting my shoulder on the doorframe as she takes the stairs slowly. I should be pissed off with myself for diverting so spectacularly from my plan. But . . .

She's still here.

She looks over her shoulder when she reaches the top. Smiles. Blows me a kiss. And I fall harder.

They say it's better to have loved and lost than to never have loved at all. I call bullshit. To love and lose is hell. I wouldn't know what it's like to love and keep forever.

But I pray I'm about to find out.

34

AFTER CALLING the local Chinese takeaway and ordering, I wipe the worktops down and go to the fridge for some water. I frown at the empty shelves, empty except for bottles of water and jars of my vice. I need Cathy back. My washing is piling up, the cupboards are bare, and the dishwasher is beginning to scream in protest for being so full. Speaking of which . . . I head for the machine and pull open the door, scanning the control panel. Simple, she said. I wrack my brain for the instructions she gave me. They're lost. Buried by other thoughts. I hit a few buttons. "Add rinse aid?" I say to myself, frowning. The screen flashes again. "Salt? You put salt in the dishwasher?"

Giving up on trying to figure out the dishwasher—there's too much else to figure out—I shut the door and go back to the fridge, reaching in for my peanut butter and quickly retracting. "No," I say to myself. "You'll ruin your appetite." Hunger is a rarity, my appetite constantly suppressed by other things. I'm quite enjoying being starving, and not just for food.

I hear the phone chime and head for the door, answering to the concierge. "On my way," I say, slipping out to go collect our dinner. The smell of good food smacks me in the face when the elevator doors slide open, and I spy a bag sitting on the desk. The concierge is pouting at it.

"Hungry?" I ask as I stride toward him, a small smile on my face. I claim the bag, and my eyebrows shoot up when I hear the distinct sound of a stomach rumbling. "Was that yours or mine?" I ask, glancing at my midriff.

Clive shakes his head and massages his tummy. "I've not eaten since breakfast," he moans. "How's Ava?"

"Sober," I grunt, reaching into the bag and pulling out a prawn cracker. "Here. That'll keep you going until you knock off." I place it on his desk and stroll off, getting back in the elevator. The doors begin to close, I glance up, and an odd shiver glides down my spine.

Someone is standing outside the glass door of Lusso, staring in, and I squint, trying to focus, but the reflections on the glass are hampering my view. Then the doors meet in the middle, and I quickly reach for the buttons and start stabbing at them, my stomach not now churning with hunger, but churning with something else. I can't put my finger on it. The doors begin to open again, and I squeeze out of the gap as soon as it's wide enough, my eyes scanning beyond the doors. There's no one now. But there was someone. Someone I rec—

"Mr. Ward?" Clive says.

I blink my burning eyes and look at him.

"Everything okay?"

I march past, my strides long and determined, my eyes back on the entrance, and when I reach the doors, I push my way outside, searching every nook and cranny of the car park. Nothing. Another nasty chill ripples through me. "No," I say, laughing under my breath, reaching for my throat and massaging the ball of anxiety away. She's locked up somewhere far away from here. Fuck, I need to screw my head back on straight. I rub at my forehead, reversing my steps back into the foyer, my eyes still darting the car park outside, until I turn and head back to the elevator. I look over my shoulder, frowning.

"Mr. Ward?" Clive says again as I pass his desk, his eyes wary.

I return my attention forward. "Thought I saw someone," I say quietly, getting in the elevator and shaking off my paranoia as I'm carried back to the penthouse. I really am going crazy.

I close the door, lock it, and lean against the wood, looking up to the top of the stairs. I can hear her. Smell her. Home.

In the kitchen, I scratch around for two clean plates, then proceed to load Ava's with a bit of everything, piling it up high, smiling, thinking we've both worked up quite an appetite today. Takeaway. My favorite girl. If only she'd have relented and said the words I need to hear, today could have been the best day of my life. I pause, thinking, as I lick some sauce off my thumb. The person outside the doors of Lusso was a woman. There one second, gone the next. I should have the cameras che…

No, I'm being completely irrational.

Ava. Where's Ava?

I grab some cutlery and am just about to go get her when I hear movement from the door. As ever, I'm rendered incapable of anything when she's before me. And now, drowning in my shirt, her hair a sexed-up mess, her face free from makeup, and her long legs bare, I'm suddenly not hungry for food anymore. "I was just coming to find you." I spend a good, pleasurable while drinking her in. "I like your shirt."

She looks down coyly, like putting that shirt on wasn't tactical. She knew exactly what she was doing. Killing me softly. "Kate didn't pack any slobby clothes."

I smile on the inside. That's because Kate didn't pack her clothes at all. "She didn't?" I ask as I finish serving up, ignoring her look that tells me she's onto me. And yet she doesn't challenge me. Doesn't scold me for performing a ramraid on her bedroom. "Where do you want to eat?"

"I'm e . . ." She fades off, and I grin like an idiot.

"Only for me, yes?" I ask, and she rolls her eyes. It's quite ironic. She's not exactly easy unless I have my hands all over her. I collect the plates and water. "We'll slum it on the sofa." We head into the lounge and I let her settle, her legs tucked under her arse, the shirt riding up her thighs. Lord, those thighs. Wrapped around my waist. *Feed her.* I hand over her plate and relish in the deep inhale she takes as I find the remote for the TV and open the doors to reveal the gigantic flat-screen.

"Do you want to watch television, or would you prefer music and conversation?" I ask, watching her shoveling some noodles into her mouth. She freezes, and I smile as she swallows, ridding her mouth of the obstruction to speech.

"I'll take music and conversation, please."

Stupid me. I shouldn't have asked. I should have put on the TV and settled down, not giving her the option to question me. Because that's what's going to happen. Questions. I look across to her, finding she's back to shoveling food into her mouth, ravenous.

"Good?" I ask.

"Very. You don't cook?"

"I don't."

She doesn't even remove her fork to smile. "Why, Mr. Ward," she coos, and I know something snarky is coming, "is that something you *don't* do well?"

Yes, as well as being honest, apparently. "I can't be amazing at everything," I say mindlessly, gazing directly at her, hoping my pros outweigh my cons.

"Your housekeeper cooks for you?"

"If I ask her to, but most of the time I eat at The Manor."

She nods, thoughtful, her mind evidently spinning. Here they come. The questions. "How old are you?"

I still, thinking, being presented yet again with the perfect opportunity to feed her curiosity. "Thirty," I say quietly, tagging an "ish" on the end.

"Ish."

"Yes." I match her small smile. "Ish."

She shakes her head mildly, only slightly exasperated, and goes back to eating, slowly working her way through the plate. My mind reels as I study her thoughtful state, wondering what's running through that pretty head.

"Ava?"

She jumps, startled out of her daydreaming. "Yes?"

"Dreaming?"

"Sorry, I was miles away." She sets her fork down, and I free her hands of the plate, putting it on the table with mine.

"You were. Where were you?" There's way too much space between us, so I reach for her and drag her to my end of the couch, tucking her neatly into me.

"Nowhere," she whispers, getting comfortable. Her weight on me feels somehow like a protective shield. We're in our bubble again. And once again, I can't comprehend the thought of popping it.

I sink my fingers into her hair and run them to the ends, twiddling with a glossy lock. "I love having you here."

"I love being here too." Her fingertip meets the silver edge of my scar and draws a line from one end to the other.

I watch her trace the jagged mark, her pretty nail looking so perfect against the ugly, imperfect mark. "Good," I whisper. "So you'll stay?"

"Yes." She swallows. "Tell me how you got this."

It's an effort not to shut her down with a straight *no*. And yet another opportunity passes me by. Or, more accurately, I run away from it, taking her hand and squeezing, my scar tingling terribly. "Ava," I say softly. "I really don't like talking about it." I feel her tense, and I know I've just increased her curiosity tenfold.

"I'm sorry," she murmurs quietly.

I curse myself and kiss her hand. She's sorry. She shouldn't be. She's making everything better. "Please, don't be. It's not something that's important to the here and now." My mouth is talking, words coming, all wrong words. "Dragging up my past serves no purpose other than to remind me of it."

"What did you mean when you said that things are easier to bear when I'm here?" she asks, lifting her head from my chest to get me in her sights. I can't bear the sympathy on her face. She could never comprehend the level of darkness I'm trying to leave behind. Trying to escape. And desperately trying not to poison her with.

She's waiting patiently for me to answer, but I can't, and my inability to spit out the words makes me so fucking angry with myself. "It means I like having you around," I say sharply, pushing her back into my chest and letting my head fall back.

She sweetly rests her lips on my flesh and pain sears me. Pain for her. And if she hurts, I'll hurt. This is a lose-lose situation.

For both of us.

35

AN HOUR LATER, she's asleep in my arms, breathing consistently and calmly. Her blissful oblivion is a stark contrast to the panic within me. I'm welded to the couch, unable to move, and I've been staring at the same spot on the ceiling for so long my eyes are dry. I'm certain if I could bring myself to peek at the woman in my arms, I'd find a blemish on her thigh where I've been stroking in circles for the past hour.

She stirs, murmurs some sleepy, quiet words, and I finally rip my stare from the ceiling, my chin pushing into my chest to see her face. The peace I find slices another piece off my heart. I'm content with her here in my arms, and yet in complete turmoil. And she has no idea.

I start to negotiate her in my hold, rising to my feet with her cradled against my chest. Her hold tightens. She snuggles deeper. "I love you," I whisper, my jaw clenched as I convince my feet to move, walking to the stairs. If I tell her enough, will it seep into her mind? Will she ever know?

"I love you too," she murmurs, and I halt, caught between shock and elation. But when I find her sound asleep, unconscious, sadness snuffs my joy. Will either of us ever find a way to speak those words to each other when we're *both* awake and aware? She's as scared as I am. How can we both be brave?

I carry her to my room and lay her delicately down, stripping her out of my shirt. Crawling in behind her, I curl every inch of me around her body, banishing all space between us. Her warm skin, the smell of her hair, the sound of her gentle breaths. It's like a sleeping pill, and I doze off dreaming of my happily ever after.

"Hey, baby girl." I drop to my haunches and open my arms, my heart swelling as her little legs run toward me. Her smiling face is like sunshine and rainbows, and one look at it rights all of my wrongs.

"Daddy!" Rosie dives at me, and I catch her, her little butt sitting just right on my forearm.

I rise and plant a kiss on her cheek. "I've missed you." It's been a matter of days, but each day feels like a week going without her. Lauren's mother approaches, her usual look of disdain firmly in place, a little pink backpack hanging from a finger. She extends her arm, passing it to me without having to get too close. The animosity is rife and yet, thank God, Rosie is oblivious to the daggers firing this way.

"Thanks," I say, accepting and swinging it onto my shoulder. As always, there are no pleasantries. No "hello" or "how are you?" Collecting my daughter is almost like a business transaction. A handover. I don't hang around. Focusing on Rosie in my arms, who's currently playing with my earlobe as she sucks her thumb, I find the smile that's so easy to locate when we're together. "You want to go to the park and feed the ducks?"

"Quack," she mumbles around her thumb, and I laugh, sinking my face into her neck as I walk us back to Carmichael's

car. When she spots Rebecca in the back, she nearly springs right from my arms. "Becca!" she sings, prompting Carmichael's daughter to start jigging in her car seat. The moment I drop Rosie into her own seat, the girls' hands join, and that's how they'll stay the entire journey back to The Manor while they have a little toddler chat about who the heck knows what. I secure her straps and kiss her cheek. "Get that thumb out of your mouth," I say, and her little nose wrinkles. It's so cute, it chokes me up.

"No."

"Stubborn," I counter, puckering my lips. She grins and lands a sloppy kiss on my lips. "Thank you."

Rebecca soon steals her attention, flashing her newest doll. Rosie's eyes widen in awe, and I reach down and pull up the bag from the car floor. Her squeal of delight pierces my eardrums, and I see Carmichael in my side vision covering his ears.

"What do you say?" I ask as she makes grabby hands, the straps of her car seat preventing her from reaching.

"Tank you, tank you."

"Welcome, baby." I relinquish the doll and shut the door on her hugging it fiercely. I have one foot in the car when Lauren's mother approaches, and for reasons I may never know, I freeze, when I should undoubtedly be getting in the car before I get caught up in something ugly.

"Get in, Jesse," Carmichael says, starting the engine.

But I'm curious. Too curious. Lauren's mother hasn't uttered a single word to me on any occasion since I won access to my daughter. Though her looks speak a thousand words that I'm certain I don't want to hear.

"I suppose you're taking her back to that whorehouse," she says, casting an evil look Carmichael's way.

I don't bother defending The Manor. Telling her it's not a whorehouse serves no purpose. "I have private space there. It's temporary until I find an apartment. Rosie doesn't leave my sight."

"You're a disgrace," she spits, and I frown, wondering where this hostility is coming from all of a sudden. I know she thinks it, but she never speaks her mind. "What kind of father are you?"

"A father who wants to see my daughter."

"Jesse," Carmichael calls, leaning across the car, jerking his head for me to get in.

"I'm many things," I say, fighting to keep my temper. "But I am not a bad father." Rosie is my only accomplishment. The only thing I have to be proud of. I will not let this bitter woman take that away from me.

I get in the car before I subject myself to more vicious words. "Let's go," I say, and my uncle is quick to pull away. I rest my elbow on the window, hearing the girls in the back chattering.

"Don't let them get to you," Carmichael says, giving my thigh a reassuring pat. "You're a good dad, boy."

I strain a smile and glance back at Rosie. She's not interested in me right now, and that's fine. She doesn't even know I'm here. But I'll always be here.

My body catapults upward, and I gasp for air, drenched, the sheets sticking to me. It takes me a few panicked moments to get my bearings. I feel like I'm suffocating.

Ava.

I turn my head, noting her sprawled beautifully on her back, and I gasp, suddenly finding the air I need. My heart seems to kick start, the beats dull but consistent. "Shit," I breathe, scrubbing my hands roughly down my cheeks and falling to my back. I let my eyes close again, feeling groggy and dozy, but my darkness is a picture show of everything I can't handle. Faces from my past. Hurt I can't escape.

I get up quickly and pull on some shorts, heading for the gym to run off the anxiety. I don't build up from a jog to a sprint. That's not going to work this morning. I need to shock my body out of these shakes, so I crank up the machine to full-whack and flick on the TV, watching the sport updates coming in. My legs work like pistons, and I zone out, clearing my head, working my heart rate up to a dangerous level.

Ten miles.

I reach down and smack the plus button, running on, and ten minutes later, I can't feel my legs, but my lungs are ready to explode from the strain. All I can focus on is catching a breath. It's where I need to be.

I keep going, my tormented mind draining, my thoughts dispersing, until all I can think about is how fucking beat I am. I hit the decrease button and rest my hands on the bars, my head dropping as I watch beads of sweat hit the treadmill. I slow to a stop, grab a towel and wipe my forehead, looking over my shoulder to the glass doors.

I blink, and it's as if that small movement clears the obstruction to see clearly. Just for a moment, though. Like wipers working fast across a windscreen, ridding the glass of violent rain briefly before more rain comes and distorts everything again. This thunderstorm will never cease. Not until I physically stop it.

I drop the towel and head upstairs to Ava, finding determination in each stride. No more stalling. No more hiding. Tell her how you feel and tell her who you are. I can't go on like this, caught in a mixing pot of happiness and dread, my sanity dictated by which direction the spoon stirs.

I enter the bedroom, my mouth loaded with words, my intention set . . .

And find the bed empty. No Ava. Panic joins my nerves, and I turn on the spot, sensing the emptiness of the room without her in it.

"Ava," I yell, checking the bathroom. No Ava. I run out of my room, checking every bedroom as I pass, swinging open doors, scanning the space, my dread multiplying with each room I find empty. "Ava?" I take the stairs fast, looking out onto the terrace. Black clouds linger in the distance, a storm on the way.

I fly into the kitchen at breakneck speed.

And I see her, just before I nearly crash into her. "Fucking hell, there you are." *Relief.* I seize her and hold on to her like my life depends on it. "You weren't in bed."

"I'm in the kitchen," she murmurs, sounding as thrown as she deserves to be. My heart instantly settles, but I can't bring myself to release her. Just hold her, and never let her go. "I saw you running," she goes on. "I didn't want to disturb you."

I feel her writhe in my hold, fighting to break free. I must be hurting her, and that's the only reason I relent, placing her down gently to take her in, to reassure myself she's actually here. "I was just in the kitchen," she says, dazed.

She was just in the kitchen. She hadn't left.

I collect her and sit her on the worktop, getting as close as I can. I'm worrying her. "Sleep well?" I ask, trying to ease her and settle myself.

"Great." Her head tilts, and she studies me with a curiosity I'm not comfortable with. "Are you okay?"

I search for the words I found in the gym and on the way to the bedroom only moments ago. No words. I'm blank. So, at a loss, I smile, and she blinks, her confusion multiplying. "I woke up with you in my bed wearing lace." *Though I was in no fit state to appreciate it.* "It's ten thirty on a Sunday morning and you're in my kitchen"—I force my eyes down her front—"wearing lace. I'm amazing." *And so fucking torn.*

Her smile is demure. "You are?"

"Oh, I am." I kiss her. Try to relocate some fortitude. Restock on bravery. "You're too beautiful, lady."

"So are you."

I gaze at her longingly and push a strand of hair away from her cheek. "Kiss me." She needs to feed me with some strength because I need it. And so will she.

Her lips on mine are life, and I lose myself in her adoring kiss, happy to follow her lead. Slow. She wants it slow and loving. It's the most peaceful kiss we've shared, which is ironic in this moment, when I'm feeling a heightened sense of panic.

My phone rings, and I curse the caller to hell, feeling on the worktop, unprepared to end this exquisite kiss. "Oh, go away," I mutter into her mouth, staring at John's name on the screen over Ava's shoulder. "Baby, I've got to take this." I tear my mouth from hers but remain with my hips cradled between her legs. "What's up, John?"

"Mike's here," he says, sounding pissed off.

Fuck. "What's he doing there?" I watch as Ava watches me, her curiosity back. I kiss her frown away.

"He wants to talk. Sort it out with you. He's calm." John clears his throat, and I hear a door close in the background. "But I'll send him away if that's what you want."

Is this an opportunity I shouldn't miss? The Manor is quiet on a Sunday morning. I'll take Ava with me. Let her eat breakfast while I talk to Mike and then show her upstairs. Show her that it is nothing like she will imagine. "No, I'll be there," I say quietly.

"You sure?"

"Yes."

"Good. It's about time this was sorted out like men."

"See you in a bit." I end the call and get on with sorting my fucking life out. "I need to go to The Manor," I tell her. "You'll come." *Ask, you dick, don't demand.*

"No," she blurts, looking horrified.

"But I want you to come."

Her eyes dart around the kitchen. She looks stressed. "You'll be working. You do what you need to do, and I'll see you afterward."

She's missing the point completely, which shouldn't be a surprise since she doesn't know what the fucking point is. "No, you'll come." She *has* to come. It's time. This half-life ends today.

Ava moves to escape, and I instinctively lock her down. "I'm not coming."

"Why?"

"Just because," she shouts.

I have no idea why she's being so obstructive, but I'm sane enough to realize that putting my foot down right now won't help.

It's time to beg. Plead. "Please, Ava," I say, giving her beseeching eyes. "Will you just do what you're told?" *Just for once, please?*

"No!"

I close my eyes and count to ten to keep my temper in check. "Ava, why do you insist on making things more difficult?"

"I make things more difficult?"

I'm trying to fucking help. To enlighten her. Prepare to give her information she desperately wants. "Yes, you do," I grate, my voice shaking with my building frustration. "I'm trying really hard here."

She snorts. It's an insult. "Trying hard to do what?" she asks, genuinely interested in what my answer might be. "Send me crazy? It's working." She knocks me out of the way, and knowing she'll fight me if I resist, I let her go, unwilling to get caught up in a physical tangle as well as a verbal one.

I sigh. "Well, this is going well," I mutter, going after her, accepting I have only one choice here if I want the outcome I'm wishing for. Let her win.

"Okay," I call to her back, catching up with her. "You'll wait here. I'll be as quick as I can." I'll sort out the shit with Mike, mark it off my list of things to do, and then deal with Ava. Hopefully by the time I'm back, she'll have calmed the fuck down and be acting more reasonably.

"I'll go home." She disappears into the bathroom, slamming the door behind her, and I, as a result, slam my palm to my forehead.

"For Christ's sake." I don't go in after her—I don't need this to escalate further, but she's not leaving this penthouse. Not until we sort this out.

I drop my arse to the bed and try to rub away the building headache, dialing Kate. "Hey, big man," she says, sounding wary. "Everything okay?"

"Not really. I could do with your help."

"What for?"

"I need to go out and Ava is threatening to leave. I need her to stay here."

"Why?"

"Can you ask questions later?"

"What's going on?"

"Kate," I say over a sigh. "Please, would you just do me this favor and come over?"

There's a long pause, and I wait, hopeful that she'll relent and kill her curiosity for the time being. "Okay," she says slowly. "I'll head over now."

"Thank you. See you in a while." I cut the call and toss my phone on the bed, getting up and looking to the heavens for strength, for help, for anything to get me through today. Yesterday was perfect. Today feels like it's going to be anything *but* perfect.

The skin on my back tingles, and knowing what I'll find, I turn to face her. She looks uncertain. Worried. I pass her, feeling her eyes follow me to the bathroom. She's wondering where my fight is. I'm running out of fight.

My hands work fast, soaping the sweat away and rinsing, before brushing my teeth. I go to the walk-in wardrobe, ignoring her static form still standing in the middle of the bedroom where I left her ten minutes ago. I stare at the rails of clothes, thinking. I can't just leave with all this bad feeling hanging like a weight around my neck.

I back out and find her in the exact same spot, looking as apprehensive as I feel. "I need to go." I swallow, stopping myself from demanding she come again. "Kate's on her way over."

"Why?"

"So you don't leave." I return to my rails and pull down some jeans, glancing up when she appears at the door.

Her apprehension looks like it's converting into rage. "I'm going home," she says, and my back teeth clench dangerously as I yank a T-shirt on and stuff my feet into some Converse. *Don't react to her goading.* She passes me and starts yanking her clothes from the rails. It's a move meant to provoke me, and if she's not careful I might just react.

"What are you doing?" I ask calmly, removing her clothes from her arms. "You're not leaving."

"Yes, I am," she yells, snatching them back childishly. All this fucking drama over . . . what? She doesn't want to come to The Manor? Fine. I gave her what she fucking wanted, bowed to her insistence, despite my good intentions, and now this?

I snap, my patience shredded. "Put the fucking clothes back, Ava," I bellow, battling with her, playing tug-of-fucking-war with her clothes. Her strength is no match for mine, and I wrench everything from her and discard it, then lock down her flailing arms, hoofing her up, and carrying her deranged form into the bedroom.

"Calm the fuck down," I shout, pinning her to the bed and

seizing her jaw, forcing her to look at me. But true to her defiant
ways, she slams her eyes closed, shutting me out. God damn her. I
need her to see me—to see the desperation in my eyes. The hurt
because we're fighting. "Open your eyes, Ava."

"No."

"Open!" I bark.

"No!"

She's fucking impossible. "Fine." So she won't look at me,
but she will damn well hear me. "Listen to me, lady," I say,
locking down every muscle, making her struggles to break free
impossible. "You're not going anywhere. I've told you repeatedly,
so start fucking dealing with it. I'm going to The Manor, and
when I get back, we're going to sit down to talk about us." She
stills. I have her attention. "Cards on the table, Ava," I go on. "No
more fucking about, no more drunken confessions, and no more
holding out on me. Do you understand?"

Her eyes open slowly, and I see desperation to match mine.
She wants all of that too. "Come with me," I beg. "I need you
with me." Walking away from her now just doesn't feel like the
right thing to do.

"Why?"

"I just do. Why won't you come?"

"I don't feel comfortable."

With me? At The Manor? Is it Sarah? I need to know. "Why
don't you feel comfortable?"

"I just don't."

"Please, Ava."

"I'm not coming."

I inhale, willing myself to stop wasting my fucking time.
"Promise me you'll be here when I get home then," I say. "We
need to sort this shit out."

"I'll be here," she whispers, and I see with perfect clarity that
she's being honest with me.

"Thank you." Exhausted, I drop my head to hers and take a few moments of peace in our chaos. I then lift from the bed and walk out.

And still, even though she's promised not to leave, something doesn't feel right.

36

I LOOK up at my rearview mirror as I approach the gates to The Manor, frowning when I see Sam's Porsche in the distance, racing up behind me until his bumper is practically kissing the arse of my Aston. I hit the remote to open the gates and slow to a crawl as I rumble down the driveway, the trees lining the way perfectly still, not a leaf moving. It feels somehow eerie, leaving me with a sensation I've never felt before. Like I'm driving into an ambush.

I get out as Sam skids to a stop behind me, kicking up plumes of dust from the gravel. "What are you doing here?" I ask, concerned by his apparent urgency.

"Why haven't you answered your phone?"

"I didn't hear it," I say quietly, almost to myself. I think back on my journey from Lusso to The Manor. I can't remember a damn second of it. I feel unsettled. Completely out of sorts. It shouldn't be a shocker after my showdown with Ava.

This time tomorrow, I'll either be walking on air or drowning in the bottom of a bottle of vodka. My skin becomes clammy, my stomach knotting.

"What's going on?" Sam asks, approaching, his laid-back persona lost somewhere on the way here. "Kate dashed over to your place. Said something about watching Ava. What's wrong with her?"

I find my feet and take the steps up to the entrance. "We had a fight."

"About?" he asks, walking on my heels. "Did you tell her?"

"I wanted her to come, and she refused. I'd planned to tell her a few truths this weekend and everyone keeps shitting on my plan." I push the door open and take a moment to absorb the silence. And maybe to rein in my foul mood. I can't walk into this *meeting* with Mike feeling like this. It'll be a bloodbath. My patience is thin at best, and my need to get back to Ava to fix this shit is all I can think of.

"You were going to bring her here to tell her about this place?" Sam asks. "Why would you do that?"

"Because she can't run away from me here," I say without thought, the deepest corner of my mind giving us both the answer. We're in the middle of nowhere. She can't walk away.

"That's fucked up, Jesse," Sam says over a nervous laugh. "But regardless, she isn't here, so why the fuck are you?"

I head for my office, and Sam is in quick pursuit. "Mike's here. He wants to *talk,* and I need this problem to be gone once and for all." It'll be a tick off my endless list.

I stop at my office door and look back, finding Sam's stopped at the end of the corridor to my office. He thumbs over his shoulder. "I'll be in the bar. Drew's on his way."

Fuck me, it's like the mounting of troops. "You called the cavalry?" Of course he has. This Jesse is not the man they're used to dealing with.

He throws his hands skyward. "I didn't know what the fuck was going on."

I shake my head and push my way into my office. Talk, resolve this shit with Mike and Coral, then get the fuck out of here. I find Sarah at my desk and John pacing circles, guarding

Mike, who's looking a bit too comfortable on my couch. It riles me, and riling me now isn't wise for anyone. "So I'm here," I say, closing the door behind me. "Let's talk." I feel John's eyes burning through his wraparounds, focused on me, and Sarah's obviously tense, drumming her long red nails on my desk. I set my keys and phone down, eyeing her. "You okay?" I mouth, and she nods, but there's no denying she's stressed.

"You going to ask your skivvies to fuck off?" Mike asks, and I turn to find him throwing a gesturing hand John's way, not looking at him. I, however, do, and the big guy's chest is rolling dangerously, his phone turning in his hand repeatedly. Call me intuitive, but this doesn't feel like it's going to be the calm, grown-up discussion that John alluded to. I don't feel the air clearing. I feel it clouding more.

"I've got it," I say more calmly than I'm feeling. Like John, I already want to rip Mike a new arsehole. But this can't get messy. Sarah appears beside me, her hand resting on my arm. "Call me if you need anything."

"Thanks."

Mike sneers at John as he backs out of the room with Sarah. Everything about my oldest friend's persona tells me he doesn't want to leave. And he won't. He'll wait outside because that's John through and through. Protective. Loyal. My rock. I give him a nod, telling him I'm good. "I won't be long," I assure them both. I have a feeling this is a waste of my fucking time, and I have far more important things to be dealing with. John nods, closes the door, silent and brooding, and I redirect my attention to the prick making himself at home, leaning back on my couch.

He points to the cabinet. "Not going to offer me a drink?"

My jaw stiffens, and I cast my eyes across to the alcohol still holding court. "Want a drink?" I ask, strolling over. It's barely midday. He doesn't want a drink, but he'll have one.

"Vodka," he says, and I close my eyes, reaching for the bottle.

People say you can't smell vodka. It's bullshit. I unscrew the cap and pour, shutting off my sense of smell. "One cube of ice," he adds.

Opening the mini-fridge, I pull out one cube, dropping it into the glass. The disturbance of the liquid makes the smell waft up. "Here," I say, turning and walking across my office to him, my arm outstretched, keeping the devil's juice as far away as possible.

Mike smirks knowingly as he accepts. "Not joining me?"

I ignore him and sit on the couch opposite, fighting to keep my temper in check. "Talk," I order shortly.

"I hear you're dating."

I stare at him with every ounce of malice I feel. "I'm not here to talk about Ava." I can feel a threat coming, and I'm suddenly so fucking glad she refused to come. This isn't going to end well. My mood was already in the gutter. This arsehole is going to send it into the sewer.

"Ava," he muses, looking at his glass as he rolls his wrist, making the ice drag around the inside. Her name coming out of his mouth feels like nails down a chalkboard. "A little birdy told me she doesn't know about The Manor."

"A little birdy like who?" Who else am I going to decimate once I've seen to Mike?

He smiles. It's cunning as fuck. "People talk, Ward."

"Then people should learn to keep their mouths shut." I get up to restrain my increasingly tense muscles before I dive across the table and strangle the fucker. "You wanted to talk, Mike. So fucking talk."

"I want you to assure me my wife won't be coming back."

"Done," I say. "And while I'm at it, I'll revoke your membership too." I'm done with both of them.

He's off the couch in a heartbeat. "I'm keeping my membership."

"Wrong."

There's a kerfuffle outside my office, and the door flings open. Sam stands on the threshold taking in the scene, John hovering behind him. "Okay?" I ask.

"Ava's here," he pants, and I freeze. *The fuck?* How? "Jesse?" Sam says, poking me from my inertness. "Ava is here, man."

I snap to life, being assisted back to reality by the sound of Mike's cackling laugh. "Who let her in?" I ask, charging past Sam and John, running down the corridor. "Who the fuck let her through the gates?"

"Don't know," Sam says.

"Where is she?"

"In the bar."

But when I land in the bar, Ava is nowhere in sight, and I inhale, fearing the worst. I back out of the room slowly, casting my eyes up the curved staircase.

And I know.

I just fucking know.

Dread builds with every step I take, my pace gaining as I go, and when I reach the bottom of the staircase to the communal room, I peer up, seeing the doors open. Rosa appears, looking stricken with worry.

"I'm sorry, Mr. Ward," she mumbles as she rushes past my static form. I take in air and climb the stairs, feeling heavy and despondent, and when I breach the entrance, I find her standing stock-still in the center of the room, silent, gazing around. As if I need to remind myself what surrounds us, I look too. Ropes. Suspension grids. Every piece of bondage gear imaginable, and also some she probably could never imagine. She looks so wrong in here. So out of place, and for the first time in my adult life, I feel out of place too. I don't want to be in here.

"Fucking hell," she says quietly, and I swallow hard.

"Watch your mouth." It's all that comes to me. All I'm

capable of as I stand here staring at the back of the woman I love, wondering how many moments I have left in her presence. Any peace I've had will be taken away . . . because I'm gutless. This woman deserved truth, not omissions. *How can we possibly come back from this?*

She flies around fast, and the look on her face is like a knife to my heart. She doesn't speak, just stares at me as I stare back. I can see her mind spinning. She's going over every detail of her time with me, piecing it all together, bringing her to this reality. Bringing her to now.

Sam crashes into the room, and I look past him to find Kate looking awkward on the sidelines.

"Oh, fucking hell," he says over a sigh. *Yes, fucking hell.* "I thought I told you to stay put," he barks at Kate. "Damn you, woman."

"I think we need to go." Kate claims Sam and leaves us alone, her face grave.

"Thank you." I only just manage to push the words past my thick tongue, my body getting tighter by the second, tension mounting. Sam shakes his head at me, his expression also sombre. He doesn't need to tell me I've royally fucked this up.

My lip gets a punishing chew as I stand, frantically searching for a way forward. A way to a happy outcome. I take my eyes away from her, unable to face her shock. "Ava, why didn't you wait at home for me?" I ask.

"You wanted me to come." Her voice isn't raised, but it's on its way.

"Not like this."

"I sent you a text. I told you I was on my way."

"Ava, I haven't received a text from you."

"Where's your phone?" she asks, looking at my pockets. I'm about to feel at them myself, but I remember . . .

"It's in my office."

"Is this what you wanted to talk about?" she asks, and I look up at her, facing her. I see her swallow. I see her eyes awash with devastation. I've imagined—or dreaded—how this might play out, but her face now? Nothing could have prepared me for this. I'm at a loss. I want to go to her, hold her, make our problem disappear. Make her forget her reality and leave only space to feel how fucking good we are together.

"It was time you knew."

She balks. "No, it was time for me to know a long time ago, Jesse." Her body is starting to shake as it turns, and she takes in our surroundings again. "Fuck."

I flinch. It's a natural reaction. "Watch your mouth, Ava," I say gently.

She spins back around, glaring at me with something close to hatred in her eyes. It's a killer, even if I know she doesn't really hate me. She can't hate me. She can't love me one second and then hate me the next. "Don't you dare." She starts rubbing at her forehead, her eyes closed. "Fuck, fuck, fuck!"

Jesus, the language. It's unnecessary, and not even my fear in this moment can make me disregard it. "Watch—"

"Don't!" Her jaw tenses to a point it could snap. "Jesse, don't you dare tell me to watch my mouth. Look!" She indicates the room, a room I'm all too familiar with. And for the first time in my life, I wish I'd never stepped foot in here. In The Manor. My sanctuary is fast becoming my ruin.

"I see it, Ava."

"Why didn't you tell me?"

I only have the truth, and it's what she deserves. "I thought you would have grasped The Manor's operations on our first meeting, Ava," I say, my mind giving me a swift flashback of her face on our first encounter. The words she said to me that completely knocked me sideways, more than she already had with nothing but her beauty and clear inability to deal with my presence. *You have a lovely hotel.* "When it became obvious that you hadn't, it just got harder and harder to tell you." And now I'm here, standing before her wondering with increasing concern if this is fixable.

Her head drops, her eyes darting across the plush carpet. I've not known someone so deeply since Jake. But I have now. I know her, inside out, and I know she's silently piecing the puzzle together. Piece by piece, she's building the picture. Not the whole picture. Now, I wonder if she'll *ever* get the whole picture. Just this part of the story is enough to end us. The rest?

"I'm going to leave now," she says with an edge of resolve I don't like, looking at me with equal grit. "And you're going to let me go."

She sidesteps me as I stand motionless, scrambling for some instruction, trying so hard to locate some sense in this madness. How do I handle this? What should I do? Beg. It's all I have.

"Ava, wait." I go after her. "Ava." She doesn't stop, doesn't give me the time of day, as I follow on her heels. "Ava, baby, please."

She pivots, and I stumble to a stop at the bottom of the stairs. Her face. I've never seen disappointment so deep. Hurt so rife. "Don't even think about it," she yells, and I back up, wary. "You'll let me leave."

"You've not even given me the chance to explain. Please, let me explain."

"Explain what?" she asks. "I've seen everything I need to see. No explanation required."

My hands come up of their own volition, reaching for her. She steps back. "You weren't supposed to find out like this." Fuck, this is a fucking mess. How did I let this happen? Why didn't I deal with this sooner?

This.

This is why.

Her face. Her reaction. What she now thinks of me. I was delaying the inevitable. Delaying this pain, this hurt.

I watch as she casts her eyes around the entrance hall. I can feel the presence of some spectators, but there would be nothing that could make me tear my eyes away from Ava, as if I need to prolong this unbearable ache in my gut by seeing her desolation.

"What a fuck-up you really are."

My shoulders tense as Mike's snide words crawl across my back and settle under my skin.

"You're no longer a member, motherfucker," John growls. "I'll be escorting you from the grounds."

Mike laughs, and I close my eyes, praying for some restraint. My fear is turning into anger. He's just one person in a long list of people who don't want me to have my peace. "Be my guest," he sneers. "Looks like your tart has seen the light, Ward."

Tart. My blood turns hot. *Tart.*

"Shut the fuck up." I hear John's warning, though it's muffled by the whoosh of blood rising fast to my head. My hands are shaking. A red mist creeps in, distorting my vision. But I still see Ava's eyes widen and her lips move, though what she says I don't know. It's too quiet. Just a breath of air.

Though Mike's next words I hear perfectly. "He takes what he wants and leaves a trail of shit behind him."

I lock down every muscle I have.

"He fucks them all and fucks them off."

Ava's welling eyes find me. "Why?"

She is my priority. I need to keep my focus on what matters, and nothing matters more than her. "Don't listen to him, Ava."

"Ask him how my wife is," Mike goes on, taunting me, pushing my limits. "He did the same to her as he did to all the others. Husbands and conscience don't get in his way."

Something inside of me gives, snaps, and all focus disappears. I swing around and yank him from John's hands, smashing him onto the floor and letting my fists loose, punching him repeatedly, roaring through it, all of my anger being injected into my strikes, my control gone.

I feel none of my stress leave me. If anything, it builds, increasing my rage.

"Jesse!" John's on my back, trying to yank me away, Drew helping him. "For fuck's sake!" I raise my arms for a second, knocking them all back with one roll of my shoulders and a roar.

My hands are covered in blood, my vision still blurry. Mike isn't struggling anymore. Not making a sound. I rein in my fists and heave above him, trying to gain some sight.

"Come here, you fucking psycho," John growls, seizing me and dragging me off Mike's limp body. He pushes me aside, and I flop back against the wall. "You'll fucking kill him," he yells, going to one knee next to Mike to assess the damage I've done. Mike starts coughing, rolling onto his side and groaning.

I blink. Look down at my bloody fists, flexing them. They don't hurt. There's another more biting pain superseding it. My heart.

"Ava." I push my back from the wall and search her out, scanning the lobby. The pain inside intensifies. She's gone. I run to the door and down the steps, taking my search outside. Nothing.

"Jesse," Sarah says, resting a hand on my shoulder. I flinch, shrugging her off. "Come on, let's clean you up."

"No." I pace to my car, hearing her running across the gravel to keep up with me.

"You can't drive like this," she argues, sounding worried.

I yank the handle on the door of my car, nearly ripping it off. "My keys," I say, feeling at my pockets. No keys. No phone. I head back inside, my head clouded, my mission clear. Don't let her end this. Fix this. Prove to her what needs to be proven.

"John!" Sarah yells as she flanks me, calling for reinforcements. "John, tell him, please. He can't drive in this state."

"I'm fine," I grate as I pass John, who's managed to get Mike on the bottom step of the staircase. Coral's husband looks up at me and recoils, scrambling up a few steps. He thinks I'm coming back for another round. If I didn't have more important things to do, I would. "I never want to see your face around here again," I say as I pass.

"John," Sarah pleads. "Stop him."

"Just leave him," John replies as I stalk on. "Choose your battles, Sarah. Where that woman is concerned, he'll do what he has to do, and you'll do well to keep out of it."

I find my keys but no phone. "Where the fuck's my phone?" I growl, tossing pillows off the couch, searching the drinks cabinet.

"Here."

I turn and see Sarah pulling it from beneath a file on my desk, but when I take it, it slips right out of my hand, hitting the floor with a thud. "For fuck's sake." I look at my keys. Covered in blood.

Sarah dips and collects my phone, grabbing a Kleenex from the box on the desk. She wipes it over and moves in, taking my hands in turn and gently cleaning them. "You'll slip all over the steering wheel," she says as I stand, silent, letting her do her thing. And I think as I watch her.

"What have you been saying to Ava?" I ask, relatively calmly, considering. "And don't lie to me this time."

She wilts. It doesn't suit her. "I just told her you're not the kind of man to build dreams on." She takes my keys and wipes those too as I laugh under my breath. *Because I'm an unstable fuck-up who can't offer anything more than lies and poison.*

"Thanks for the vote of confidence." I withdraw from her, stepping back, and she looks up at me, her face tortured. But I bet it's still nowhere close to the ruin embedded into mine.

"This is our life, Jesse. You, me, and John. I'm just looking out for you."

"Well, don't, Sarah." I snatch my phone and keys and walk out, pacing through The Manor, my whole body shaking. I try to take a moment in my car to calm. No calm.

I race down the driveway toward the gates, and I can't help feeling like I'm driving toward my end.

37

I KNOW DEEP DOWN she won't answer, but a glimmer of hope inside has me calling her repeatedly on my drive into the city. When I see Sam trying to get through, I abandon yet another attempt to get hold of Ava and take his call. "I'm on my way to Kate's," I tell him. "I assume she's there."

"Yeah, I'm thinking you need to let the dust settle," Sam says.

"No."

"Jesse, she's not in a good way."

"Neither am I. Don't tell her I'm coming." She'll run. She *can't* run.

He sighs, and I hang up, not giving him another opportunity to try and talk me out of this. Nothing will talk me out of it.

I'm banking on this drive to give me time to cool down and gather myself, but with each call she rejects and with each mile under the tires, I'm nowhere close to being together by the time I pull up outside Kate's. I mindlessly leave my car in the middle of the street and jog up to the door, letting my fists loose again. Desperation is controlling me. Fear rooting so deep I'm certain I'll never dig it out. "Ava!" I bellow. "Ava, open the door!" After two minutes straight of hitting the wood, I go back to my phone, dialing her, as I reverse my steps, looking up at the house. "Come on, baby. Give me some time."

"Hey, mate, you gonna move your car?"

I look up, seeing a guy pacing toward me, waving his arms, gesturing to the line of traffic up the street. I have no intention of moving my car, but I'll move him if he comes too close.

"Jesse, what the fucking hell?" Kate yells, coming out and traipsing down the path toward me.

"Kate," I breathe, meeting her on the pavement. "Kate, please, tell her I need to see her."

She shakes her head at me, and the disappointment in her eyes hurts. "Move your car," she orders gently. "I can't think with all these car horns screaming."

"Hey, is anyone going to move the car?"

"Be patient!" Kate yells. "There's a tragic fucking love story playing out here."

Tragic. Ain't that right? She's not ordered me away, so I'm going with this. Will do anything she says. I go to my car and park it up the road, and Kate joins me. I lean against my Aston, head dropped, feeling so fucking ashamed of myself as Ava's best friend stands before me.

"You should have told her."

"I know," I grind. If she's just going to simply state the fucking obvious, she's of no help to me. "It's not something that tends to come up in general conversation between two people who are falling for each other, Kate. Jesus," I breathe, my hands going to my hair. "She's just a regular woman." Regular but spectacular. "And I am far from regular, Kate." My damn bottom lip wobbles. "I need her to let me fix this."

Her eyes drop, and I can see I'm breaking through her thick skin.

"She's everything to me, Kate. I can't lose her."

She sighs, looking past me. "I'll see what I can do."

"Thank you." I exhale the words, so fucking grateful. She could have told me to fuck off. She could have shut me down, and the fact she hasn't sent me packing gives me hope. Because she's Ava's best friend and she wouldn't try to help me if she knew with certainty that Ava truly hates me.

Kate heads back, and I follow obediently, using the time to pray. I pray on everything. I call on my brother to help me. I call on Carmichael. And I call on Rosie. My little girl. She'd be nineteen now. Nineteen years old. And if she was still here, I wouldn't be in this position. I can only hope that my path still would have led me to Ava though. I have to believe it would have, because to know I would have to lose one love of my life just to find another is unthinkable. It's cruel.

I climb the stairs to her flat, more nervous than I've ever been in my life. Kate looks back at me, and I see in her expression that I should wait here, so I stop, nodding, swallowing, willing to do anything she says if it means I get this chance. She disappears into the lounge, and there's a prolonged, unbearable silence before anyone speaks. It's Kate, and what she says is defensive. It tells me maybe I was wrong with my assumption. Ava really doesn't want to see me.

"Just hear him out, Ava," she says softly, and I rub at the ache in my chest. "The man's a mess." I could laugh. I'm not a mess. I'm fucking broken. Destroyed. "You, get in the kitchen!" she snaps.

"I can't fucking move, you evil cow," Sam retorts, and the next minute they appear at the door. Sam's limping.

"Don't ask," he mutters. I don't bother telling him that I wasn't going to, but if I were to hedge my bets, I'd say Kate's let her fury out on his balls. I'd take that over this. I'd take a cricket bat to my nuts repeatedly. The pain would be more bearable.

I breach the opening of the lounge and find her by the window, her back to me. It's a tactical move on her part. She knows the affect we have on each other with just a look. Just a touch. She knows I can eliminate her despair. If she'll only let me. "Please, look at me, Ava," I beg, trying to adopt a gentle approach. Give her space. Tell her rather than show her that we're meant to be. "Ava, please." And yet despite my better judgment, my hand lifts and feels her arm. She jerks away, and it's like a knife to my heart.

"Please, don't touch me," she says, facing me. I momentarily avoid the sheer determination in her stare, unable to face it. But I must face it.

So I look up at her. I see detachment.

"Why did you even take me there?" she asks, her voice worryingly stable.

"Because I want you with me all the time," I admit unashamedly. "I can't be away from you." *Because I love you. I need you.*

"Well, you'd better get used to it because I don't want to see you again."

"You don't mean that," I say, feeling my eyes stinging. "I know you don't mean that."

"I mean it."

"I never meant to hurt you," I whisper. I was trying to protect her. From me. From my reality.

"Well, you have," she snipes coldly. "You've trampled into my life and trampled all over my heart. I tried to walk away." Her jaw rolls angrily. "I knew there was more than meets the eye. Why didn't you let me walk away?"

"You never really wanted to walk away."

"Yes, I did." She loses her battle to retain her emotions, her eyes brimming. It's both relieving and crushing. "I fought you off.

I knew I was heading for trouble, but you were relentless. What happened? Did you run out of married women to fuck?"

I flinch. How could she say that? "No, I found you," I say, moving forward, but she maintains the distance, stepping away. She's scared of my touch.

"Get out," she orders, making her escape. I reach for her, missing her arm, her pace too fast for my lagging, worn-out muscles.

"I can't. I need you, Ava."

"You don't need me!" she shouts, flinging her arm out toward the door. "You want me." She pulls up, gasping for air, the pure level of her anger exhausting her. "Oh God, you are a dominant, aren't you?"

"No!"

"Why the control issue then?" she asks. "And the commands?"

Oh, Jesus, where do I even begin explaining this without filling her in on every fucked-up detail of my past? I'm snookered. Because the reality is, I can't. And what I'm dealing with now—what we're both dealing with—is set to end this. "The sex is just sex." Just sex? It's never just fucking sex with Ava. It's earthmoving every time. "I can't get close enough to you. The control is because I'm frightened to death that something will happen to you." *Because everyone I've ever loved has been stolen from me.* "That you'll be taken away from me. I've waited too long for you, Ava," I go on, finding words in my bedlam, letting them roll out. "I'll do anything to keep you safe. I've lived a life with little control or care. Believe me, I need you." She needs to take my word for it. She has to. "Please. Please don't leave me." She must see the despair as I approach her cautiously. There must be a small part of her that wants to help me. But she steps away again, avoiding me. "I'll never recover."

"Do you think this is going to be any easier for me?" she

yells, her eyes overflowing, tears rolling down her cheeks. No. I don't think it'll be easier for her. If anything, it'll be harder, because I would put my life on the fact that she won't find numbness in alcohol like I will.

"If I could change how I've handled things, I would."

"But you can't. The damage is done."

"The damage will be worse if you leave me." So much worse. There's still a chance this can be repaired. If I walk out of this room, there will be no going back for me.

"Get out!"

"No." I will not give up. "Ava, please, I'm begging you."

She looks away.

"Ava, look at me."

"Goodbye, Jesse."

I will not let her do this. "Please."

"I said, goodbye." She swallows, and the shift in her persona is like a punch to my gut. And I see it. Resolve. I see the end.

I'm not enough for her. And I absolutely cannot risk spilling my agony, my entire fucked-up story, for her to reject me. I can't confess my love for her to throw it back in my face. It would destroy the idea of her. It would make me hate her, and I have no energy to hate.

She's taken away my choices.

It really is the end.

Numb and beaten, I turn and walk away, my despair fading, my anger returning. I pass Sam and Kate in the hall. I don't look at them.

"Jesse?" Sam calls.

"It's over." I say, swallowing hard. *I'm* over.

I make it to my car and stare at my reflection in the window. This feeling of loss, of grief. It's embedded on every inch of my worn face. It's familiar. It's excruciating.

It's all my fault.

Again.

My lip curls at the man staring back at me. A man I hate.

And I launch my fist into his face.

38

I PUSH the door of my penthouse closed behind me and go to the kitchen, sliding the box onto the counter and bracing my hands on the edge, staring at it. My heart hasn't slowed. My pulse is still booming. Has been since I entered the liquor store and bought enough vodka to kill me. I've ignored endless calls from John, Sarah, Sam, and Drew. Everyone in the fucking world is trying to get hold of me except the one person who could stop the train crash that's about to happen. But this pain. This anger.

With no Ava, there is only emptiness without a cure.

I pull out a bottle and unscrew the cap, breathing in deeply, staring at the clear liquid. My nostrils flare. I snarl and take it to my lips, swigging, clenching the side of the worktop with my spare hand, closing my eyes. The burn isn't so familiar anymore. It hurts, and I gasp, slamming the bottle down on the counter, breathing hard.

More anger.

More pain.

Drown it.

I gulp back more, wiping my mouth with the back of my hand, gasping for air in between mouthfuls. And still, the agony remains. "Fuck you," I spit, taking more, determined to be rid of this noose around my neck. I carry on swigging and pluck another bottle from the box before loading the rest into the freezer and heading for the stairs. Every single thing in my home is a trigger. It all has her name on it, and worse, I see her everywhere—on the couch, on the stairs. I finish the bottle, drop the empty at my feet, and make fast work of opening my fresh one as I take the stairs slowly, inspecting my abused, swollen fist. There's blood every-where, and stupidly, I don't want to get it on any of the walls or furnishings. It'll smear her hard work with my pathetic-ness.

I go straight to the bathroom, avoiding the bed and the vanity unit, and flip on the shower. Her shampoo stares at me. I reach for it as I take another swig, before lifting it to my nose and smelling it. My stomach turns. My head booms. I discard it and strip down slowly, stepping in the stall, and I spend just enough time under the spray to clean up the blood before exiting and finding my vodka. I avoid the mirror, getting my phone and putting some music on to blanket the unrelenting silence. *Angel* comes through the speakers, and I still, listening, the part of my mind that the alcohol hasn't reached yet telling me to turn it the fuck off. But that's a small part of my mind. I turn the volume up to max and put it on repeat. I deserve to be tortured.

Wrapping a towel around me, I go back downstairs. My only escape from the visions of her all over my apartment is the terrace, so I go there, collapsing onto a sun lounger. I have time to make up for. An oblivion to find. I stare up to the sky while working my way through my second bottle, the fuzz in my head becoming thicker with each swig I take. Yes. Nothingness is within reach, but I frown, the bottle pausing at my lips when the music shuts off. I swallow and start to push myself up, set to find my phone and put it back on. I was enjoying the torment.

"Fuck," I mutter as I fight and struggle with my unresponsive body. "Fuck, fuck, fuck." I finally make it to my feet, and when I stagger, the alcohol now replacing the blood in my veins, I find Ava standing on the threshold of the terrace. I blink. Once, twice. She's not a hallucination.

She's here.

And she looks shocked. What's with that? What the fuck did she expect? For me to head to The Manor and fuck my way back to normality? "You're too late, lady," I mumble, feeling nothing but contempt for her. Because she did this. What she's staring at now, she did it. So the fact that she's looking so fucking stunned is a fucking insult.

"You're drunk," she says.

Yeah, I'm drunk. But not drunk on love anymore. I'm drunk on my faithful friend Vodka. Love obviously doesn't suit me. Vodka, though? It feels good. She can't touch me now. She can't hurt me. Nothing she could say will sober me up and take me back to where I absolutely cannot be. "That's very observant of you." I raise my bottle and have another needed swig, being sure to maintain this emotionlessness. "Not drunk enough, though." I pass her, going to the kitchen to source more medicine, since she's taken herself off the menu.

"Where are you going?" she asks.

"What's it to you?" Don't tell me she's worried about me now? I grab another bottle and sling the empty in the sink. "Bastard." I wince, trying to unscrew the cap, my hand hurting. A lot. Why the fuck does it hurt? It shouldn't hurt. Nothing should fucking hurt. I fight my way through the pain and swig in a panic.

"Jesse," she says softy. "Your hand needs looking at."

My hand? She should see the state of my fucking heart. And on cue, it cracks a little more, pain radiating through me. What the fuck is this? "Look then," I grate, showing her the mess. "Yet more damage you've caused." She has the nerve to look insulted. Is she fucking blind? Didn't see The Manor for what it was. Didn't read all the signs. Doesn't know how much I love her.

"Yeah, you can stand there," I snap, anger returning to join the pain, "stand there looking all bewildered . . . and . . . and . . . confused. I fucking told you. Didn't I warn you?" I can't breathe. Can't see. Can't bare this agony. "I . . . I warned you!"

She stares at me blankly. It's another knife in my gut, twisting repeatedly. "Warned me about what?"

Unbelievable. And so fucking ignorant. "Fucking typical."

"I didn't know," she says quietly, and I laugh.

"You didn't know?" I hold up my bottle, and her eyes fall to it. "I said you would cause more damage if you left me, but you left anyway. Now look at the fucking state of me." I manage to get my legs moving, and she backs up, wary.

"That's it, run away. You're a fucking prick tease, Ava. I can have you, then I can't, then I can again. Make your fucking mind up!"

"Why didn't you tell me you're an alcoholic?"

I back her up into a corner. "And give you another reason not to want me?" Wait. *An alcoholic?* "I'm not an alcoholic."

"You need help," she whispers, looking at me as I breathe down on her.

"I needed you," I slur. "And . . . you . . . you left me."

Her hands push into my bare chest, and I flinch at the warmth of her palms. I mustn't take comfort in that. Not if she's going to rob me of it again. So I move back and take more vodka. No one can take my vodka. "Sorry, am I invading your space?" I start laughing, sounding deranged, unhinged. I'm close. "It's never bothered you before."

"You weren't drunk before," she counters, looking at me with nothing but contempt.

"No, I wasn't. I was too busy fucking you to think about having a drink." I match her derision. "I was too busy fucking you to think about *anything*. And you loved it." My dirty smile is natural. She's hurting. *Good. Welcome to the fucking club, baby.* And an unreasonable urge in me wants to make her hurt more, because she's here now, stamping all over my attempts to rid myself of my agony. "You were good. In fact, you were the best I've had. And I've had a lot." My head snaps to the side with the power of her slap, and again, it fucking hurts. I breathe through the sting, laughing at the irony. Seems I'm not immune to her like I'd hoped. She has this power over me, the power to destroy me, and I realize in this moment that nothing can save me from my fate now. Not even my trusty vodka. "Fun, wasn't it?"

"You're one fucked-up sorry state."

"Watch your mouth." She just loves seeing me tortured.

"You don't get to tell me what I can say. You don't get to tell me how to do anything anymore."

Anymore? Whenever did she fucking listen to me anyway? "I'm. A. Fucked-up. Sorry. State. And. It's. All. Because. Of. You."

She's suddenly gone, and the second my drunken eyes register her absence, my heavy legs start to follow, dropping the bottle on my way. The damn stuff isn't having the desired effect anymore.

By the time I make it upstairs, she's got armfuls of clothes. She stops outside the walk-in wardrobe and studies me for a few moments while I frown. Then she's moving again, going to the bathroom. I follow, coming to a stop by the vanity unit where I fucked her for the first time.

"Does this bring back memories, Ava?" I ask as she stuffs her toiletries into her bag, the memories of the first time I truly got my hands on her flooding my drunken mind, burning away the alcohol, making more room for more pain. She doesn't answer, and instinct has me moving to the doorway, blocking her escape.

"You're really going?" I ask, looking at her arms full of all her things that looked so perfect in my home. She's taking it all.

"You think I would stay?" she asks, almost on a laugh. Yes, I think she would, if she'd only stop for a moment and acknowledge my grief. Accept that she can repair the mess that I am.

"So, that's it?" I ask. "You've turned my life upside down, caused all this damage, and now you're leaving without fixing it?"

Her eyes remain glued to mine for a few moments, her chest expanding. "Goodbye, Jesse." She shoulders her way past me, and I stumble, hitting the doorframe.

She's going. *No, she can't leave.* "I wanted to tell you," I bellow, righting myself and staggering after her. "But you had to be your usual difficult self." I have nothing else to help me, my loyal vodka betraying me. "How can you walk away?" I yell, ricocheting off the walls, unable to find any speed or coordination to chase her down, to stop her. "Ava, baby, please!" I catch my foot on the doorway as I exit the bedroom, slamming into the wall on the landing, taking a picture off the wall as I do. I crash to the floor and try so hard to get back up, but I'm all out of strength. The vodka's done me over this time. Not helped. Not been my friend. It's hampered me.

I pathetically crawl to the top of the stairs, my throat clogged, making it impossible to call for her again. "Ava," I mumble, seeing the door slam.

And she's gone.

Taken my heart with her.

Now I'm just . . .

Empty.

"No," I whisper, rolling to my back. She was meant to be my angel. My redemption. "Come back, Ava." I beg. "Please, come back."

I can't hear her. I can hear nothing.

Except for the beats of my heart slowing down.

Silence.

Darkness.

I close my eyes.
I hope they never open again.

The End . . . for now

Jesse's story continues in With This Woman.

This Woman is also available in Audio - read by the incredible Shane East. Take the story to another level. Download from Audible now!

ABOUT JODI ELLEN MALPAS

Jodi Ellen Malpas was born and raised in England, where she lives with her husband, boys and Theo the Doberman. She is a self-professed daydreamer, and has a terrible weak spot for alpha males. Writing powerful love stories with addictive characters has become her passion—a passion she now shares with her devoted readers. She's a proud #1 *New York Times* Bestselling Author, a *Sunday Times* Bestseller, and her work is published in over twenty-five languages across the world. You can learn more about Jodi & her words at www.jodiellenmalpas.co.uk

ALSO BY JODI ELLEN MALPAS

The This Man Series

This Man

Beneath This Man

This Man Confessed

All I Am – Drew's Story (A This Man Novella)

With This Man

The One Night Series

One Night - Promised

One Night - Denied

One Night - Unveiled

Standalone Novels

The Protector

The Forbidden

Gentleman Sinner

Perfect Chaos

Leave Me Breathless

The Smoke & Mirrors Duology

The Controversial Princess

His True Queen

The Hunt Legacy Duology

Artful Lies

Wicked Truths